THE

BEN LEECH

THE BIDDEN

PAN BOOKS

LONDON, SYDNEY AND AUCKLAND

To my friend Douglas Hill
for points and pints

First published 1994 by Pan Books

an imprint of Macmillan General Books
Cavaye Place London SW10 9PG
and Basingstoke

Associated companies throughout the world

ISBN 0 330 33540 5

1 3 5 7 9 8 6 4 2

A CIP catalogue record for this book is available from
the British Library

Phototypeset by Intype, London
Printed and bound in Great Britain by
Cox & Wyman Ltd, Reading, Berkshire

Contents

Prelude

The coastal waters of Japan form the habitat of *Dorippe japonica*, a crab made remarkable by the resemblance of its shell to caricatured human features; specifically, to the fierce severity of a samurai warrior's face.

Modern evolutionary biologists suggest that these resemblances are a normal consequence of natural laws. Julian Huxley maintains that:

> The resemblance of *Dorippe* to an angry traditional Japanese warrior is far too specific and far too detailed to be merely accidental: it is a specific adaptation, and can only have been brought about by means of natural selection operating over centuries of time, the crabs with a more perfect resemblance having been less eaten.

Local legend maintains that the crabs are reincarnations of a Japanese warrior family who, having suffered defeat in battle in the year AD 1155, committed mass suicide by hurling themselves off a cliff into the sea. For reasons of superstition and respect, fishermen will not catch the crabs nor eat them, even though they are edible.

Both explanations point to a close and subtle relationship between *Dorippe japonica* and man. And whichever is true, the crab survives . . .

Chapter One

God hath given you one face, and you make
yourselves another.

Hamlet, III.i.145

The sun went down in flames and left a smoky twilight. A long insectile freight train pulled by two big diesels hauled itself slowly out of the yards and accelerated on the gradual upward gradient that took it out of Calverton and away to the west. Denny Crane counted forty wagons; almost a half-mile of rolling stock, as the train rattled and clanked its way into a distance made hazy by the dust and pollen kicked up on this sticky late-June afternoon.

The day had been languid, easygoing, unrushed: Crane wished he felt the same. He had chain-smoked his way through the duty shift and now took the last cigarette out of what had been his third pack of twenty. Jesus, but the strain was going to kill him, before the cancer could! He lit the cigarette from the smouldering stub of the last one, which he flicked away – then checked to be sure it had not dropped into spilt oil or a bone-dry tuft of wasteland grass. Only last weekend a furniture warehouse had gone up like a tinderpile, the fire-crews reckoned because some careless employee had dropped a roach-end into a wastebin. Damage was estimated at two million, and one of the warehouse staff had died, suffocated before the flames ever reached him.

Crane imagined that death now: that black agony of suffocation, the ecstasy of helplessness as your brain, deprived of oxygen, closed down: perhaps, in the final moments, the indescribable pain of superheated air scalding over your skin, taking off your hair and eyebrows, crisping eyelids and lips into non-existence; blackening nostrils and making the subcutaneous fat of the face bubble and fizz, before you literally melted into flames that you fed with your own substance . . .

Crane chuckled oddly at the vivid horror of his vision: the fear he felt kicking an adrenalin boost through his blood as he made his rounds, flaring a flashlight into corners turned purple in the dusk. The sky was warm and heavy like a blanket, filled with sickly diesel smell and late midges: the white walls of the warehouses, huge as airplane hangars and as featureless, radiated the heat of the day, pumped it out into an atmosphere already laden with too much of it, together with the rest of the shit the human race vented from the arse-end of its so-called civilizations.

For a brief moment, Crane's tension shaped itself into a curse against all the evil that men do – that he himself was contributing towards, however indirectly. Then he realized that his nerves were getting the better of him, and that he was more likely to screw things up in a panic if he allowed himself to go on like this.

He finished his smoke, ground out the dropped filter and walked more purposefully towards the barriered zone of the yards that carried a Grade-A security tag. This was where he would spend the rest of his shift tonight. This was where Risico and his men would strike, twenty minutes before the teams of watchmen changed over.

Ten yards from the inner gates, Crane stopped and stood looking up at the armoured surveillance camera on its house-high pole. He was dazzled by the multiple sunrise brilliance of floodlights; could hear the hum of high voltage through the two-mill diamond link of the zone's fencing. After a few seconds of this exposure, he continued up to the gate, where an amber light in a five-colour sequence was glowing at him. Now he took out a plastic ID tag and ran it through a magnetic reader. There was a heavy click of opening locks, and for five seconds only, the killer current through the gates was stilled.

Crane stepped through with careful alacrity, pushed the gates closed and walked on to the small but specially adapted Portakabin that housed his team-mate and the nucleus of the security net that cobwebbed the yards.

Miller was making coffee. At twenty-six, he was twelve years younger than Crane, which was the least of their differences. Miller, Crane reckoned, was a product of the Millennium; born at the end of the eighties and raised with computer and video technology, he put a lot of store by machines; had a strength of faith in them that Crane could never summon forth. Jez Miller was young, able, intelligent and on the way up. Crane, in contrast, with a little over a decade separating them, had become soured by cynicism and convinced that the world had passed him by. He'd bought himself some training in the general field of security and worked for six years in the then recently privatized prison service, jacking it in when he and his superiors realized he was not promotion material. Miller had undergone the same training, but used a succession of jobs since then as stepping-stones; his own personal stairway to the stars, projecting the achievement of director of his own company by the time he was Denny Crane's age.

He turned as Crane entered, and smiled, never for an instant realizing the hatred the man harboured for him: never suspecting that he in his innocence personified all that Crane envied but could never, now, attain.

'Some coffee, Den?' Crane nodded and made a cursory scan of the monitor array decked against a side wall. The room smelled of plastic and Miller's crisp aftershave. No doubt the little bastard would have a cheena lined up for later: take her to a club, have a bit of a dance and a drink, then back home for some in-out and a long sleep in a perfumed bed before the next day's shift began. Crane himself lived in a rented three-room a mile from the railyards. His landlord was German, his neighbours French and Ugandan, and most of his meals came out of tin trays cooked by a Chink. Sometimes, Crane felt like a stranger in his own land. No doubt Miller was much more cosmopolitan.

Miller made the coffee as Crane liked it, milky with plenty of sugar.

'Bloody hot night to be cooped up in this hut,' he said, a reflex complaint that Crane had been making regularly for the past week: Miller gave his usual reaction now, a tolerant nod and a mumbled response that neither of them thought was funny or clever; meaningless talk between two men who had nothing in common.

Crane sat on a castored chair before the bank of monitors and rolled up the sleeves of his pewter-blue uniform shirt. He loosened his tie, checked the time – 23.32 – and gave every appearance of doing well what he was paid to do. Miller spent five minutes routinely logging the progress of this quiet night, then took a seat at a computer terminal against the opposite wall and began typing with a swift and quiet clatter of keys.

Twenty minutes passed with nothing changing, save that a huge orange moon rose in the east and the last faint traces of violet drained from the opposite horizon.

At 23.55, Crane yawned, stretched and stood up. He rummaged in his holdall behind the door, perhaps looking for his sandwich box or a smoke (never alcohol: that was strictly forbidden). He lifted something from the bag as

6

Miller went on writing, lost in the words he was making. Crane turned, took two steps over to his team-mate and drove the syringe needle deep into Miller's neck before he had time to begin to react. Crane pushed the plunger home: Miller's body stiffened and a sustained shudder ran through it. Then abruptly it lost all tension. The man's head lolled sideways. Crane released his hold and stepped away, the hypodermic still protruding from Miller's carotid artery.

Crane realized that he had stopped breathing as his companion had died. Now he dragged in a lungful of warm air that was stale with the sweat smell of two bodies, exhaling it with a racking sigh. He checked the time again – just on midnight – and tripped the master switch that would deactivate the whole surveillance system, exactly according to the plan he had made with the man called Risico, three months earlier.

'Risico's' real name was Patrick Joseph Peters. He was edging forty and looked it, his naturally boyish face now irretrievably lined, his fair hair thinning. His pale-blue eyes still held the same cold fire that had burned a path for him thus far through life, but there were dark bags beneath them these days, hung there as much by nightmares as by age.

He was sitting in the passenger seat of a matt-black Ford transit, parked half a mile from where Denny Crane had just committed his murder. A pale-green seven-segment digital display on the dash flicked from 23.59 to 00.00. Without being told, the man seated beside Peters started the finely tuned engine, kicked on the lights and moved forward.

Calverton's railyards lay on the west side of the city, nested within a post-industrial sprawl that was the phoenix emerged from the ashes of a pre-Federal Britain. A hundred years earlier Calverton was the most prosperous city in the country, fully exploiting its central position and, even then, its excellent transport links. The place was warrened with canals, railway lines and roads: in the fifties, an airport had been built fifteen miles to the northeast, and enlarged two decades later to accommodate transatlantic routes. But by then the trading infrastructure of the nation was being weakened by bad management on a grand scale: billions were being poured into social engineering projects as though Treasury funds were limitless: corruption and laxity reigned: the great wave of the country's wealth crashed uselessly towards the start of the eighties, much of it gurgling down a vast and hitherto unsuspected drain. Tory austerity followed, powered by ideologies diametrically opposed to the 'All Animals Are Equal And Have Rights' philosophy of the left and neo-left. The aim as the century flowed towards its cynical close was to make the country leaner and meaner, putting a competitive cutting edge to British industry and innovation through the force of economic natural selection. Coupled with increasing commitments to European unity, the result thus far was a significant influx of industry and manpower funded by co-member nations taking advantage of governmental incentives and sweeteners. Once more, Calverton's prosperity bloomed. As far as Peters was concerned, most of that money was pouring into the wrong pockets.

The driver of the van, a huge bull-necked man called Conway, glided the vehicle in neutral along the short side-street to the corner that offered a first view of the railyards' outer boundary. Hundreds of vehicles from executive autos to fifty-ton juggers moved to and fro across the complex all day, and well into the night. Calverton Yards formed the nucleus of a continent-wide transport network owned by

scores of private companies. Administratively it was impossible to co-ordinate: logistically it was impossible to secure. It
was like all big bolt-on systems – crawling with parasites and
bleeding badly. Despite the presence of the top half-dozen
security firms in the country, and supposedly regular patrols
by a state police force (stretched to homeopathic dilutions),
anyone could walk in, around and out of the place at just
about any time and go largely unchallenged. If a job was
well-planned and coolly executed, it would probably succeed – especially if you had an inside man in your pocket.
That, of course, had been the first of Risico's priorities.

'Go on,' he told Conway quietly. Then as the transit
moved towards the high-security area, Peters turned to the
two remaining members of his hand-picked team, their faces
softly shaded by the pastel lights of the dashboard.

'I want it quick, I want it clean. Crane will have switched
off the current by now . . . He'll switch it on again at mid-
night-five, then off for a further five minutes at midnight-
thirty.' Peters stared hard at one of the men. 'You know
what we're looking for?'

'I've been through it with him a hundred times . . .'
Cernan shrugged. 'Besides, I didn't study archaeology for
nothing – '

Peters hissed quietly through his teeth, a sound of such
serpentine evil that both men seated in the rear shrank back.
Conway just drove, smiling to himself. These were new
guys, but he had worked with Risico before and knew the
bastard was a psychopath as well as a genius.

'You think a hundred times is better than one time?'

'What?' said Cernan, missing the logic. He felt afraid
suddenly for his life.

'A hundred times makes you complacent. One time with
proper attention and direction is enough . . .'

Cernan gave a shit-eating grin, understanding something of the mind behind the pale and pain-washed eyes that stared at him and through him; consuming him in their quest for something utterly beyond his comprehension.

'I know what I'm looking for, Risico,' he acquiesced, praying inwardly that this statement proved true.

'And you?' Peters swung his glance to the other man, the one who liked to be known as the Electrician.

'No problem. The zone is protected by a standard Centrel Surveillance system: nothing very high-tech – Centrel have gone for solid reliability. Works too, except for, ah, human error.'

'Or human greed . . . I want to be sure the deactivation is not detectable . . .'

'I can reprogramme the mainframe clocks and wire up a video loop to cover the blind spots when the cameras were switched off. Don't worry.'

'I never worry,' Risico told him. 'I simply eradicate the cause of any mistakes, so that they don't happen again.'

And the Electrician believed him, absolutely. On both counts.

Crane saw the van emerge like a shadow from the greater shadow of the side-street. Its forelights flickered off, and on, then blinked off once more. He opened the access gate to the zone automatically, then walked to the threshold of the Portakabin to wait for Risico's arrival.

Presently he saw the van's bulky silhouette slide through the pools of floodlighting as it approached. Crane lifted his hand as if to say, 'It's OK – it's me. Don't worry . . .' He had met Risico once, briefly, in a city-centre nightclub, where the deal had been offered and accepted. They had shaken hands, Crane recalled, but it felt then and now as though he'd signed on the line in blood – his own, if he didn't tread very warily indeed.

Conway parked the van at the end of a row of vehicles and killed the engine. The four occupants stepped out. Risico broke away from the group and came towards Crane, who remembered vividly the verminous, dangerous look of the man whose rapacious, distant eyes, catching the light at a particular angle, hardly seemed human.

'You've killed him,' Risico said, with no lift of the voice to denote a question. He had expected nothing less.

'Inside.'

'We'll get him in the van. Then my man can work on the surveillance equipment. Now, take me to the warehouse.'

Crane nodded. 'It's this way.'

After disposing of Miller, Crane walked ahead of Risico and his team, while the fourth man entered the cabin with his bag of tricks. Crane felt suddenly drained, as though all of his energy had been spent running through varied scenarios of what might happen if it went right, if it went wrong, if Risico had failed to show . . . The reality seemed almost mundane by comparison.

'Here.' Crane stopped at one windowless block among many. There was a single white steel door of pallet width, protected by more Centrel standard kit: a red light burned steadily in the smart-lock; a wall-mounted videocam pointed directly at the men, but by morning would show no trace of their passing.

'You.' Risico indicated to Conway, who had been the last out of the van after dumping Miller. The big man produced Miller's ID card and ran it through the reader. The light switched to amber, then to single-green. All guards in this zone had clearance through any doorway – but there were added safeguards . . .

Crane realized this, and almost panicked, as Conway lifted something wrapped in linen and pressed it to a glass panel in the lock. Then the panic turned with the speed of strong acid to something else – to more than disgust.

'Oh God,' he moaned, as his stomach clenched. 'It's his hand . . .'

'How'd the fuck you expect us to get in? Talk nicely to the door, maybe?' Conway gave a low greasy chuckle as the single-green doubled and the door slid back.

They stepped through into momentary darkness splintered by flickering neon as the lights turned on automatically. The warehouse smelt of new boxwood and electricity, and a strange pungent chemical smell like hot plastic. The air held so much of the day's heat that you could almost chew it. Crane felt sweat beads spring out on his skin, and his armpits itched with it.

'OK, let's do it,' Risico said, swinging his glance towards Cernan, who was already scanning the stacked crates, searching hawk-like through their trans-shipment codes.

Crane's work was about done, he knew. All he had to do now was steel himself for a crack on the back of the head, making it seem as though he'd disturbed the gang and been overpowered. The evidence of Miller's absence, and the handprint recorded by the smart-lock, would implicate him utterly in the robbery. There was time for a final smoke, Crane mused – although his curiosity was pricked by the object of this operation. He knew from the manifests that nothing of immense value was left here overnight: cash, bonds, precious metals and stones – these passed straight through and on to their impregnable destinations without pause: most often stuff like that anyway was flown in, or brought by personal courier. Crane seemed to remember that there was a lot of imported art in the warehouse; or statues, antiquities, that kind of crap . . .

'Yes,' Cernan said, grinning. He pointed at a certain crate. 'Yes, yes!'

Crane thought; you'd think the guy was coming, the way his excitement showed.

'Open that one,' Risico directed the big man, who dragged a jemmy from his holdall and broke his way expertly into the box the younger one had indicated. Together they pulled out swathes of packaging; polystyrene beads, then foam pads and finally a carefully wrapped object that Cernan laid with reverence at Risico's feet.

'Show me.'

Cernan worked with trembling hands, unwinding the sterile wrappings as though they swaddled a bomb or the Baby Jesus. What emerged was a statue of green bronze; a grossly bloated woman whose huge belly and orbed breasts swelled in grotesque disproportion to the rest of her body.

'Wrong,' Risico snapped. Cernan, on his knees, glanced up and giggled with pure fear. He had found out from Conway that Risico had a short fuse: Cernan suspected privately he had none at all, and would kill him now as soon as look at him. But his summer-blue eyes did not yet have murder in them, only frustration.

'Try another. Break open this whole row, here.'

Conway produced another crowbar and tossed it to Crane. The warehouse filled with the noise of smashed wood, Conway's grunts, and Cernan's increasingly panicky mutterings as the correct artefact failed to appear.

'What the hell are we searching for, anyway?' Crane wondered aloud, as he and Conway dragged out the entrails of another crate.

'A stone . . . A stone,' Conway repeated, amused by

Crane's open-mouthed look of incredulity. 'With writing on it.'

'I'll be buggered,' Crane said. Conway smiled.

'After the pay-off, you can afford it nightly.'

Crane grinned up into the big man's face, then watched it transform with horror as Conway threw himself sideways, a second before thunder broke through the building and the backdrop of stacked boxes disintegrated, showering splinters.

Cernan screamed, scrabbling on the floor like some absurd cartoon animal. Crane was in the process of turning – had time enough to see the ugly rictus grin of failure on Risico's face, and the tall uniformed silhouette of a state cop limned by moonlight, with a second officer hovering behind.

Then Cernan, mad with panic, flipped himself over and fumbled inside his denim jacket.

The cop shouted a warning, aimed and fired, all according to the book. Cernan's body jerked in a spasm, his chest opening up. Crane recognized the style of devastation and the peculiar boom of the gun in that confined space: the cop was using a Wildey 9mm self-loader, probably modified to take lower powered ammunition, which would be cheaper for the force and in compliance with Government regulations . . .

Crane smiled inwardly at these thoughts running inconsequentially through his mind, as the man died painfully in front of him. But it was the end for all of them, one way or another. Risico and his gang were pinned fair and square, while there was no way that Crane could plead coercion to account for his presence here.

The officer stepped forward and Crane squinted for

details of his face. Did he know this man? Was there even the slimmest chance of making a deal . . .

'On the floor, slowly, spreadeagled. Now!' The voice echoed crisply, calmly. Crane noted with a certain admiration the cop's balanced stance, gun held double-handed, its laser-sight pointed unwaveringly at Conway, in appearance the most dangerous of the gang . . .

A mistake, Crane thought: the cop's focusing on the wrong one.

But Conway started to ease himself around, sinking to his knees: Risico, apparently, going through the motions also.

Without warning smoke bloomed beyond the doorway, a choking ammonia fog. The second officer yelled. Both Conway and Risico began moving with desperate speed.

The first cop shouted again, but now the command was gone from his voice. Conway snarled, his hand already delving in the holdall at his feet, hefting up the stubby menace of a sawn-off pump-action shotgun.

A machine-gun chattered a dozen rounds in the night outside as the first burning tendrils of fog needled into Crane's eyes. The second cop slammed into the wall of the warehouse, already dead. His partner opened up with the Wildey, and Conway's face turned into a mask of blood.

Risico's body was a blur: Crane barely caught sight of the gun levelling up as a flash of fire spurted from his hand. The bullet caught the cop high up in his chest on the right side, spinning him round like a doll. He stumbled, shooting in a spasm, as Risico fired again, again – kept firing until the man's back was a ragged landscape of blood-fringed craters and he lay still.

The Electrician stumbled through into the warehouse,

startling and alien in a gas-mask that muffled the shrill elation in his voice.

'The system's rigged. Our faces are not on the tape. But hurry, there's a vanload of filth on the way . . . Hurry! Oh Jesus Christ!'

Risico had gone back to searching, tearing at the wall of damaged crates in a frenzied disembowelling.

Crane found himself in a dilemma, poised at a point where the future divided on wildly diverging paths. He could choose to go along with the plan as laid down, at least until the police arrived, when he would need to vanish pretty fucking quickly . . . Or he could take Risico out now, easily – and the Electrician, who had moved to the doorway to search for approaching headlights. Two men, easily kill-able. And Crane's career would be assured, as well as the fifty per cent down payment Risico had already made in cash for Crane's co-operation thus far.

There were few such moments in a man's life, when circumstances were malleable to conscious decision. Crane felt the world fall silent around him as he reached inside for an answer, for the best way forward from here.

Then he heard sirens wailing through the hot night, and the man at the door beckoning crazily and yelling.

Crane lifted his right hand to the holster on his hip.

Risico was watching him, gun already in position.

He fired without hesitation.

The security guard flopped backward into the gathering gloom; an acrid, lung-burning combination of dispersing ammonia and smoke from packaging that had caught light somewhere from a stray bullet. Risico heard Crane's head thunk on the concrete floor, and there was a great deal of blood spread in a black splash across his shirt. If he wasn't dead, then he'd wish he was when he woke. Risico had deliberately gone for a gut shot, the cruellest form of retribution; worse than knee-capping, worse than anything Risico could imagine. They said the pain could turn you mad – but then, plenty of things could do that . . .

Risico calculated that he had two minutes at most, by which time the law would be here in force, and the warehouse with its fortune in relics would be well ablaze.

Now, in this moment of extreme danger and on the brink of calamity, Risico felt wonderfully calm. The strange rapture of frustration that had seemed to scrape at his skull from within was over: he felt no urge to rage against Fate, or to destroy the human instruments of its will. Ironically perhaps, here on the lip of the new century, he was standing amongst the remnants of a culture for whom Fate had been an intensely real and powerful influence. Greater minds than man's decided the fall of one's fortunes, judged and arranged the spill of human life and death across the face of the world . . . It was said that God does not play at dice, but Risico reckoned that if He had a heart at all capable of love, then the thrill of the next throw would be irresistible . . . And the same would be true, of course, of Satan.

Risico covered his mouth and nose with his sleeve and pulled over the last few crates in the row that had stamped on them the code numbers Cernan had been looking for. Maybe the number for the particular box he wanted was wrong; but his information was of a high quality – he had paid plenty for it: it had to be right.

He set to work again, knowing it was his last bid. The sirens were right outside, shrieking like harpies; and flames were visible now, showing as a random pinkish-orange glow through the blossoming palls of smoke.

Risico ripped at a box that had been partly opened by its fall. He delved inside with both hands, careless of the acidic fumes that scalded down his throat and flamed into his lungs. He did not recognize his own screaming: paid no heed to the blood and fluids pouring from his burst and blistering mouth . . .

His fingers closed around something cool and solid and cylindrical – he tore it free of its wrappings and held the stone up to his blurring, melting eyes . . . Yes, it was the stone that lay at the centre of a legend: the Rosetta of Ancient Greece – a 4000-year-old keystone by which the translation of a previously indecipherable dialect would become possible. To a collector, it was worth several millions: to historians it was priceless . . . To Risico, unless he could get away with it, the stone held no value at all.

Visibility was down to a couple of yards now. The warehouse was dark and suffocating, and growing unbearably hot. Risico's body was a mass of pain, he could barely see: but his mind was clear and his purpose as sharp as it had always been. He tucked the stone into a pouch in his jacket and hunkered down below the boiling underbelly of black smoke. The air was filled with the thunder of the fire, but through it he could hear men shouting – and then the clatter of the machine-gun as the Electrician fought for his life at the expense of others.

Maybe he won, Risico thought, maybe he lost. It hardly mattered. All he cared for was to reach the blessed quiet and cool of the night that lay beyond the walls – to run and to keep running with his prize. Once he was clear of this zone, no amount of searching would find him out. The railyards were a labyrinth of sheds and streets, canal tunnels, factories . . .

A figure emerged from the gloom, a shadow on which

proximity painted the badge and standard-issue kit of a state officer. He was walking warily, a step at a time, with his regulation Wildey held before him in one hand, a less than useless flashlight in the other. His protective mask lent him an insectile look . . . And Risico had loved to crush bugs as a boy . . .

He never normally carried a gun. Rather, he slid from his belt a scalpel-sharp blade and waited for the target to come to him. The cop was peering into the murk at head-height. Risico rose from the ground and drove the knife under the man's ribs, deep in, piercing the chest cavity and puncturing the heart.

The cop fell with a sigh, dead before his last breath was finished. Risico ripped off the gas-mask and struggled it over his face, clamping his teeth as scalded skin and flesh came away at a touch.

He dropped to a crouch again at once, knowing that state cops always worked in pairs. The efficiency of his kill-ing meant that the dead officer's partner would probably not realize he was alone; would come in as unprepared as his friend had been.

And so it was. Through the pouring smoke, backlit by flames and the sparks of bursting boxes, the second cop appeared a moment later.

Risico tensed himself.

He stood to deliver his blow.

Then he screamed.

The cop was not moving warily, but staggering forward with his hands flung up to his face, his mask dangling by its straps around his neck.

In the second of Risico's hesitation, the officer let his hands fall away . . . Risico imagined he'd see a face ruined by fire, some charred and blackened thing . . .

Instead he saw Beauty – a smile of unsurpassing enchantment; eyes of a wonderful clarity, blue as a lagoon; fine cheekbones, flawless flesh . . . But the cop's head was fringed with writhing pink serpents, as thick as his fingers, that quickly clamped themselves to the skull and seemed to meld with the skin and the bone . . . And the appearance of that face was changing in the space between heartbeats; sprouting black hair above the top lip, etching strain-lines around the eyes, pushing blood into lips that grew fuller . . . A transformation in living clay into something that was merely a man.

The police officer looked steadily at Risico and smiled with the knowledge of the gods.

Long afterwards, when the body was healed and imagination caused Risico his only agony, he thought back to that moment and wondered why the cop had not killed him where he stood. Perhaps he – it – had also been terrified and confused just then; or possibly Risico had not been the primary target.

He would never know. But two things were absolutely clear and absorbed his every waking hour, of which there were many . . .

The stone he had stolen and still possessed held more secrets than he had the wit or courage to dream –

And, without a doubt, if he had not been before, Risico was insane by the time he broke free of the burning warehouse.

Chapter Two

I hold up my mirror, and seeing my face, I
am troubled.

Po Chu-I, Chinese poet

James Parco stared hard at the face that stared back at
him from his rearview mirror, and for the first time ever
he thought he was getting old. The laugh lines around
his mouth and eyes, that once had betokened a friendly
approach, a convivial manner, now to him indicated merely
the passing of too many years. The 'distinguished' touches
of grey in his hair that Theo said she found attractive had
become more than touches: Parco wrestled mentally over
whether to dye-and-lie, or just to grow old gracefully – as
his dad had done, and then died at sixty-four of a coronary,
a year off retirement and with a small nest-egg in the bank.

Parco was forty-one, almost; but by God he'd not regard
himself as such until the fateful day had come and gone. His
estimation of whether or not he looked his age varied with
his mood. Last weekend, when he and Theo had gone to
the theatre (her friend had let her down at the eleventh
hour, and she hadn't wanted to waste the ticket), he'd felt
like a kid just out of his teens: he'd felt young and alive and
almost in love – and would have tipped the brink and given
his future to Theo Vines if she'd suggested it. She hadn't.
But today, at the tail-end of a six-hour stake-out, his head
buzzed with exhaustion, and stiffness had seized all his
joints in a painful vice-lock. Worse maybe than that, he
quietly stank in his two-day-old shirt and underwear, and
his suit trousers were itchy and damp. The car smelt of
the one small cigar he'd smoked that day at the start of the

watch, and of his hamburger lunch: its polystyrene wrapper lying like a plastic oyster, open-mouthed on the passenger seat.

Parco yawned, screwing his eyes, and stretched as well as he could in the car's confines, cracking the pain from his elbows and knees. Right now, if someone offered him an easier way of making 40K annually than being a hassled PI, he'd take their hand off along with the contract. Tomorrow it would all look different – and *he'd* look different. God would be in his heaven, and his fee for this case would hopefully be in the bank.

It was an infidelity job, the husband of Parco's client allegedly playing away with his wife's PA; an affair which began, it was claimed, when the two met at an office-moving party arranged by the wife. She was Managing Director of a clearing house for TV and magazine special offers, a business she'd inherited from Daddy. But to give the lady her due, she'd run the operation more tightly than the old boy had done for the past six years. She was intelligent, wealthy, not bad looking though just a shade cold, Parco felt: no sound reason in itself to lay some pipe at the risk of losing it all . . .

And this goon looked set to do just that, Parco reckoned. He'd logged the couple in and out of three different motels during the past week, noting times and locations, licence plates (Department of Motor Vehicle checks had confirmed the car as his on two occasions, hers on one), and iced the cake with a couple of close-up kissy shots which, really, were incontrovertible. Tomorrow, or maybe on the next day, Parco would call Mrs Carthew and suggest an appointment in his office: there he would present her with the slim sheaf of evidence and, if she wished, recommend a class lawyer;

the lawyer being a close friend who reciprocated the good word when his customers needed detective work doing.

Just as these plans ran leisurely through Parco's mind, the door of apartment number six of the Calverton West Motel opened and two people stood for a moment framed in the amber light that matched the cheap lampshade of the room. One was Anthony Carthew, whose tallness and five-hundred-pound blue pin-stripe actually did evoke the adjective 'distinguished' when noting the silvery streaks in his hair. His partner, twenty-five, stunning and blonde, was Carianne Sutton, whose bust size in inches, Parco estimated, easily beat her typing speed in w.p.m. Or perhaps he was simply feeling vindictive tonight.

Whatever: as Carthew slid his arms around Carianne's lean waist and down to the tight roundedness of her backside, Parco took a few more night-shots with the old Minolta that had been a faithful and reliable companion to him for most of his professional life . . . More fucking faithful than most of the folks its photographs were destined to damn . . .

Parco waited until the couple had driven away in Carthew's BMW, then he went to the reception desk to ask if a briefcase he'd left behind a week ago had by chance been locked away in the motel's safe . . . To tell the truth, Parco admitted, sheepishly, he couldn't even be sure if this was the right motel . . . He was sure the guy on reception appreciated how hectic life could be: but if he could just check, Parco would be very grateful . . .

He gave the desk clerk a fiver and the man went away with what he tried to suggest was a knowing grin. Parco photographed Carthew's entry in the register (at least 'Albert and Mrs Hall' was original), then he left.

He arrived back at his office just as his illuminated desk-clock display changed from 21.59 to 22.00. Not too late – time enough for a drink down at The Manor, then a cab home rather than drink less Scotch and risk being picked up for driving himself home.

Theo had gone home a couple of hours earlier, it seemed, and would by now most probably be curled up on that cosy sofa of hers with a generous glassful of Bushmills and crushed ice, and her cat asleep on her lap. Parco grinned tiredly, envying that blasted cat for the thousandth time since Theo had joined the firm four years earlier. Parco had always regarded himself as a confirmed bachelor, previously more out of selfishness than natural inclination: his work rarely fell into a routine pattern of hours, and when he worked, he did so with diligence and pride. For the sixteen years he'd been a PI, since leaving the state police in search of greater challenges, he'd survived by his own wits and sheer doggedness. It was not something he could easily abandon or even change for a regular hot cooked meal set before him at the table, and a regular bosom against which to rest his weary head.

Even as he considered it, Parco wondered if that was true. Might it be, now, that he could not give up his bachelor ways because they were too deeply ingrained in his life – in him? And was it just possible that no female would take up with this almost-middle-aged loner with a warm heart that, after all these years, still turned cold upon contemplating the hurt and evil in the world . . .

Probably not. Lately, Parco had dwelt on the problem more persistently and more deeply. He guessed that if he didn't marry soon, or at least set up shack with a willing lady, it would be too late before he knew it. He had made it an aim to retire in his mid-fifties or earlier – and yes, it was true that people of that age formed new relationships and sailed around the world, but by then his habits would have ossified to the point where the daily company of another would be mutually intolerable. Simply, he would have missed that particular boat . . . But the ocean was large, and its far and unknown shore not too many years away . . .

Almost angrily, Parco ran through the message pad that Theo had prepared for him earlier; a crisp abstract of fax and telephone calls received that day, plus, where necessary, cross-references to other files and databases; together with the little personal reminders that lifted her from being a good secretary to a brilliant one.

He scrolled down the screen, noting that the social scan on Anthony Carthew had come through from Parco's regular information-processing source. The data included employment, medical, credit and other details on Carthew for the past few years, all made accessible through the magic key of the man's social security number. While Carthew most certainly guarded the privacy of his bank-account numbers and numerous other financial dealings very fiercely, his SSN was common knowledge to all manner of organizations, and opened the doors to many other safes, both literal and metaphorical, that would otherwise be locked tight against Parco's probing.

Following Mrs Carthew's instructions, Parco paid particular attention to her husband's medical record, which showed that he had taken an HIV test at a private clinic in London three months before, about the time he and Ms Sutton started their clandestine dating. The results were negative. When the girl's scan came through, probably tomorrow, and if that too showed clear, Parco would be able to reassure Mrs Carthew, who could then begin the job of destroying her husband in another but no less painful way.

Parco sighed, reflecting on the varieties of human deceit; the spectrum of human betrayal and cruelty. Why, for instance, was Carthew such a two-faced bastard that he needed to do this to the woman whom he'd vowed to love, honour and cherish? Why promise, when promises crumbled against the first assaults of lust or greed . . .? Couldn't he at least have told her?

This sudden high moralizing made Parco chuckle aloud. No one was beyond reproach: no one could ever justifiably cast the first stone. He himself had done things that were best left to lie in the dark undercroft of his memory. When and if there came a Judgement Day, Parco knew, neither he nor any of his kind could face their Maker with a pure heart or a clear conscience.

But saved or damned, Parco had to get through another working day tomorrow. He pressed on through the messages, smiling absently at Theo's asides and comments, until the final note rose up to fill the screen:

Your first appointment tomorrow is with a Mrs Eleanor Van Allen (if you like classy broads, you'll love this one!). She is very concerned that her husband is no longer her husband – That is to say, he does not appear to be himself. She told me when she called at the office that, 'Richard looks the same and behaves the same, but somehow I know it's not him: his spirit has gone.'

I reckon we can charge top rate on this one, and there's always the escape clause of recommending psychotherapy – for both of them, probably . . .

So be here by 8.45, Parco: watch *Invasion of the Body Snatchers* if you've got it on the cable database; and wear your best tie. And, for pity's sake, don't drop your aitches or she'll think we're too down-market.

See you in the a.m.
Theo.

At ten-thirty that same night, the clouds that had been building all day became substantial enough to release a warm autumn rain which sparkled in tinsel veils under the streetlights. The pavements and roads were soaked within minutes. Traffic sizzled through the city centre, and cinema-goers and drinkers on the move were forced to shelter in shop doorways and beneath trees whose leaves had in the past week been touched gold by the change of the season.

Two miles south of the centre, on rising ground that overlooked the bowl of the valley, Calverton University stood proud amidst trees. The campus had grown since the turn of the century, to the point where virtually all of its gardens and grounds had been given over to new labs and lecture complexes. Likewise, the accommodation for its burgeoning student population had increased, such that many of the late Victorian and Edwardian streets around had been bought up and converted to dorms and flats.

One such street was Eastleigh, an avenue of three-storey buildings and silver birches that curved with quiet grace around to the north and west. The road and pavements were empty on this wet night. The trees lifted their skirts in the strengthening wind, and rain swished at windows like handfuls of flung beads.

Inside one darkened room in a house that was no differ-ent from any other on Eastleigh, William Howard Jnr. paused in his love-making as the weather rushed at the window. He had been lost in lust, driving like a machine into the girl beneath him, so that he was surprised now, as he came back to himself, that the room had grown so dark.

Howard pushed himself up above her, feeling the sweat

27

cooling on his bare back. He looked at Helen's gold hair splashed across the pillow, and at the pale smudge of her face, but could not tell if her eyes were open or closed . . . If the damn bitch had fallen asleep during the performance, he'd never forgive her!

Howard ran a hand across her breasts and squeezed at a nipple. He was amazed anew every time these circumstances arose at the softness of women; warm velvet in which he loved to sink, redefining himself within another. He felt the nipple tauten, puckering; lowered his lips and licked it.

'Finish what you started, Bill,' the girl said out of the darkness, an edge of frustration in her voice. 'I was almost there . . .'

He laughed as he geared up into his rhythm. 'You asked for it: you got it . . .'

They came quickly, within the minute, she taken to an exquisite peak that tore through her, gently bruising her soul; he pulsing with a groan as he spilled himself inside, blessing and cursing this moment that, of all moments, he wished would last for ever.

Then they moved apart like the sea sliding off the land. Howard felt he could slumber now in that warm and satisfied aftermath of sex. Sleep surrounded him, ready to overwhelm.

Helen switched on the bedside light and fumbled for her glasses.

'Bloody hell!'

'Well, I can't see a thing without them – '

'What's there to see?' He was annoyed at the sudden glare and at her for taking control of things; his restfulness in ruins around him.

'Mugs, kettle, coffee jar – unless you'd prefer tea?'

She was serious, he sensed, and he wanted to yell at her –

then laugh at his own anger. Helen Remmick was too pretty to yell at; too sensitive to laugh at. So Howard sighed quietly and propped himself up, plumping pillows behind him, as Helen found her glasses, put them on, and looked once more like the studious undergrad that she was.

She rose from the bed and walked naked to the sink in the corner. The light cast her body into contours of shade and pale profiles, arousing Howard once more. He was always like this during the first few weeks of a relationship, so freaking horny that desire crowded his every waking moment, so that he wanted only to screw and screw again, even when his machinery had given all it had to give and screamed at him to desist. Besides, Helen was far and away the most beautiful girl he'd ever dated, and intelligent too. Many fresher-girls came on to university as much to hook a husband as to train for a career: it was the same for plenty of the boys, too, although perhaps with marriage not set so firmly in their minds.

Howard, with his Masters behind him and on a generous Ph.D. research scholarship funded by the European Association for the Advancement of Archaeological Studies, was able to enjoy the best of all worlds. His work was practical and fulfilling, he had no worries over money, there was most likely a job at the end of it, and he had enough freedom in planning his schedule to spend as much time with Helen Remmick as he liked (or his body could stand). She, for her part, seemed to like him for himself, notwithstanding the academic benefits accruing to her by their friendship.

Howard reckoned it was a good deal all round, especially if she made coffee in the nude more often.

He leaned across, reached into his side-table drawer, and took out a reefer, already rolled and wrapped in a twist of waxed paper. He lit up and tilted his head back, letting the smoke trickle into his lungs like a warm liqueur.

Helen turned around at the new smell of sweetness in the air.

'Smoke?' Howard offered. He could not feel more relaxed, more at peace with the world in which he was embedded – and yet with a perception of it that seemed razor-sharp. He felt a powerful sense of the rightness of his life: an intuition that destiny was carrying him on towards purposes unknown, but purposes that would eventually justify his existence and exalt it.

'I don't know . . .' Helen smiled. 'I mean, I've never . . .'

'The caffeine in that mug will do you more harm. Go on, take a puff – humping is even better after one of these . . .'

'It's against the law,' she pointed out, with a mock coyness that delighted him. She put the coffee down and her small breasts gleamed in the light flung upward against them.

' "Every law is an infraction of liberty" – Jeremy Bentham, 1748 to 1832,' Howard quoted, drawing another deep breath.

'Damn show-off. Oh, all right. Hey, love and peace, man!'

Howard laughed and made the still-famous Vulcan hand sign.

'Live long and prosper, fellow traveller in time and space . . .'

An hour later, Helen said she needed to get back to hall: there was an early lecture tomorrow, and besides, she didn't feel she could handle all the gossip if she was seen sneaking into her room any time after midnight and before 6 a.m.

'Tell them you've been out earning extra cash to supplement your grant,' Howard suggested glibly, regretting it at once as her expression darkened.

'I'm sorry, Helen, that was plain stupid – '

'Is that what you think I am?' Her anger and hurt surged up suddenly, tingeing her cheeks, making her eyes flare.

'Don't be ridiculous: it was just my loose mouth. I like you a lot. Really . . . Please, I do. Believe it . . .'

'I believe it,' she said, 'I think.'

'Listen, love, actually I can't stand your body – '

She spun at him, then paused at the gleam in his eye.

'It's just that you make such great coffee,' Howard said. And Helen laughed, and Howard breathed a deep and inward sigh of relief.

They showered – not together; that would have delayed them another hour – and Helen wondered if he'd call a cab for her.

'I'll walk you back – '

'I don't mind going in the taxi,' Helen said. She was standing in front of the mirror, her reflected face looking back at him, busy combing out her long blonde hair. Howard marvelled at it once more: it was white-gold, its longest strands reaching to her waist, almost glowing now against her black roll-neck sweater and dark-blue 501s. When Howard had initially seen Helen Remmick, that unique and fleeting moment of first meeting, his breath had caught at her beauty; such a clean and uncomplicated loveliness. Nineteen and fresh from home, knowing almost no one in this strange new town: easy meat, Howard thought, for the hungry dogs on campus. He was in a very real sense saving her from them, as much as saving her for himself . . . It was a dark and depressing truth that the suicide rate for students had for many years been significantly higher than that for the population at large. Book-based knowledge itself was not so dangerous, although the pressure to absorb it could be extreme: what killed more kids than drink and drugs and fast cars was their failure to cope with the new world that had been opened to them; out of the nest now and exposed to the rapacity of those whose flight was direct through the bones of the living.

Howard didn't want it to happen to anyone, least of all to this girl with whom, he suspected with a shock, he was starting to fall in love.

He walked over to her, slid his arms around her waist and nuzzled her ear. 'The rain's stopped. What could be more romantic than a walk back to hall through the park on a late summer night with someone you admire and like a great deal?'

'Show-off!' She twisted around to face him.

'I was talking,' he said with quiet sincerity, 'about myself . . .'

He kissed her, allowing it to linger, reluctant to let go of the evening they had spent together. Eventually it was Helen who broke the intimacy and eased away.

'Come on, let's go, before you persuade me otherwise.'

Eastleigh and the streets around were separated from the campus by Elizabeth Park, an open area of grass and treed walks given over for public recreation in 1953. Streetlighting had been installed after a rape there in the early sixties, and upgraded after an assault and robbery in 1984. These days, the place was more or less clear of students (except large groups walking together for safety) by nightfall. Between dark and dawn you'd find a few drunks, a scattering of girls or guys hoping to turn a trick; maybe a mugger or two. Perhaps once an hour, a state patrol car would cruise around one edge of the park boundary; very rarely a pair of beat cops might check out the footpaths. For all that, Howard was quite fond of Lizzie Park: he'd spent many summer afternoons here soaking up sun or exploring the limits of what was possible or known with groups of students or lecturers: spent many hours walking, thinking – and not a few occasions gentling girls with smiles and whispers into his bed.

None of them truly compared with Helen, however. In her he'd found a happiness that was somehow richer and more substantial than all of the hungering that had gone before. He felt that so strongly, that he did not even trust a cab to get her back safe – not after the cop had been killed downtown, just two months earlier.

Start of term was still six weeks away, but Howard had returned to Eastleigh early to begin in earnest on his thesis. He had access to the University Library, and to the City Museum, which housed a unique collection of artefacts pertinent to his researches. That aside, he liked Calverton; its atmosphere was different from London, where he'd been raised, and it was small enough to get to know. Whereas the capital would always be very largely a monstrous unknown, Calverton had assumed in Howard's mind a certain identity. It had become, almost, home.

The cop killing had unnerved him; had scared everyone for a while. Not that such slayings were rare in cities now, but the nature of the murder was repugnant to Howard and, indeed, to the public perception of how a police officer's death should occur. Very little was released to the media, but rumour was rife and embodied the belief that the man had been mutilated, in particular about his face. No official statement confirmed this, but the image held a powerful horror in the mass mind and was thus taken as truth – as was the apparent lack of motive for the act. Such extreme and purposeless brutality caused everyone to take care. Howard never mentioned the murder to Helen, but since the killer had not yet been found – and could therefore be anyone – he was reluctant to let her out of his sight.

But it was more than that. Death was no longer an abstract thing to Howard since Neil Cernan had been amazingly, appallingly killed at the railyards in June. Even now, Howard could hardly accept the fact, much less the implication touted by the press that his friend was involved in the robbery. Howard knew that Neil was close to Richard Van Allen, Director of the Calverton Museum, among other things: so the likelihood was that Neil's purpose was to supervise an incoming shipment of Van Allen's, and nothing more . . . No way would Howard ever consider an alternative – unless it was that Neil's death had been planned. Somehow, considering him as a victim made his slaughter more bearable.

Howard walked Helen to the door of her hall of residence, kissed her quickly under the porchway light (it made him feel like an adolescent all over again!), then hurried away once he was satisfied there was a locked door between her and the night.

Howard jogged it back home. The wind was behind him, skittering first-fallen leaves along the path, through glinting rain puddles and on out of sight. He did not run, nor let the panic that was lying there waiting blossom in his chest. But never for a second did his hand let go of the knife that he held by the hilt, ready and sharp, in his coat pocket.

He let out a shuddering breath as he pushed his front door closed. The large chilly hallway of the house was lit by a low-wattage bulb that cast a tired amber light across the chequerboard of stone floor-tiles, the trim noticeboards and the red polished pine of the stairway banister. Against one wall, the rows of staff and student pigeon-holes loomed like empty sockets. Howard checked his mail and found a late message from the Director of the Museum asking him to come by next morning . . .

He frowned. There were no details, but the note was personally signed. It could be anything; good news, bad news. Howard decided not to let it trouble him. Tonight he would sleep like the dead, waking in the light to the thought of the girl that meant so much to him.

The tenement was filled with rats and darkness, of which he was a part. Or rather, he thought, that were a part of him. These days it was difficult to decide what lay within and what without. For when the night came on, Risico's mind too seemed to drain of light. That was not so bad – it was bearable: but what set him screaming, despite his best efforts to keep the terror tied on a short line, was the chemical pungency of burning that might have been in his head . . . Or in his destiny. He was never sure. At such times, when he felt suffocated by fire, and more by horror, the urge to find its source became irresistible. Then he must reach the face behind the face. Then he must dig down behind the cherubic smile out of heaven and seek the devil beneath . . . There was beauty at the heart of the beast, Risico knew, but not a human beauty. No, nothing that had a soul.

The street bum Risico had found made the call willingly at knifepoint. Inside the cramped phone box, he had all but been choked by the stink of the tramp; but behind the wiry whiskers and gin-raddled eyes had been the remnants of a keen intelligence. More façades, Risico thought. It didn't matter. The bum had spoken well and reported the gang of kids shooting up in the old abandoned building: not that that was reason enough for a unit to be despatched, of course – but it looked like a few of the girls had been under-age; probably there while their parents were going quietly frantic ... And with the Mayor up for re-election in the spring, mightn't it be a good idea to send ...

The officer on the line asked for details, and the guy read convincingly what Risico had previously written out on a card. The address was a boarding house he had never roomed at; the driver's licence number belonged to Conway; poor Conway, who would never need it now ... Maybe they'd run a check at the station, in which case the use of the ID would bring them out anyway. Or maybe they'd just come. City cops, naturally. The private force wouldn't bother with a general social problem like this. While their job also was to protect property and people, the reckoning was that nothing but dross was in danger here – and then by their own hand – and that if the faceless owner of the block had not tidied it up or bulldozed it flat, then it must be for a reason, probably tax related ...

No, the private boys would stay out of it and the state units would come in, perhaps. Which was just what Risico wanted. It had been the face of a state cop that had smiled at him with a look of such terrifying evil and power on that night in June when, by some awful turn of magic, the universe had opened up and shown Risico its guts. He still couldn't figure it now, as he sat waiting, crammed under worm-eaten stairs, just what had occurred. Something other than a man, something more, had filled the eyes and the mouth and the ears of that cop ... The noise and the fire, the dreadful pain of the flames, all had conspired to confuse his perception and judgement. Risico, despite long questing hours, still did not know what he had seen. But he had seen something, something that had been till then hidden from human sight . . . Something ancient and obscene.

He saw it now, fleetingly in his mind's eye, before the sound of voices disturbed his fantasy and brought him back to the cold and uncomfortable present.

Risico rose, all his survivor's street instincts aroused, and moved away from his hiding-place.

Outside, the wind had gotten up, but the rain had eased to a few gusted specks on the windshield of the patrol car that sat in the roadway, its blue light flashing.

The two officers, Spears and Harris, standing nearby, were debating their course of action. Something stank here besides the cats' piss in the decaying hallway of the tenement. It was suspicious enough that someone should call in reporting a skag den in some God-forgotten downtown slum – what the hell was he doing there anyhow, to witness it? But when the driver's ID belonged to a corpse lying in the city cemetery these past few months, there was cause enough to look into the matter. So the desk sergeant said: Harris and Spears themselves would have preferred to forget about the whole damn thing.

'You think it's a set-up?' Harris wondered now, his attention drifting between his partner's response and the crumbling hallway into which he knew he would soon be stepping. Spears, four years his senior and one grade above, was in no better position to judge.

'Why – you got anything to be scared of?'

It was a standard come-back in place of an answer. In these hard times, two thousand years after Christ had died for man in the name of love, bastards still killed cops because they were cops. Or just because they liked killing, which was worse. There seemed no point in it, beyond the celebration of evil for itself. Witness Mike Fisher's killing in

July, and the frightful raking of his face . . . Neither man had seen the body, but they'd heard from others what it had been like. Hardly a face at all, when the killer had finished his work.

Which was why Harris shrugged and, against the superstitions of the force, said, 'Yeah. I got a lot to be scared of . . .'

Spears's expression hardened into something like contempt. He was feeling like shit himself about this, and Harris wasn't helping.

'We go in anyway,' he said to his partner. They both drew their guns, aimed their flashlights and stepped out of the wind.

Risico heard them coming; saw their shadows behind the glaring Cyclops eyes of the torches. He smelt them. He could almost taste the presence of these men . . . It was what living like this had done to him: existing like a sewer-dweller in the cellars beneath the seethe of the city's commerce, surfacing occasionally at the beck of the internal tides that motivated him now. He recognized that he had become an animal – but that was still preferable to what the officer in the burning warehouse had been. Angel. Demon. Something between both.

For all his rough living, Risico had kept himself in good health physically. He was lean through choice, not deprivation, and strong. And fast. He moved in and out of the darkness with a silence that still surprised him, his senses spread out through the filthy spaces of the building like a net, already cast around these two doomed bluefish who had taken his bait. He looked down through rotted floorboards a storey above, listened to the cops' conversation, saw them split apart to cover the ground more quickly and be done with this place . . . Neither man felt safe, but their own fear had ironically reassured them that no one would lay a trap in this abandoned ruin at this time of night . . . And, anyway, they could keep radio contact, and they had the guns and the night-sticks . . .

Risico smiled as the wave of triumph crested inside him. He slid his knife from its keeping place, unsheathed it like a claw, and moved in on the first of his victims.

Harris hefted the weight of the Colt in his moist hand and felt marginally reassured by the silver-blue gleam of light along the barrel. The gun was a Cobra .357 Magnum, low-priced, mass-produced, reliable, carrying six shots. That should be enough. He put in a couple of hours' practice weekly, regular as clockwork, using the same weapon; and his scores were good. Not that the practice-room resembled this gloomy cavern, rich with the stench of rot: but Harris trusted to the wisdom of his body: the reflexes were drilled into him so that he did not need to think in order to act, and act effectively. Even if some crack-ruined crazy came out at him, Harris knew that he could register the attack, aim – and blow the fucker's head off before the assailant got within swiping distance. Then, OK, so there'd be a day's paperwork to deal with, and he'd need a couple to wind down after the shock, but it would be good for a few sessions in the station R&R lounge, and the guys would stand him drinks all night just to hear the story again, once he was out of this, if it came to anything at all –

And theories are fine until they're proven wrong. There was a writhing movement in the darkness before him, gleaming eyes and a face of such fear and hatred that Harris opened his mouth to shriek – and died before that shriek was born. Risico's knife, plunging inwards and at a slightly upward angle, slid through intercostal muscle between the fourth and third ribs on the left side; punctured the left ventricle of Harris's heart and severed the aorta before being withdrawn. Massive haemorrhaging started at once.

Even as the huge bleeding began, blackening the royal-blue police uniform, Risico swept the blade in a precise arc that slit the cop's throat and dropped him where he stood. He crashed down among sodden planks and rusty cans, among fetid rat droppings and foul water, and felt none of it. His whole being was concentrated for a second on the face of the man who had slain him. Such empty eyes: such a driven and wearied paleness . . .

Then Harris's attention turned inward and he reflected momentarily and with an endless sadness on all the things he had not done in his time . . . Life was such a trifling game, so brief and disappointing. But it was all, and now it was over.

The officer died of shock and rapid cardiac arrest; flooding of the lungs with blood being a secondary cause. And perhaps if mercy existed, his death was merciful, for he was no longer aware of Risico using his blade once more, this time to see if Satan lurked beneath.

Spears used his radio to contact Harris a few minutes later. There had been sounds some distance away: nothing identifiable, nothing sinister. But Spears's bad feelings had grown. Blithely Harris had suggested splitting up, dovetailing the suggestion with an instruction to make a standard search pattern through the building's empty spaces; working front to back, a floor apart, easily within yelling range if something happened.

OK, Spears thought; something has. Someone had moved below, and Harris was not answering the call . . . He tried again and was answered by the tearing cloth of static. With a quiet curse he stopped moving and pondered whether to go on, or return to the car and request backup.

Spears did not take long to choose, telling himself that common sense and not cowardice tipped the balance of his decision.

He backstepped a few paces, turned, and the figure of Harris's killer leaped in the glare of the torchlight.

Spears had time for one shot, a thunderous detonation in the closeness of the hallway. He saw the psycho stumble as the darkness returned like a closing iris: but the flashlight was smashed and not working – no – it was snatched from him – and now – and – now . . .

The pain hit him instantly and completely. It was an agony that he thought no man could imagine, let alone endure. Spears was not even sure where he was hurt, for it erupted everywhere, like a petrol fire, and he collapsed under it and lay face down in the muck.

Risico turned the man over, grateful that the intensity of his wounding had silenced the cop. He worked quickly, switching on a lamp of his own; hurrying back through the tenement for his bag. Returning, he took out the steel timber nails and the hammer, and staked Spears out on the soaking boards; arms first, then legs . . . The man began sobbing, gurgling out some stillborn plea to live, to live, to die . . .

Risico turned a deaf ear, but not for a second did he look away from the officer's face. He had rendered the body useless and put it through intolerable pain. So, if there was anything possessing this hulk of weeping, pitiful flesh, it would now show itself as it sought escape and freedom . . .

Risico waited for an hour, which was as long as he dared. By then, the cop was dead and his face was dead, and stayed so, except that in ironic parody, the black lips pulled back in rigor mortis into a final, awful grin.

Chapter Three

And wet my cheeks with artificial tears,
And frame my face to all occasions.
King Henry VI, Part 3, III.ii.184–5

Parco heard the news on his way to work the following morning. The cab driver was tuned in to a local FM rock station, and Parco had been amused that the music was turned down low for the benefit of any passenger: Theo, whose philosophy was 'if you're gonna live – live!', would have complained and asked for the dial to go to ten – and why didn't the cabbie have a better set of speakers in the back . . .

The car was caught in a city-centre rush-hour snarl and the band had climaxed its song in a cascade of thrash. The linkman's voice was a whisper; and then the cab driver swore softly and brought up the volume for Parco to hear.

' . . . double police killing in an abandoned tenement block in the High Fields area of the city last night. This follows the murder of State Police Officer Charles Golding last June, and an early statement from City Police Head-quarters suggests a possible link between the slayings.

'The dead men have not been named, nor further details released. Police are asking for any information in connection with the incident, and for possible witnesses to come forward; they have issued an alert to members of the public not to walk alone in any part of the city after dark.

'A release from the Mayor's office confirms that extra patrols will be targeted to High Fields and the surrounding areas. An official enquiry into the murders has already begun . . .'

'I tell you, I don't know what this fucking town is coming to!' The cabbie part turned to make this observation. Parco saw his face in half-profile and noted that the guy was unshaven and that his breath smelt stale. He was probably on the butt-end of an all-night shift, and Parco would be his last fare before he returned to base. Since this was the start of Parco's day, he did not want to waste time and effort either agreeing or otherwise with the driver. Sure, the news was shocking and depressing, and the outspreading ripples of what had happened might in some form brush past the world in which Parco operated: a PI could find himself up some pretty strange avenues. Parco knew that he would take time to reflect on this act of savagery. But not now, not with this dork.

'Drop me here,' he instructed, passing over his credit card and not caring that the driver seemed offended by his brusqueness – which was ameliorated a little when Parco told him to take a tip which was likely to be the most generous he'd see during that week. From Parco's side, you never knew when paths would cross again. He might one day need this man's help in a hurry, so it paid to pay, as it were.

He offered the driver a friendly enough smile and agreed that Calverton was not the place it had once been. Then he stepped out and walked the last mile to his office, turning quickly off the main street with its traffic din and fumes and taking a cut-through to the quiet pedestrianized walkway, lined with sycamore trees, on which his and a thousand other offices were situated.

Theo was already in and busy, of course, and not mad with him – because he'd obeyed her message and was here in plenty of time to see Mrs Eleanor Whatever-it-was.

'Been out on the piss again, Parco?' were Theo's opening

words to her boss. They both knew she could get away with it; that the remark was part of the close working relationship they shared. Parco did not take offence – and in any case could hardly deny the accusation when his car was still parked in the underground garage beneath the formal lawns which his inner office overlooked.

He shrugged, grinning like a schoolboy caught on the skive.

'Theo, it was a heavy day. A boring day. I needed that drink.'

'I thought you loved your work?'

'Certain aspects of it. But waiting for a man to finish copulating with his wife's secretary hardly constitutes life in the fast lane.'

Theo laughed, beautifully to his eyes. ' "James Parco's my name – danger is my game." I'll have some new business cards run up!'

'You can mock,' Parco said, 'but it pays your wages – '

'Which reminds me: now, about my raise . . .'

'Maybe if the Mrs Eleanor – um – '

'Van Allen.'

' – Van Allen case pays off, we'll negotiate. But I have to warn you, I'm at my most malleable over a candlelit dinner . . .'

Dammit, Parco thought; that was clumsy, and far too heavy a suggestion for so early in the day. But I wouldn't need to resort to these tactics if she paid more attention to what I'm trying to say to her . . .

Theo was smiling gently, realizing well enough what Parco was trying to say to her.

'I'm no good at candlelit dinners, I can never see what I'm eating.' She added, just as his expression started to turn: 'I like bright and cheerful restaurants, and to save the candlelight for conversation afterwards . . .'

That satisfied both of them without committing either. Parco felt better; let down gently – if he had been let down. Theo was too intelligent, and maybe too well-meaning, just to say no, or just to say yes.

He nodded, then asked her to run through the day's schedule, which she did in her standard crisp and concise way, though her perfume worried at the edges of his concentration and distracted him.

Theo Vines was twenty-eight years old, a redhead (soft copper rather than fiery bronze), with green eyes of intense clarity, and a determined look to her that a lot of people had found offputting – thus, ironically, sometimes blunting Theo's intent to go far and go fast. She'd worked her way determinedly through the educational system, compensating for its broken-down machinery by hundreds of hours of private study and clear-sighted goals that her parents did not completely comprehend; but they helped her where they could, with a room of her own and what money they could spare for the books and materials she needed. Their reward was to see her win a place at one of the London colleges, where she majored in media studies, specializing in televisual language structures in advertising campaigns.

A hundred doors opened for Theo after graduating. Most of them led to the bowels of one or other of the TV networks, where she would never be seen or heard of again. A few led directly to a sweaty director's penthouse sofa, cushioned with promises but oddly bereft of contracts. Theo wanted none of it: there were other ways to the top besides the back door or working up from the basement.

She took a job at twenty-one with Datafax, a major information-gathering organization based in London but with branches spread across Europe. In a world where facts had replaced dollars or yen as the major currency, Theo used her skills to make plenty of dollars and yen for herself and her company. She was quick and she was reliable, swiftly mastering the techniques of database access, public-document searches, medical-information retrieval, and the more subtle arts of telephone persuasion, working under the adage that if it's not on file, then someone, somewhere has it in their head.

Within four years, Theo was a highly paid insurance investigator for Datafax, one of their top operatives in Britain, and with the chance to work abroad whenever she liked. She found the job challenging but not daunting, exciting but not stressful. The money pleased her and the prospects were excellent. She more or less had reached where she wanted to be before the age of twenty-five, and was prepared to give it a few more years yet before thoughts of marriage and home-making and kids changed the direction of her life.

For someone who relished being in control, the situation she found herself in that summer four years earlier was particularly frustrating. She did not then and would not now call it love: lust, infatuation, foolishness – yes, all of those. She could not even immediately identify just what it was about Tim Leason that she found so compelling. He was not especially good-looking, nowhere near as considerate and appreciative as James Parco: he was mercenary, a user and sometimes a brutal one; socially, sexually, intellectually ... But now as Theo reflected on it, she understood just why she had stayed with him – because she had enjoyed it; the utter contrast of being dominated for once by someone who could dominate her skilfully. The humiliations she had suffered at Leason's hands burned in her memory still, but they had excited her then; proven to her that she was not the cold and calculating careerist she had built herself up to be, in her mind and the minds of her colleagues. The bitch at work became the compliant slave in Leason's bed, and not before or since had she been so aroused.

But the final act of using had been hers, ditching him and his cul-de-sac life when she'd satisfied herself – most importantly in the respect that she was going nowhere with this man, that he meant nothing to her at all.

Theo moved north, answered an ad in the *Calverton Times* for a secretary and assistant, placed by one James M. Parco; passed the interview with flying colours and was hired over the phone that same evening. She recognized at once that Parco, a bachelor, was a lonely man, and that working with him (not for him, that was a distinction they clarified early) could be difficult. But she offered no come-ons, always dressed smartly but never provocatively, and attempted to maintain the standards that Parco demanded, and that she in her own mind had set herself anyway. It worked fine. She had of course taken a sizeable drop in salary, but the future was rich in potential opportunities: and, at the same time, Theo was still stretching her wings, seeing how high she could fly. She decided that she liked things as they were, for the time being . . .

After running through the details of the Van Allen case, as much as Mrs Van Allen had offered during her brief preliminary phone call, Theo outlined a couple of other propositions, including a missing person's which, if Parco decided to take it, she could work on while he probed into Mr Van Allen and finished off the Carthew affair.

'Sounds great,' he said, and smiled at her. They had sat together on the same side of Theo's desk, she in her green, leather-upholstered executive chair, he in a more modest chair with castors that he'd moved up close – but not too close – to see her notes.

'At this rate,' Parco added, not entirely glibly, 'we'll need to take on more staff.'

'Whatever you say, boss.' Theo was pleased, because the matrimonial (it was suspected that the father had snatched his little girl from his estranged wife) had been a referral to her personally, based on similar work she'd done previously in that field. It gratified her more that Parco considered letting her take that load, which he would not have done if there'd been any lack of faith.

'OK.' Parco stood up and straightened his tie. 'Show Mrs Van Allen in when she arrives. If the job looks right, I'll chase that and leave this other to you.'

He walked to his door, turned. 'And thanks, Theo. You're good for me – more than you know.'

'Thanks, Parco,' she said. And, to cover her embarrassment: 'That raise had better be a good one . . .'

Parco went through and closed the door. He sat at his desk, swivelling the chair around to look out over the gardens, and scribbled a few initial notes in a leather-bound pad.

Eleanor Van Allen, he thought, would most likely be mid-fifties, prudish, upper-middle class and an incipient neurotic, worrying about her altered husband when, in fact, it was just her passing through the menopause . . .

She turned out to be late thirties, amber-blonde and with exquisitely classical features. Her pale complexion was thrown into contrast by bright-red lipstick that easily avoided garishness, and by eye make-up expertly applied. She was powerfully attractive, elegant, assured, poised, intelligent and controlled. Parco began to take her assertions seriously.

'And you first started noticing changes in your husband when, Mrs Van Allen?'

'I suppose it was early in July . . . It was that terrible hot spell: both of us were on edge . . . Richard was so busy at work . . . I had various pressures . . .' She smiled in a way that Parco found ambiguous.

'You sound as though you're trying to talk yourself out of this, if I may say so . . .'

Her smile, that first hesitant crack in her cool façade, was a breakthrough for both of them. Now, whether she realized it or not, the information content of what she said would rise.

'It's difficult to talk about – '

'Of course it is.'

Eleanor Van Allen chuckled.

'No, you misunderstand me, Mr Parco. It's difficult because I'm not sure the language exists to frame what I want to say. You see, you're asking when I first noticed things, but I'm not sure there were "things" to "notice". Even now after these two months of worrying about it, I don't have a shred of evidence, let alone proof, to back up what I feel.'

'Which is why you've come to me, presumably.' Now Parco was on more familiar territory, dealing with uncertainties in his clients: uncertainties that had grown more influential than the instinctive wish to leave well alone, to let the humdrum life roll on, a wish that lies inside everyone.

'Let me put it to you like this, Mrs Van Allen,' Parco said, following up his advantage. 'I like to go in fast, get the job done and close the case. You've seen my charges: my clients can't afford for me to dither about looking for clues that may or may not exist. I can't afford it either. If I take a case just to screw money – I'm sorry, just to maximize my income – and don't produce fast and definite results, then folk lose faith in me and I lose customers.'

Parco smiled, a smile so professional it had become natural.

'I've met you and I trust your judgement. I believe that something about your husband has changed; that it's serious, and that you need an explanation, if only for your peace of mind. If, after this consultation, you still feel you want to go on, then I'll ask for an initial fee of seven hundred and fifty pounds, which is seventy-five an hour for ten hours, including this morning's meeting. Now, by that time, Mrs Van Allen, I will either have wrapped the matter up, or I will have uncovered depths to the case which will require me to refer to you for further instructions. You are in control of the situation at all times. I report back to you whenever there's a break in my investigations, and, of course, these are conducted with the utmost discretion and the highest respect for your privacy.'

'Then I can say we have a deal, Mr Parco. You must agree that it can seem pretty foolish to meet with a stranger and confess that your husband is no longer the man you married – though I still can't say how . . .'

'Then let's proceed carefully, unpicking the details as we come to them – '

'Do you mind if I smoke? It puts me at ease . . .'

'We, uh . . .' Parco was about to enforce the no-smoking rule that had existed in his office, inner and outer, for the past three years, since he'd given up himself. That was primarily due to Theo's influence. At the time of the painful transition, he'd complained that, at this rate, he'd have no vices left to fall back on. Theo had replied that that was no bad thing, and had not enquired what his other vices might be, much to Parco's chagrin . . .

He opened the bottom drawer of his desk, where he kept an untidy miscellany, including a glass ashtray and his old Ronson lighter, which he maintained in working order for reasons of nostalgia – and in case he ever got bitten by the nicotine bug again.

He placed the tray on the desk in front of the woman and then walked around to light her cigarette, which was one of those long, dark, exotic types with a thin gold band that smelt, he always thought, like hashish. Theo was not going to approve of this!

'Can I tempt you, Mr Parco?'

Parco looked at Eleanor Van Allen's eyes before he looked at the packet she was offering him. She blew smoke slowly into the air between them, keeping her lips pursed. She'd unbuttoned her coat and sat relaxed, leaning back, with her legs crossed. She was wearing a simple dark-blue dress, made by Raynor's of London, Theo would later confirm, with a skirt that was a shade short for someone of Mrs Van Allen's age, but not for someone of her figure. She had positioned herself to the maximum advantage as Parco came around to her side with the lighter. Her stockings were of black silk, her blue Gucci shoes had a high polish, and there was nothing false in her tiny pearl ear-rings and the simple gold-and-diamond jewellery she wore around her neck and on her wedding-ring finger.

'It would distract me too much right now, but thank you,' Parco answered. 'I like to keep my head clear when I'm opening a file.'

'Very businesslike.'

'Right.' Parco sat and looked at his notepad. When he

glanced up, he was in control of himself once more, and learning fast.

'Tell me about your husband's work, Mrs Van Allen, if you would.'

'Richard is the Director of Museum Services for the region. He's based at the museum here in Calverton, but his responsibilities lie further afield. Have you ever been to the City Museum, Mr Parco?'

'Years ago . . . Enjoyed it . . .'

'It hasn't changed much, at least not as far as the public is concerned. Over the past twenty years, many museum bases have closed their public facilities entirely as council and Government fundings dried up. That is not to say that they've ceased functioning as organizations: a number of directors have chosen the path of specialization to maintain the museum's infrastructure – I mean by that the work has gone behind the scenes completely.'

'What does that involve?'

'Usually, establishing affiliations with academic organizations; developing restoration facilities; acting as consultants in a range of capacities – from advising antiques' dealers on the authenticity of certain items, to liaising with governments on renovation work of buildings and suchlike. But Richard has fought hard to keep the public facet of his profession going. He believes that the shape of the future is embodied in the form of the past. Me, I think you shape your own destiny, regardless of the bygone mistakes of others . . .'

'I never realized so much went on underground – if you'll pardon the pun.'

'On this one occasion, I will.' Eleanor Van Allen smiled at him, and in that moment Parco's intuition told him a great deal. Perhaps this woman's husband had changed in her eyes, simply because he had discovered her appetite for other men, or had grown tired of it. But the same principle had been operating in him – to let life roll comfortably on: to let – Parco excused himself a second pun – to let sleeping dogs lie.

'It is, in fact, big business,' she said. 'Ever since the Tory influence of the eighties exhorting private enterprise and the entrepreneurial spirit, public organizations all over the country have been changing the direction of their operations. Ironically perhaps, people like my husband – experts in looking at the past – have become experts at looking to the future. Richard has built up a business worth forty million in the last fiscal year, with many branches – '

'Such as?'

'The things I've mentioned to you – restorations, architectural renovations – as well as building up important databases and collections of antiquities. We're very lucky that we have a major university here in Calverton. They use us a great deal, and pay well for the privilege.'

Parco nodded. 'OK, that's all useful to me, Mrs Van Allen. But – '

'Eleanor, please . . .'

'Right, Eleanor. Um, and in which area does your husband specialize?'

She shrugged. 'Well, these days it's administration. But his field of knowledge is Ancient Greece, specifically, the island of Crete before 2000 BC . . .'

Parco frowned. 'I seem to remember – there was an attempted robbery down at the railyards awhile ago. Late June. A couple of policemen were killed . . . and a security guard; another was injured. Wasn't that to do with – '

'You're right, Mr Parco. The criminals were after a shipment my husband was importing: mainly Minoan items, very old . . . The pity of it is that they were probably after gold jewellery and plate, whereas the most valuable pieces were simple pottery and scriptural tablets – I'm talking about academic value, of course. Potsherds and fragments would not fetch a great deal either on the open market, or from a collector. But their research value could be priceless.'

'What were the details?' Parco asked. 'What did your husband lose?'

'Some amphorae were smashed. A number of smaller items were never recovered . . . There was a fire, you'll recall. The warehouse was largely destroyed.'

'Yes,' Parco said. 'I remember. A bad business. Could it tie in with this change in your husband?'

'Possibly. I know that the pressures have been getting to him lately – well, and not so lately. You see, Mr Parco, our relationship has deteriorated somewhat over the past few years. That's not to say I don't love him, you understand. But he has been so busy with his work . . . We've not enjoyed the intimacy that bonded us at the start.'

'I see.'

'I hope you do.' Eleanor stubbed out the remains of her cigarette and looked at Parco squarely.

'I suspect you are a very shrewd man, Mr Parco, and I'm sure you've learned a great deal more during this interview than I've told you. But for all that, I'm convinced Richard Van Allen is not the man I married: I mean it literally, and not just in terms of the distance that has developed between us. In fact, I will go so far as to say that he is not Richard Van Allen. Not any longer . . .'

'It's a hell of a thing to . . .' Parco began, but the woman had not glanced away. Her gaze, as far as she wanted it to be, was frank and sincere. And frightened. That's what convinced Parco that he would take up the case: the same instincts that had told him so much about her, persuaded him now that Eleanor Van Allen knew just as instinctively her husband was a different man.

'I'll do what I can, Eleanor,' he told her. 'Give me a few days to map out the territory and get the picture clear in my mind. Feel free to call for an update, although I have to confess your problem is new to me . . . Does your husband have a police record, by the way?'

'Oh, drink-driving, I think. That's about it.'

'All right. And I'll need to have access to your house at least once, preferably when there's no chance of Mr Van Allen being there.'

Eleanor caught the shift in Parco's eyes, and delighted in the fact that the man was discomfited. She decided, since he had committed himself now, not to spare his blushes.

'Why, Mr Parco, whatever will the neighbours think?'

When the hell have you ever worried about that, lady? Parco wanted to say to her.

But he smiled instead, letting silence be his reply.

Calverton Museum had been built in 1847 by a far-sighted city council with big dreams. All over the country, the Industrial Revolution was growing apace, and the influx of people from the fields to the towns continued unabated. The university had been established just ten years earlier, the boundaries of its extensive grounds brushing by the fringes of museum land, where a select cluster of houses had been built for the first director and his executive staff and servants.

The museum, like the city itself, had prospered throughout the century and well into the next. More recently, a partial rechannelling of money away from the public educational budget had allowed the building to assume a rather faded and forgotten look.

William Howard thought that was a shame, because the substance of the building's modest Victorian grandeur was still imposing despite the weatherworn paint and badly maintained guttering. He approached from the south, turning off the main northbound road into Calverton on to the trafficless avenue, lined with sycamores and silver birches, on which the museum stood. It had been constructed in a mock-Grecian style with a four-columned façade and triangular arch above huge metal double-doors. Memorial benches and tidily kept flowerbeds flanked the cobbled walk leading up to the portico. The front area was fringed by iron railings, with small private ornamental gardens beyond: all of which blended in Howard's mind to create a fond impression of slightly sad elegance; a sort of lost echo of past greatness and endeavour, a little misplaced now in this runaway world of infotech, cyberpunk and Muzak made by machines.

He walked through the modern steel-and-glass doorway constructed under the arches of the old, and dropped his regular donation into the big Perspex collection-bin placed just inside the lobby. Most public facilities now charged an entry fee, but one of the Director's hobby-horses had always been that the splendours of the world and its history should be freely viewed and appreciated. Howard grinned, wondering in the cynical way he had cultivated over the years what old Van Allen's ulterior motive might be. He did not doubt that there was one; this conviction partly arising through Howard's overall attitude towards the inevitable reaction of money on men; partly through what little he knew about Van Allen as an individual. Simply put, he did not trust the bastard an inch, this opinion albeit based on campus rumour and hearsay – which was often exaggerated, but rarely wrong entirely. There had been vague stories of large investments made, using museum money, in deals that were legal through loopholes: this created cash for Van Allen's work, true enough, but it was more than evident that he'd creamed off a generous percentage in 'commission' for himself. Howard wondered how many other curators could afford a ten-bedroom mansion in the executive belt at the top end of town, and four cars which included a Daimler and two BMWs? Not much had been proven, of course; and what had been proven was legitimate. These days, the boundaries between public functionary and private businessman were sometimes blurred – and as Van Allen himself would no doubt argue, the skills used to create his personal wealth also kept the museum and its arms in existence.

Howard tried to put it out of his mind as he walked through the familiar rooms towards the private quarters of the building where the Director's office was located. Normally he would make his way across the small but effectively staged display of Ancient Egyptian antiquities, through a side-door and down a flight of steps to the labs and workshops. Today, he passed by Fine Arts without a glance, along a blue-carpeted corridor lined with a variety of modern sculptures, to the tall oak door of Van Allen's office.

His knock was answered at once, by Vaughn Castillo, who was the Deputy Director.

'You're punctual, Mr Howard. We appreciate it.'

It was all Howard could do to avoid retching in the man's presence. Castillo made his skin crawl. He was an arrogant poseur, in Howard's view; a leech that clung to Van Allen's side, enjoying his superior's reflected fame and reciprocating with a treacly sycophancy that revolted

Howard utterly. Quite evidently Castillo was also homo-
sexual; not that that fact influenced Howard adversely or
otherwise – one man's meat, as the saying went: but the
Deputy Director all but paraded his proclivity by his effemi-
nate manner and the camp extroversion he affected to make
others ill at ease. It was all front, Howard had concluded
long ago, an attempt to shock when what Castillo really
wanted was to be left alone to enjoy the flesh of men and to
be enjoyed in turn. Perhaps through self-shame he made a
song and dance of it, and that's what grated on Howard's
nerves and on his moral senses, liberal though they were.

Richard Van Allen was something different again; deeper
waters by far, Howard decided as he obeyed the Director's
gesture and sat facing him across the broad expanse of his
desk. It had been made for Sir Charles Wallace, the first
director of the museum, over one hundred and fifty years
ago, and was Van Allen's only pretension. While Castillo was
all sham, all powder-puff prancing and shallow sarcasm, Van
Allen's comments cut to the bone of things. He was a terse,
intolerant man whose few words reflected profound and
comprehensive calculation of a problem or a plan. Howard
found that characteristic impressive, even occasionally
unnerving, especially when coupled with Van Allen's
imposing physical presence. He stood over six feet tall, and
for a man touching fifty maintained an enviable physique
and stature. He was always immaculately dressed, usually
in a suit from Jermyn Street that would swallow most of
Howard's annual grant: no one ever saw Van Allen in anything less formal than a roll-neck sweater and slacks. He
kept his dark hair brushed back and brilliantined, which
added to his look of severity, at least as far as Howard was
concerned: he guessed that a certain type of woman would
find the trait irresistible – and maybe Castillo did too, come

to think of it; which was why the mincing fairy was rarely absent when Van Allen was around . . .

Howard stifled the smile that threatened to get the meeting off to a bad start, and accepted the wine that Castillo had brought over with as much grace as his distaste for the man would allow. Van Allen also took a glass, and Castillo a third, as he sat in the bottle-green leather chair to the left of the Director's position.

'No doubt you are wondering why I wanted to see you so urgently, Mr Howard,' Van Allen began.

Howard was in mid-sip and, in nodding, almost spilt the Bordeaux down his shirt front. He noted Castillo's small smirk, and wanted to break the man's nose.

'I'll come to the point. Your work at the university, and indirectly at the museum, has impressed me greatly. I will go so far as to say that the research you have conducted on the written language of the Palace Civilizations of Crete and Mycenae is the best I have seen. I feel quite confident that you can take your line of enquiry on to achieve your doctorate and, if the circumstances fall right for you, to a professorship, quite probably at the university here in the city . . .'

Van Allen paused to drink delicately from his glass, leaving Howard stunned by the magnitude of what he had said. His head spun with the opportunities that could open up for him now; of the money, of the trips abroad to Greece, to Crete and the Aegean Islands and beyond. And what would Helen think? It would be a boost to her academic career also if Howard's prestige was enhanced by a public endorsement from Van Allen . . . He began to think of the fellowships that might follow this, of the offers of research associate . . . And then his perspective swung back as Van Allen's possible motives began to gather in his mind like shadows.

None of this showed on his face, and Howard was careful to keep it so. He allowed himself a smile and stared for a long moment at the paperweight resting by Van Allen's right hand. It was a bronze, dating back over a century, showing a chimpanzee sitting atop a pile of books, with a pair of pliers gripped in one foot, and holding a human skull in one hand, its other hand cupping its chin, as though in deep contemplation. It seemed somehow apt for the occasion.

'That's a fine compliment, sir,' Howard said. 'I'm very flattered.'

'Nothing to be flattered about, and I was merely stating a fact. Professor Quinn from your department has shown me some of your preliminary notes on the cross-correspondences between Cretan Linear A and Linear B scripts. You have gone as far as any man, and possibly further, in deciphering Linear A; and I know that privately you have hinted at a breakthrough on the horizon . . .'

Van Allen's tone invited Howard to elaborate. It was true that through a mixture of luck and perseverance he had made inroads into the strange, almost runic hieroglyphs the Minoans used four thousand years before: and yes, in a rare moment of over-confident boasting he had intimated to Quinn that his thesis might contain the most complete decipherment yet presented . . . But this was still by no means certain, and even if it was or became so, he did not wish to have the kudos snatched from his hands by a man like Van Allen – who would certainly steal or plagiarize Howard's findings if he could discover a plausible way of doing so.

All of Howard's instincts told him that this was the purpose of the Director's invitation this morning; to sound out the depth of his research and pitch a deal that would benefit Van Allen himself.

Suddenly the wine was sour in Howard's mouth, and he was on the point of getting up and leaving . . . And it would mean leaving in every sense, for such a snub to Van Allen was tantamount to washing his hands of the museum, the university and his scholarship.

'A – breakthrough,' Howard mumbled, caught like a speck in a hurricane. 'I don't – know – I – '

Van Allen was watching him closely. He smiled and reached for something beside his chair, out of Howard's sight.

'Perhaps this will clarify your thinking, Mr Howard.'

Howard took what the Director held out to him. It was a roughly oval piece of plaster casting, about the size of a hardback book; light, chalky and covered with closely written pictographs in several different styles, most of which Howard recognized at once: the others, as he stared, frowning, suddenly grew in significance that blazed through him like bright electricity. He almost dropped the cast in his shock.

'My God . . . My – God . . . Do you realize what this is?'

Howard glanced up sharply, face filled with excitement and suspicion, both. Van Allen's manner remained relaxed.

'As well as you do, Mr Howard. It is a code-key that will enable you to decipher Linear A within a few months. Or rather, would allow you to do so if it were complete. As you see, a significant portion of the cast is missing . . .'

A hundred questions clamoured at the front of Howard's mind, and frustration as well as wild elation tightened in his chest.

'Yes,' he said, 'but I can make real progress with this. Even as a plaster facsimile, this is incredibly valuable . . . We must discuss further how my final work should be accredited. I don't feel that—'

Van Allen stopped him with a raised hand, which he then held out for the return of the cast. Howard handed it over as though it was his mother's life.

'I am not concerned about accreditation, Mr Howard. A simple acknowledgement when you have finished your thesis will be sufficient. I am more interested in the source of this casting – in the original stone from which it was made.'

The idea bloomed in Howard's imagination. But of course, there would have to be an original. But where was it found? And where was it now? And why hadn't he read of it in the literature? The whole world of archaeology would be buzzing with such news, unless . . .

'I see,' said Van Allen, 'that you have come to understand the nature of my dilemma. Your face tells me. You are quite correct in thinking that the removal of the keystone from a shaft grave near Hagia Triada was illegal. That is not ulti- mately a problem. Once I have acquired the stone, I can have copies of its textual content made before contacting the appropriate authorities with news of its existence and an offer of its return. Diplomatic entanglements will not interfere with your work . . .'

Howard finished his wine and looked down into the empty glass. He felt he knew what was in Dr Faustus's heart when he made his pact with the devil – for it was surely true that Van Allen would never simply hand the artefact over to the Government of Greece for the price of a thank you and a few column inches in *The Times*. There were other forces working here; the ulterior motives Howard had earlier sus- pected. And yet, to hold that stone in his hands, just once, and be able to read a language that no human mind had understood for thousands of years . . .

'. . . you realize that we will need to work together to procure the stone,' Van Allen was saying smoothly. 'I will need an assurance of your co-operation in this affair, Mr Howard. Timing will be very important, and secrecy of course . . .'

Howard sighed, knowing he was in deep whichever way he turned. Van Allen was offering him the choice between fame and obscurity, between fulfilment and academic oblivion.

'I'll help you all I can, Mr Van Allen,' Howard said quietly.

Van Allen nodded, and allowed Castillo to pour him another drink.

Later, when the other two men had gone, the Director rose from his chair and looked out across the small, leaf-strewn lawn at the back of the museum. It was a private, quiet piece of ground with the blue-brick walls of the stately Edwardian houses beyond forming its far boundary.

The day was mild and dry, with a weakening sun spilling its light through hazy September cloud. But the past few nights had been a little chilly, the ground cooled by rain; and soon the winter would come on and there would be frosts and sleet and long dark nights.

So different from home, the voice whispered in the Director's head. He felt a surge of sadness through him that was not his own.

'You know sun and bright skies, and dreams of gods that are nothing like our noise and machinery; the filth of this modern world . . .'

There are still dreams of gods. They are clever enough to be what men at any time imagine them to be.

'You are right. Men are men in any age – lustful, greedy, fearful of the heaven's thunder; fearful of their own ending.'

It need not be so. The mark of any god is control over the inevitable.

'In return for celebration and worship. Man and the gods. It is a union. The sky and the clouds: the snow and the mountain.'

Then so shall it continue to be.

The voice fell silent and Van Allen put his fingers to his face – which smiled in triumph of its own accord.

Chapter Four

All, all are gone, the old familiar faces.
'The Old Familiar Faces', Charles Lamb

Theo worked all day at her desk on the missing-child case that Parco had allowed her to handle. She exchanged a few brief words with her boss as he showed Eleanor Van Allen out of the office (but plenty of time to catch up on the details afterwards, maybe!), and barely noticed when, two hours later, Parco went for an early lunch. He stayed out for most of the afternoon: Theo guessed he was 'mapping the territory' as he liked to call it – getting a feel for the places where Richard Van Allen would dine and drink, as well as his place of work. Perhaps Parco would talk casually to folk, casting for information, or it might be that he'd just stroll and think and lay his plans of action. Theo knew as well as anyone that such time was rarely wasted. Parco would be, among other things, assessing the information offered by Mrs Van Allen, and retesting his own reactions to it. Theo smiled as she paused in her work to bite at a sandwich and swill it down with her third cup of tepid coffee of the day. Whatever else the Van Allen woman was or was not, no one could doubt that she was a bombshell. Not one of those startlingly pretty or even glamorous females whose looks come out of a handbag. Eleanor Van Allen's attractiveness operated on deeper levels; a dark and underlying sexuality that Eleanor would have come to recognize early, and use to her own advantage from then on. Theo wondered if Parco had accepted the case for the reasons he usually gave – it's possible and it's profitable: or did the lady in question have something to do with it?

Even as she felt the mildest pang of jealousy and regret threading through her, Theo was glad that Parco's attention had been diverted away from herself. She had become very sensitive to the little courtesies and compliments he had been paying her lately; the oblique requests for a date . . . The little word game about the raise and the candlelit dinner had been just that, a kind of half-serious subtext that left more unspoken than said, and created problems for the future rather than merely leaving doors open for either or both of them to step through later. Theo sighed. Why the hell couldn't Jim Parco simply date her, woo her and screw her? In her surprised-by-joy state, she might even let him get away with it! But all of this uneasy compromise within the context of a job that required her total concentration and all of her skills, was a pain that she knew she could not tolerate indefinitely.

Theo surfaced from her reverie and found that she was angry. The final mouthful of coffee at the bottom of the cup had gone cold, stone-cold. She drank it anyway, tossed her sandwich crust into the wastebin and got back to her keyboard.

Parco's first port of call after Eleanor Van Allen's departure was the reference library in Calverton civic centre, where an assistant who was charmed by his mildly scruffy good looks and polite enquiries provided him with all the material he could have hoped for at this level of probing.

He sat at a table set by itself in a window bay looking out over the civic square. Opposite him rose the self-important redbrick magnificence of City Hall, with ornamental fountains flanked by a quartet of bronze lions between. It was another of those late summer/early autumn days when the changing season had lightly touched the trees, and the sky looked white and washed-out by months of bright sunlight. Parco liked this time of year: it had a quietness to it, a calm before the busyness of autumn and the bleakness of winter began. He set to work in a mood of calm confidence, happy to be doing what circumstance had brought him here to do.

Two hours' effort yielded several pages of notes on Richard Van Allen, the man and his reputation. An initial check in *Who's Who* led Parco on to more specialized listings: *Cale's Directory*, a kind of phone book in reverse, supplied not only Van Allen's home number, but two located at the museum and another for Dashwood's Club close by; a place that Parco had heard about but never had the contacts, fees or professional reasons to visit.

Moving away from the volumes piled in front of him, Parco asked for a telephone and called up the computer service he habitually used when skimming information prior to engaging top gear in a case. He identified himself to the operative of Fax Manifest Incorporated by his subscription number, then self-accessed the database with the user code that, like the pin number on a cash card, was known only to Parco himself. Luckily for him and his clients, unluckily for those whom he was investigating, freedom of information law coupled with the proliferation of registers held on disk allowed any legitimate paying customer, such as a hassled PI short on time, to pick up all manner of facts relating to the person in question. Parco soon had details of Van Allen's academic and business careers; his achievements and standing in the archaeological world; via yearbooks, of his interests and activities; and by scanning his credit transactions of the past year, of where he shopped, what he bought and how much he spent.

Parco quickly built up a picture of an astute and charis-

matic man who had reached a certain, rather modest, position in museum administration and then, rather than
moving up a narrow and very finite ladder in that area,
had spread his interests wide by forging links with other
organizations and, by commercializing his expertise,
accumulating wealth and prestige through the transhipment
of antiquities, mainly from the Mediterranean.

That gave Parco what he called his surface summary of
the target. He thanked the FMI operative, asked for the files
to be faxed in full to his office, and settled by VisaCard. He
was pleased to have made rapid and useful progress, but
realized clearly that he had not gone deep enough; yet this
early assessment was based on information gleaned about
Van Allen, and not on first-hand experience of the man
himself. It was also true that he was not investigating him
for any supposed wrongdoing. As far as Parco knew at that
moment, Van Allen was not a criminal – although it would
be interesting to see what kind of dirt could be dug on his
so-called import business: no end of suspect merchandise
could be brought in under the guise of 'Artefacts for
Research', and with the protection of authenticated documentation, validated by museum and university stamps . . .

Parco smiled, realizing that a shadowy corner of himself
almost wanted to pin something on Van Allen, for no other
reason than he was successful and, in his own way, powerful.
He must have been both to have hooked a catch like
Eleanor, Parco surmised, recognizing with a deep and familiar pang of envy that this man had something he didn't.

Rather than ruin his amiable mood by further thoughts
along these lines, Parco decided to stay busy. At some point
he would need access to the Van Allen household in order
to give substance to his initial impressions. He also felt
inclined to poke into Van Allen's antiquities business, start-

ing with a reassessment of the warehouse incident ten weeks
earlier. His investigations confirmed Eleanor's assertion that
Van Allen had lost items in the fire: by probing in that direction, Parco hoped he could speak to Van Allen personally
and get to nose around at closer quarters. He felt that one
interview would likely decide in his own mind whether
Eleanor's suspicions – her fears – were groundless or not . . .

It was now mid-afternoon. Parco felt peckish again, and
could do with a drink. He thought he should also check
back with Theo. Increasing her caseload was all very well,
but she was not a trained PI and it was unfair to leave
her floundering.

He left the reference library, grabbed a burger and ate it
as he walked back to the office, deciding to kill several birds
with one stone by stopping by at Burly's Bar later that
evening. It was a place where most of the city cops went to
do their social drinking; so Parco could re-establish some
old friendships, while at the same time ask around for the
information he wanted. Also, the beer was good and the
Scotch was not watered. And the place stayed open late,
very late, for known faces. He would not need to spend
another entire night solely in his own company.

Theo was reading a magazine when Parco walked into the
office. It was *Cosmopolitan*, and so made for a double surprise. He had never before known her to idle time in
working hours, and would have thought anyway that a
highbrow novel or even a book of non-fiction would have
been more her style.

'What are my stars for the week?' he wondered, keeping
his tone completely non-critical. Parco hoped his smile was
simple, straightforward and not disapproving.

Theo dropped the magazine down at the side of her chair. Her returning smile was not quite so uncomplicated.

'Couldn't say, Parco; but mine mention a tall, dark, handsome stranger . . .'

'Lets me out,' he said, 'but if you had occasion to meet Richard Van Allen, I'm sure he'd fit the bill.'

'I reckon you're right.' Theo handed him a slim folder. 'These came through on the fax a while ago. He reminds me of George Sanders – do you remember that actor?'

'Before my time,' Parco teased. They both laughed, what thin ice there had been now broken.

'There're also a couple more consultations to fit in – I made appointments for Thursday; and Mrs Carthew's been on the line asking for an update.'

'OK, Theo, and thanks. I'll read this stuff before I leave, and type up my final notes on the Carthew case. Um, about the mag – I don't mind, you know, an unscheduled break . . .'

'Actually, Parco, I've done all the paperwork on the child snatch,' Theo said, crisply cutting through Parco's fumbling words. 'I was waiting for you to get back or call in, so's I could check on what you want me to do next.'

Parco nodded, feeling foolish. Theo's tableau of an open *Cosmopolitan* and feet up on the desk had been staged to make a point – that it was no good letting her pull her weight if he didn't do the same.

'Theo, I apologize, I really do. I should have checked back. I never thought for a moment you were slacking . . .'

'Apology accepted, boss – but I didn't want one anyway.' She ran a hand through her hair self-consciously, sensing the atmosphere tensing between them; another awkwardly intimate moment Theo couldn't handle right now.

'Fill me in on the snatch.' Parco had picked up the vibes

also, and there was work to be done that could *only* be done if their conversation was emotionally uncluttered.

'It's pretty definite that the natural father has taken Betsy Cline and is holding her in a rented flat.'

'Where's that?'

'London. Wood Green. I ran some credit checks on the guy and found he's been buying stuff at London Zoo, Hamleys, MOMI – there's an exhibition of kids' TV on there at the moment . . .'

'It all seems pretty clear. He's bribing the girl with gifts, showing her the excitement of the big city. Is he working?'

'Freelance TV producer, would you believe? He's on contract to a small private company at present, splitting his time between a studio in Fulham and home. There also seems to be a live-in lover,' Theo went on. 'Marcia Symmonds, twenty-three, brunette, aspirations to be an actress . . .' She finished the thumbnail sketch, then grinned at Parco's reaction.

'Jesus wept. Can't you see it – the guy is hoping for the big time himself, so moves to London where the contacts are. He carries on with the bread-and-butter jobs but will, no doubt, be on the sniff for the one break he needs to get the girls and the glory. Right now, Ms Symmonds is both exciting and useful, in so far as she can keep an eye on the kid while Cline is at the studio. But that's an unstable structure. Pretty soon she'll get bored with him if his contracts don't come along; or he will with her if they do. To cap it all, he takes revenge on the wife he's left behind by snatching the daughter . . . It makes me sick, Theo – the petty-mindedness, the sheer meanness . . .'

'You're reading it right, Parco,' Theo replied. 'The Clines tried some marriage counselling about three years ago, but stopped attending the sessions after a couple of months. Peter Cline then moved out and began making things difficult for his wife – refusing financial support, pestering her and the daughter; the usual crap. She successfully obtained a court injunction preventing him from going near the kid, meanwhile filing for divorce on the grounds of an irretrievable breakdown of the marriage. There was a fight over custody, but it was a foregone conclusion that Anna Cline would get it. Her ex-husband was granted very limited rights of access to the child, and after a short phase of what you might call terrorizing Mrs Cline and Betsy, he vanished – only to reappear in the frame when the girl went missing at the weekend.'

'Right. It's simple, then. We garner a little more on Peter and his starlet – run a DMV, and – '

'I did that,' Theo said. 'In between *Cosmopolitan* articles. He doesn't own a car currently, but hired through Hertz last Friday and returned the car yesterday morning. The manager of the rental shop told me Cline had clocked a little over two hundred miles.'

'A round trip from London to Calverton.'

'That's right. Marcia Symmonds owns a Mini Piccadilly, metallic-gold with blue leather upholstery ordered especially. More mobile than a casting couch, but not as much room to spread out . . .'

'You're a cynic, Theo, and wicked to boot.'

'Sorry, it's my media training coming to the surface.'

Parco shrugged. 'It may be that Cline is expecting the law to call round, or a PI, if his imagination stretches that far. Could be he only wanted to give his ex a scare.'

'I don't know. He sounds a mean bastard . . . Which is why I was wondering if you'd come down to London with me tomorrow, Parco? I mean, if you have time: I know this Van Allen job has intrigued you . . .'

'What are you suggesting?' Parco wanted to know, amiably enough; but he could feel himself getting hot under the collar.

Theo's turn to shrug. 'Seems like Eleanor has legs men would kill for.'

'I'm happy with the legs I've got,' Parco replied promptly. 'And I'd be glad to travel with you. I can work on the train anyway . . . In this case, I think *you're* reading it right. This is not just some scare tactic. In my experience, when the non-custodial parent steals a child from the ex-partner, it's for keeps. Cline could get nasty over this one – and I wouldn't want you confronting him by yourself – '

'I might do him too much damage?'

'Something like that. Look, Theo, why not take an early cab home after reserving a couple of seats on an early train for – '

'Done that too. We're booked on the eight-fifteen Intercity out of Calverton. Standard class – but close to the restaurant car so you can buy me breakfast.'

'Theo,' Parco beamed, 'you're priceless!'

'But perhaps underpriced,' she came back without mercy. Parco held her gaze with a grin.

'I'll bear it in mind. Believe me.'

At a little after eight-thirty that evening, Parco locked up his office, set the alarm and strolled down towards the city centre. He was acutely aware that for the second night running, he'd left his Saab garaged because what he most needed to do was relax over a whisky or four. Not that he believed creeping alcoholism was a problem: not yet, anyway. He had read long ago that it wasn't just the amount one drank that was significant, but the reasons behind it. Lonely drinking, secret drinking, peer-pressure drinking – these were the danger signs. Well, he hadn't quite reached that stage. He liked to loosen up at home, sure; run a video or play some rock music. And loneliness didn't come into it. Hell, if he was lonely there were a hundred places he could go for company; not that all of it was wholesome, not that all of it was free. But such people could fill his hours amply enough, and had done so on any number of occasions. As for peer pressure . . . Most of the folk who knew he liked a glass never forced more on to him, out of respect for his wishes rather than as a nicety of drinkers' etiquette, Parco was glad to realize. In this city that was really no different from any other; within its vast and anonymous concrete sprawl, Parco knew he had friends, and some close ones. He had a life here that occupied him, even if it didn't always satisfy or fulfil. He knew happiness as much as he knew pain.

What more could any man ask for, Parco thought; without dwelling on it too much . . .

He reached Burly's Bar and walked inside. The place was quiet this early on, having not yet become the hot, smoke- and noise-filled den that he both loved and hated. It would get that way around ten to ten-thirty when the regulars rolled in.

'Burly's Bar' was its unofficial name: the sign above the door read 'Team of Oxen', but the present landlord, Bill Burly, had run the joint for the best part of twenty years, so that the style and ethos of the place had come to assume his character. Bill's family had strong police connections. His grandfather had been a cop, his father had been a cop, his mother had been a civilian secretary employed by the force, and Bill's sister still counselled the families of officers killed in the line of duty. Bill himself had trained at 'Riot City' in Hounslow during the mid-seventies and stayed for five years as a beat cop in Calverton, before protesting at the cut- backs in basic police provision and the insidious flourishing of private forces during the nineties by quitting. It was still a topic that he chose never to talk about.

Feelings generally ran strong and deep in Burly's Bar on all matters related to law enforcement, generating a sense of camaraderie closer and more powerful than any other emotion Parco had ever experienced: it led to fights, sure enough, when there was a difference of opinion; fights which Burly settled swiftly and judiciously with a cricket bat – and it led to friendships that lasted for life, and beyond. The ghosts of dead cops haunted the tobacco-yellowed wallpaper and the dark and secluded bays of Burly's Bar. And Parco sensed that they were here around him now, as he leaned against the counter and waited to be served.

Bill noticed him and came across.

'Jim . . . Good to see you again. You OK these days?'

'I'm alive and it's pay-day on Friday,' Parco said, reciting what was a ritual greeting whenever a friend at Burly's enquired after your well-being. He was as glad to see the tall, balding landlord as Burly was to see him. 'I'll take a glass of best and a whisky chaser, Bill, if you please . . .'

'Malt?'

'Blended will do, it's only a chaser. Have one yourself.'

'A half of beer, Jim. Thanks. Seriously, it's been a long time.'

Parco nodded and watched Bill Burly pull an expert pint. 'Haven't sampled your wares since April–May time. It's your prices, Bill. Too high. I've been saving for tonight . . .'

'Then have this first round on me, you tight-fisted bastard.' Bill laughed and Parco smiled a little tiredly. 'You can't tell me private-dicking doesn't bring in plenty of green.'

'Not that much after taxes and overheads. And please,

Bill, "investigatory services" not "private-dicking": you could create entirely the wrong impression . . . Cheers.'

Both men took a long swallow of their ale, and in Parco's case it was a grateful one. He tossed down the Scotch, took a deep breath and felt much, much better.

'Are you here as part of an "investigatory service",' Bill wanted to know, 'or is this a social call?'

'There's been a complaint about sawdust in the sausages, actually. This is official.'

Parco delivered the line with such deadpan sincerity that for a moment the big man over the counter looked worried, then angry, before a broad smile broke across his weathered features.

'Seriously,' Parco said, 'I just thought I'd come in to see a few old faces. To, uh, you know . . . show my respects.'

'It's a sad time at Burly's. I don't think I've seen morale so low for years.' Burly shrugged, his hands busy beneath the bar as he soused out some glasses. 'And as for the old faces, most of them are working extra time to try to catch the crazy fucker who's behind all of this . . . But a few discerning punters drop by occasionally. How you doing, boys?'

Parco turned at Burly's greeting. A group of four police officers, just off duty and just out of uniform, had come in and, after exchanging a nod and a wave with Parco, headed for a tucked-away table; one of the men breaking away a moment later to buy the round.

'Good to see you, John.' Parco registered the tiredness in the cop's eyes; and not just the physical tiredness of a long shift.

'Can I buy you one?'

'Thanks, Jim. Give me a Jack Daniel's, Bill, will you? And

four pints on a tray to take back . . . Long time no see. How are you?'

'Doing OK . . . I was sorry to hear about Harris and Spears.' Parco felt awkward as he said it, knowing there were taboos here when it came to mentioning cop killings yet to be solved. On the other hand, silence would be unforgivable.

'Yeah,' Pearcy said, without looking at Parco. He raised the tot glass Burly put before him and drank the bourbon in a single shot. 'To absent friends. "Gone, all gone; the old familiar faces . . ." It's a quote. But don't worry, I'm not feeling sorry for myself.'

Parco grinned at his friend: it was a grin tinged with sadness. Pearcy had always been a good cop: once he had been a young cop, filled with fire and the drive to see justice done and wrongdoing beaten. Now Parco saw, not the thinning hair or the eye lines of age, but a weariness that soaked right through to the man's bones: a world-weariness Parco had heard it called; one that you couldn't sleep off.

Parco finished his beer and Burly poured another without being asked.

'You partnered Harris for a time, if I remember it rightly . . .'

'Two years, when I first joined the job. The Super liked to use Col to break in the raw recruits. He had a way with him, a gentle way, you know? But by Christ he could bawl you out if you put a foot wrong.'

Now Pearcy did look at Parco, who could hardly stand to face the man's pure, unashamed grief.

'Upstairs they'll talk about the due process of law – but I hope a couple of us corner this psycho with a gun in his hands. Of course we'll give him the proper warnings . . . Then we'll cut the bastard animal down like he deserves.'

For a moment the passion burned up through Pearcy's blood and found echoes in Parco's bones. The old dilemma of what was right against what was legal surfaced again: he met it himself many times in the course of his own work.

The sudden fire died on the instant as Burly loaded the tray and pushed it solemnly across.

'I'll, uh, be taking these back to the lads. Sorry, Jim.' Pearcy's expression of apology was almost heart-breaking. 'Here's about the only place we can let off steam, y'know? All of this – this damn business – it brings out the worst in people . . .'

'You take care,' Parco said. Then: 'You're riding with Bakker now, aren't you? He isn't in with you tonight . . .?'

'Bakker likes a drink, too, and a game of snooker.' Pearcy made a throwaway gesture with his hands. 'It's changed us all. I hardly know the guy these days. He's not the partner I teamed with . . . Still, stay well – don't go eating any of Burly's food.'

'See you.'

Parco grinned and Burly, ignoring the insult, started talking sport. Pearcy's comment about Bakker was forgotten, until it sprang into Parco's mind much later; and much too late.

Unlike Theo, Parco hated trains and wished for the twentieth time that he'd offered to drive to London. Not that British trains weren't fast, clean and on time these days, but Parco felt frustrated by the fact he was trapped for the next hour and a half without the option of changing his plans, or even stopping off at some cosy country hotel for a proper breakfast. Doubtless Theo could have matched his protests with the logical arguments that he still had plenty of alcohol in his blood after his binge at Burly's; that they could profitably use this time to discuss the Cline case, or just to get through some necessary paperwork; and that, in any event, getting to the centre of London by car was going to be slower than using Intercity. Parco conceded these points in his own mind before they were ever mentioned, leaving Theo mildly surprised by her boss's docility.

They ate light in the restaurant car, then returned to their seats, where they finalized the details of the operation. The main difficulty in any re-snatch job like this was gaining the child's trust when contact was made. Short of bringing the custodial parent along – a move which often caused huge problems of its own – the only way was to couple communication skills with a swift and definite sign that they were who they said they were. To this end, Theo with Mrs Cline's help had prepared a letter and audiotape explaining things simply to Betsy. Mrs Cline had also given Theo the daughter's favourite soft toy, a teddy bear called Charlie, in the hope that the child would respond positively when the time came. The difficulty always remained that the child might prefer to stay with the person who'd snatched her, in which case the mother's only recourse was through the courts. That was one reason why Parco limited the number of missing-children cases he took on board: there was rarely a clean conclusion to them, and sometimes outright failure that did nothing for a PI's self-esteem or reputation.

He said none of this to Theo, whose face still glowed with the pride of being asked to do the work – as well as with the determination that it would be done effectively. When they talked through the encounter, Parco suggested that he dealt with Mr Cline while she, Theo, approached Betsy to gain the kid's trust.

The sun was out and the sky was blue when they arrived

in London. Parco got his own way at the station, hailing a cab to get them to Wood Green, rather than using the tube as Theo suggested. He had to admit to himself, as he stood outside St Pancras linking arms with this attractive woman for whom he felt such affection, that the day away from Calverton would probably do him good. The city, with its dark streak of violent tragedy, felt oppressive, despite his love of the place. He had sensed that keenly at Burly's Bar, which he'd rolled out of at 1 a.m., leaving Pearcy and his mates still knocking them back. There was death on the streets, death directed at them for no reason they could see: it touched them personally, and during those hours Parco had experienced something of their fear . . . Now he was glad to be clear of it for a while; and the hazy sunshine and Theo's light and positive mood helped him in that. He loved her: Parco reaffirmed it as the taxi pulled away and she looked at him with just the tiniest hint of apprehension. Even though he'd never said it straight out, and in truth had not fully admitted it to himself until just a few days ago – now he let the wonder of it pour through him, and decided that before long he would need to tell her. It would make or break the relationship, he knew. But he had to tell her.

The shopping mall and main street at Wood Green were typically bustling. Theo used a photostat road-map to locate Cline's apartment before leading Parco into side-streets and away from the crowds.

Soon after they reached the address Mrs Cline had given them, which turned out to be a well-kept Georgian house in a respectable-looking terrace. The house had long ago been divided into three self-contained apartments, Cline's being situated on the top floor.

'Tricky,' Parco said. 'This main door's locked, so we can't even get into the hallway. There's also a door-phone, so we'll need to state our business before we ever reach Cline's flat . . .'

'I've considered it,' Theo replied. 'EWO – Educational Welfare Officer,' she added as Parco frowned. 'Neighbours have seen the little girl coming and going; we're just checking to make sure her name's down to attend the local school.'

'Which is?'

'North Street Junior,' Theo said, beaming. 'I rang the borough council, said I was moving here and asked which was the nearest school with places available . . .'

'So who's a little marvel, then!'

'Don't patronize, Parco. It's either go in with a sound cover story, or with metaphorical guns blazing . . . Don't forget we need to be aware of the child's feelings in this: she's been through enough trauma recently.'

Parco held up his hands, recognizing the onset of the peculiar friction which was both a strength and a weakness between them, but which seemed to be an inevitable chemistry of their characters.

'OK, OK.' He looked her up and down, openly admiring her white blouse, dark knee-length skirt and brown leather jacket. 'Just thinking, Theo – you look remarkably like an EWO. Well done.'

'Some day, Parco, so help me . . .' Theo muttered ominously, and pressed Cline's door buzzer.

There was no reply, and no metallic-gold Mini parked nearby when they checked. Theo's face showed disappointment and frustration.

'Blast and hell, Parco! I was all psyched up to do this.'

'Part of the job, honey. They could be gone all day. We'll walk round the block and make a couple of passes to see if Cline or Symmonds return.'

'Then?'

'If they do, we follow Plan A. If not, Plan B.'

'What's Plan B?'

'Lunch,' Parco said brightly. 'Followed by another try this afternoon. If there's still no joy, we hit the centre and see some sights. I know a great little Cantonese restaurant at Covent Garden. They do a fantastic Crispy Barbecue Pork . . .'

It was Plan B, to Theo's annoyance and Parco's quiet delight. Peter Cline got home a little after seven, and he was alone: Marcia Symmonds did not return until 8 p.m. that evening, with the little girl in tow and in tears.

'Probably parked her with a child-minder all day while she went in search of fame and fortune,' Theo said, displaying an instinctive and open dislike of the woman who was the willing partner in Cline's crime. Meanwhile Parco had taken a few shots of Symmonds hauling Betsy into the flat. He checked his watch.

'Too late now to use the EWO front. Do you want to go for it anyway, Theo, or wait until the morning?'

'I don't like the office to be empty . . .'

'Yes,' Parco said, 'but we need to be aware of the child's feelings in this. She's been through enough trauma recently . . .'

'You bastard, Parco,' Theo whispered, but she stepped up close to him anyway. 'OK, we wait overnight. Now, how about you take me for that candlelit dinner you promised?'

Mr King's was everything Parco had built it up to be. It was a small establishment tucked back among publishing houses and financial consultancies on Henrietta Street, ten steps away from the piazza. Inside, the décor was subdued; subtle softlights casting pastel glows across delicate bamboo arrangements, paper-thin porcelain vases and plates, and stern dragons wrought in green bronze. A fierce china lion gazed down at Parco as he ordered for himself and Theo; starters of chicken satay and rice wine, a main course of assorted dishes with plenty of plain rice, all helped along with green Chinese tea. Waitresses with flawless blue-black hair and beautiful, delicate faces refilled the tiny handleless tumblers each time they passed. The music was so softly fragile that it barely touched the air, trembling notes spilling from unseen speakers.

'This is lovely, Parco. Thank you.' Theo smiled at him, the nature of the smile changing as she saw the difficulty he was having with his chopsticks. Her efforts were confident and successful.

'Bloody things,' he said quietly. 'I always have trouble. If I'd known we were coming, I'd've brought a fork along.'

'Use the rice spoon.'

'Then I'd look a bigger berk. Anyway, my mouth isn't that big!'

Theo chuckled, refraining from making an obvious comment. What pleased her was the spontaneity of the occasion – given that Parco hadn't had 'Plan B' up his sleeve since his suggestion to travel down with her! She dismissed that: the chances had always been good that they could have confronted Cline and his daughter at the first attempt, recovered her and travelled back within a few hours. No, this dinner was out of the blue, a show of courtesy and affection from James Parco that touched her deeply. She decided, then, that tonight, if he asked, she would sleep with him; the gift of herself for all he had done to help her, and a statement of her own fondness for a rare man who wanted her as an aim in itself, and not as a means to a selfish end.

The meal concluded with 'Fruit on a Snow Mountain', fresh exotic fruits heaped on crushed ice, served with a champagne that Parco must have specified when he telephoned the table reservation. Theo was delighted.

'Thanks, Parco,' she said again, amusing him with the use of his surname, a habit she had never broken. 'It's wonderful – I love all of it. I love the food, the atmosphere; I love these superb little paintings . . . Chinese art always impresses me, the way the few strokes offset the white background. The explicit revealing the presence of the implicit. It's like, what's unsaid is as important as the words that are spoken . . . Don't you agree . . .?'

Parco, playing the game he had started, said nothing, but looked round and indicated to a waitress nearby. Moments later, the girl brought a white bowl of rosewater, on which were floating waxed paper flowers cupping nuggets of wax and wavering central flames, the final element of the meal he'd promised.

'Parco,' Theo breathed, reaching across to touch his fingers with hers.

She stripped for him slowly, using pace and movement to create an agony of anticipation. Two of the water-candles trembled a faint light on the bedside table in a tiny hotel room that no one in the world knew they occupied, apart from the polite middle-aged proprietress who had watched Parco sign the register. The air smelled tantalizingly of Theo's perfume (Impulse, Parco noted wryly), the pleasant taint of wax, and the sex that the proximity of their bodies generated.

Beneath her blouse and skirt, Theo was wearing a silky pale-blue chemisette with darker blue lace frills, very brief blue panties and stockings. She turned her back on Parco, undid the ties of the chemisette and let it fall away: it lay on the plain grey carpet like a pool of quicksilver. Parco moaned and his breath caught in his throat.

'Theo – I – '

'Parco,' she told him gently, 'I'm a modern girl in a modern world. I want to do this. It doesn't have to mean an automatic commitment either way, you understand? Take me for what I am . . .'

Now she turned to face him, letting her arms uncross away from her breasts.

'Just take me . . .'

His loving was passionate and hard, almost cruel in the force of what he wanted to express to her. Theo's, no less passionate, was gentler, an exploration of desire rather than the will to see it simply and swiftly satisfied.

After Parco's initial intensity ebbed, the tender brutality of which flattered Theo, she took the initiative and guided him on, revealing secrets of her body and his that brought him to the brink many times, and then led him gently down. He had never realized love-making could be such an art – as much an art as the waterwash landscapes they'd admired at the restaurant. What Theo did *not* do counterpointed her actions; her silences made her moans of pleasure that much more erotic and complimentary to her man. He loved her for it, loved her with his soul as well as with his body that was tautening now as she bucked above him, her eyes closed, her face set in a snarl as she rode herself to climax.

'Theo – ah, God!'

Parco felt himself coming and grabbed her hips to maintain the exquisite, ecstatic rhythm of it, the pain he could endure a million times and not be satiated.

At the last moment, Theo's eyes blazed open to take him in. He shuddered and jerked beneath her as she cried out in her orgasm.

And at about the same time, a little over a hundred miles away in Calverton, another man was dying.

Chapter Five

For by his face straight shall you know his
heart.

King Richard III, III. iv. 55.

Helen caught much of William Howard's excitement
but little of the reasoning behind it. They sat
together in the airy vestibule of the university
library, a low glass coffee-table between them. He'd met her
after a morning lecture and walked with her here, chatting
as they went, making promises and half-formed plans that
sounded crazy to her ears. He was like a small boy who'd
met Santa Claus for the first time, or an adolescent who'd
never been in love before until now.

'Wait a minute, Bill. OK, I understand that Mr Van Allen
has offered you this chance to extend your work and – and
that's great. But I can't see why he's done it. From what
people have said, he isn't the kind of man to do something
like this out of generosity alone – or even in the name of
academic progress . . .'

Howard held up his hands to forestall further criticism.

'Helen, really, what do you know about him? Maybe for
once he is doing something out of altruism. Besides, you're
underestimating my abilities. Van Allen couldn't translate
the script himself – I doubt if anyone in the country could,
except me. Oh, maybe Parkhurst at Edinburgh could do it,
or Pope at Warwick – but they couldn't do it quickly; not as
quickly as me. Anyway, for anyone to decipher the script,
they'd need the full text, either the original stone or a complete cast . . .'

The girl smiled at him, and Howard wondered if she'd

seen through the lie. Or rather, the truth he'd left out. OK, so what he'd said about the difficulty of the translation was accurate enough: Van Allen couldn't do without him. But Van Allen was clever; he had many fingers in many pies, maybe one of which was connected to Neil Cernan. Quite possibly the Director had linked Cernan and Howard and wanted to see where the link led . . . Nothing more sinister than that . . .

Howard outlined the meeting he'd had with Van Allen and Castillo.

'So even he doesn't have the original stone yet?' Helen asked.

'No, but I think he has a good idea where to find it – and it's close. It's in Calverton.'

'How does he know that?'

Howard shrugged. 'I can't say . . . But Van Allen has contacts, he's into grapevines, yeah? He left some addresses for me to check out; said they were dealers who sometimes handle this kind of material. You know, specialist stuff for collectors and institutions. He also gave me a note of authorization to purchase the stone . . .' Howard unfolded a sheet of heavy, high-quality vellum notepaper that bore the museum crest and the coat of arms of the city and county. Helen whistled quietly at the figure Van Allen had quoted.

'Jesus, he wants the thing badly!'

'Even this amount doesn't come near what it's worth,' Howard explained. 'If we get the stone, make the translation and be the first to publish, the prestige and honour we receive will be phenomenal . . .' He sighed impatiently at the girl's obvious lack of comprehension. 'Look, it's like being the discoverer of Tutankhamun's tomb, or the man who found the *Titanic*: it's like owning the *Mary Rose* . . . Do you understand, Helen? It'll set us up for life.'

'Us?' She smiled at him, smiled at the contrast between these grand dreams and the man who sat opposite in his slightly worn and rather baggy jeans, and the chunky home-knit turtle-neck sweater with the hole in the left elbow. Howard's hair was uncombed and his dark beard needed cutting: he could have looked clownish, and maybe did, to the other students on campus. But now, as he returned Helen's smile, she felt a surge of fondness for him, and the faintest tingle of apprehension that he was out of his depth, blinded by glory.

'I want you to be a part of it,' Howard said simply. 'I realize we haven't known each other long, but I like you a great deal, Helen. I – think – I – '

Her eyes lost their softness as she saw the nature of what he was saying. My God, he *was* like an adolescent with his first crush, offering her the world on a plate when all she had given him was a good screw and a few hours of her attention. She wondered fleetingly whether his hesitant protestations of affection derived from emotional immaturity or were sincere. Either way, she was not convinced she felt quite the same. Howard was fun to be with, made love with great expertise and greater vigour, and might yet do her career some good. It was not time to burn her boats and wave goodbye.

'Bill – if you want me with you, fine. I'm happy to help you all I can. Are you checking out these dealers today?'

'I thought I would, yes.'

'Then why don't I come too? Not that I'll be able to recognize what you're looking for; but we can make a day of it. I haven't seen the sights of Calverton yet, and I'd love you to show me round . . .'

They made the date, arranging to meet after lunch back at Howard's apartment, where his car was parked.

Helen stayed on at the library as Howard left, watching him walk away along the gently curving pathways towards the museum. She also watched another man, shortish and stocky, around forty years old, stare at Howard as he passed by. The man rose from the bench where he was sitting, paused to light a second cigarette from the stub of the first, and sauntered along behind him.

The pain in Risico's flesh was nothing. It could be controlled. His body was his own. His face was his own; all under the control of his will. The second cop's lucky bullet had passed right through his arm, luckily missing bone and major blood vessels, and the muscle, though still intensely sore and tender, was healing. He was not to be stopped yet, not yet: his guardian angel still hovered at his side, singing insanely in the night's lonely hours, of horrors hiding behind the backs of shadows, of mantraps camouflaged by smiles.

Risico stood at the grimy sink in the room he had rented and finished cleaning out the wound. He'd used a strong antiseptic that felt like hot needles, and applied the dressing as best he could one-handed: now he lifted his eyes and laughed at himself in the mirror. There was a crack running jaggedly through the glass, and the silvering was decaying with age, so that his reflected face looked distorted and strange. The laughing stopped and Risico turned away, terrified again.

He stumbled to the bed and sat down to the discord of creaking springs. There was a half-empty bottle of Black & White on the cheap side-cupboard within his reach. Risico snatched up the bottle and took a swig, knowing that this way out was no way out; he needed his senses sharp and his purpose honed to get to the bottom of the mystery that had stared him in the eye all those weeks ago . . . But the burn of the Scotch in his throat and its warm blooming through his guts soothed him so; and the buzz in his head, the way the liquor relaxed him and cradled him closer to sleep . . .

Risico knew he would sleep, even though he had lain unconscious all the previous day and the night before that, since he had dragged himself home from the killing. Some all-but-forgotten corner of his heart found room to feel sorry for the men he had murdered. Those cops, in the end, had not needed to die; neither of them harboured whatever it was that Risico felt he must exorcize from his black imagination: neither was infected by that fearful possessor of souls he had glimpsed at the railyard warehouse . . . That one look – it came to him now, unbidden, in all its awful beauty – that one look would always be worth killing to find again, in order to claw it off, to rake out those wonderful terrible eyes which saw more than a man should ever see . . .

Risico drew a shuddering breath, took another slug of whisky and thumped the bottle back down. He tried fleetingly to gather some threads of a game plan together for the next few days. His safety lay in his anonymity, and in the lack of motive for the murders, as far as the police were concerned. There would, to be sure, be intense investigations progressing to find the city's cop killer, but no one would be looking for Patrick Joseph Peters in particular. He was hidden behind Risico, on file as a simple blagger for money, being of sound mind and body and with no reason in the world for cutting off the faces of the noble boys in blue . . .

Laughter bubbled up in Risico again, dissolving into sobs. Sweet Jesus, that it should come to this! He had never imagined his mind would go as well as his nerve . . . But not yet – not yet! Not until the work was finished . . . As it would be, in the name of all that was decent and human.

On an impulse, Risico pulled open the door of the side-cupboard and took out the last item he had that held any value to him. All his money was gone now; on the bag of food by the window, on room rent for the next few days, on a new jacket, the old being ruined by his blood. No, only this remained, a fortune lying heavy in his hands, if he could but realize it.

He unwrapped the stone from its protective cloth and stared hard at it, appreciating the worn smoothness and weight of the object, but making nothing of the etched lines and symbols carved there. Some of them, Risico thought, looked like a kid's scribblings: here was almost a house, there was nearly a man. He pondered on the lost meanings for several minutes, marvelling at the mind that had conceived them, all those long ages ago. Ah well, what mattered was that someone saw potential here, and was prepared to pay for it. Cernan had told him that this artefact was worth a fortune in certain quarters . . . Cernan . . . Risico recalled the young man's face and again felt a stab of regret. He had been a promising kid, a real brain, into books and learning . . . He had enrolled at the university and was studying the worlds of the ancients. He used to go to the museum at the town's top end, he'd told Risico, and spend hours just staring at the stuff in the glass cases and reading the labels . . . He'd helped a lot in finding out which items of the shipment were worth taking. It had been during one memorable conversation with the boy, the result of a chance meeting in a city pub, that the germ of the idea had been born. Calverton was the centre of a spiderweb: millions of pounds worth of freight passing through each week. And not just the mundane cargo of the world. Risico himself knew of gold consignments coming down the line from repository to repository; and diamonds and bonds, cash, antiques. It almost made his mouth water to imagine them – to visualize his hands dipped in such wealth.

Both he and Cernan, strangers to each other but not to this world of dreams, had drunk enough to loosen their lips and imaginations. Risico remembered the moment when the kid paused in his talk, and frowned, and looked squarely into the other's eyes, knowing him for what he was.

'So you've thought about it before? Stealing stuff, I mean?'

Risico grinned, amused at Cernan's naïvety, flattered by the admiration implicit in his voice.

'Son, I was born with a job in mind. I was always a street kid, you see; never had enough, forever wanting more.' He took another drink, so the anger at that truth didn't show too pure and too raw. 'But it's harder than you think to break into one of those armoured trains . . .'

'What about the warehouses?'

Risico shrugged. 'Not so bad, but the transferable items don't stay there: bullion, diamonds and suchlike are deposited in vaults if it's not a straight-through transit.'

'Have you considered antiquities?'

'Not worth it. You've got to know what you're looking for, and a lot of the stuff is breakable – I mean, loading it into a van can ruin a day's work, right?'

Risico chuckled at his own little joke. The kid shook his head.

'I said "antiquities", Mr Risico, not "antiques" . . .'

'So, what's the difference?'

Cernan had explained the difference, and had gone on to say more, a lot more, about how archaeological shipments were generally low profile, and about plenty of them being borderline legal anyway. 'That means,' Cernan explained, 'that if we knock off some Mayan jade statues from Palenque, or gold funerary equipment out of the Valley of the Kings, the importer is not going to kick up a fuss, since the likelihood is they've been smuggled out anyway. Every year, thousands of valuable artefacts are lost from the developing world, into the hands of private collectors who will pay plenty to lock them up in a private safe. And I mean plenty, Mr Risico.'

Cernan mentioned some figures, and the slight glassiness cleared from Risico's eyes.

'These collectors – they don't mind who they buy from?'

'As long as you can offer the documents of authentication along with the item, I'd say not. And as long as the price is right. No one likes to be taken for a ride.'

'That's right. Including me, Mr Cernan.'

'I haven't spent all of my time at university working towards a degree,' Cernan said. 'We could sell any merchandise that we acquired: I could tell you just what to acquire, and when it's coming through . . . And even if, for whatever reason, a particular collector shies off, there are dealers who would fence the items for us: specialists. There are a few in Calverton, actually, because that's where the traffic is.'

Cernan finished his lager and put his empty glass down in front of Risico, whose temper rose at the impudence, but whose expression remained cool.

'It seems like we've got the potential here for some business, Mr Cernan. And I'm impressed with what you know. But remember that you're in my world now – boy – and that if you want this to be more than hot air, you start listening to me. Now,' Risico said quietly, 'you get up off your arse and refill my glass. And if you fuck me about at all, ever, I'll cut your bollocks off and feed them to you one at a time or both at once, it don't matter to me. Get it?'

Cernan's smile wavered a second before his gaze did. Then he nodded slowly, got up and went to the bar.

Risico felt deep inside himself that there was something to be made out of what the boy was saying: he was a clever kid, and knew his place now – at the end, his eyes had held the appropriate glint of fear. And sure he was drunk, but Risico knew men, knew that Cernan was drunker yet with greed . . .

The memory faded. Cernan was dead now and no investigation had connected him with Risico, or was likely to. But the outcome, apart from those deaths, was meagre. This stone was all Risico had to show for it; and without the documentation the kid had talked about, it would be much harder to fence. Yet he would have to try, if only to raise enough cash to survive another week, another month – to dig to the heart of the puzzle that haunted him.

Risico dropped the stone back into the drawer. The alcohol was working now, its effects peaking through his body. He lay back, let his breathing slow, and steeled himself for the night.

Parco felt great, twenty years younger, as he walked with Theo beside him towards Cline's apartment. The woman smiled at her partner's childlike buoyancy. Let him enjoy the triumph of his conquest, a voice in her head said softly; he hasn't looked beyond to the problems; hasn't realized that by taking you once, he has not come to own you for ever . . .

'All right?' Parco asked, breaking the bubble of Theo's thoughts. She nodded.

'Just thinking.'

'Yeah, me too . . .'

'Thinking about the job, I mean.'

'Oh. Right. Nervous?'

'A little. I hope Betsy Cline comes with us, that's all.'

'Don't worry. You've got her soft toy – Charlie?'

'Yep.' Theo pulled it out by the ear to peep from her pocket. 'Charlie says, "Good morning, Mr Parco. Theo tells me you're a great boss – and a really hot lover. Grrrr!" '

Parco blushed and Theo giggled delightedly. 'And James Parco says that although Theo Vines looks gorgeous today, why doesn't Charlie mind his own fucking business and go back to sleep in there . . . Anyway, we're about here.'

They turned into the avenue and increased their pace as they saw the front door of Cline's house open and the three of them, Cline, Marcia Symmonds and the little girl, come out and start down the steps.

'Bit of good fortune,' Parco muttered. It looked as though Marcia was about to leave with Betsy. Cline would be working at home today. He saw the woman fumble in a purse for some keys; saw Cline glance up the street towards them, look away, then look back at them once more.

'On to us – ' Theo said.

Parco broke into a run and reached the group first.

'Mr Cline – Mr Peter Cline?'

'What do you want?' His expression was one of suspicion and hostility. Theo, a few paces behind, noted Symmonds holding tighter to Betsy's shoulders.

'I'm a private investigator, Mr Cline, employed by your ex-wife to trace the whereabouts of her daughter. Looks to me like you've taken her illegally, sir . . .'

'Piss off,' Cline snapped. He flashed a glance at Marcia. 'Take her back in the house – '

'Not a good idea,' Parco said, keeping his tone level and

pleasant, playing the game for now. 'I have authorization from Mrs Cline to bring Betsy home, and I remind you that you have no custodial rights over this child at all. I would therefore suggest, Mr Cline, that – '

'You have fuck all!' Cline snapped, trembling both with anger and the fear of discovery. 'You have no rights at all, you fucking bastard.'

Parco regarded the man with an outward show of calm, maintaining the professional façade that was expected of him. Inside he was seething, his rage moving beyond mere temper to the hatred he harboured for people such as these; knowing that child snatchers do what they do, not out of love for the child, but because they have a vile and pathological need to torture a lover or spouse. And now, to cap it all, he, Parco, was being mouthed off by this animal about the rights of the matter.

Cline was tall and lean: Parco reckoned that maybe he worked out a few times a week. Cline's reddened face was stretched back tight in a sneer, and he had tensed himself to act. The odds were not all stacked in Parco's favour, but he had a few tricks up his sleeve and was guessing that Cline didn't. Hoping so, at least.

'Theo . . .' Parco said, without turning to her. Marcia took this as a signal too, and struggled with the lock of the Mini's driver's door, trying to hold Betsy at the same time.

Theo took a step closer, pushed her right hand into the girl's tumbled ringlets of blonde hair, and pinched a long and elaborate ear-ring between forefinger and thumb.

'What's your game?' Marcia demanded to know. Theo tugged and Marcia squealed.

'Do you know how much a ripped ear *bleeds*?' Theo asked in a friendly way. 'I'll tell you, Marcia, I've seen it done and it's awful . . .'

'Y-you wouldn't . . .'

'Yes, dear, I would. I can assure you that as well as ruining your pretty mini-dress and your hairdo, ripping this earring out will also give me a great deal of pleasure.'

'Bitch!'

'Maybe, but at least I have a conscience. Now be a sweetie: let go of the little girl and get your bony arse out of here. OK?'

Marcia complied without further argument. The interview she had lined up for today had taken plenty of swinging, and her prospects looked good, if the bulge in the casting director's pants had been anything to go by. She stepped down into the car, revved the little engine to a scream and drove quickly away. Theo pulled Charlie from her coat pocket and offered it to the child.

'Here, honey, Charlie's come to see you. And I have a note from your mummy. Want to hear it?'

'Betsy!' Cline snapped, a final attempt to bludgeon.

Parco made his move, stepping a pace closer, transferring his weight to his left foot, hooking his right around Cline's left leg, then following up by pushing him squarely in the chest. Cline toppled backward, sprawling awkwardly and banging the back of his head against the railings flanking the steps. He started struggling. Parco came forward with him and brought his knee down on to Cline's chest.

'I'm taking her home, Cline – uh-uh – don't try it now, because with my other knee I'll squash your balls like overripe tomatoes, and I mean it.'

'I'm getting a lawyer!' Cline's face was suffused with rage, his neck tendons bulging like taut cords. Parco glanced at Theo and saw she'd turned Betsy away and was helping her to read her mother's letter. Later, they'd play the tape before taking the first train home.

Parco used both hands to force Cline's head further between the railings. The man gave a throttled cry.

'I will stay in touch with this case, Mr Cline – for no extra fee, because I want to see Betsy and her mother happy and left in peace. If you make any contact over and above what's laid down, I'll come back and do then what I'd like to do now. Goodbye, Mr Cline. I hope we don't meet again.'

A little extra pressure jammed Cline's head pretty solidly between the iron verticals. He whimpered with pain as Parco walked away, taking Betsy's hand while Theo took the other.

'Fancy a packet of sweets, love?' Parco said. The little girl smiled. Theo didn't.

'They're bad for kids. An apple will do.'

'Yes, darling, whatever you say.'

Three people, Parco reflected, out on a sunny morning walk. Anyone would think they were a family.

Carl Shelton was twenty-eight years old, tall, dark, handsome and moving fast up the ladder of success. He had joined the force straight from college, worked hard, made a good impression and soared through the internal examinations, transferring from the uniform branch to plain-clothes investigations two years ago. As detective sergeant on the drug squad, Shelton found that his salary had improved, and that the work was challenging and exciting. He had a steady girl who loved him, a second-floor flat down at the wharfside development, and a Golf GTI Ghia that could leave most other motors floundering in its dust. He was a happy man.

He left the singles' bar shortly after 11 p.m. with a couple of tenuous leads to follow up, either right away or tomor-

row night, as he chose. The word was out that the ard
stuff, crack, PCP, angel dust, was starting to appear vi. new
avenues of supply; one such being through pushers masquerading as lonely hearts hanging around singles' bars, gay
clubs and maybe even students' union bars on university
and college campuses. Shelton's hunch led him to check out
Melvin's first. As the most recently opened singles' bar in
town, Shelton had a thin suspicion that drugs money might
even have been used to get the place running. He thought
about the folks who frequented it and its like: lonely people,
sure, who would be easy pickings for pushers offering company or solace or a new experience. When you're down, he
reasoned, you're at your most vulnerable. A man or woman
struggling through the nightmare of divorce; a kid whose
plainness has made him/her an outcast among peers; a basi-
cally normal guy just out on the razzle, using Melvin's as a
meat market, picking up what he thought were ladies desperate for some male attention, open all hours, as it were . . .
All of these might become prey for a clever pusher promising happiness but delivering death. The whole thing stank,
and needed to be nipped in the bud before it bloomed into
yet another fungal growth rotting the social structure of the
city. Shelton had come to realize that he had a conscience
about such things – no, even more than that: a driving sense
of purpose that yearned to see the end of such quiet and
underground atrocities. Not that he pictured himself as any
kind of white knight coming to the rescue of the common
people in a blaze of glory and brilliance. No, the bottom
line was that but for the grace of God, he'd be part of the
world his job required him to inhabit. He'd been lucky, and
had played that luck for all it was worth; but not once
forgetting that luck is fickle, that you never, ever take it
for granted.

Even so, Shelton walked out of the cellar club and on to one of Calverton's city-centre streets with a thoughtful smile on his face. While he'd been making ostensibly idle conversation at the bar, a lady had tried to pick him up. She'd been on the far side of forty, pale, with a plain black dress showing plenty of cleavage from generous tits that fifteen years before had been her fame and fortune. Now they needed a little more support as, Shelton mused, did her soul. When she offered to buy him a drink, he'd felt an echo of the sadness that resounded through her empty life, and he'd accepted. Her gratitude was almost heart-breaking.

They talked a while. She was called Beverley, a name most likely as false as her eyelashes. She had been married to an accountant named Stu, who'd died of a sudden and massive heart attack out on the golf-course a year ago. He'd been well insured, leaving her with all she needed . . . Or all he thought she should need. But she had never really moved in his circles, never really been a part of the social scene Stu had involved himself with, for the job's sake, of course . . . Now that the hurt of his passing was over, she was spreading her wings a little, seeing what life could offer a rich lonely lady who was, she hoped he'd agree, still a bit of a looker . . .

Shelton listened attentively and used the body language he'd learned to make her feel that he was attracted to her and would like to get to know her better. He used his thin cover story of being a computer programmer up from London to help install a mainframe at the new TransGlobe Insurance headquarters that were opening up near the station . . . It was all crap, of course, lies swapped for lies: but Shelton was hoping that Beverley, in the act of offering herself, would throw in a peace pill for good measure: at no extra charge this first time, but from then on he'd need to pay for them, OK . . .

101

' . . . so if you wanted to date, I'd be willing. What do you say, Steve?'

Beverley was looking at him hopefully, her pale-blue eyes almost lost in haloes of dark eyeshadow. Her fair hair had swung forward as she leaned towards him, to touch his knee with a thin-fingered hand. Her breasts jutted creamy smooth but showing hairline stretchmarks in the skin.

For a moment Shelton was disconcerted and did not respond to his cover name. The woman's face was a tragic picture of hope, her eyes moistening like beads of antique glass. He felt a strong and sudden doubt that he'd misjudged her – but then, maybe she was just cleverer than he'd at first assumed.

Shelton put on his most winning smile, leaned to meet her and slid the flat of his hand between her legs, past warm stocking-tops and beyond.

'I'm game, love, but I'd want something special, you understand?'

Hurt and hate crashed together in her face, a look of pain and shock that convinced Shelton he'd made a mistake. There was no point in explanation or apology, though he wanted to explain . . . No, he'd just have to take the backlash; a Martini thrown over him, a scene . . .

Beverley leaned back, her arms flopped at her sides, struggling with tears. Her voice, when it came, was very low, thick with a dark cocktail of agonies.

'You are a bastard. Leave me alone. Get out of here.'

Shelton nodded and got out, reaching the exit steps before Beverley's voice floated across the smoky, jazz-laden air for all to hear:

'Listen, I've just put my hand on that man's crotch. And you know what, everybody – he's got no dick!'

Laughter splashed like a languid wave on shingle, then

ebbed away. Shelton looked back at Beverley, who had turned to tackle another Martini. Then he climbed the steps out on to street level.

He'd decided to call it a night. The encounter with Beverley had affected him, although he was loath to admit it. After all, his existence revolved around the wish to protect people – people like her included. Although clubs such as Melvin's were open until the still, early hours of the morning, Shelton felt that the edge had been taken off his appetite for success now. He'd walk towards the station, where there'd be more chance of picking up a cab; then a quick shower, a sandwich and some sleep. He'd speak with DI Hammond in the morning and get that man's opinion on his hunch. He'd made a blunder with the lady tonight, and did not want to blunder on a larger scale with his theory of pushers in bars.

Shelton knew Calverton moderately well, but especially this end, where the shopping areas gave way to a maze of light-industrial premises, countless offices and a few shops; these in turn blending gradually into heavier industry as the ground sloped down towards the railyards. The train station lay at the extreme north end of the yards, about two miles from the city centre.

Shelton used his mental map to trim distance off his journey. Knowing side-streets, you could reach the station in less than ten minutes, when normally it would take you over twenty.

He moved at a brisk pace, signalling an accurate impression of a man who knew where he was going, in all senses of the word. He replayed the night's work as he walked, thinking of Beverley's face lost in its own hurt, of how it would be with her, if he'd accepted her offer – or she had accepted his . . .

Shelton's crisp footsteps echoed back from the street's tall buildings, their sightless doorways and windows sunk deep against the bland orange cast of the sodium roadside lamps. He was twenty yards from the corner of a brighter street, where he would see the station swing into view. Good job; he was dead-beat now; would he even bother with a sandwich or—

Someone stepped out of a doorway as Shelton passed by and drove a needle-pointed knife into his left ear and through into his brain. Shelton saw a vivid flash of white light, an incredibly dazzling flower of fire that lit up the world and all its wonders. Then, a darkness so complete it suffocated him. Sadness came before pain. There was no pain. Shelton felt his balance going and began to fall, and was dead before he hit the ground.

Risico watched the young man's body collapse, stiffen, then relax as all control was relinquished. A faint sweet smell of human excrement rose up to meet him. Blood that looked viscous and black under the streetlighting oozed copiously from the man's ear as Risico withdrew the shiv and wiped it on the smart blue blazer his victim was wearing. He turned the head so that the blood would spill over his hair and the back of his head, leaving his pale impassive face in clear sight. Would this be the one, Risico wondered? Or would he need to put another and himself through this agony again.

Shelton was dead. No part of him squirmed to be free of the cooling corpse. Risico rose – then a million volts of fear shocked through him as headlights swung into the street's gloomy corridor and illuminated the scene.

In the patrol car, Pearcy did a double-take at the sight of

the men on the pavement; one down and motionless, the other up and running.

'Holy shit! Will you look at that, Dave – it's him, it's the killer!' The realization squeezed a fist in Pearcy's chest: anger, terror, triumph. But mainly anger.

Pearcy kicked on the sirens and high beams, downshifted and sent the car spurting along the street trailing veils of blue tyre smoke. He accelerated fast, but the running man had a good start and was fit. It would be a close one.

'Put in a five-eleven. Tell them we've got this psycho in view, moving down Redman Road. We need back-up now to seal off the area.'

'Done,' Bakker said, and started to make the call.

Pearcy raced the motor until he was level with the speeding figure – at which instant the man swerved into a narrow side alley between buildings and streaked into the blackness.

'Fuck it! Fuck it!' Pearcy said, handbrake-turning the car, then fumbling the gear-shift so the engine roared.

Without discussion, Bakker kicked open the passenger door, leaped out and gave chase. The alleyway was blocked by a concrete bollard; there was no way the patrol car could follow.

As he ran, he withdrew his flashlight and Wildey 9mm, bringing both to bear as he focussed on the just-seen shadow ahead of him. Bakker stopped, fired a shot in the air and turned on the torchbeam.

Risico froze and turned into the flashlight's powerful beam, then went on running before Bakker could issue his warning. He reached the end of the alley and was gone within a couple of seconds. Bakker considered pursuit, but decided against it. He holstered the Wildey and walked back to the car.

Pearcy had taken off, he found on his return, but reappeared a few minutes later, trembling with fury and cursing like an expert.

'Bastard got away,' he said. In the distance came the screams of the back-up units racing to the scene too late. 'We'd better take a look at the poor sod who got it . . . He's not in uniform . . .'

Pearcy reversed the car until it was level with Shelton's body. Recognition drained all the colour from Pearcy's face.

'Oh my God . . . It's Carl Shelton . . . That bastard – that bastard knifed him!'

'Leave him, John,' Bakker said quietly. 'Leave it to the homicide boys . . .'

The older man wiped at his eyes roughly with the back of his hands. He looked across at Bakker.

'Did you see him, Dave? Any details at all?'

'Just a fleeting glimpse. Saw nothing of his face . . .'

And the lie would never be discovered, Bakker knew, as he thought back to the railyard fire and the man who had witnessed the birth of a new age.

The soft purr of the telephone trilled through the darkened bedroom, waking the sleeper instantly. He had in any case been only half unconscious. Now he picked up the handset, noting that the nearby illuminated clockface gave the time at 2.16 a.m.

'Hello.'

'It's Bakker. There's been another one; DS from the drug squad. I was there seconds after. And I saw him. I saw the one who is the threat to us.'

'Yes,' said the other voice passionlessly.

'Patrick Joseph Peters. Grand larceny, robbery with violence – he was in the warehouse at the time of the fire.'

'Ah. I understand. You didn't destroy him?'

'No,' Bakker replied, 'there was no chance. But now we have an identity – now we have his face.'

'It needs to be soon.'

'I know that as well as you do. We must in any event move quickly.'

'Do you suppose he has the stone?'

'It's likely,' Bakker said. 'So we cannot kill him until it is in our possession.'

'Find him then, in his hiding-place. I will implement the search for the stone from this end.'

'I'll get back to you.'

Bakker hung up. At the other end of the line, Richard Van Allen replaced the handset, closed his eyes and returned to his dreams.

Chapter Six

Why, what's the matter
That you have such a February face,
So full of frost, of storm, and cloudiness?
Much Ado About Nothing, V. iv. 40–2

There was nothing more depressing to Parco's eyes than shunting yards in the rain. The mild, bright weather of the past few days had given way in the night to chilly overcast and an early downpour that had slackened now to a dismal drizzle that seemed to paint everything, the whole picture of the world, in drab shades of grey.

He'd been back in Calverton by 11 a.m., leaving Theo to deliver Betsy Cline to her mother while he went back to the office to reply to urgent messages and generally to catch up on a day spent out of town. There was nothing of any consequence on the Ansafone, except a brief and garbled message from John Pearcy, the gist of which was that the killer had struck again late last night, and that he, Pearcy, and his road partner Bakker had almost witnessed it.

Pearcy's voice was slurred, his sentences rambling. It was easy to tell that the man was in shock as well as being half-blitzed. Parco guessed that he, that all the state cops in Calverton, would be feeling personally in fear of their lives, as well as having to cope with the rage and anguish of seeing another one of their own go down so violently.

He dialled Pearcy's home number but there was no reply. Parco decided to call in at the station later, after he'd made a solid start on the Van Allen case, as his conscience prompted him to do.

Now he watched the grey-black bulk of an endless freight train crawl past and vanish into the rain mist, dwindling like some clanking ponderous brontosaur out of sight. He waited on a minute or two, listening to the lazy flick and backflick of the wiper blades clearing water, then eased the car forward to a convenient parking niche close to the yards' administration offices.

Parco was confronted inside by a pleasant but fiercely protective middle-aged secretary whose bluish hair tint Parco thought had gone out of fashion twenty years before. Talk about validating stereotypes by conforming to them! He introduced himself, flashed his EAPI card and told her he was investigating an insurance claim relating to the warehouse fire in June, on behalf of the British Museum Authorities. It was a smooth piece of bluff, the kind of thing he had gotten away with hundreds of times in the past.

The name-tag on the secretary's cashmered bosom announced her as Mrs E.P. Sunderland. Mrs Sunderland now offered Parco a smile of surpassing disbelief, and her grey-green eyes cooled by several degrees.

'But your card says you are a *private* investigator, Mr Parco. And it's been almost three months since the fire caused by that robbery. The damage has been rectified – so surely the insurance has been settled . . .'

Parco's confusion was momentary. His face quickly cleared and he nodded, beaming at Mrs E.P. Sunderland in his most charming style.

'I can see where we've got our lines crossed, Mrs Sunderland – is that "Eleanor", by the way?'

'Edith, if you must know.'

'Edith, yes. May I call you Edith?'

'No, Mr Parco . . .'

'Please, call me Jim. Now, it's true I operate privately,

which essentially means I'm freelance: and in fact a large percentage of my caseload is work done on behalf of other organizations, who either can't spare the personnel at the time, or who don't have a representative in the area. People rely on me for my local knowledge and contacts; and, when the case is of a sensitive nature, such organizations prefer the friendlier, personal approach. Which is why I was employed, Mrs Sunderland, and which is why I've come to you first . . .'

'Oh?'

Parco caught the gleam of self-importance and pleasure his comment was designed to engender. He pressed on fluidly.

'The fact is that the insurance claim I'm talking about is nothing to do with the structure of the warehouse, which comes under the ambit of the Federation of British Railway Companies. As you rightly say, that's been agreed and settled. No, I'm referring to a separate claim made by the BMA in respect of the losses incurred during the fire, of items belonging to them. Specifically, a number of artefacts in transit to Calverton and other museums from abroad. These artefacts include pieces of pottery, statues, weapons, and so on. Some of them were badly damaged, others were destroyed outright. And of course, the robbery itself – or should we say the attempted robbery – has not yet been fully investigated: it's still an open file.'

During Parco's explanation, Mrs Sunderland had been nodding appropriately, as though understanding every word. Now she frowned.

'I still don't see how I – '

'Mrs Sunderland, I have to confess that without your help, this whole matter will drag on for months. The point is that the insurers of the BMA consignment are not happy about the security arrangements made to protect the items at the time of the robbery. Now I understand that a number of private security firms are operating across these yards?'

'Yes.'

'What I would like from you, Mrs Sunderland, is simply the name of the company employed on the night of the fire, together with a list of the personnel on duty at the time. I also need access to any transactions made between your office and the persons who hired space in the warehouse, and who therefore are involved in the claim for compensation.'

'Mr Parco, I'm really not sure I could do that.'

Parco pursed his lips and looked serious.

'I understand your dilemma perfectly, Mrs Sunderland. All I will say is that my employer will now be forced to seek authorization from higher authorities to obtain the information I'm requesting. The whole affair will then become public, and highly embarrassing for a number of people, including your superiors, whose job it is to vet security companies operating on these yards.

'It can all get very messy,' Parco concluded sadly. 'Men died in that robbery – policemen, security guards: it would be awful to dredge up the details of those deaths, just to settle a dispute about money . . .'

Parco watched the woman hesitate as she wrestled with these complexities, most of which had just been generated in Parco's head. After a few moments, she glanced up at him.

'I'll give you the information, Mr Parco. I wouldn't want those old wounds to be reopened.'

Parco smiled. 'I am deeply grateful, Mrs Sunderland. And I can assure you the matter can now, most likely, be concluded privately to everyone's satisfaction . . .'

The woman busied herself at her keyboard, accessing the files Parco had asked for. She tilted the VDU towards him, so that he could note the information as it appeared. He dutifully jotted down names, times and reference numbers, none of which he might ultimately need – but memorized the access code to the backing store where all of these facts, and millions of others, were kept.

Parco drove from the yards directly to police headquarters, where he identified himself to the desk sergeant and asked if officer John Pearcy was available to see him, and if not would the desk sergeant ask him to call Parco at the earliest opportunity.

The sergeant's face registered nothing, neither friendliness nor the hostility Parco thought was more likely, given the traditional relationship that exists between PIs and the state police: his own inclusion within the fraternity was more to do with his personality, the particular officers whose friendship he'd cultivated, and the fact that he'd provided some discreet and positive help on a few occasions in past years. But this man didn't know him from Adam, was not impressed by his ID, and was still ringing from the aftershock of another death in the ranks; one of a wave of killings that seemed no closer to being stemmed.

'Officer Pearcy is not available to talk to you,' Parco was informed. 'I can tell you that he is off-duty at present, so I'm not sure when I'll be able to pass on your request for him to call.'

'Couldn't you ring him at home?' Parco wondered. He could do it himself of course; this piece of provocation was for the mean and simple pleasure of needling the desk sergeant, whose faceless, by-the-book attitude Parco deeply detested.

'I have plenty to do without making calls for you, Mr – '

'Parco.'

'So if there's nothing else . . .'

There was plenty else: Parco would like to give this jumped-up beat-boy a mouthful, about how friendships matter, not procedure; about how systems are meaningless abstractions without people responding to people at the core of them; about how Parco's heart had been scalded by the grief of these killings as much as any cop's . . . But the sergeant had returned to his routine notes, head down, scribbling, and did not look up until Parco was out through the door and halfway across the car park.

Because he'd not let off steam at headquarters, Parco's temper was short by the time he got back to the office. Theo had been in for an hour or so, after dropping off Betsy Cline and offering the reassurances to Mrs Cline that Parco had insisted upon. If her ex stepped over the line just once, just slightly, Parco wanted to know about it. Then he'd do to him what he'd felt like doing the day before, and damn the consequences.

'Hi,' Theo greeted him, smiling pleasantly; moderating the smile when she picked up Parco's own mood. 'You OK?'

'Yeah. Fill me in, will you: I've got a lot on today.'

'Fine,' Theo said stiffly. She gave her boss a rundown of the telephone messages he'd already listened to earlier, plus those that had come in since, and abstracts of ongoing cases that needed attention.

'That all?'

'Well, there was one other, but – '

'So let's hear it.'

Theo's cheeks coloured. Parco was rarely like this, but

when he was she hated it. At such times he treated her like some kind of secretarial machine, a skivvy whose only value lay in doing the dogwork so he could swan off on the jobs that appealed to him.

'A call from a Mr Hartmann who's discovered that his wife's been having an affair with a bisexual, and wants us to find out if her lover has had contact with any HIV positives or AIDS victims. He – '

'Jesus,' Parco breathed, shaking his head slowly. 'Jesus Christ, is there no end to the filth that people will wallow in? Are there any limits to the deceit one human being will subject another to? Sickening, right?'

'Sickening,' Theo agreed, 'but business. You want me to turn him down?'

Now Parco heard the hurt in her voice, and saw it in those bright-green eyes that had mirrored such ecstasy by his hand last night. He clenched his teeth and his fists, closing his eyes for a fleeting moment.

'Theo, I'm sorry – '

'OK, Parco . . .'

'It's lots of things, not least these cop killings. What's the world coming to, eh?'

'Nowhere it hasn't always been,' Theo said. Parco smiled.

'Yeah. I guess that's right . . . OK, this Hartmann call: it'll cost a bundle for us to check out his wife's lover's lovers – all phone work, but time-consuming.'

'I don't mind doing it.'

'I know, Theo, but it's tiresome stuff. Look, give Hartmann an estimate of how much it'll cost – no, make that a lower ceiling, and make clear, will you, that it could be a great deal more. If he's still willing to go ahead under the circumstances, we'll take the case.'

'That's fine. It's a job I can do in spare slots anyway.'

'Anything else?'

'Oh yes. Mrs Van Allen rang just before you came back. She says that if you wanted to look through the house, then her husband will definitely not be there this afternoon: apparently she checked his schedule last night, and he'll be busy until late evening at least.'

'OK, thanks. Is she leaving a key, or – ?'

'I think she'll be there in person, Parco.' Theo's grin was mischievous. 'So be careful, or she'll get you.'

'That's all I need right now,' he said wearily. 'What time?'

'Any time after two p.m.'

'Right.' He checked his watch. 'It's coming up for two now. I'll get straight off.'

'See you later.'

'And, Theo,' Parco said, pausing at the door. 'Thanks – really. For everything . . .'

'That's all right, Parco,' Theo replied. She was not quite able to add 'anytime'.

William Howard walked into Richard Van Allen's office and sat down at the man's invitation. Vaughn Castillo was present again on this occasion, but did not pour drinks as he had done before. Howard got the impression that the first meeting had been to tempt him into complicity, but that now it was down to business, and these pleasantries could be dispensed with.

'I have the addresses I mentioned to you previously,' Van Allen said. 'It would help me a great deal, Mr Howard, if you could find time to visit these people in the next day or two and make enquiries as per the arrangements we discussed.'

'No problem.' Howard smiled. He was eager to seem co-operative as well as competent, but did not feel inclined either to give too many of his reservations away, or to make demands that might cool Van Allen to the whole deal. He decided that the obvious question – why Van Allen didn't check these dealers out himself, or send Castillo to do it – could wait for now. The obvious answer, that Van Allen's numerous other commitments didn't allow him time, some-how did not satisfy.

'Are you still happy to offer the sums you mentioned?' Howard wondered. It was a pointless question, he realized as he asked it: Van Allen seemed like a man whose mind, once made up, stayed made up.

'Of course. You need only to convince the vendors of our sincerity to purchase. Once they have seen the note of authorization I gave you, there will be no doubt that the money exists to support the offer: you may recognize one or two of the signatories to the letter, apart from myself . . .'

Howard didn't, as it happened, but guessed that they'd be prominent businessmen or speculators whom Van Allen would have met and won over, probably without too much difficulty.

Howard nodded and Castillo rose as Van Allen handed across another sheet of his pale-cream notepaper, this time with three addresses written on it. Howard scanned them and folded the sheet into his pocket.

'I'll see to this today, Mr Van Allen. I know how keen you must be to procure the original of the stone.'

'Yes indeed.' And Van Allen smiled, the first time Howard had seen him do so. He found it somehow chilling, in part because it brought out the full force of the man's charisma and was, for the Director, a rare event . . . But more than that . . . The smile was oddly knowing; strangely

116

– evil – in a way Howard could not identify. It was the smile of the rapist as he lures the little girl off the sunny pavement . . . It was the way that Hyde might smile, knowing he was safe behind Jekyll's eyes . . . It was –

'So, if that's all,' Van Allen said, glancing towards Castillo to usher out the guest. The smile turned out like the light that allows the moth to fly free.

But Howard sat on, determined to push through with his request, and not surprised to feel a prickle of sweat under his arms and on his top lip.

'I am also keen to begin translating the texts,' he said, speaking into a silence that suddenly deepened.

'Naturally.'

'So, since I'm helping you in this way, Mr Van Allen, I was hoping you'd grant me access to the casts you showed me – '

'I'm not sure that would be a good idea,' Van Allen said quietly, and if Howard hadn't been prepared for that reply, he would have felt threatened by its tone.

'It would certainly give us the edge in this field. It's a fact that Professor Parkhurst and Doctor Pope are working along the same lines – '

'It's a matter of security. If the casts are seen by others with vested interests . . . Or if you . . .'

Howard's sudden temper was not entirely feigned. 'If you don't trust me with the casts, Director, then how can you trust me to negotiate for the original? I might simply locate it, take it and vanish.'

Van Allen looked as though he wanted to reply, and forcefully. His eyes flared hotly and he leaned forward, barely controlling himself. But he thought better of it, and the kraken, Howard observed, failed to surface.

'It's a fair point, Mr Howard. Very well, I will allow

you to examine the casts in more detail – but with certain conditions attached.'

'Fair enough.'

'There is a small storeroom, currently unused, adjoining the workshops in the museum basement. You will have access to the casts only in that room, and under supervision.'

'OK.'

'Moreover, I request – no, I demand – that you bring nothing into that room, nor take anything out. All the writing materials and other items you need will be supplied for you. I also reserve the right to request a search of your person if I feel that you are not being completely honest in this matter.'

Howard grinned as Van Allen ran through his stipulations. This was taking the wish to be first into print to paranoiac levels. He glanced at Castillo, and noted surprise even on his face, though carefully concealed by the loyalty he felt for Van Allen.

'Well?' the Director asked. 'Those are my terms and I will not waver from them.'

'It limits me,' Howard admitted. 'I won't be able to work from home, or exactly when I choose.'

'Unfortunately, no . . . Of course, I may even insist on more stringent measures once we have the original stone, and thus the complete texts, in our possession.'

Howard made a show of considering, shrugging his shoulders after several seconds.

'Well, if that's the way it's got to be.'

'That's the way it must be.'

'Right then, Mr Van Allen. With your permission I'll start translating tomorrow.'

'That is acceptable. I'll have one of the staff clear the

room for you. There's a power-point, I seem to recall, so you'll have hot coffee and the facility of a computer.'

Howard rose, hesitated about offering his hand, and then decided not to. He inclined his head to Van Allen and followed Castillo's prim little gesture towards the door.

He left the museum, grabbing a takeaway sandwich at the coffee shop nearby, and made his rendezvous with Helen on time.

Howard drove an orange VW Beetle, an original built in Belgium two decades ago, that he'd restored himself from a wreck. As they motored away from the university towards the south flyover, he gave Helen a résumé of his conversation.

'The man's over the top, a raving nutter,' she concluded. Howard grinned.

'Eccentric to say the least.' The grin vanished. 'What worries me is that he'll ask Castillo to do the body searches . . .'

In Van Allen's office, Castillo poured a coffee for himself and his superior. He guessed that the Director was worried, since Howard, although fulfilling a necessary function, was a potential weak link in a chain that could lead the police directly back to the suppliers of the smuggled artefacts Van Allen handled – and on in the other direction to the purchasers, many of whom were influential enough to have them both destroyed if they became implicated in any scandal.

'I can tell you don't like this arrangement,' Castillo ventured to say. He placed the delicate coffee cup close to Van Allen's hand as it rested on the polished red leather desktop, then sat and absorbed the details of the man's strong jawline, the clear and purposeful set of his eyes, those deep and brooding eyes, and the quiet power implicit in his body. To be taken roughly by such a man would be sexual nirvana . . . But Castillo let his gaze flicker away as Van Allen swung his head to look at him.

'We cannot be connected with anything lost from the pipeline. Although using Howard is a gamble, at least he's anonymous, and the man has a powerful motive for going along with our suggestions. His future as much as ours depends upon the recovery of the stone.'

'That's true,' Castillo conceded. He sipped at his coffee, crooking his little finger. 'But I'm not happy that you gave him a document with your name on. I think he should be watched.'

'Crane can do that. I've already set him the task of noting Howard's movements. He can supervise him while he works, also.'

'Ah. Yes. What happens, though, when we have the stone and Howard completes his translation and publishes? Won't the fact of the work be an admission that he used the stone – an artefact illegally imported out of Crete?'

'That,' said Van Allen, 'is a bridge we'll cross when we come to it.'

He looked away from Castillo's tightly serious but fawning face and stared through the window, noting with a part of his mind how weak and low the sun seemed in this corner of the world; and how damp and languid seemed the air. And this man Castillo – in the Old Country he would never have been tolerated, with his inane comments and twisted outlook . . . He might yet need to be removed, or controlled, Van Allen thought. No need to tell him anything: no need to tell anyone that he, Van Allen, already knew precisely and in every detail what was written upon the Sacred Stone of the Gorgoneion.

Parco had to confess to himself that he felt the slightest bit nervous about standing here in Eleanor Van Allen's porchway, waiting for the lady herself to answer the door. Before he'd rung the bell, Parco took a minute or two to notice the big turn-of-the-century house in its setting of similar upmarket detached properties, all built well back and shielded by trees; in this instance limes, with ancient rhododendrons lining the curved macadam driveway. There was a double integral garage converted from original outbuildings, its outlines blurred by a vigorous ivy: the house itself was three storeys high, pebble-dashed over the upper two, with steeply sloping roofs and ornate tall chimneys of patterned blue and red bricks.

Parco let his gaze travel beyond the sharply pointed gable-end to the pale-blue afternoon sky, stitched now with swallow song and clear of the clouds that had brought the morning's rain. The ground still smelt damp and loamy here, and the small front lawn, north-facing, gleamed with a pelt of silver droplets.

An inner door opened. Parco saw the woman's rippling outline behind the textured glass of the outer door, which she opened for him with a bright and welcoming smile.

'Mr Parco, good afternoon. Thank you for responding so promptly.' She stepped aside to let him enter.

'No problem, Mrs Van Allen. We aim to please,' Parco said, and could have bitten his tongue off an instant later. He noted that Eleanor was wearing a long peach-coloured bathrobe, and probably very little else beneath. The air around her was subtly scented with the shower soap she had evidently just used. Her still-damp hair was several shades of gold darker than he'd remembered; and, devoid of make-up, her face looked softer, less severe, but just as compelling as before.

He was shown in to a large hallway floored with a chequerboard of small black and white stone tiles and quite bare except for a tall coatstand and a circular hall table holding a large thriving pot-plant.

'What would be of most use to you, Mr Parco?' Eleanor asked. It occurred to Parco that the woman's manner now was altogether different from that which he'd been sub-jected to in his office. There, she had seemed hard and unyielding, unapproachable, distant. Parco had disliked her then, but was allowing this initial impression to mellow as she showed him through to a large front lounge, warm, almost too warm, with an open fire burning in the hearth. The furniture was expensive without being ostentatious – like Eleanor's jewellery and clothes, Parco thought. She is someone who keeps her wealth in the background, using it for herself quietly without shouting about it. He liked that, and decided that he'd help this woman as far as he could.

'I'd like to talk to you a while,' he replied. 'I may ask specific questions – which will save me a lot of time and you a deal of money if you answer them honestly and fully. And, if you feel like it, I'd like you to chat generally about your suspicions and concerns over your husband. Just impressions – stream-of-consciousness stuff, you know.'

'I'm happy to do that, Mr Parco. Anything else?'

'The nature of my job is to pry, Mrs Van Allen. If you will leave me alone in your husband's study for twenty minutes, I can probably clear this case up within the week.'

She raised her eyebrows at this show of confidence, which was no sham on Parco's part. He knew that almost all guilty secrets, whatever they were, left traces that men could not hide. Very often the traces were much more than that, and deliberately kept for any number of reasons: photographs, letters, mementoes; files, documents, ledgers . . . Everyone carved a path through life in paper and left footprints on the sands of time, however carefully they tried to cover them afterwards.

'Very well, though I must say I feel very ashamed to be doing this behind Richard's back.'

Parco accepted that. He said, 'If you asked him straight out what was wrong, would he tell you?'

Eleanor considered a moment, then looked at Parco squarely.

'No, I'm sure he would not.'

'Then you are doing nothing to be ashamed of, Mrs Van Allen. Nothing at all.'

Parco sat on the sofa at her invitation. Eleanor crossed to a drinks cabinet and poured out two neat Scotches without asking Parco his preference.

'You look like a whisky man,' she told him.

'As long as I don't look like a bitter man. Cheers.'

'Cheers.' Eleanor watched him sample the drink, then tilted her glass and closed her eyes as the whisky flamed in her mouth.

'That was excellent.' Parco all but smacked his lips at the malt's velveteen fire. 'Not one I'm familiar with . . .'

'It's made by a small distillery at Banff – you can only get it through the independent bottlers. Cadenheads have a whisky shop in Banff itself. We bought it there.'

'I see.' Parco smiled, feeling that Eleanor was trying to break ice between them as much as converse on a topic of mutual interest. For his part, he relished the whisky's flavour without knowing a blind thing about its origins. 'You holi-dayed there?'

Eleanor nodded. 'It was a holiday for me, a working holiday for Richard. Two years ago. We went on what I suppose you could call a safari, in this case to look at holy wells. Richard was helping to compile a catalogue of them in the British Isles – the one at Fergan, near Banff, is supposed to cure skin diseases.'

'And does it?'

She glanced at him sharply, searching for sarcasm; found none, and shrugged. 'I never found out if analysis was done on the water. Maybe whether it cures or not depends on your attitude.'

'Attitude is all important,' Parco agreed. 'Your attitude towards your husband, for instance.'

'It's a case of his towards me, Mr Parco . . . I have to say that the tour we made to Scotland was one of the last I enjoyed with Richard: actually, one of the last we shared. From that time on, he seemed so busy with his work and I – well, I began to follow a life of my own. This house became little more than a convenient meeting-point for cross-check-ing our Filofaxes.'

It was an old story that Parco had heard a hundred times before. In the past, listening as he had done to these familiar patterns of divergence, he had both sympathized with the sufferers and condemned them by turns: had they made their own bed of nails, or were they simply victims of career pressure in a society that made youth, wealth and power the only aims worth fighting for? Parco's view now was ambivalent, realizing as he did that the question was not to be tackled intellectually; could not be unpicked by reason.

'And yet you allowed the relationship to drift, not taking action until now – '

'You misunderstand me,' Eleanor said firmly, stopping Parco in his tracks. 'The increasing distance between Richard and I did not trouble me greatly. To be frank, he married me for particular reasons – ' She laughed at that, a little wistfully. 'And I married him for reasons that were just as specific. None of them were really connected with love. The fact is, Mr Parco, that Richard can go where he likes and do what he wishes. I don't care. But I do care about maintaining my lifestyle and my freedom. It is no secret, and I have never made it one, that I enjoy a variety of lovers. As far as I know, Richard does too. Neither of us is bothered by this – '

It was Parco's turn to interrupt, with a mixture of frustration and bewilderment: 'I don't understand this. In what way *has* he changed, then?'

Eleanor poured a second whisky; Parco refusing one for himself. She considered for a moment, staring into space.

'There is a superstition that everyone in the world has his *doppelgänger*, an identical double who is also a kind of shadow self – similar in every particular, but with a tilt of emphasis; a twin seen through distorting glass, perhaps. That's the closest I can come, Mr Parco, and I'm sorry it's not helpful. All I can say is that the man who says he is Richard Van Allen is not the same man I travelled with in Banffshire. It is his *doppelgänger* – it is a darker facet of the same jewel.'

Parco terminated the conversation fifteen minutes later, feeling that he was getting nowhere. Eleanor still struck him as being eminently sensible and well-controlled in every way, and yet he began to wonder if some twist in herself, a

125

deep neurosis, wasn't the cause of this insistence that Van Allen was *not* Van Allen.

Parco made no judgements. He decided he needed to get to see the man himself, to let his instincts work their magic before he could wrap the case or drop it. Meanwhile, Theo could do all the necessary scans and searches, digging what dirt existed.

Asking Eleanor's permission for a second time, Parco went upstairs to Van Allen's study and spent a productive twenty minutes taking photographs and a set of fingerprints with a polymer film manufactured specifically for the job. He also took a blank diskette from a boxful on Van Allen's desk, and copied a selection of files that, he hoped, would give him some inroads into the man's business affairs. Since the sexual angle did not apply, it seemed, Parco's only avenue was to explore the man's wider activities. There might be something, but he had to admit it was all starting to look like a longshot.

He left the house shortly after with a promise that he would get back to Eleanor within the next couple of days. He did not tell her what he'd taken from Van Allen's study, nor that he thought she might be the cause of her own problem. Not that he was entirely sure – but ninety per cent convinced was a hell of a long way towards proof in Parco's book.

Go to a well-appointed uptown antiques showroom and the chances are that what you see is what you get. Dealers of this calibre have too much to lose to become involved in fraud, and are usually too intelligent to be led to it inadvertently. It is true enough that the items on display, rare and costly though they are, do not represent the best that such men can offer. Behind the scenes transactions are made for treasures that are literally unique, and whose value is measured in millions, if not tens of millions of pounds.

This is the powerful torrent of trade behind the placid high-street river, as far as ancient objects are concerned, and it was the kind of place that William Howard and Helen Remmick expected to find as they scouted for the first of Van Allen's addresses.

Howard followed Helen's navigational instructions, turning off the plush shopping street where Calverton's main antique dealers were to be found, and into a jungle of side-streets containing smaller and more anonymous premises, often without a recognizable shopfront or name.

'Just here,' Helen announced eventually. Howard complied, cruising the Beetle up to the kerb as he slowed; but his face registered his uncertainty.

'Are you sure? – Give me the map.'

'Take the bloody map,' she said, flaring, and pushed it into his chest. 'I know how to read it just as well as you do!'

A few seconds' checking convinced him she was right, and yet a less likely location for a reputable dealer in antiquities he could not imagine. The street, Thursday Street on the map and on the faded name-plate high up on a corner wall, was a cul-de-sac. The far end, a hundred yards away, was walled off, with a concrete office-block beyond. Other tall complexes had replaced the original textile factory, pub and few houses that had once stood here. The blank, bland windows of some kind of municipal building – a register office or suchlike – gleamed like bronze brought to a high polish in the late afternoon sun opposite where Howard had stopped. Next door was the address he was seeking, a single-fronted shop premises with a solid, oak-panelled door painted gloss black with burnished brass furniture, and a small display window containing only a bronze cherub reaching heavenwards, surrounded by spilled blue silk to offset the statue.

Howard scratched his head and frowned.

'Place looks like it's been closed down for a month . . . And I'm sorry, Helen. I wasn't anticipating quite such a downbeat location.'

She took the apology without acknowledging it, and followed the line of Howard's gaze. 'I don't know . . . There's a light on inside . . . And Van Allen wouldn't send you on a goose chase, would he?'

She unclipped her seat-belt and opened the car door.

'I think it looks kind of exclusive. I mean, you'd need to know what you wanted to come here, right?'

'Can't argue with that,' Howard conceded.

They crossed the road together and read the inscription on the brass plate attached to a varnished wood base beside the door. 'M. Schliemann: Dealer in Fine Arts & Antiquities'. The door was not open; Howard had to knock.

The man who answered was short, plump, very smart and had eyes like old pewter. He absorbed the details of his two visitors without appearing to look at them. Howard, in turn, openly gazed at the man's dark, crisply creased trousers, his blue satin waistcoat, white shirt and blue bow tie: he reminded Howard of a snooker player. Howard grinned, while Helen had the good sense to maintain a serious façade.

'Mr Schliemann? Oh, good afternoon. I'm William Howard Junior, and this is my assistant, Miss Remmick – ' Howard paused, feeling Helen's infuriated gaze singeing the hairs on the back of his neck. 'We are here to enquire about a particular artefact that you may have purchased recently. It's a cylindrical stone carved with pictographs –

128

Minoan, around 2000 BC: good condition, but with a transverse fracture extending from the bottom upwards for half the length of the stone . . .'

Throughout Howard's opening preamble, Schliemann had remained impassive; most likely contemptuous of these ragged, childish people intruding upon the dark elegance of the world in which he moved. But now, as the young man continued, Schliemann's face registered some interest. The grey patina of his eyes, like a lake's lustre on a still winter day, shifted towards life, as though ruffled by an unexpected breeze.

'Please,' he invited, the word accented richly, 'come in, will you?'

They allowed themselves to be ushered through into a long thin room extending the full length of the shop. Bare floorboarding shone richly, like metal brought to a dull heat, under decades of conscientious waxing. Strange ornate examples of statuary broke the room's simple symmetry; and on the wall to Howard's right, individually illuminated paintings hung without price-tags. The left-hand wall held an open staircase done in black wrought iron leading to an office and storage areas, Howard guessed.

Schliemann led them to a roll-top desk, at which he had evidently been working. He took the desk chair himself and invited his guests to bring up two Sheraton chairs that were standing side by side against the back wall.

'So, you are interested in the Hagia Triada Stone,' Schliemann said, opening with a frankness that Howard found both surprising and refreshing.

'Well, yes, I am. Or rather, the people I represent are interested in it.'

'Can I ask why?'

'I don't understand – '

'I mean, your interest must be purely academic. Such a stone, if it truly exists, would never be allowed out of Crete, let alone sold like some common painting or sculpture on the open market. Can I enquire,' Schliemann went on, 'who it is that has persuaded you to chase moonbeams?'

Howard sighed and opened out Van Allen's letter of authorization, which Schliemann read carefully and then handed back. His eyes now were brighter, and his small mouth, the mouth of a hedonist, Howard judged, smiled with tight reluctance.

'If you will excuse me for just a moment, Mr Howard, Miss Remmick . . .'

Schliemann rose and mounted the stairs, which groaned alarmingly under his weight, and climbed ponderously out of sight.

'What the hell is he playing at?' Helen wanted to know. Frankly the man gave her the creeps, partly because, she realized, she was beginning to have reservations about the entire affair. Howard tutted dismissively.

'The whole thing stinks, doesn't it? Schliemann knows as well as I do that the stone exists, and, as well as I do, that it's been smuggled out of Crete.'

'How do *you* know that?'

'Because the stone is only ever mentioned in very specialist literature, the kind of obscure stuff that I've been sifting for my work. And the way that he calls it "the Hagia Triada Stone" suggests a certain familiarity with it also – as though he knows for a fact it's more than a legend or a rumour. My guess is that he thinks we're police – CID, or maybe Customs, checking out a possible route the stone might have followed on its way to a purchaser . . .'

Helen's face looked strained. 'You mean Van Allen is

getting you to do his dirty work – making you stick your neck out while he sits in safety in his damned office!'

'I never thought anything else,' Howard said. 'But I'm beginning to work it out: I reckon – '

'Shh,' Helen cautioned him. 'He's coming back.'

Schliemann returned, still smiling, and resumed his seat. His wet mouth gleamed, pursed and apologetic. His small shrug dripped with insincerity.

'I'm sorry, Mr Howard. Although I accept that your interest in the stone is genuine, I'm afraid I do not have it in my possession. I will, however, be happy to contact you if the opportunity for me to acquire it arises.'

Schliemann stood up. 'Again, my apologies.' He held out a small plump hand.

'No problem,' Howard replied. He ignored Schliemann's empty gesture, looked at Helen, and walked to the door without turning back.

The second address lay about a mile away and was easier to find. By now the light was going: a clear violet sky over Calverton showing as a narrow band between the buildings as Howard pulled up and killed the Beetle's headlights. He turned to Helen.

'You might as well stay here. I suppose this place will be a rerun of the last. Won't be long – '

'There's someone coming out.' She pointed to a slight figure hurrying from the shop.

'A late customer. Stay put – and lock the doors, OK?'

'OK.'

Helen watched Howard stride across the street with a certain misgiving, a kind of coldness that lay in the pit of her stomach. She recognized it as a response to the first hint of danger in what they were doing, delving more deeply into a dark and unfathomable realm beyond the sight and caring of the everyday world.

Fifty yards behind her, a car's headlights blazed on suddenly as the engine revved up to pull away. Helen jolted, but took no further notice as the car sped by and swung left at the end of the street without indicating . . .

Inside, the man that had once been Denny Crane kept his eyes fixed on Risico as he hurried from corner to corner, blending with shadows, trying to stay hidden.

Crane's eyes glowed the most remarkable blue in the reflected light of the dash display, the only life evident in the passionless mask of his face.

Chapter Seven

What have I learnt?
The Lord of Nothingness
Has a dark face.

> Layman Yakusai, Zen poet

Dave Bakker dropped the handset of the telephone back into its cradle, slipped on his jacket and left the flat. He did not hurry, since Crane had told him there would be plenty of time. Risico, having been turned away by the second of Van Allen's regular fences, was on his way to the third. Risico and Van Allen knew that these three dealers, and only these three in Calverton, would handle an item such as the Hagia Triada Stone – Risico because he had dealt with such people and their kind all his life; Van Allen because, over the past few years, he had built up a certain trust in Schliemann and his ilk, supplying items that fetched the highest of prices, coming through a pipeline so well camouflaged that the police had never even sniffed suspiciously in their direction. Bakker also knew via Crane that Risico's third contact would keep him talking a while, probing for proof that the stone was in Risico's possession, haggling over a price, reiterating the dangers of handling such unique and traceable merchandise ... By the time Risico left, frustrated by refusal, Bakker would have crossed town and joined Crane, and working together, after so many weeks of waiting, the Children would have Risico and the stone in their hands ...

And then the Spawning could begin.

*

Bakker's journey was uneventful, by cab through a quiet city to the corner specified by Crane in his phone call. He paid the taxi-driver, offering no tip: the cabbie pulled away without comment, relieved that the man was out of his car. The cabbie's face was pale and sheened with sweat; he found himself frightened for the first time in his career, and by God he had ferried the worst of society's freaks, weirdos and crazies around without turning a hair. But there was something about that silent, blue-eyed young guy that put the shivers through him: something . . . He could not pinpoint just what it was . . .

Crane was parked fifty yards along the road from the run-down backstreet premises of the fence. Unlike the previous ones, the owner of this place, a man called Tony Emiliani, fronted his major operations behind the screen of a pawn-brokerage: a brash, big-windowed establishment garishly proclaiming an End of Lease Clearout – Everything Must Go! Residents of the street would confirm that those signs had been up for at least five years. The window displays themselves were as crass and, in general, as phoney as the advertising. Shelves and racks were packed with Sony Walk-mans that had never seen the inside of a Sony factory; onyx chess sets made of plastic; fur coats that owed everything to the efficiency of the cat-catchers in some Far Eastern slum, and solid gold watches whose gilding must have been about a molecule in thickness. Ironically, Emiliani made a sizeable percentage of his turnover by selling such crap: an occasional high-profit item from someone like Van Allen was a comparatively rare event.

Crane and Bakker sat together in the car, watching Emiliani and Risico through the brightly lit window of the shop as they haggled. By the pantomime of Emiliani's body language and facial expressions, it was obvious that he was treating Risico's assertions and then pleadings with total disbelief – moving slowly towards the possibility that, yes, he would consider fencing the item, if Risico could assure him of its authenticity: did he, for example, possess official documentation to that effect? If not, it would take Emiliani time – and money – to find an expert who could confirm the stone's origins, and keep his silence for a fee. Risico's responses swung between violent threats and pitiful begging. Bakker could see that the confrontation was moving to its end.

'I'll follow him on foot, you trail him in the car – but carefully: although we have Peters, we do not know where he has hidden the stone.'

'I understand,' Crane said tonelessly. The men did not look at one another as they spoke. There was no need. Although they had never met before, each knew the other in his entirety. There were no secrets between the Children.

Bakker stepped out of the car and hid in a doorway until Risico emerged a few minutes later. Once he was out of sight, Bakker began to follow. Crane reversed the car and took another route round, to rejoin Risico's trail later.

For almost three months, Risico had lived as though death was at his heels – as, indeed, it might have been in a very literal sense. Now, though, he was tired, exhausted by today's failure as much as by the trauma of what he had seen and done. He was wearied by blood. He glanced over his shoulder many times, but listlessly, carelessly, never once noticing Bakker's tall frame among the growing evening crowds.

His lodging-house stood on a street of anonymous clones, a turn-of-the-century terrace whose purpose had once been to provide cheap and efficient housing for the work-force of Calverton's then-thriving industries; textiles, light manufacturing, the railyards. Now their usage had changed out of all recognition, just as the industries that supported them had been swept out of existence, with the exception of the railways, wherein lay the origin of all Risico's nightmares.

On his hurried way down the street, Risico passed an Asian foodstore, striplights blazing whitely inside, the front garden paved and crowded with racks and boxes of vegetables, ninety per cent of which Risico couldn't name. Nearby was a solicitor's office; next door a fortune-teller's studio; then a mail-order firm offering God knew what assortment of exotic items . . . Risico grinned crookedly to think that this had once been the kind of street his parents had lived on: normal little houses for normal little people. He had grown up knowing the territory – a street kid, as he was proud to call himself. Now, it was all changed around him, an alien place masquerading behind redbrick and discretely laced-over front windows.

He used his tarnished Yale key to enter his lodging, taking a final both-ways glance before stepping through into the short gloomy hallway that smelt of cooked dinners and lavender Pledge. Mrs Kennealy, he guessed, would be in the front room, watching one of the many soaps she loved so much. On his first day there, Risico in a rare flash of humour had said that he didn't share that enjoyment; he'd washed his hands of soaps on TV. Mrs Kennealy, fat, fifty and set in her ways, had neither understood nor laughed at his comment. Risico had said little to her since, and she to him.

'That you, Mr Joseph?' came the usual call through the hardboard-panel door.

'Aye.' Risico started up the stairs, smiling tightly at the name-juggling he had to employ to stay hidden. 'Just for a wash and a change of shirt. I'm going back out.' He paused momentarily, wondering if the woman had found any trace of his bleeding in his room, or had rifled through his meagre belongings and found the stone . . . But no, she had lapsed into silence: all Risico could hear through the door were muffled Australian accents, a man and a woman quarrelling. The landlady had discovered nothing and was now sunk back to her usual state of mental torpidity.

Risico had a second key for the room, one of two that Mrs Kennealy rented out very cheaply, with no questions asked if you paid in advance. He stood outside the door, knife drawn from its sheath and held ready, and listened for five minutes, until silence satisfied him that no one was waiting for him inside. These precautions, he felt, were necessary for, over the past few days, Risico had begun to ponder on the nature of the creature he had seen; at least, whether or not it was unique. Quite conceivably there were many of these beings, these men that were not men; and that while his quest had been for the individual glimpsed amidst the fire, there could be others seeking him, as eager to destroy him as he was to finish them. That thought was as unnerving as the thing's actual existence, but it had the effect of transforming Risico's blind panic terror into the kind of emotion he could handle. Now, more and more powerfully, his fear was turning to determination that he would live, and fight to do so. Whatever the monster was in whose eyes he was lost for so long, now he knew that they could be cut out with an ordinary blade, or burned out by fire, or torn out bare-handed by a man with the will to do so. There were no qualms in Risico's mind that he would use every means open to him to preserve his own life.

Having reaffirmed this resolve, Risico entered his room, bolted the door behind him and attended to his toilet, changing the dressing on his arm, then strip-washing at the sink. He had two shirts, and now put on his clean one unironed. The other he dropped into the sink, ran the hot tap over it and squirted in some shampoo. The night was turning chilly, so he pulled on a sweater and dragged a scarf out of the battered Adidas holdall he kept on the dowdy lounge chair in the corner.

Next, Risico took out the stone and loosened the wrapping so that he could look again at the unknown script it displayed. The surface had been worn to a dull polish over the centuries, so that now it resembled greyish metal, iron or lead, rather than rock. It amazed him that such an intrinsically worthless item could fetch so high a price in the right circumstances, given that Cernan was correct in his estimations – as Risico was sure he had been. And yet, the only possible outlets would hardly listen to his description of the stone, let alone the paltry sum he was asking for it. These were men he had dealt with before, men with whom he had established a certain dark trust, based as it was on the law of the survival of the fittest at any cost; the primal law of the underworld. Many times, he had supplied the goods and they had paid a fair price, sometimes putting money up front to finance his operations. They knew he was good trade. So what, Risico asked himself, had changed in them now?

He ran his mind round the question as he repacked the stone in its cloth wrappings, then in a plastic carrier bag that he tied with string. There was enough money in his pocket for a decent drink and a curry take-away, with perhaps enough left over to stake on a snooker game or a hand of poker, and Risico knew a few places where he might find such action and so increase his fortune.

Still working through the avenues the question opened

for him, he relocked his room, called a brusque and unanswered goodnight to Mrs Kennealy, and started off down the street.

Only when he turned the corner out of sight did two figures emerge from the busy Asian foodstore. One began to follow him, the other walked in the opposite direction, to the house Risico had thought safe.

'If he's a crook, he's a damned clever one.' That was Theo's conclusion as she slapped Van Allen's file closed and cleared the screen of her work station. Parco, who had come through to the outer office, allowed himself the gentlest of sighs. If Van Allen's sheet came up clean, it made the whole problem far more complex; the implications being that either he was a better crook than he, Parco, had taken him for – in which case the time-and-money factor rocketed; or there was some other aspect of the man's life or personality that gave Eleanor grounds for her worry; or, and most disturbing of all, Eleanor's judgement was badly awry . . . You'd do well to cut loose and fast, James young man, Parco thought as he scanned the last printout just emerging from the machine. But that would mean admitting a certain kind of defeat; it would mean not seeing her again . . .

'We haven't covered all the ground, though: there're plenty of documents to delve into yet.'

Theo gave a strange, unpleasant smile that was part exhaustion, but heavily tainted with annoyance.

'What's this "we" angle, Parco? What've you been doing for the past four hours, eh?'

'You're out of line, Theo,' Parco came back, though with little heat. They both knew well enough that she had spent double that time today investigating Van Allen's business affairs with all the skill and all the guile she could muster. For the better part of the day, Theo had been exercising what it pleased her to call her 'interpersonal telephonic sorcery' to extract more information from the data Parco had taken out of Van Allen's study. She was good at this work, very good, in fact; but it still took enormous energy and concentration to project a persona, often false, down the phone line to some busy clerk or secretary; strike up a relationship and then winkle out the favour that was the purpose of her call. She had of course made full use of the national databases and information services available, and had used contacts previously known to her – Datafax being her first option. Even so, Theo had needed to reach further, connecting with the Post Office, Customs and Excise, City Hall, the Inland Revenue at their Cumbernauld office, and the Uniform Commercial Code among others; this last providing her with information on loans, liens against property and other data. And now she was tired. Now she had no time for Parco's wisecracks, meant or not.

'I'm sorry for being as out of line as you are, Parco,' Theo told him. 'I'm sorry it doesn't please you that all of this boils down to a successful businessman of great acumen and daring. Over the past couple of years, Richard Van Allen has developed a highly profitable – and, as far as I can tell, a strictly legal import business, specializing mainly in Greek antiquities, some of which he sells on to institutions such as other museums or universities: others he appears to keep for himself, while some I can't trace at all – but I suspect that's due to my limitations and not nefarious dealings on his part.'

Theo looked up at Parco and smiled, her tired eyes warming a little as she took in his crumpled suit and his loosened tie, the knot skewed to the right. Poor Parco, he was a natural scruff, any set of clothes somehow degrading to his general level of presentability. He could impress people for just about an hour with his dress, after which time he began to look ragged around the edges. That was the man: he couldn't be anything other than himself.

'I think he's legit, Parco. At least, I'd say I was seventy per cent sure.'

'Is it worth digging any deeper, Theo, or are we chasing our own tail here?'

She shrugged, rippling the silky material of her blouse. Parco hadn't even noticed how good she looked, maintaining her professional image in every way. He hadn't noticed, and he hadn't complimented her. Some lover! he thought, with a vicious self-reproach.

'Well, there is one lead I was going to follow up. Since the outset, Van Allen has done business with a Greek named Nikos Michaelides. Now Michaelides used to work for a company called – wait for it – Theodorus Antiquities Ltd, based at Athens but with branches across Greece and the Aegean. Their principal function seemed to be the manufacture of replicas of Ancient Greek artefacts – coins, war gear, statues and so on, which were sold to tourists. Van Allen used to place pretty large orders with the company, and made a tidy sum outletting this merchandise through museum shops – in particular the Age of Fable Experience in London. Have you heard of it?'

Parco nodded. Theo went on.

'OK, so far so good. Now, from what I can gather, Theodorus Antiquities made its replicas from blueprints or even moulds taken direct from the original artefacts. Since the company has built up a huge turnover during its existence, it has been able to acquire on loan the most precious items, with the full support of the Greek Government, who cream off plenty through taxes. Apparently the stage has even been reached where Theodorus technicians are invited along to archaeological digs, to advise or even take casts, and so on, as a cache of ancient treasures is uncovered . . .

'So, what we have is a link between Van Allen and precious Greek artefacts via Michaelides. Do you follow me?'

'Constantly.' Parco grinned. 'This is better than *Book at Bedtime*, Theo. Do go on.'

'Right. Well, a couple of years ago, Michaelides quit his job – for no reason that anyone could work out. And it was a good job, too; highly paid, with excellent pension and perks – a bit like you get being a PI's assistant –'

'Theo . . .'

'OK, OK. Sorry. Michaelides dropped from sight for a while, but then re-emerged, working independently, but this time supplying Van Allen with real antiquities. It meant less through-put, of course, but Michaelides never failed to produce an artefact of high quality and rarity – right at the time when ancient treasures began soaring in price, due mainly to the recent crash on the global economic scene, plus the fact that the market in rare art has dried to a trickle.'

'So, is this guy Michaelides on the level or not? That's the key question.'

'I agree,' Theo said. She pressed the 'Off' stud on the computer. 'And tomorrow I'll check it out.'

'I might do that myself,' Parco replied. He was feeling guilty that while Theo had been piecing together this complicated puzzle, he'd been wasting time on introspection and daydreaming. 'In fact, I'll definitely do it, right now – and tomorrow I'll try to talk to Van Allen himself . . . I thought I'd use the same story of investigating an insurance claim. What do you think?'

This was Theo's area of expertise, and she was doubtful.

'Someone of his calibre will have that all tied up, Parco. He only needs to phone through to check your credentials, and you're sunk.'

'Well, I've got to see the man sometime, face to face.'

Theo smiled, stood up and kissed Parco gently on the cheek. 'Face to face, Parco, it's the only way . . .'

He laughed softly, and with a subtle trace of sorrow that Theo was too tired to notice.

Five minutes later, and alone in an office that seemed painfully empty without Theo's presence, Parco dialled the London number for the World Association of Private Investigators, and asked for some names and addresses of PIs operating in the Athens area. He was given four, and asked if the London connection could recommend one in particular: Parco explained that he was investigating a possible smuggling ring in and around the Greek Islands, and needed someone with appropriate experience. He was given the name Vito Mylonas and a direct-dial number that Parco tried on the off-chance.

After ten minutes and one misdial, Mylonas's secretary answered and Parco explained what he wanted. A few seconds later Mylonas came on the line and introduced himself.

'I'm happy to take this job, Mr Parco,' he went on in English that was better than Parco's Greek: 'Of course I have heard of Theodorus Antiquities, but not of your Mr Michaelides. I can check criminal records through one or two friends I know, you understand; and I can ask around. How complete do you want the evidence against this man to be, given that there *is* any . . .?'

'At the moment, Mr Mylonas, I'm just following leads.

To be honest, my case resembles a matrimonial more than anything else: I think my client would rather turn a blind eye to criminal activities, if they're proven – although if I find some mud that sticks, I'm in a dilemma. Reporting my suspect will compromise my client's interests.'

'Fortunately that is not my problem,' Mylonas said with laughter in his voice. Parco grinned, warming to the man. Mylonas said, 'Give me two days, Mr Parco, if you will. I have one or two high-priority jobs I must see to.'

'I understand, and I thank you, Mr Mylonas – '

'It's Vito, OK?'

'Fine, Vito. Call me Jim. Really, anything you can come up with will help me . . .'

Mylonas offered an estimated fee, which Parco accepted, adding that if, when Mylonas rang back, no one was in the office, he could leave a message on the Ansafone; and of course Parco would get back to him.

'Nice talking to you, Jim . . . It must be getting late in England. Are you stuck at your desk?'

'Not any longer today, Vito. I think' – Parco decided as he said it – 'I think I'll go and sink a few beers. How about you, Vito – you an ouzo man?'

Mylonas made a choking sound. 'None of that, Jim. I'll drink lager tonight – what do you say, "I wouldn't give you four crosses for anything else"!'

The men laughed and Mylonas wished Parco goodnight. Parco rested his finger on the cradle to break the connection, then dialled John Pearcy's home number. Talking about beer had suddenly made him rather thirsty . . .

Risico knew the darkest corners of Calverton; its every street and alley and littered yard. In the early days – God, how many years ago they seemed! – he had built up a 3D mental map of the city and its immediate environs. It was a question of survival when you're outrunning cops and rival gangs and whoever else you think has a reason to slit your throat or beat you senseless with a night-stick. And because Risico had never moved away from Calverton for any length of time, as the place altered, he had kept his knowledge updated: he still knew the territory. It was only the people that seemed to've changed . . .

He took the most tortuous route he could think of towards the old industrial heartland of the city: a heart that had stopped beating now, whose remains were ever more rapidly being cleared for bland office developments, smart yuppie apartments along the river, new enterprise areas . . . Risico inwardly sneered at the city's new money that seemed, to him, to be taking the place of Calverton's ancient soul. Communities were giving way to commuters, he judged bitterly: simple trading of real things for real money at street level was now surpassed by 'financial services', deals done on the fifteenth floor without the gleam of gold crossing from one palm to another. Risico swore softly and spat in the gutter, hating the Filofax culture even as he left it behind, delving more deeply into a wilderness of factory corpses, overgrown wasteland and filthy canals.

Risico lost the benefit of the last of the streetlights as he pushed through a crumbling wall of prefab concrete panels and scrabbled down an earth bank on to the towpath. Below him in the darkness, something splashed away suddenly. A rat, Risico thought. No more than that. He stood silently for a minute, trawling for sounds that were closer than the muffled thunder of ring-road traffic, the unending language of a world that never sleeps. And he let his eyes adjust, watching shapes half-defining out of the orange sky-glow and the liquid glimmers on the gently heaving surface of the water. He felt safer, because he was alone in this place. No one knew of him here. It was Risico's old stamping ground and it would protect him.

He walked quickly along the edge, avoiding those puddles he saw, listening to the soft mashing of cinders under his heels. The canal stretched its long sinuous hieroglyph through the city, curving left, then right, bringing hazy skylines into view at every turn. Then, a shadow obscured the distant high-rise blocks ahead – the bridge that was Risico's destination. Built in the 1850s of bricks that were surely eternal, the humpback still carried traffic, a steady flow in the daytime, none at all now.

Risico smiled as the rough, arching silhouette brought a wealth of memories softly into his head. He had smoked his first joint here, fucked his first girl – Rosemary Clark – with her pressed against the curve of the arch, skirt up, knickers down, hot as an oven to Risico's inexpert probings. They'd gone to the cinema after that, and Risico had thought himself in love. Two months later, they'd split: soon after, Risico had lost touch and never heard from her again. He'd hurt then, but now felt only a nostalgic fondness for Rosemary Clark, and he wished her well, wherever she might be . . .

Life, Risico thought, was a little like the canal itself; its twists and turns, its new sights being brought into view, the people passing each other by, or drifting a while together, before they parted . . . No one had shared the whole journey with him so far . . .

He untucked the wrapped stone from inside his jacket, felt for and found the niche of missing bricks he remembered, and jammed the package in the space. Very few people came down here, except maybe to drown a dog . . .

Not any longer for the purposes Risico recalled. Now kids sent their parents out of the house if they wanted to screw, and shot their smack openly in the park, or in certain cafés the police left alone: better the trouble all in there than on the streets . . .

Risico tutted, checked the package was secure, and turned for home.

The torchbeam blinded him, a scald of light in his eyes. He fumbled for his knife, an ecstasy of fear spilling through him.

'Don't bother.' The voice rose out of the darkness behind the light. 'I can blow you away right now . . .'

Risico knew it was true. He cursed himself for letting his caution lapse – too busy leafing through his own past. And now he was caught. The end of the road . . .

Seconds passed, and Risico wondered why the stranger didn't finish him. Why wait? Was there anything to say between these two? Was there any chance that Risico might persuade . . .?

He was on the point of speaking, when the man uptilted the torch and cast his face in an eerie underlight. There came a moment when Risico's mind couldn't connect. Who – where – ?

Then he screamed, the scream splintering back at him from the bridge's dripping underhang.

Crane laughed.

'You thought I was dead, didn't you, Peters? You thought I'd died in the fire . . .' The ghastly grinning face looked barely human. There was something, some awful thing going on . . .

'You bastard,' Risico spat, jabbing an accusing finger. 'You were all set to put me out when the cops came in. You thought you'd finish me and the Electrician and pick up a commendation for your bravery . . . You fucking snake!'

Crane shrugged, and Risico's skin crawled – because *Crane's* skin was crawling. His face, his entire head, was undergoing some kind of agitation. What . . . What the fuck! . . . Risico's raw passion of hatred was blunted by a dreadful fascination. What was this? Maybe Crane had suffered in the fire: plastic surgery that was now, somehow, sliding loose . . .

'Crane . . . What happened to you?' The question came out tremulously. Risico tensed his body.

'I survived. Oh, I lost plenty of blood from the bullet you shot into me. And I was burned, Peters. You should have seen the state of me – just raw weeping flesh on my face: I could peel it off with my fingers – you did it to me, you cunt!' Crane shrieked. Then that terrible smile once more. 'Until I was saved . . . Until the Children saved me . . .'

Risico knew all too well that insanity does not necessarily put a man at a disadvantage. What was left of Crane's mind would not stop him from killing. But Risico's searching eyes could not see the gun Crane threatened. And the torchlight, still glaring upwards into his own face . . .

'I went to see Van Allen. He understood. I just knew to go to him. He gave me a job. The Children, Peters, look after their own, you see – '

Risico took his chance, this risk being better than the certainty of death.

He lunged forward with a groin kick that Crane did not have the speed or wit to shield. Risico's boot connected with the man's balls and the point of his pelvis with a thud. Crane gave a strangled howl of pure agony and doubled, retching.

Risico brought up his knee into the man's face, snarling.

He found the flesh over the bone was soft and spongy, oddly muscular and moving under his kneecap. And then – Crane's face tried to wrap itself around Risico's leg.

With a sound of disgust he stepped away. The flashlight had dropped from Crane's deadened fingers. It cast light at a crazy angle across the towpath. Crane was staggering, his crotch soaked in blood, and blood pouring from his open mouth . . .

But his eyes, the awful blue clarity of his eyes . . . And Crane's head. Risico groaned.

Crane's head was crawling with snakes.

Risico sobbed and kicked again, kicked like a kid mad with the urge to smash an enemy; a soul-consuming revenge.

Crane stumbled under the blows, went down, cracking his skull on the wall of the canal. He spasmed, then his body, quivering, relaxed.

Risico half-turned away and vomited, rejecting the contents of his stomach as his brain tried to reject what he was seeing. With an oath he stooped and hefted Crane's body, a warm dead-weight, over the lip of the ledge and into the water: watched it sink into the foul black depths in a spiral swirl of blood trails . . .

But then, quickly, as Risico stared, something came back at him. A pale smudge rising . . . Risico's laughter was shrill and hysterical as the thing surfaced. It was a many-fingered hand; a great grey hand with Crane's twisted face stamped upon the palm.

That was Risico's first impression, as the fingers scrabbled at the canal wall to heave the face out of the water.

Still laughing, stupidly now, Risico searched for a heavy stone, found one, and brought it down on the hand. The blue globes of the eyes, soft and seductive as a woman's gaze in love's aftermath, burst and spattered Risico with their fluids. The nose fractured and tore. The mouth with its long lashing tongue filled with dark blood, and the thing sank back, turning over to reveal a palpitating mass of red tendrils dropping slowly away and out of sight, spewing bubbles.

Risico found himself alone and strangely empty. Thought itself seemed to have ceased as a result of witnessing this thing. He was not sure, now, of what to do.

And the world – the world for the first time to him ever, felt godless.

Crane had no gun, and Risico failed to see the point of the man's bluff. But then, the thought occurred to him that perhaps it had not been Crane at all: certainly, at the end, nothing human had risen from the canal to terrorize him with its strange and alien haunting. Still, at least one question was answered: the thing that Risico had glimpsed in the warehouse was not unique. There had been the cop, and there had been Crane ... And yet Crane was himself at the end; from when he rendezvoused with Risico and his team, to the moment when Risico had put the bullet into him. After that, then: when the man was lying there, half-dead of blood loss and smoke inhalation, some transformation had overwhelmed him – as it must have overwhelmed the cop as he stumbled through the blazing warehouse corridors ... Something hiding among the imported crates that had the ability to change people into what Crane had become. And he had been seeking Risico to silence him, as much as to put an end to his murderous search for the secret of – what had Crane called them? the Children.

My God, Risico thought, the Children of what monstrous parents?

On his way back to the lodging-house, he was tempted several times to dim the light of his knowledge with alcohol. Public houses looked so comfortable behind their coloured frosted glass; the beery blast of hot air through street-level extractors, the sound of human laughter. It was as though Risico had moved into some other realm of understanding, a kind of limbo, as though he had lifted a stone and witnessed something concealed and secret, something from the deep collective memory of mankind. It was a knowledge not to be borne without price, and even as Risico hurried along street after street, he felt his control slipping away. A numbness of reactive terror stiffened his limbs; his mind was sluggish, his wits brutalized.

At the lodging, he fumbled with his key, dropped it, then felt light-headed when he stood again. Inside, the TV set was still on, swamping the living-room with silver light and inane kitchen-sink babble. The main light was off.

Risico wondered whether to disturb Mrs Kennealy or not. He was going to pack and get out fast, knowing the old bag would neither care nor complain. She was paid to the end of the month, and that was all that would trouble her.

The front-room door was ajar, and Risico halfway up the stairs, when suspicion drew him back down. He unsheathed his knife, put the wrapped stone on the bottom step, and pushed open the door.

'Mrs Kennealy?'

TV light splashed frantically over walls and ceiling. Risico could see the landlady's bulky silhouette in the armchair she pulled into the middle of the room, to gain the benefit of the television and gas fire equally. He noted that the woman's hair looked mussed – a mass of tangles. And her hand, resting on the arm of the chair, seemed to be glinting, as though blistered . . . The room otherwise was unoccupied and normal.

Risico turned on the light. He walked over to see whether Mrs Kennealy's eyes were closed in sleep.

But she had no eyes. She had no face.

The front of her head was a cocoon of silvery slime, hardened now and crusted over, like rough stone. Globs of the material had run down the front of her cardigan and congealed on her hand: her lap was filled with the disgusting viscid stuff. Risico had no doubt that she was dead.

Slowly, and with revulsion stirring in his guts, he slid the knife-blade into the facial mask and prised some loose. An ooze of half-coagulated blood and plasma dribbled forth, where it dripped from the corpse's chin in a thin string down to the neck.

Risico stepped away from the body. Crane must have been here first, and then followed him on to the canal. So, it was more imperative than ever to get away – to get right away and have done with this horror.

Risico left the room, then realized that the hallway light was turned off. In the gloom, he saw that the stone was gone from the step, and caught a movement behind him –

He spun, lunging with the knife, and drove it deep into Dave Bakker's body. Risico felt the gush and smelled the stink of ruptured intestines. He made to withdraw the blade – but the cop grasped his shoulders and pulled himself deeper on to the steel, his face coming closer and closer to Risico's own.

Risico recognized his doom too late, and had no time to act.

A mere handspan in front of him, quicker than he could follow, the cop's whole face was writhing, ripping loose.

There was great activity in a fringe all around his head; a slithering stir of tendrils.

Something strong and muscular pushed itself bonelessly between Risico's lips and into his throat. Other fingers, if that's what they were, pressed his eyeballs to an unbearable agony, and then beyond. Risico heard the right eye pop, spurting juices ... There were busy scrabblings in his ears ... And someone was running curious fingers through his hair ... Tubes crawled rapidly into his nostrils and down, deep into his head ...

He was dumb and he was blind and he was terrified.

But soon, the terror was replaced by something other, by something wonderful. He could hear again, and he could breathe – though the air tasted strangely metallic and heavy to his senses.

And he could see again, and Risico smiled. Now he looked upon the world not as one man, but as many.

And as something more than man – something more wonderful, and more ancient.

Parco and Pearcy were both drunk. Up until then, their reminiscences had torn nostalgically at their insides, and they had wept quietly and self-consciously together, as men do, over the deaths of Spears and Harris; and this grief had turned slowly into hatred for the killer, and then a deep disgust with the world that had nourished it.

Rambling a little now, Parco confessed to Pearcy his love for Theo Vines, and the sharper, wickeder lust he felt for Eleanor Van Allen, and what problems that caused. For his part, Pearcy said he just loved women, full stop, but could never leave Karen and the kids; though, boy, did some chicks go for a man in a uniform ...

Bill Burly watched all of this from his all-seeing vantage-point across the counter, and sent drinks over without being asked. Until, that is, he felt his two friends had exorcized enough demons. Then he went across personally, said he was chucking these two drunken bums out, and that they had to drink at least one cup of his special black coffee by the time the cab, which he was about to call for them, arrived.

Before it did so, even before Parco was halfway through his first coffee and hating every mouthful, a couple of on-duty cops burst in and broke the news to Pearcy that Dave Bakker's body had been found downtown.

At least, people were assuming it was Bakker.

Chapter Eight

Thus saith the Lord,
Set thine house in order, for thou shalt die, and
not live.
Then he turned his face to the wall.

2 Kings 20:1–2

The sight of what remained of Bakker sobered Parco up instantly. Pearcy, probably sober as well by now, looked stunned, all but drained of any response. For his part, Parco preferred feeling blitzed.

The little terraced house was crammed with forensics' people, homicide people, a couple of sharp-nosed reporters whom nobody had yet noticed enough to throw out, Pearcy, Parco, and a long-time neighbour of Mrs Kennealy: the neighbour *was* thrown out – politely – before she had seen anything, by the white-faced patrol cop who had first answered the call to investigate suspicious comings and goings at number fourteen.

'What the hell's happened here?' Pearcy demanded to know, of anyone who was within earshot. He was standing beside Parco in the cramped hallway, squinting through the glare of the portable spotlamps that the pathologist needed to make his on-site observations. 'Who could do that to his face . . .?'

Parco's mind, reeling through nightmare possibilities, spinning at superspeed along many meaningless dead-ends, thought crazily that his friend's question was misphrased. No one knew, strictly speaking, what had happened to Bakker's face, because the face was missing. All that was left was the ruined skull, pitted as though with sprays of acid, the

155

flesh eaten away to nothing, save where traces remained under the chin and at the sides of the head; this looked torn, and had freshly bled over Bakker's jacket and shirt collar: grotesquely, tufts of his hair were still intact, hanging by scabs of skin from a brainpan that likewise displayed the tiny pits, like the boreholes of some obscene carnivorous worm.

The pathologist, whom Parco knew slightly by sight and more fully by reputation, came through from the kitchen. The man was painfully thin, as tall as Parco, and sported a goatee beard that emphasized the angularity of his whole body. He was wearing a green disposable plastic apron over a chunky sweater and cords.

'There's not a lot more I can do here. We'd best get them shifted down to the morgue.' Then, as the spotlamps flicked off, he noticed Pearcy. 'It's a bitch of a way to lose your partner, John. I'm sorry about this . . .'

Pearcy shrugged. Words to talk about the way Bakker had died didn't exist in his vocabulary at that moment. The shrug somehow said it all.

'This is Jim Parco,' Pearcy said, shifting the subject. 'Jim's a PI, and also a close friend of mine . . . Jim, this is Barry Hanlon, he's—'

'I know,' Parco interrupted. 'I've heard about some of the cases you've cracked.'

'Well, fame at last.' Hanlon smiled, to say he was not being ironic. 'I'm not sure I'll be cracking this one, though. I've never seen anything like it.'

'Any theories, Barry?' Pearcy asked. Hanlon picked up the grief in the cop's voice. 'I mean, anything at all?'

'You know my methods, John. I never give opinions unsupported by facts – '

'So what are the facts, then!' The sudden whiplash in

Pearcy's voice killed conversation in those nearby. Parco put a hand on his friend's shoulder.

'Cool off, John. The man's doing what he can. We're all working in the dark here . . .'

'Yeah . . .' Pearcy wiped the back of his hand across his eyes. 'Yeah, I know. I apologize. It's just that this – I mean, it's like the way Harris and Spears died – except – '

'Except forensically,' Hanlon added, 'there are major differences. The mutilation to the faces of those men was inflicted with a knife: I'd stake my reputation on that. But this . . .' Hanlon shook his head. 'It's as though Bakker's face was pulled away like a Velcro patch – but cleanly. The facial bones seem undamaged; yet all the overlying musculature is gone . . . It's crazy. And where are his eyes?'

'I beg your pardon?'

Hanlon looked away from Bakker to Parco. 'Well, the eyes are direct outgrowths of the brain, attached to it by the optic nerves. Now, given that it's possible to tear a face off a skull so completely, the eyes would be left behind: they're attached to the brain, they're held in the orbits by quite powerful rectus muscles . . . I can't see why they aren't here.'

'The killer – Jesus, this is awful . . . The killer, maybe, cut them out afterwards . . .'

'Interesting conjecture,' Hanlon said, ignoring the nausea stamped on Parco's face. 'Once I've looked closely at the orbits I'll be able to tell. Initial examination shows they're pretty free of tissue. If your idea is correct, Parco, the murderer spent a long time cleaning out the sockets – not at all like Harris, Spears and the others.'

The three men moved aside while the horror was covered over and placed on a stretcher. Parco stared into the street as the front door was opened and, amidst a flicker of newshounds' flashlights, saw the crowded faces of neighbours and passers-by, babbling and excited by the atrocities. Police officers moved in to clear a way to the ambulance. The front door was closed again.

'I would say,' Hanlon went on, disobeying his own rule, 'that this terrible injury to Bakker was not inflicted *post mortem.*'

Pearcy jolted. 'What! You mean his face was cut—'

'Either before or as he died. There's plenty of blood on him, John: he was bleeding as the face came away, which means that the heart was still beating – though not for long. I think massive trauma and the knife wound are what killed your partner.'

Parco felt sick to his soul. He had almost hardened himself to the betrayal and hurt he saw each day as part of his job. But this kind of inhumanity was on a different scale altogether. This destruction was simply not human.

'And what about the landlady?' Pearcy wondered. 'Mrs Kennealy – what happened to her?'

Hanlon scratched at his beard.

'Completely outside the realm of my expertise, I would say as a first impression.' He stripped off the plastic apron and stuffed it into a safe-bag. 'All I can say with regard to her, gentlemen, is – welcome to the Twilight Zone . . .'

It was late by the time Parco had gotten John back to the Pearcy household. He had phoned his wife earlier to explain the situation: Karen was waiting for them both, with hot coffee perked and a meal in the microwave if they could face it. Parco ate a little, but Pearcy declined both food and drink. Instead he dug in a drawer of the bureau and pulled out a pack of Marlboros. He had given up smoking six months before.

'The kids all right today?' Pearcy wondered. He asked it for something to say, and did not register his wife's reply with any meaningful expression.

'John,' Karen said tentatively: 'John, maybe you should go to bed now, and ring in sick in the morning – ' Parco stayed quiet, sympathizing with her completely, but knowing what her husband was going through. He was familiar enough with this territory not to feel embarrassed by the painful tableau. He smiled at Karen, noting the prettiness smothered by the worry; the beauty beneath the strain of living with a streetcop.

'I'm all right.' Pearcy glanced at Karen and she barely recognized him. 'I'm all right, OK. Just let me sit here a while. I just need to think.'

She turned to Parco. 'Jim, I'm worried about you, too.'

'Karen, I'm fine.' He was far from fine. His stomach churned, and his head throbbed due to the downslope of the alcohol high. He felt like shit.

'Stay with us tonight, please, Jim. The bed's made up in the spare room . . . I'd feel better if you were here. To be frank,' Karen said, with a tiny half-smile, 'I'm scared . . .'

'Then I'll stay,' Parco said. 'And thanks. It'll save calling a cab.' The truth of it was, Parco thought to himself, that he was scared too; scared witless of this unknown that had come into his life with such dreadful purpose, wielding its blades.

He retired to bed ten minutes later, leaving Karen and John together in their troubles. Parco showered under water as hot as he could stand it, climbed into the bed, put the light straight out, closed his eyes, and failed to find sleep.

*

Next morning early, Parco walked into his office like some bum who'd staggered in off the street. Theo's face was stamped with shock momentarily, but then she pushed her chair back from the desk, came round and hugged Parco like a wife: and Parco, wrung dry of response, felt her trembling and did nothing.

'Oh, Parco . . .' Her wet eyes were alight with a complicated fire. 'Karen Pearcy left a message to say where you were. And she said there'd been more killings last night, and you were there. What's going on? Why is this happening?'

'Questions no one can answer, Theo.' He stroked her hair and, touching her cheek, lifted a tear on the tip of his finger. 'At least, we can't answer them yet. But I reckon that, since it's my job to find answers, I'm as good a man as any to try . . .'

Now the hurt of the present was tainted with future danger in Theo's expression. 'You're going to search for the killer? Parco, you can't do that!'

He shrugged. 'Why not?' The extremity of his disgust had put everything into perspective. Yesterday's problems were, today, not worth entertaining.

'What about the business – it can't run itself . . . And where do you start, anyway? I mean, Parco, you have commitments to clients – Mrs Carthew phoned last evening, and—'

'Oh, fuck Mrs Carthew!'

At last, Parco thought, a normal, human annoyance to give him back the anchor of the mundane. And Theo was laughing.

'I think that would be better coming from you . . .'

He had to grin in turn, his face as pale as paper.

'OK, you win, Theo. But you must understand that I can't let this go. Something's happening in Calverton.

Something we've not seen before. There are no comparisons: no similarities . . .' Parco went on to tell her a little of what he had learned, a little of what he had seen. But not everything. The worst he kept screwed tight in a corner of his memory.

As Parco talked, quietly and without elaboration, his tone easing the dreadfulness of the crime, Theo put coffee on and broke open her lunch-time pack of sandwiches. At first Parco declined, but then at her insistence he accepted the food and discovered how hungry he really was.

They spoke together for an hour. Theo for the most part was silent, her face strained, but gradually she began to quiz him gently, to draw out the stinging shock of his experience; rather as a balm to his wounds than simply to find out more for herself.

'The point of it all,' Parco said in conclusion, 'is that it's more than psychopathic. The mutilations lack the mad ritual of the Ripper's killings. These murders were done in haste, as though the perp was looking for something . . . Except for Bakker and Mrs Kennealy . . . But why . . .?' Parco frowned. 'But why were *they different*? And what was covering the woman's—'

The phone rang, a gentle burr that Theo answered by reflex, passing the handset to Parco a second later.

'Yes?' Parco listened, nodding minutely. Theo could make nothing of the mosquito-whine voice at the other end, and was intrigued by the way Parco's reactions changed. Life was coming back into him, she saw. His purpose was returning.

'OK, thanks.' He handed the phone back to Theo. 'DS Cavanagh, phoning from Headquarters, passing on some information that he and John Pearcy thought I should have.'

'John's back at work?'

'When have you ever known him listen to Karen's advice . . .?'

'Yeah.' Theo looked at her nails. 'Men are so bloody-minded . . .'

'They found another body, floating in a canal down near the Basin – same state as Bakker.'

'My God, Parco . . .'

'The word at the station is that he and Bakker died around the same time; quite late on last night. And they have an ID.'

'But – '

'No face, but ten perfect fingers, Theo. And the prints match up to a guy called Denny Crane . . .'

'Means nothing to me,' Theo said.

'Nor me – until now. He was a security guard working for Hi-Seal Security at the time of that robbery down on the railyards: he was, in fact, on duty the night the heist took place . . .' Theo still looked blank. 'Crane was burned in the blaze,' Parco explained. 'And there was a serious wound, also – probably stumbled on to the gang, who opened fire.'

'I still don't see – '

'I am reliably informed that Crane, and another guard called Jeremy Miller, who was killed that night, were protecting a consignment of valuable antiquities from Greece. At least, that's what the record states was in the warehouse. Apparently, due to his injuries, Crane had to quit his security job, but was offered a post at the museum by Van Allen. Crane was still employed there at the time of his death.'

'And so do you think Van Allen gave Crane a job out of conscience, feeling sorry for him maybe?'

'From what I've learned about Van Allen, I'd say there was not a chance in hell of that. But it's a connection; it's a doorway into the Van Allen case and, perhaps, a lead on these killings.' Parco grinned, and Theo knew exactly why.

'Theo, would you please phone through to Richard Van Allen's office and make an appointment for me to see him as early as possible this morning – tell him it's in connection with the warehouse fire, in particular with an employee of his who was present at that time.'

'Denny Crane?'

'Yes. I'm counting on the police not having contacted Van Allen yet, and him not knowing of Crane's death . . . Though even if he does, the most he can do is tell me to push off.'

'I'll do it now.'

'Fine.' Parco looked down at himself in distaste. 'I intend to revisit the railyards for another talk with Mrs Sunderland, but first I'll drive home for a shower and a change of clothes . . .'

Theo, deadpan, stood up and flicked on the Expelair.

'I think that's a marvellous idea, Parco,' she told him.

Edith Sunderland had changed the colour of her cashmere sweater, but not her attitude of stony reticence at Parco's return. He had put on his best blue pin-stripe in anticipation of his meeting with Van Allen, and thought this might make some impression on the lady. Parco found himself a little disappointed.

'Really, Mr Parco – '

'Jim, please.'

'Really, Mr Parco, I can't see what help I can be with regard to Mr Crane. The poor man suffered terribly in that fire, what with burns to his body, and the gunshot wound . . .'

'Did you know him to talk to at all, Mrs Sunderland?'

'Just to say good morning to. He was rather quiet. Kept himself to himself. Not as outgoing as Mr Miller . . . Such a cheerful young man: such an awful way to die.'

'Indeed,' Parco said. 'But did you ever—'

'I don't know why I'm talking to you at all,' the woman interrupted crossly. 'What can this have to do with your insurance claim – the fact that I said good morning to Mr Crane?'

Parco restrained himself and explained patiently: 'I simply want your impressions of the man, Mrs Sunderland. It's very important.'

'Why is it important? Tell me why! I gave you what you wanted when you called before, and now here you are again pestering me with these silly questions!'

The woman's voice had risen almost to a shriek, so that one or two clerks beyond the glass partition in the next room glanced up. Edith Sunderland's right hand fluttered to her bosom in her agitation, and then moved towards the internal telephone.

Parco leaned over the desk, bringing himself closer.

'Mrs Sunderland, Mr Crane was murdered last night and his body dumped in a canal—'

'Oh – oh – my—'

'He was badly mutilated – I can't say more: but I'm sure you'll appreciate that any details you can supply, either to myself or to the police if they call, could have a crucial bearing . . . Now, tell me please, is there anything about Denny Crane that you can remember, anything that I can use in my work? I assure you that any relevant details will be passed on to my contacts at Police Headquarters . . . Mrs Sunderland, your personal impressions are very important. Possibly vital. Do you understand?'

The woman nodded, gulping for breath. A high colour had come to her cheeks, and her right hand shook as she placed it back in her lap.

'There – there's not a lot, Mr Parco . . . As I said, I didn't know him very well . . . Though I did go to see him in hospital. Mr Galbraith – he's the yard Administrator – asked me to drop by with some fruit and flowers . . .'

'Yes, very thoughtful. And you spoke with Mr Crane then?'

'Briefly. He seemed – oh, abstracted, I suppose. Distant. Not like himself . . .'

'The shock of the fire, perhaps?'

'Yes, probably that. Odd. But he didn't seem like Mr Crane at all.'

'In what way, Mrs Sunderland?' Parco was interested to note that his pulse-beat had quickened, and the skin at the back of his neck was alive with electricity.

'I can't really say. Oh, it was Mr Crane, sure enough. But he was even more silent and withdrawn . . . He hardly said a word. And when I got up to leave, he – he looked at me and smiled, Mr Parco . . . That wonderful smile, and those blue, blue eyes . . .'

Edith Sunderland shivered.

'I'd never noticed how attractive his eyes were.'

'His face was not badly burned, then?' Parco asked.

'Why no, Mr Parco. That was a blessing for him, at least. His face was not touched at all by the fire . . .'

What had been Risico sat before Van Allen, and smiled. The face was not Bakker's, nor did it resemble that of Patrick Joseph Peters: neither of theirs, nor anyone's. Even someone used to the grotesque and deformed would not have watched that face easily, nor could readily have delivered up the words to describe it. Part of the difficulty lay in its ever-changing nature; the restlessness of features not yet guided by the memories of the brain beneath, not settled by a single identity. What might, then, have been taken as a smile was no such thing, for the mouth twisted suddenly, skewing sideways, opening to a red cavern filled with writhings, closing to an agonized grimace. Meanwhile the body, slumped until now in the chair, stiffened and shook; its hands gripped the chairarms as shudder after shudder ran through the flesh –

Suddenly one hand flew free and ripped at the scalp, tearing madly, uprooting a tangle of muscular tubes that immediately delved back down into hair, skin, bone. Blood ran thinly from the nose, and a black fluid more viscously from the clamping mouth, which now stretched back in a shriek of final pain.

It was Risico's last human scream.

After that, the thing in the chair quietened and the white eyelids slowly lifted. Blue eyes, blue as lapis lazuli, gazed across at Van Allen, and a profound adoration spilled into them.

'There is no difficulty now?'

'No.' Risico's head calmly moved from side to side. 'It is done. He is subdued . . . The other was not like this: he came easily under our influence.'

Van Allen shrugged, a gesture that the other did not yet understand. 'They are individuals, for all they follow the herd: unpredictable beings who will sometimes fight and die for unfounded and thoughtless beliefs. The Mothers found this out to their cost.'

'Blessed are They.'

'Blessed are They,' echoed Van Allen, then, after a moment's contemplation of past glory, he attended to the business before them.

'Now we are two. Peters destroyed the third, as the body of Crane was destroyed. And you allowed Bakker to die . . .'

'But we have the stone – '

'But we have lost the freedom our secrecy allowed. Now the police will intensify their investigations. Your destruction of the woman at the house is a mystery to them, and they abhor the unknown – giving it the image of their own face whenever they can . . .'

'Fools!'

'Perhaps,' Van Allen reflected. 'And yet their success is unprecedented. Look at what they have achieved, Brother, since the Old Time.'

'The world is dying,' came the simple, irrefutable reply.

'Yes, it is dying and their most powerful cultures are decayed almost to the point of collapse. But still, I say, they will investigate the mysteries we have created. So we must plan, and take the utmost care.'

'I agree. If only our numbers were greater . . .'

'There is another consignment.' Van Allen glanced at the documents on his desk. 'It will be arriving later today. I am told by Michaelides that a small number of eggs will be contained therein, and one cocoon, which is mature. We can build our strength within a very few weeks. And so,' Van Allen glanced up, 'to the practicalities of the matter . . .'

'A host for the Brother?'

'Yes. I have an idea whom it might be—'

'And a hatching place . . .'

'That will follow shortly after. For now, you must lose all resemblance to your hosts: search Peters' memory for that. And I should not need to remind you to be careful, until you are fully established.'

'Even so,' said the other, 'I am not sure I could attain your degree of control.'

Van Allen lifted his hands and gazed at them, then used them to straighten his tie minutely and plane across his already immaculate hair. He laughed.

'You know, I have grown quite attached to him . . .' The smile dropped away. 'Now attend to yourself!'

The face opposite relaxed, losing all expression, the mouth hanging slack, then thinning to a white line. A convulsion rippled from forehead to chin; strangely, not following the musculature of a normal human face. The nose thickened, reddening; the ears enlarged slightly in a moment's flowing change; cheekbones bulged outward and moved to enhance thicker jowls that sprouted dark-brown hair bristling around fleshier lips. What could be taken as tendons stiffened and shifted like cords in the neck, finding firmer purchase, and the brown hair spread upward, displacing Risico's pale blondness. These major changes were swift, a melting transformation, but now, as the final alterations were made, they slowed and became more subtle. A tinge of colour flowed across the countenance as a scattering of small blemishes appeared; the jawline blurred fleetingly and drew back to seem less heavy and jutting; the forehead acquired frown lines, and now a mock pulse began to beat at each temple.

'It is good enough,' Van Allen proclaimed. 'And you will be Mr Patrick, who is an old acquaintance of mine. I have employed you in a casual capacity to clean and tidy up around the museum. The regular janitor is away ill, so rather than trouble the employment agency, I have taken advantage of your offer to help me out . . .'

'I understand,' Patrick said. His expression wavered slightly like animals stirring beneath.

'You must take care,' Van Allen repeated. 'I don't want the plague of suspicion here more than is necessary . . . Soon, I will show you the stone, and together we will reaffirm our purpose and courage. For now, make yourself familiar with the layout of the building. Introduce yourself to Castillo and say that I have asked him to show you the janitor's room and your list of duties . . . Go now. I have a man to see who wants to talk to me about Crane.'

'What of Crane? Is this the police?'

'No, not the police. I expect they will also want to interview me shortly. This man is a private investigator. His name is Parco . . .'

Parco sat across from Richard Van Allen and knew exactly what Eleanor had meant. It was a complex and subtle reaction on Parco's part: he knew that something was amiss, but it was as though all of his investigator's instincts were screwed up suddenly, everything wired wrongly. The man certainly had charm, panache, and a powerful presence that answered all of Parco's unspoken questions about how Van Allen had got what he had and where he wanted to be. Simply put, Van Allen was compelling, had a charisma you could almost taste . . .

Parco found himself mildly jealous, which in turn shortened his temper.

'Crane . . . Crane . . . I seem to remember him . . .'

'You ought to, you employed him personally . . .' Parco sketched in the relationship that, he knew full well, Van Allen recalled in every detail. 'Maybe you felt sorry for him after the attempted robbery at the warehouse. After all, he was pretty badly injured.'

'Ah, Crane.' Van Allen looked up from his desk and drove the full force of his gaze into Parco's eyes. 'My hiring him was nothing to do with his misfortune. He was good at his job, Mr Parco; a man of long experience and an impeccable record, and, since I happened to have a vacancy on the security side . . .'

The blue . . . Thoughts and dreams . . . Terrors . . . Wonders . . . Out of the blue . . . The liquid sky . . . Seas with no end . . . Ancient awe when the world was small . . . That blue slumber . . .

'Mr Parco?'

'I'm sorry,' Parco said. 'I was thinking of something else.' He wondered if Van Allen knew yet that Crane was dead: guessed that he did with his likely contacts in City Hall or elsewhere. Van Allen confirmed it a moment later.

'I notice from your card that you are a *private* detective: I cannot see how your presence here constitutes part of any official police investigation . . .'

'My enquiries are coincidental, Mr Van Allen. This has nothing to do with Mr Crane's death.'

Van Allen said nothing, and in the silence the mesmerism began again, so that Parco had to pull himself together with an effort.

'I am working on behalf of an insurance company under-writing certain consignments that Mr Crane was protecting when he worked for Hi-Seal.'

'Oh?'

'Electrical components, actually; nothing you were importing.'

Van Allen smiled. 'You have done a bit of background reading on me, I see.'

'Thoroughness pays.' Parco's smile in return was vir-tually a sneer, which he regretted: it weakened his cover, for one thing, hinting at more than a purely objective pro-fessional search for information. Van Allen appeared to ignore it.

'The components had been bought by Tesla Industries,

an American corporation with an assembly plant at Kenniston Newtown—'

'I'm aware of that.'

'The point is that discrepancies were found between the shipment and the consignment manifest, mailed separately. In short, items were missing, Mr Van Allen – '

'So why come to me?'

'Because I can no longer interview Mr Crane personally, and because I thought you might be concerned that an employee of yours was under such suspicion. Looking around your museum, I can't see many signs of sophisticated security. It would not be difficult for a pro to take whatever he wanted . . .'

'The second point is now hypothetical,' Van Allen pointed out. 'As to the first: all I can tell you is that Mr Crane came to me with perfectly satisfactory references, both from Hi-Seal Security, and Carl Galbraith, who is Chief Administrator for the railyards where Crane worked. Apart from that, I judged him to be reliable, Mr Parco – and I can tell you that I am an excellent judge of character.'

Parco knew then that Van Allen had not believed a word of his story: the fabrication had been too loose, too clumsily pitched. He would be wise to leave now with his dignity intact; in any event, he had gained the impression he came for.

'I'm interested to know why you were employed by the insurers, Mr Parco. With respect, a small-time PI can't match up to the big guns employed by large corporations . . .'

Parco rode the affront with a casual shrug. His cover might be hanging from him in shreds, but no way was he handing the admission to Van Allen on a plate!

'There's such a thing as PR, Mr Van Allen. It *would* be possible for Tesla Industries to bring in their big-time professionals in five-hundred-pound suits and accents learned at Eton: but any investigation that stirs the mud can smell. I think Tesla decided not to embarrass local companies, frankly. Besides, this is a small leak in a very big pipe. It was not worth the company's time to crack this nut with a steam-hammer. It *was* worth their while, however, to let the guilty party know that someone was on the case.'

'I see. Well, Mr Parco, I'm sorry I can add nothing that would be of any help. Denny Crane carried out his duties entirely to my satisfaction, and I deeply regret his passing. Now, if you would excuse me . . .'

'You are a busy man.'

Parco stood, infuriated that Van Allen had dismissed him by dropping his eyes back to his work. He stared at the top of the man's elegantly barbered head, then walked out and left the door open.

Outside, he checked the time. Not yet 10 a.m. What were his options now? Theo might have more data he could use from her scans . . . Was it worth visiting Eleanor once more, he wondered? Parco rejected the idea, knowing it would not be for any reason that would enable him to close this case and quickly. Now that he was out of Van Allen's presence, the fact of Bakker's awful death and that of the landlady pressed back into his mind. He realized that the deep revulsion he felt as a human being had involved him in it, as much as the circumstance of being at John Pearcy's side when the word came down.

Parco left the museum and sat outside on one of the benches. The approaches were all quiet at this time of day. In the distance, a couple walked arm in arm, and an old woman was sitting fifty yards from Parco throwing breadcrumbs to the birds. He saw no point in tracking down Pearcy again, who had in any event promised him updates on the PM from Hanlon as they were released. Another trip to the railyards, then, just to ask around more generally . . .?

Parco realized he was grasping at straws, wasting his own time. He decided to close the Carthew case and one or two others he had pending, all of which he could do from his desk, down the phone line. He'd wait for Vito Mylonas's call on the Michaelides/Van Allen connection before making another move in that area.

That call came a little after nine hours later, confirming that Nikos Michaelides was under suspicion by the Greek police for illegal smuggling of ancient artefacts out of the country along what was thought to be an extremely well-sealed pipeline, which began at Piraeus to the west of Athens, and ended in Calverton. Mylonas was able to tell Parco that the case against Michaelides was shaping up strongly, but the authorities would make no move until they had unequivocal proof of guilt, nor until they had traced the pipeline through from end to end, to see what shit scattered when the heat was turned up.

Mylonas's news depressed Parco as much as it pleased him. He could not, now, wrap up this one cleanly: but it had brought him a step closer to Van Allen, and thus he was committed to seeing it through.

At 19.45, Parco locked up his office and decided to delay his trip to the railyards until the next morning.

At about the same time, Van Allen himself and 'Mr Patrick' were finalizing the documentation on the shipment they had been expecting. Van Allen was making pleasant conversation with the clerk who was dealing with the hand-over, while Patrick supervised two railyard workers as they manhandled a heavy box into the boot of the Director's Daimler.

Chapter Nine

How I long to see
Among dawn flowers
The face of God.

Basho

Face to face was Van Allen's favourite way, and always had been. Eleanor now, eyes squeezed tight, was reminded of her husband's old joke, long since bleached of any humour: 'The missionary brings solace to an untamed corner from a position of rectitude and the will to please . . .' She was whimpering with a fear that had been building since his arrival home, but which she hoped he'd take as the voice of ecstasy as his cold passion grew with the mechanical regularity of his fuck.

He breathed hot husky laughter into her ear and followed it with his tongue, its tip prodding and probing at the whorls and galleries of flesh. Eleanor all but cried out in hysteria. This had become an act of hostility and hate, and not of love, she knew. Whatever cause had convinced him of her wickedness, he was taking a painful revenge: and the bastard was making it last. Sweat covered Van Allen's body with a slick sheen and his grunting increased with metronomic desperation. His tongue, trailing snail-like across her cheek below her right eye, found the corner of her mouth and pushed apart her lips; they resisted momentarily before allowing him entry. He flickered it over her clenched teeth, pushing, insisting. She let him through, losing the last of her dignity as he came with a cry inside her that drowned out Eleanor's own choking sounds of nausea and the ragged sobbing that was love's aftermath.

Van Allen pushed himself up and stared down at the twisted wet face of his wife. Her hair was messed, spread untidily across her peach satin pillow. Her eyes were closed, long lashes matted, tears leaking between. Her upper lip, bitten by herself or by him, was bruised and swollen; blood smearing her button teeth with pinkness. He knew that she had loathed and detested the act she had just suffered, but an obsolete part of his ego was flattered that her face was flushed and her pulse was racing. He felt her spasm in waves around his subsiding cock, and pinched a nipple with a quick viciousness, so that pain interrupted her pleasure and forced her moaning to splinter with a sharp involuntary cry.

He pulled away, rolled off the bed and took two steps to the unlocked tantalus on an ornate Georgian dresser, where he poured two good measures of Scotch, drank deeply himself, and returned to Eleanor, still spreadeagled like a slut across the rumpled sheets.

'Drink, my darling . . .' He held more of the liquor in his mouth, dribbled it over her breasts, then moved to her mouth and poured in the rest. Eleanor jerked upright, coughing violently, her hands flailing him away.

'You – you bloody disgusting – b-bastard!'

'Don't say you didn't enjoy it . . .'

'There's no point in saying anything, is there?'

'Oh, I don't know. Communication is the essence of reconciliation . . .'

Van Allen had walked to the long mirror and was regarding himself critically, planing back the hair over his temples, smiling darkly.

'Damn your so-clever fragments of philosophy, Richard. You came home hoping to catch me with someone else – although why you're troubled now, suddenly, I can't imagine.'

'I simply wanted to enjoy my wife. It's been long enough since we pleasured each other . . . You're still very desirable you know, Eleanor . . .'

She threw back her head and gave a bitter, contemptuous laugh. 'What do you mean, "still"? Do you regard me as used goods, perhaps – looking a bit raddled after all the wear and tear these past few years . . .?'

'No, not that.' Van Allen turned around and looked at her. 'He still loves you—'

'What "he"? Who are you talking about?'

'I meant I – I still love you.'

She tried to summon up a sneer, to reject him utterly in a single supreme instant of liberating hatred. But it was difficult. It was impossible. Aside from the security and freedom inherent in his wealth, as a woman, Eleanor still found Richard Van Allen compelling. With every other man, and occasionally with other women, *she* had decided, *she* had controlled. The power of that intensified the mere physical pleasure of her intercourse. But with him it was different. He wanted her, he took her. It had always been like that. Nothing had changed.

She watched him now as he moved across to replenish his glass. The down of hair across the shoulders, the leanness of his flanks and the tightness of his buttocks were as she remembered them, and set her tingling. He half turned and noticed her appraisal. His cock hung thick and pendulous, still half engorged with blood; and now, in a renewal of desire, it rose at the sight of her – and at Van Allen's vision of how he wanted her this second time.

The look in his blue eyes, Eleanor feared, belied what he'd said. How could he love her? She'd read his intention and was shaking her head slowly from side to side, dreams and denials both caught in that one gesture. She remem-

bered the last time, the soreness that had lasted for days: the
recollection that still burst like a wound in half-sleep, in
some lost hour of the pre-dawn dark.

Van Allen's big hands hauled her up and spun her round.
This time, unlike the last, she did not bother to fight him.
His fingers clenched on her hip bones and pushed her over
and down on the bed. He began to plough doggedly into
her, aware now that another was watching with him, con-
taminating what fondness was left with a black and alien
disdain.

'I'll tell you what: you don't know you're born!'

William Howard cast his eyes around Helen's room. His
voice held a note of irritation that was totally unfeigned. She
poured boiling water into two pot noodles and handed one
across to him. Howard accepted the container and glanced
at the bubbling mass of coloured powders and fragments.
He made a face.

'Stir it yourself,' she said shortly. 'It's curry flavour.'

'Great . . . I mean, when *I* was an undergrad, I roomed
for two years with this beer-swilling womanizer from Leeds
who broke wind in his sleep every night and filled the place
up with rancid socks and beaver books – '

'With what?' Helen's frown was genuine.

'Oh. I mean, he was disgusting. The room hadn't been
painted for a decade; the veneer was crumbling off the built-
in chipboard cupboards, and the central heating was broken
down half the time! Jesus – just look at this. Proper dormer
windows, new carpet, a posh desk, shower unit . . .'

'You're only jealous.'

'Well, of course I'm jealous. This is better than the room
I've got now – and I'm on my way to a doctorate!'

'I'm not sure if that's boasting or not.'

'It's not. It's complaining.'

'Well, shut up and eat your supper.'

'I've had a hard day – and this is what you serve up for me!'

'I'll serve it over the top of your bloody head if you carry on . . .' Now Helen's temper was flaring, she and Howard like two flints with these words of acrimony sparking between them. Her expression softened.

'Look, Bill – if you like we can go over to the Union Bar and grab some supper. The food's not bad, though most of it's fried. And they've got lots of real ales on. There's this new one . . . um . . .'

'Well?'

'Old Fart.'

'Thanks a lot. There's no need to get personal!'

For an instant Helen felt the return of her temper, then realized that Howard's high dudgeon was faked. She crumbled into laughter.

'You idiot . . . On the other hand, if you're paying, we can ring for a pizza. They deliver from The Pizza Piazza in town. Actually, I fancy a ten-inch broad-base . . .' Helen licked her lips, and Howard was tempted to forget all about the cares of the day. Almost, but not quite. He nodded briefly to indicate that any plan would suit him.

'OK, if you like – and yeah, I'll pay. We'll ring soon. But I was wondering, Helen, if you'd do me a little favour?'

'What do you think I've been hinting at?' she said, exasperated. But she had seen that serious look come over him, a look she knew well by now. It dated back to the day he'd accepted Richard Van Allen's offer. The promise of glory had changed him, she reflected . . .

'Oh, go on then. What do you want?'

Howard rolled down the sleeves of his white shirt, and Helen was amazed to see the cotton covered in writing. He grinned at her sheepishly.

'It was the only way I could get my notes out of that damned basement workroom . . .'

'I'm sorry, I didn't ask about your day.'

Howard shrugged. 'The day was fine. I arrived. The place was cleaned up like Van Allen said it would be. The Deputy Director, that fucking queen Castillo, brought in the casts of the Hagia Stone, and I set to work. Castillo went after a while, and this other guy took over the watch. He told me his name was Patrick, Joe Patrick – and would you credit it, he was the new janitor!'

Helen's eyes mirrored the surprise Howard was expecting. 'So why was he put in charge?'

'Beats me,' Howard said. 'All round it's the strangest arrangement I've ever come across. Well, anyway, Joe Patrick doesn't hang around continually. He comes and goes. But I had a hunch that Van Allen wasn't joking when he said he wanted this work kept hermetically sealed. At the end of the afternoon, Patrick asks me to turn out my pockets. He checks my jacket himself . . . But the heating's on high and my sleeves are rolled up, and he doesn't think to look there. I managed to scribble down a few fragments . . . And it's the weirdest stuff you ever heard about . . .'

'What I can't understand,' Helen said, spooning up the last of her noodles, 'is why Van Allen didn't send you – us – out in search of the original stone again. There must be other places where it could turn up?'

'No doubt.' Howard passed his plastic pot, half-full, over to her. 'I don't know. This runs deep, Helen. God knows what Van Allen is really up to. My guess is he's playing his

179

cards close to his chest, so that nobody has a clue what his hand really looks like.'

'Do you, um . . .' She smiled uncertainly. 'Do you think it could be dangerous, Bill?'

'To tell you the truth, yes. Ever since I met the man, I've had suspicions about the legality of his operations: it's pretty clear now he's got some kind of traffic going in smuggled antiquities . . . Which is why I want you well out of the way – '

'Oh, come on!'

'I'm serious, Helen – ' She could see he was. Howard stripped off his shirt and spread the sleeves out before her. 'Look, you can help me best by chasing the leads these fragments throw up. Now, the Linear A script, of which this is an example, usually seems to be reserved for administrative details; records of taxes, incomings and outgoings, stock lists . . .'

'Christ, the world hasn't changed much.'

'True enough. But the point is that *these* pictographs are concerned with fantasy, folklore, legend . . . And they are not representative of straightforward Linear B characters. I mean, this resembles B, but it's not the same. From comparative studies on the evolution of Egyptian hieroglyphic texts, I'd say this was older – maybe much older. Which is as much of an academic bombshell as the discovery of the Hagia Stone itself!'

Helen smiled, and as the intensity of Howard's excitement abated, so did he. He could see that she was bored by his talk of old stones and ancient languages. Right now she was interested in pizzas, and in him: Howard reckoned he should take advantage of it.

'OK, Helen, you win . . . But will you please go to the library and check out some references . . .?'

She had stood up and stripped off her shirt, which she dropped over his.

'Helen – '

'Of course I'll help. Tell me what to look for.'

She leaned forward, placed her hands on his knees and kissed him.

'Euryale . . . Stheno . . . Mmm, that's good, lover . . .'

She touched him, taunting, tantalizing.

'Roromandare . . . The Evil Eye . . .'

Helen gently pushed against Howard's shoulders, pressing him down on to the bed.

'Helen – I'm . . . Phorcys and Ceto . . . The Gorgoneion . . .'

Her hands were everywhere. Howard's determination to continue gave way to sighs.

Theo served Parco some coffee. The sight of him slumped in his desk chair staring idly out of the window with his mind elsewhere brought a hot, frightened gleam of tears to her eyes. He was a changed man, wrung into a new shape by events not entirely clear to her. She felt adrift, lost without him as he was.

'Parco.'

He took time to respond, swivelling slowly round to acknowledge her: and Theo noted with brief disappointment that his eyes did not admire her as they had done since – well, Theo admitted with no false modesty, since I joined the goddam team.

'Coffee.'

'Thanks, Theo . . . Thanks.'

'Parco, are you OK?'

'I'm fine.' His face told otherwise. Theo had noticed the

shadows and lines, the glassiness in his eyes that spoke of too little sleep.

'Eleanor Van Allen will drop by before lunch, she says: remember you asked me to fix an appointment.'

Parco roused himself, forcing out the clamouring thoughts; the undercurrent of nightmares. He wanted to see John Pearcy again, and Hanlon: he wanted to get to the heart of this darkness quickly – and then still that heart for good.

'Right. I'll make sure my hair is combed . . .'

'Parco, that's enough of it!' The whiplash made him glance up. Theo was furious. She leaned towards him and jabbed at the air with a finger.

'It's enough. I know there're pressures – and what's happening in the city is unspeakable. But I can't work with you like this.'

'What—'

'Hear me out. I don't know what it is, Parco: I can't figure what's worrying you. These killings, the Van Allen case, us . . . But I know that you're operating at about fifty-per-cent efficiency, which is just about enough to make the slide into bankruptcy long and painful. I've worked hard for you, Parco – hell, I've worked hard ever since I can remember. And I'm not giving up that foundation because you can't handle yourself. I mean it. If you don't shape up, I'm cutting loose – and you can – you can fuck off!'

Parco summoned up a smile; found the heart in himself that was still beating and alive. Now he responded to Theo's flaring, flaming eyes and her angrily reddened face.

'What can I do?'

'You heard me, Parco . . .' The storm was abating. Her anger had peaked and crashed against him and now drained away. 'You can fuck off,' she said more gently.

'That's what I thought you said. Let's take a holiday, Theo.' He grinned at her surprise. 'I mean it, too. You're right. I've been taking on the problems of the world, rather than just the problems of my clients. And those have gotten to me: it's not the professional way . . .'

'Involvement makes for slow solutions. You taught me that yourself, Parco. Do it fast, do it right, close the case.'

'Yeah.' Parco gulped a mouthful of coffee. Theo came round and squatted at his side, putting her hands on his.

'A holiday would be lovely, Parco. Where?'

'Anywhere you like.'

'Scotland. I love Scotland. The heather will still be flowering now . . .'

'Scotland, then.'

'But after all this is over, Parco. Let's come back to a clean slate. If the Van Allen case looks protracted, you can always refer it on to Paladin Associates – although I know you're going to tell me you want to see it through yourself . . .'

Parco shrugged. 'It looks more and more like a police matter anyway. The pipeline Van Allen's set up is international. If Pearcy or someone like him can access the police national computer, we can smash the operation fast.'

'We?'

'I mean, the boys in blue . . .'

'That's better.' Theo kissed him lightly on the lips.

'When it's over, then,' he promised. If it's over, he thought.

Shortly before Eleanor Van Allen arrived, Parco debated with himself how much to tell her. The more he considered it, the more he became convinced that things were moving out of his ambit, as well as out of his league. His connection with her had caused him to lift the stone unseen: now he really ought to turn the matter over to the CID before the bugs began to scatter. Van Allen's carefully constructed machine was beyond Parco's abilities to destroy: he probably couldn't even damage it with his limited powers. That convinced him. He'd tell the woman what was necessary; that her husband was involved in the illegal importation of smuggled antiquities, and that, in Parco's opinion, accounted for the change in him that she had noticed. He would apologize, offer what help he could (though recognizing this would likely be an empty gesture), collect her cheque and wave goodbye to the whole affair. It would do him good to have it finished. In his present emotional state – scared, frankly, of the murders in Calverton, and still not entirely sure of Theo's intentions – he could not withstand the power of Eleanor's heady seductiveness. Tangling with her would be wonderful – before Parco or any other man lost the last few threads of their self-control. Women like her ate up lovers and spat them out. Driven by whatever urge – anger, loneliness, a need for love they could never fulfil – they destroyed what they touched as they slowly destroyed themselves. Parco imagined Eleanor in ten years' time, or fifteen, and felt a profound sadness that remained with him throughout the morning.

He was calm enough and friendly as she sat before him, however; and intrigued by her stylish hat, the latest fashion from Paris, with its gauzy blue veil covering her face. It looked as though she was in mourning; an impression that Parco found faintly disquieting.

In quiet, formal tones he outlined some of what he had learned, but was careful to offer no advice. This was the dilemma he had foreseen. Even by explaining thus far, he was giving Van Allen the advantage, should his wife tell him; allowing him time to close down or modify his operation, or cover his tracks effectively. Parco decided to speak with Chief Super Maynon directly Eleanor left. He could not shoulder the weight of this knowledge any further.

Eleanor listened without comment as Parco ran through what he'd found. He took it for granted that she would see this as the cause of her husband's transformation. Maybe he was planning to seal the pipeline and disappear while he was ahead: or perhaps there was a particularly import-ant consignment coming through ... Parco didn't know, and no longer cared. He had done what he had been paid to do by Eleanor Van Allen, and now the file could be closed.

'So you see, Mrs Van Allen – Eleanor – this has become an official matter of the most serious nature. Your husband is in very deep, here. Obviously I will continue to respect the confidentiality of the meetings we've had, but I have to say that I am bound to inform the police of the details I've uncovered. I'm sorry, truly.'

The woman inclined her head slightly to acknowledge what Parco had said. He found it disconcerting not to be able to see her face; shadows within shadows behind her veil. As he concluded, he experienced the strangest sen-sation that she was grinning at him.

'I will ask Miss Vines to prepare your account, since my work has taken me slightly over the ten-hour limit we agreed.'

Parco half rose to open the door.

'Don't do that,' Eleanor said. 'I fear the matter isn't settled at all, Mr Parco.'

'I don't understand ...'

'When I say that my husband has changed, I mean just

that. I'm not talking about some kind of emotional strain he may be suffering – or me, for that matter. I'm telling you that he is not Richard Van Allen: someone else is occupying his place. As to the illegal activities you mention, I have known about them for some time – a marital bed loosens the tongue more effectively than any confessional box, Mr Parco.'

Parco found himself floundering. And then Eleanor lifted her veil.

'Jesus Christ! Eleanor, what in God's name – '

'Now,' she continued. 'If we could discuss this a little further . . .'

She left an hour later, leaving with Parco a letter containing a phone number where he could reach her if he made more progress. She actually felt sorry for him. The man's shock upon seeing her beaten face had been deep and sincere. He, like the others, was under her spell. But not Richard, never Richard.

She walked out of the office-block into a warm early autumn afternoon. The forecast had promised rain and lower temperatures, so Eleanor decided to stroll in the park and then shop before returning home to finish her packing. Maybe the change in the weather would hold off during her journey.

She smiled at a young mother calling to her children not to wander too far . . . Said hello to an elderly gentleman who lifted his hat to her . . . Ignored the weirdo who stared openly at her legs as she passed him by.

Joe Patrick turned to watch the woman walk away down the avenue, turn into the park gateway and vanish from sight.

*

Parco's frustrations were increased considerably after his conversation with Chief Superintendent Maynon. He had met the Super on a couple of occasions, both informal, and had not been impressed then by the man's rigid and by-the-book approach to policing. Maynon fought crime with what he believed to be tried and trusted procedures that left no room in the equation for individual initiative or the gut sense that every good cop uses while on the street. Maynon's view of the world was coloured by budget sheets, stats and governmental legislation that, in Parco's opinion, had stretched the force tissue-thin across the country, to the point where holes showed through in many places. There was also the negative factor of the private police forces, also running to the bottom buck line; a kind of 'protect-as-you-pay' policy that left huge swathes in cities and rural areas inadequately covered. This, of course, simply served to reinforce Maynon's attitude, his motto being: 'The system is sound, it's people that balls it up for you'.

And so, after fifteen minutes of hard telephone talking by Parco, during which time his temper had been barely restrained, Maynon agreed to read an abstract of the Van Allen file that Parco had prepared, and to find time to contact his counterpart in Athens for any likely connections.

'You'll understand, however, Mr Parco, that this is not at the top of my priority list. While officers are getting their faces slashed by a psychopath right here in Calverton, I can hardly spare the manpower to investigate a possible antiques' racket . . .'

It's 'antiquities', Parco thought savagely. And it's more than a fucking racket. And there was already a link between Van Allen and the killings in the person of Denny Crane, lately deceased.

He said, 'Well, sir, I'd be grateful if you would do that. I feel very strongly that crime of whatever sort should be properly dealt with, and the perpetrators punished.'

'An admirable sentiment, Mr Parco. But when it comes to a choice, you must surely see where my loyalties lie.'

'Absolutely, sir – '

'Good-day, then.'

'And stick your system up your arse, you pompous shit-eating, pencil-necked ponce!'

'Anyone I know?' Theo asked lightly, coming through to Parco's office.

'Chief Super bloody Maynon – don't worry, he'd already hung up. No doubt he'd find the manpower to do me for slander if he'd heard that lot!'

'No doubt.' Theo smiled. 'John Pearcy's on the other line. He says he'd like you to meet him at Headquarters . . .'

'Thanks, Theo, put him through, would you?'

Parco spoke briefly to Pearcy and left his office shortly thereafter. He asked Theo to prepare a copy of their findings on Van Allen and to have it sent personally to Maynon by private courier; then take the afternoon off.

'You deserve it, love. If you work much harder you're going to start looking like me . . .'

'That's not funny, Parco. Hey – ' she added as he reached the door. 'I'll be at home later if you want to drop round, OK?'

'I might just do that,' Parco said.

A different desk sergeant handed Parco a note from Pearcy, asking him to go straight up to the officers' lounge on the first floor. There he found John Pearcy and Barry Hanlon sitting in a corner of the room. There were a few off-duty cops playing snooker and the games' machines; another guy was talking to the bartender, who pulled Parco a pint and told him Pearcy had already paid for it.

Parco took his drink over and sat down. He found the others in serious mood. Pearcy still looked tired, but his spell of leave had done him some good: Parco guessed he'd followed advice and spent plenty of hours in bed. Hanlon, on the other hand, seemed quietly excited and yet, as he spoke, Parco realized that this was mixed with puzzlement.

'You were pretty insistent on the phone, John. What's the news?'

'The scene-of-crime boys have come up with fingerprints already on our files – Patrick Joseph Peters . . .'

The name meant nothing to Parco. Pearcy continued. 'He's a local boy with a few minor convictions and one or two spells inside: although he's suspected of having pulled off a couple of larger jobs in recent years. Nasty piece of work; clever, violent, a thinker who doesn't mind putting his plans into practice with the help of a knife or occasionally a gun.'

'A knife? You think—'

'The injuries on the earlier victims are consistent with the use of a knife,' Hanlon interrupted. 'I'm having my assistants look again for Peters' fingerprints, and there's an APB out on him as of this morning.'

'The Chief Super sure runs a smooth machine.' Both Pearcy and Hanlon missed Parco's irony.

'Point is,' Hanlon continued, 'the killings at East Street don't fit the pattern. Bakker's injuries are like nothing I've ever seen, as I said at the time: the Kennealy woman's death was caused primarily and immediately by a neurotoxic venom, similar to cobra venom; and secondarily by a powerful acid that destroyed the tissues of her face: there was not a lot left by the time I peeled away that muck on her head.'

'Jesus, acid.' Parco sipped at his beer and didn't taste it. 'Sounds like a Mafia-style revenge killing – but on a landlady?' Hanlon lifted his hand.

'Wait, I haven't finished. Preliminary tests reveal that the acid has some distant molecular relationship to gastric acid, the stuff we produce to help digest our food. The neurotoxin, I suspect, was injected directly into the carotid artery, where it was transported within a couple of seconds to the medulla oblongata: this part of the brain controls breathing, and once damaged, an instantaneous cessation of lung action is caused. In simple terms, this kind of poison injected in this spot kills as effectively as a brain shot from a .38 at close range.'

Parco shook his head, frowning, trying to understand. 'But how does this tie up? A snake venom, a stomach acid, that crust of matter on the woman's skull . . . How do they dovetail, Hanlon? And how was Bakker's death different?'

'From here on in,' Hanlon told him, 'it's pure conjecture, OK?'

Parco nodded. 'Go on.'

'Imagine an animal – don't ask me what sort – small, tenacious, hungry. It targets a victim, attaches itself and delivers the neurotoxin, which works within a few seconds. There is not even time for the prey to claw the thing off, or otherwise move from the spot where the attack occurred. Remember that Mrs Kennealy was found in her armchair, and the TV set was still on.

'Meanwhile, the creature busies itself secreting a copious amount of mucus over the victim's face and head. This mucus reacts swiftly with oxygen and hardens into a tough, stone-like crust that serves two purposes. The predator uses something like a proboscis to drill through the crust and spray acid into the chamber it has created: the crust localizes the effects of the acid, and protects the creature's own body from being damaged by it. Skin, blood, muscle are all liquefied by this substance, which is short-acting and is soon neutralized. Once this process is complete, the animal draws up the nutrient fluids through the same proboscis and feeds to satiation, at which point it drops off . . .'

'And goes where?' Parco's skin was crawling. He had an in-built dislike of insects and a positive fear of snakes that folk had always said was irrational. Now, he couldn't help flicking his gaze to the shadows under tables and in corners.

'Unclear,' Hanlon said. 'Most animals that feed something like this usually burrow below ground or find a safe niche in which to sleep. In certain instances, feeding precedes egg-laying. It may be that this creature was about to reproduce itself.'

'As you say, Barry, pure speculation,' Pearcy said. He gave a splintered laugh that stopped the conversation at the bar. The skin around his mouth looked grey.

'The method of science is to formulate hypotheses based on observations of the perceived world,' Hanlon remarked. 'And then to test those hypotheses through further observations. Experimentation follows, and if the theory, as it then becomes, passes the test of repeatability, it is elevated to the status of a law. At the moment, we are struggling in darkness – a new kind of darkness which can mean one of two things. Either I'm completely wrong in my assessment of these murders – in which case I'll quit and retire to a cottage in the Cotswolds; or else I'm right, and what we think we know of the world is incomplete – that we've missed something, an aspect of nature that is new to us.'

'Or ancient, and we've never noticed it until now.'

'As you say, Mr Parco.' Hanlon raised his glass and drank.

'If your ideas are right,' Parco continued, 'then Bakker's death must be tied in to the theory somehow.'

'Yes. There is in nature a phenomenon known as symbiosis – the association of two dissimilar organisms for their mutual benefit. There are hundreds of examples: nitrogen-fixing bacteria that live in the roots of leguminous plants, the tic birds that peck at a rhinoceros's skin, remora fish that attach themselves to the bodies of sharks . . . Even we are symbionts, Mr Parco: living in our gut are millions of bacteria that help to break down the food we eat, and, in return, we provide them with a protected environment and all the nourishment they need. The creatures inhabiting this world are much more closely interdependent than most people realize . . . Of course, this is officially outside the provenance of a police pathologist: I shouldn't even be talking like this. But I have to, Mr Parco; to someone who will at least listen, and may be able to do something about it. I fear that Chief Superintendent Maynon would throw me out inside a minute of mentioning the idea.'

Parco smiled wryly. 'I've a feeling you're right. But Bakker – '

'Right. If such a hypothetical creature can feed off a human, it could probably also live on one. In this case, the mucus membranes of the animal would secrete a thin film over the host's face, temporary protection while the acid was used, not to destroy but to *sculpt*; a process allowing the creature access to the deeper regions of the head.'

'My God, Hanlon . . . But what would we, that is, the host, get out of the deal?'

'Your guess is as good as mine – and I mean that literally, Mr Parco.'

'Before it happened,' Parco said slowly, 'any normal person would be horrified by the prospect. Even someone mentally unbalanced might be – and might also go searching for such a creature. Seeing one, finding one, could tip you over the edge completely!'

'You're talking about the killer?'

Parco looked at Pearcy. 'Cutting into faces to see what lurked beneath. It fits the hypothesis . . . The killer has reached the same conclusion as ourselves, and goes looking for this animal . . .'

'But the victims were all cops, until Crane was found.' Pearcy finished his beer and wiped his mouth, allowing his fingers to rest a few seconds on his chin, his cheeks . . .

'OK, let's go slowly. So Mrs Kennealy was a victim, food for this obscenity. And Bakker – Bakker was a host, willing or not, for the same animal.' Parco glanced sharply at Hanlon.

'But why that way round? Why wasn't the landlady the host human?'

Hanlon stared at Parco and beyond him, his face grim.

'Maybe pure circumstance. Or maybe the creature has the ability to choose . . .'

Eleanor Van Allen found that she needed all of her will-power not to hurry. She recognized that there was a pressure building inside her, the pressure to panic and simply run blindly away from whatever her husband had become. *Whatever* – it was still an unknown. James Parco had been unable to find out; and even she, subjected to the perversity of Richard's desires, knew only that something black and dreadful had come to lodge in his soul. She admitted to herself that Richard had always been rough in his love-making, enjoying her cries of pain and humiliation to the point where she found them erotic herself, climactically so. Blood and joy had almost come to seem normal whenever the two of them coupled: and if she was true to herself, Eleanor knew that this influence had twisted her heart, so that she, like a pale mirror of the man she married, needed to hurt as she loved; wanted to dominate as she desired. It had sent her in search of many lovers – and she had found them aplenty. But never once had any of those panting, sweat-glossed faces belonged to a partner. In her own way, she'd loved them all, but trusted none of them one bit.

Perhaps that was what had sharpened the edge of her suspicions to the point of paranoia. First Richard, and now, this afternoon, the man outside Parco's office. Those same blue and penetrating eyes; the dreadful contrast of open lust and otherworldly coldness . . . She had almost fled from him then, as dread rose inside like a flame that burned away all traces of rationality . . .

But for all her weaknesses, Eleanor knew that she possessed a certain strength, and had used it to move her silently screaming body sedately around the park, as though on a pleasant afternoon stroll: then on to some shops where she'd bought a set of lingerie, a bestselling paperback, a piece of jewellery . . . And now, alone in the house, she allowed herself a few minutes to weep in fear for her sanity; perhaps, she reflected, for her life, which suddenly seemed precious since she had gazed into the unhuman face of death.

Her self-control was such that she did not even sneak a look through her windows, though she knew the stranger would be waiting there. It could be no coincidence that she'd seen him after discussing her husband with a detective: Richard must have some deep connection with this man and had sent him to spy out her secrets. Her primary worry now was that the man had reported back, and that Richard would arrive to find her packing – to find her leaving him at last.

She had it planned: a cool and calculated sequence of events that would give her the best chance of escaping without detection. Far away from Calverton. Far away from

Richard, to a place he didn't know. Somewhere out of her past. A kind of home. It had been in her mind for a while, but this afternoon had seen her certainty consolidate into action. Deeds, not thoughts, Eleanor reminded herself, as she packed some essentials into a single Samsonite suitcase, washed and changed into casual slacks, a sweater and a leather jacket. It was a different style for her, but it somehow symbolized the new life she was beginning.

She walked across the kitchen and through the connecting door into the integral garage. The room was dark, warm, smelt sickly rich of oil and metal. The few cars parked there, her own Rover and Richard's 'weekend motors', bulked like huge animals in the gloom.

Eleanor put her case in the Rover, then got in and found the garage door-remote on the glove-shelf. She felt desperately grateful that she always took the trouble to manoeuvre in the drive and reverse into the garage. It would make her departure easier and smoother. Quicker.

The engine fired at once as Eleanor jabbed at the remote. The up-and-over door drew slowly open with a quiet whine of servos and the squeal of sheet metal: bright afternoon sunlight blazed in like the opening of a glorious eye. Eleanor put the engine into gear and moved off, thinking to engage the door-lock as she accelerated down the drive, pausing briefly at the bottom before speeding away down the road.

She drove smoothly, and with a certain plateau of tension that felt oddly like a dream, towards the city centre. Halfway along the busy approach road was a cut-through Eleanor knew that joined up with the outer ring, trimming miles and minutes off her journey. She took it, negotiating side-streets and local one-way systems without error: ten minutes later she was on the fast lane of a quiet dual carriageway, heading north-east.

At first she found herself continually checking the rear-view mirror, fully expecting to see Richard's powder-blue Daimler powering towards her, lights flaring; or perhaps some more anonymous car that trailed her more discreetly, but with the same unshakeable tenacity, to her destination. But once past the suburbs, she was able to reassure herself that there was nobody on her tail. Long stretches of quiet motorway convinced her that she was alone, and free. Free – the concept and its reality arrived in her head as a gentle revelation, half frightening, half exhilarating. After years of weaving Richard's world around her, she could now barely believe that she was breaking out of the cocoon. And it was a total break: what she'd brought she'd earned, one way or another; a meagre bag of possessions after all those years of effort. Yet there were no regrets. A little sadness perhaps, fading echoes of anger, a fear that still clenched her insides . . . But no regrets. Her absence was her only good-bye to the man.

She drove without a break for two hours, with the sunset pouring its honey over her left shoulder. The hills ahead, and their downy summer grass, reminded Eleanor of the naked curves of women asleep under the sky. She smiled. She began to make plans.

Soon after, she pulled in at a RoadChef for some coffee, and a sandwich she picked from a poor end-of-day selection. On impulse as she was leaving, she also bought herself a CD, the kind of ringing West Coast rock that she so much enjoyed, and Richard so passionately detested. Inside the car, she loaded the disc and turned the volume up loud.

The world darkened around her as it rolled by beneath her wheels: Eleanor held to a steady ninety on the road's unravelling grey ribbon. The music played on: her mind idled through daydreams, letting go its fears, gently, one by one.

Some time later, by the glare of her headlight beams, she saw the sign she wanted and slowed into the turnoff lane as she indicated. Now she found herself on minor roads and heading for the coast. The thinner, more sinuous roadways were chalky white; the russets and greens of the field-edge trees strangely off-shifted in the car's high beams. Eleanor drove confidently, smoothly through fond and familiar territory; her mental picture of the land revealing twists and turns before they arrived in reality. She smiled at the thought of the known landscape around her.

The CD's final track finished.

In the silence, Eleanor realized she wasn't alone.

The jolt froze her hands to the wheel momentarily, so that she almost failed to negotiate an approaching tight right-hand bend. She swung wide on the corner and felt the offside wheels judder and bang along rough roadside verges, spraying dust. The view ahead was crazily angled; an oncoming car blared its horn, lights flickering anger and fright – all of it obliterated by Eleanor's accelerated heartbeat at her conviction of company.

But there was no one in the car.

She slammed on the brakes, skewed the Rover sideways and craned a look behind at the empty rear passenger seats and the dark deserted roadway beyond.

'Jesus . . . Jesus . . .' She whispered it, laughed it. 'Oh Jesus Christ!' Eleanor felt foolish at spooking herself – and making such a thorough job of it. The first flood of adrenalin had pulsed like voltage, and now she went through the process of starting the stalled engine and moving off slowly in the aftermath of melting relief that always follows such a shock.

It occurred to her to think why she had been so convinced of another's presence in a car that could only contain herself. The old urban legend of a mad axeman sneaking aboard at a stopoff was just that; a contemporary nightmare to tell over coffee, along with the story of the microwaved poodle or the phantom hitch-hiker. Strip off the cloak of the night and such tales became ludicrous, full of daytime holes that the rational mind soon spotted . . .

Anyway, Eleanor told herself firmly that she was half an hour from home; the seaside cottage of a girl friend who'd made a standing invitation for Eleanor to stay. They'd known each other since schooldays, and had kept in touch during all the years between. Natalie knew something of Eleanor's troubles by her letters, and had written of her own times of doubt and disappointment in a way that had bonded their friendship rather than made it burdensome to both. Eleanor guessed they were of like mind: but whereas Natalie had uncovered the truth of herself years before, choosing a quiet and quietly creative life on the coast, Eleanor had taken the path of her greed inland to London and Richard, and the bitter realizations that followed. It had been a symbolic as well as a practical gesture for her to leave virtually empty-handed. The best decision she'd ever made.

Eleanor crested a hill, took a left turn and drove slowly along the ridge, savouring her first sight of the sea, or what stray gleams of it were visible in the moonlight. She slowed right down to appreciate it more, to get used to the idea that now this was hers: glanced in the rearview mirror in case she was holding up any other car – and saw the face.

It moved in the instant she screamed. Eleanor felt fingers tangling in her hair, sliding around her neck. But there were too many fingers. And they felt strange. Long. Boneless.

Her body spasmed uncontrollably in the sudden dread of

the vision. Eleanor only half understood that her right foot had stamped the accelerator pedal, and that the Rover was speeding diagonally across the road, shrieking in low gear. Her hands – her hands were not even on the wheel now, but grappled with whatever was throttling her. She felt the thing's mouth – and – eyes – and – screamed again as her left hand plunged into a squirming nest of living tendrils that explored her skin busily like insects' antennae or the questing palps of some flowering sea anemone.

There was no more. The headlights allowed an instant's glimpse of a tree's uprushing trunk, then the car struck with a bang that imploded glass into Eleanor's writhing face: she felt it shower into her mouth; her lips were slashed by the fragments, her gums peppered with splinters. Needling agony burned her from forehead to chin; and with awful clarity, she was aware that her left eye had burst, gushing blood and liquids down the front of her blouse.

Silence came, and stillness. The crumpled front-end of the car settled with a final tinkling of metals and the cab filled with petrol vapour. In a parody of Eleanor's own injury, a single front light shone out into the darkness. It enabled her to see the damage to the car – everything distorted and broken – and the state of her own body; her lacerated hands and bruised and dirtied arms. The blood on her chest was shocking. And below . . .

Eleanor looked down in disbelief, and her one eye clouded over with tears, heavy with the weight of seeing. She began to tremble as the face gazed back up at her, stunning in its blue-eyed beauty, surrounded by fingers of flesh that palpitated softly. She could feel the weight of the thing in her lap; did not dare deny its existence. This was no near-death nightmare. Despite the pain and trauma, her mind was blazing with a crystal clarity. This was real, utterly real . . . And there in the mangled car, on a little-used road between nowheres, the face began to speak.

It spoke to her of many things that, later, Eleanor could not consciously remember. But gradually it soothed her with promises, seduced her with dreams beside which the aspirations of humankind seemed pathetic and pale. The face spoke of glory to come, a natural consequence of the glory that had been. Its span of ambition was world-wide and reached across many, many centuries. It talked of civilizations as though they were structures of mist, swept away by the first fires of each dawn. And individuals seemed to have no place at all in the picture it painted of its universe.

Syllables spilled liquidly through Eleanor's mind. Most of the time they were meaningless, though their poetry and tone were a balm to her pain and disquiet. What was about to happen, she was told, should not be regarded as death; any more than a drop of water dies as it enters the ocean. By losing what belonged to one, she would gain what was shared by the multitude. The Children looked after their own, and soon Eleanor Van Allen would dwell in a million minds – a billion; living on for as long as any one of those minds yet remained in existence. Essentially, she was eternal . . .

It was too much; too great a gift to renounce. Eleanor's left arm was numb now and agonizingly cold. She understood that without help of some sort, she was finished. And this creature, this dreadful and beautiful thing, was inviting her to perpetual life free of human failings.

She believed it, and she was calmed; accepting gladly as the face that was hers hauled itself slowly up the cliff of her body towards her bleeding head.

Chapter Ten

MENAS: All men's faces are true,
                whatsoe'er their hands are.
ENOBARBUS: But there is never a fair woman
                has a true face.
              The Rape of Lucrece, 1252–3

Helen Remmick somehow felt better sitting amid the bustle of the Students' Union Bar: more comfortable. Safer. With a couple of hundred people chattering and laughing around her, and she in plain sight, the stuff Howard had asked her to check out did not seem so perverse. She'd accumulated twenty pages worth of notes, some of it pretty weird shit that mixed carnality with philosophy, metaphysics with murder. Not bedtime reading, unless you were into pain as a way of achieving bliss. There were a lot of oblique references to the subjugation of the will, of the soul; and two sourcebooks had talked about the validity of the Christian God in light of the antiquity and richness of belief in pagan deities in an animistic universe . . . Helen had just about grasped those higher reaches of reasoning, which, brought down to her everyday level of understanding, seemed to suggest a kind of undercurrent of non-human power, dating back millennia, around which an elaborate weave of superstition and legend had been created. Eventually, weariness as much as revulsion had driven her home, where she'd slept fully clothed, with every light blazing.

Howard crossed over from the bar with a second round of drinks; cider for her, while he stuck with that awful flat and watery beer they only seemed to serve in the SU in Calverton.

'I reckon they brew it over in the labs.' Helen reiterated the old joke.

'Made out of rats' piss – '

'No.' She shook her head. 'They add that later to make it stronger.'

It was banter between them to lighten the weight of Helen's mood. Howard had detected something changed in her as soon as he'd met her out of morning lectures. Her first words had pinpointed it:

'I didn't know the Ancient Greeks were such a bloody sick bunch!'

'I feel dirty, just reading it,' she'd confessed later, as she ran through the gist but not the detail of what she'd found.

'Paganism often seems strange to us.' Howard tipped back a gulp of his beer and licked his lips in relish. Helen couldn't keep back a smile. 'Our view of religion is soaked in the imagery of latter-day Christianity – Sunday-evening TV scenes of nice middle-class people massed in well-kept churches singing "Now Thank We All Our God . . ." The little girls have bows in their hair, the boys are wearing ties. Can you imagine any of those thoroughly decent folk even farting, let alone—'

'This is your politics showing,' Helen interrupted, scoring more of a bull's-eye than she realized. 'A lot of people recognize that some of the Christian symbology is built on older images, feast days, festivals . . .'

'OK.' Howard conceded with a shrug. 'Let's take another tack. What's fashionable today in Green and Alternative ideas? Gaia – the unified Earth; a planet grossly damaged by Cartesian mechanistic thinking embodied in the Industrial Revolution. We are flaying the world alive for our own ends – killing it through our own excess – destroying a living and interdependent multiorganism through ignorance and greed.'

'I'll go along with you so far . . .'

'Right. Imagine a way of thinking not based on consumerism or competition, or even upon modern conceptions of progress at all. Imagine a cosmos ruled by a hierarchy of discarnate beings that all, somehow, were united in maintaining that cosmos as it was created – in its natural state. Step out of line, and you incur the wrath of a local god. What you can and cannot do is laid down for you in a rich mythology that keeps you in touch with the past and the future, with the here and the elsewhere. You understand that you are no more than a cell within the corpus of All There Is . . .'

Helen lifted her hand, shutting Howard off in midsentence.

'The idea of achieving Oneness is common to most religions, but – '

'There's more than that!'

'Damn right! I was reading about S and M masquerading as worship at ten o'clock last night. And sacrifice – living sacrifice, Bill . . .' The memory darkened Helen's eyes. She looked away.

'All right, love. I won't go on about it. But I must get the nature of these texts clear in my mind if I'm to make progress with the rest of the translation . . . I still find it amazing that the stone deals with this stuff, and not with day-to-day commerce . . .'

'Unless this *was* everyday commerce – the commerce of common belief, and an acceptance of it.'

'That's not a bad idea,' Howard said. 'Belief should be a kind of currency, an ordinary commodity. Every true

Christian lives with the coinage of God every second of every day ... OK, we'll keep it in mind.

'Now ... There was once a brother and sister; Phorcys and Ceto, who were the children of Gaia the Earth and Pontos the Sea, and parents of both the Graeae and the Gorgons. The Graeae we know are the sisters of the Gorgons; their name means 'the grey ones' and they seem to be the personification of age. They are blind, save for a single eye which they share between them, mainly in order to guard the Gorgons themselves ... I got that out of my *Kids' Bumper Book of Folklore and Fables*.' Howard grinned.

'The legend of the Graeae is not as familiar as that of Medusa and her two sisters, Stheno and Euryale. These last two are immortal, and do not feature as powerfully in the modern imagination as Medusa – the only mortal of the three. She was once beautiful, and Poseidon fell in love with her. They went one time to the temple of Athene to make love, thereby outraging Athene, who transformed Medusa into a frightful creature with glaring eyes and serpent hair: she had a gaze so horrifying that men were turned into stone. Medusa was later destroyed, beheaded by Perseus – the archetypal hero who has come down to us through the centuries as a thoroughly good guy. Personally, I spit on his values ...'

'There's a lot more, Bill,' Helen said. 'We're only scratching the surface.'

'I know that. But let's look for a moment at the ideas *within* the stories. We've got the idea of disturbing the universe – offending the gods: the idea of beauty and ugliness, and the strange way these melt and blend one into the other ... We've got the concept of good and evil tied up with the human need to destroy what is *not* human – even though, let's face it, Perseus would've fucked Medusa willingly before she was changed by Athene . . . All of these strands of legend twined around human impulses and perceptions.'

'I'm still not clear about this.'

'Nor me, not yet,' Howard confessed. 'But as you say, there's more. We have, for a start, the distinction between the Gorgons and the Gorgoneion – a concept that might be much older, and one from which the story of the Gorgons may derive. You OK for a drink?'

'I'm OK.'

Howard flipped through Helen's notes, and turned to a page in his own notebook.

'Right, let's tackle this. At the heart of the matter is the notion of the Evil Eye – a gaze so dreadful that a man's mind is unhinged, its power taken from him. From this we get a multiplicity of ideas about hexing, the subjugation of the will, masquerade and concealment, empowerment . . . And for thousands of years amulets have been worn to divert the Evil Eye – often by portraying a frightening face. In this way, the gaze of the enemy is deflected: in a metaphorical sense, bad fortune is turned aside.

'We have links already between the story of Medusa, the Graeae and eyes . . . King in *Gnostics* states that the most efficacious amulet of all was one depicting the face of Medusa. She is the prototype of masks, a hideous grotesquerie. She is connected also with the Eastern idea of the Bhavani, the Destructive Female Principle . . . But I wonder, Helen, if "destructive" relates only to a patriarchal society; one that seeks to dominate through power; one that upsets balances for gain and individual glory?'

'Do you suppose that Bhavani and Gaia are connected?' Helen wondered. 'I'm puzzling over how the archetype of the Destructive Female and the unitary concept of a world-organism can be dovetailed . . .'

Howard shook his head. All of these ideas, he felt, formed a rich lode in the bedrock of mythology. With Helen's few references and the fragmentary scribbles he'd smuggled from the workshop, they'd taken a tiny step into a different land; glimpsed foreign minds that were distant in both time and space. They had touched a wonderful unknown here, something so strange that it seemed meaningless.

Howard related to Helen a story a schoolteacher had told him, years ago, of when the conquistadores had first made contact with the Peruvian tribes in the 1530s. The Aztecs and Incas had not been able to recognize the European ships for what they were: they simply did not register upon their minds, since the native boats were so much smaller. Later, the galleons appeared as incarnations of the Bird God, and only slowly did the conquered South American peoples come to see the Spanish ships for what they were.

'They had to learn the new perceptions: they had to enlarge the frame of their thinking to accommodate this invasion into reality.' Howard finished his beer and ran his eyes down the pages he held. 'I get the feeling that that's what we have to do now.'

'Learn a new reality? Or an old one,' Helen corrected. 'The events in your translations go back four thousand years.'

'Yeah, I know . . . How wonderful it would be to travel there and stand by the shore on a sunny day in Ancient Minoa. Would there be gods in the sky, Helen? Would there be any chance of stumbling across a cliff cave and to hear, echoing from the depths, the harsh cries of the Graeae: or one moonlit night, to see – reflected in my shield, of course! – the unspeakable face of the Medusa?'

He glanced at her and smiled.

'Oddly enough, while early images of the Gorgoneion were incredibly fearsome, with serpent-wreathed heads and razor tusks, by the advent of the Augustinian Age in Rome, the same symbols were represented as being incredibly beautiful. Did perceptions change?' Howard asked. 'Or had reality itself altered as the Greek Empire crumbled and faded and gave way to the splendour that was Rome?'

'Do I get another cider if I answer it correctly?' Helen grinned and pushed her empty glass towards him.

Howard's voice was subdued as he replied, 'My guess is, love, that whoever answers it will be able to write his own ticket, and earn a place in history . . .'

The weighty oak desk had been cleared of all its accoutrements. The curtains were drawn. A single spotlamp spread a pale fan of illumination into one corner of the room, which was silent save for the sound of slow breathing.

Eleanor sat unmoving on a straight-backed chair that she had placed to face the desk. A corner of her consciousness registered the soreness across her chest where the seat-belt had cut, and her neck was painful to move too suddenly; her arms throbbed and stung still from the cuts she had suffered, and from the antiseptic Joe Patrick had used on them . . .

She smiled, though her face failed to register the expression. Of course, she needed to get used to the new way of thinking: they were not *her* arms any longer, nor her neck or chest. Her body was no longer her own. Indeed, the very notion of 'she' as an individual now held no meaning at all. Even as she sat there alone in Richard's office, Eleanor sensed the company and proximity of the Children, those that were manifest and the others – the countless thousands of others – latent in the spawn of the Bidden. How deluded she had been to think of home as a time and a place – as somewhere apart from her Brothers and Sisters. How lucky she felt now, to have learnt.

A side door opened and Richard entered carrying the stone. He placed it reverently in the centre of the desk, but let his fingers stroke and caress its surface for many seconds before stepping back and taking his own chair to Eleanor's right.

Joe Patrick followed soon after. He was carrying a green bronze head of Adonis, a little larger than life-size, fixed atop a bronze spike attached to a heavy marble base. This he stood beside the Hagia Stone and facing Van Allen. Then he took a third chair and joined the silent conclave.

After a few seconds' silence, Van Allen spoke. His voice held all the old authority and confidence that Eleanor remembered, but now she recognized a new note of purpose and anticipation there; and was caught up in it, her hands gripping the edge of her seat tightly.

'We few are the first, our eyes open again after a span of many centuries. The Fates have granted us life in this new time, here in a place that is so unfamiliar and so hostile. Our Brothers in the Old Land also have their chance of life, and we wish them a rich and flourishing destiny. It is they who have allowed us this opportunity to rise from the dust, these two arms of the Gorgoneion's great existence separated for safety. Mankind, we recognize, has not changed: he is no more dangerous now than in the days of Agamemnon – but no less dangerous either. Together, then, we ride the Beast into the future, cherishing the hope of life in this fair and flowering world. Blessed are Phorcys and Ceto – '

'Blessed are They.'

The three fell silent once more, their eyes swinging slowly to the metal mask on the desk. The bronze was moving, tendrils appearing on its left side like a crest of serpents testing and tasting the air, feeling forward around the shadow-profiled features of the most beautiful mortal the world has ever known.

A thrill ran through Eleanor's body at this miracle of life. Evidently the head was hollow and cut away at the back, out of her sight. The Bidden must have been resting within, but now chose to show itself in this gesture of gratitude and respect.

Van Allen sighed with pleasure and an immeasurable fondness as the creature slid smoothly over the face of bronze, its body contouring the curves and planes of Adonis. For one exquisite second, its limbs lifted in a sunburst of living rays, the true and original echo of Medusa, before curling around for secure purchase. The substance of the thing rippled and heaved, melting, moulding itself, so that what had been hideous to mortal sight was soon transformed into flesh fairer than the imagination of any man or woman.

The beloved of Aphrodite opened its blue eyes and the Bidden smiled at its sparse but loyal gathering of acolytes.

'Out of me shall come the millions. But we must act quickly to find a place of hiding where the spawning can begin. I sense from you that the people here suspect our existence. There have been mistakes. One of our number is destroyed. It was a pointless death, and not one to be countenanced. The Children are yet only strong in determination, but not in number. Go then, prepare a spawning ground and cover your tracks well. The Fates have looked fondly upon us: the world is still a rich and plentiful place: we the Children of Phorcys and Ceto may yet stand again with the gods, in dominion over all its creatures.'

'So shall it be,' echoed the three as one voice. They watched and waited while the thing around the bronze head crawled back into its biding-place and out of sight, leaving the face of Adonis perfect again, but merely human.

Burly's Bar was empty at this time of day, kind of cold and unwelcoming. Parco and Pearcy, sitting at a two-chair table at the back, did not mind in the least. What they had discovered needed to be chewed over in peace, out of the swing and bustle of the world; a world that seemed diseased to them now, infected by a greater evil than anything they had dared to imagine before. That morning, Pearcy had told his wife to phone in and tell them he had taken to his bed; his headaches had come on worse and he would most likely be off the rest of the week and maybe longer . . . When Karen had questioned him, Pearcy had yelled at her, red-faced and shaking and completely out of control. She had shrunk back, terrified of him for the first time in their married life. At that moment he could have hit her, only some fortunate spark of self-will making him turn instead to the door and walk out.

He'd phoned her soon after from town, and apologized. By what few words Karen said, Pearcy could tell she'd been crying. Her meek unchallenging acceptance of his apology had hurt him badly: he wondered if she and the kids would still be there when he returned. It was common for officers' wives to suggest spells apart – or sometimes even just to vanish for days or weeks, with maybe a letter mailed through to suggest that this was the best thing: to see if the gravity of the love they'd felt at the outset could still draw them back. Sometimes it did. But there were plenty of cops living alone these days, carrying this weight of failure on their already overburdened shoulders.

'It's all a lie of course – phoning in sick, I mean,' Pearcy explained, ignoring the glass of fruit juice Bill Burly had put before him, on the house. Licensing hours had been tightened several years before as a measure to curb city-centre violence, and Bill was a stickler for the law, as he told his customers regularly, sometimes tongue-in-cheek, but usually not. Pearcy hadn't the energy to argue, but he'd be damned if he'd swallow orange juice in any bar!

'You see, I daren't go into the station, y'know, Jim . . . I find I can't – trust – any more – it's hard for me – to—'

Parco looked at his friend momentarily, before the mutual pain in the eyes of the two men broke apart the contact.

'You don't have to explain this. I know it. Who could stand to walk the streets and talk to folk when any number of those "animals" are out there? Hanlon called them symbionts . . . But who's affected?'

'And how? For God's sake, those things must be big, Jim! We're not talking about bacterium-sized. A creature needs to be substantial to manufacture sufficient poison to kill a man, or to rip into his face like it did into Bakker's . . . Where in people are they hiding?'

'Yeah. And then there's this idea of the egg-laying. That's what scares me most. There can't be too many of the muthas around right now, or we'd surely have seen more of the damage they do. As far as I know, Denny Crane, Bakker and the landlady were the first. So, we've got a small number of the animals showing themselves for the first time.

They've come in from somewhere recently; been activated somehow . . . But if they were to breed . . . Millions of them burrowing into whatever humans were around at the time . . .'

'Or *choosing* their hosts.' Pearcy looked nauseous. 'Remember Hanlon said they could do that.'

'He was theorizing,' Parco said. 'Like we are now. There's no proof for any of this—'

'Only Bakker's head half-eaten away . . . Come on, Jim, we might as well face the fact that even if Hanlon isn't bang on, he must be pretty close. We're facing some new kind of organism here – maybe a genetically engineered breed, or something built from scratch – God help us . . . Either way, it's loose in the city and it's costing lives.'

'Right, then, we'll work on that assumption. I think our first job has got to be to track back to the initial appearance of the creatures – their point of origin here in Calverton. We know that Denny Crane is implicated, and a customer of yours, Peters—'

'Patrick Joseph Peters.'

'Anything else on him from memory?'

Pearcy shrugged. 'Not a lot. But I can tell you he's not an airhead like plenty of his kith and kin seem to be. Peters was always an organizer – it was his talent, to map out a job and buy in what specialist talent he needed. Invariably Peters was netted because of a failing in one of his team, rather than something he'd missed himself. He tends to go for medium-security premises; shops, warehouses, and he is never too greedy . . . The man is a thief who knows his limits, which makes him hard to catch – and very successful.'

'No joy on the APB?'

'Nothing I've heard.'

'What we have here is a start. If we can trace an occasion

when the paths of Crane and Peters crossed, we'll have a direction to follow. John, do you suppose you could get that data? I realize it'll mean speaking to someone at HQ, or—'

'Or going there myself. You know what you're asking of me, Parco?'

'I'll be happy to come along too . . .'

Pearcy gazed at his fingernails, slowly curling them under to make a fist, white-knuckled and trembling.

'I would never want to end up . . . I don't want to be like Bakker, Jim. Kill me first.'

'You make the same promise to me, and you've got a deal.'

'Then it's a deal. Shake, friend.'

'John – ' The smile Parco managed was totally without mirth. 'I'm already shaking.'

Parco watched Pearcy out of sight on the pavement outside Burly's. The cop had insisted on going alone to the station, telling Parco he could beat the fear barrier. If anyone there was infected, then there was no point in them both being put into danger. Besides, Pearcy by himself, pottering around his locker, talking idly with the guys on the night shift, boring them with his ills, would arouse less suspicion than if Parco was hanging on his arm. They agreed to keep in contact: Pearcy would call Parco's office later that night, or else come in person. Parco said he would not go home, but would stay at his desk until they'd cracked this thing. Mutually reassured, albeit briefly, they'd separated.

Parco walked across town to his premises, without knowing whether or not he wanted to find Theo still there. He desperately needed the warmth of her company and, again, of her body: but the horror that was opening up for him was not something to be shared. Not yet. When the time came that Parco was sure of what he was facing, he would either tell her fully, or at least ensure she was out of town while he or the powers that be purged Calverton of its infestation. Or, if that wasn't possible, then Theo would be out of it and able to enjoy her life while the rest of the world was still clean and free, and the smiles of children meant nothing more than smiles.

The dusk closed around Parco as he walked, and swathed him in veils of drizzle that had him saturated by the time he reached the office and found it empty. He guessed that Theo would've left him a message, as usual in a coded file in his PC. He remembered also that she'd invited him round to her place that evening: there was still time – except his promise to Pearcy kept him tied here until they'd collectively gathered enough data to move the investigation forward . . .

'Investigation'; the euphemism made Parco smile. If they'd judged it right thus far, what they had here was a battle – a bloody war against an enemy as insidious as any. Parco tried to picture it – them – as his imagination swung between colonies of bacilli flowering virulently in agar, and swarms of rats or ratlike things seething through a sewer; and then on to dark and vaguely visualized monstrosities that were an amalgam of all he feared. Which was plenty.

His mind offered up nothing that he could use. Besides, he was no expert. Hanlon had been able to tell plenty from the injuries left on Bakker and the others, and even he fell short of any definite reconstruction of the creature, or creatures. Parco knew he would only suffer a failure of nerve through any triumph of imagination. Better not shine false lights in that awful darkness until he had to – and until he had a weapon gripped firmly in his right hand.

He switched on his desktop computer, loaded up the file that he and Theo always used for personal communication when they missed each other in the flesh – oh yes, Theo, I do miss you in the flesh! – and waited for the screen to fill.

Dear Parco – Bit of a non-day, really. You realize that our caseload is lighter now than it has been since I joined. At this rate I'll be buying some nail-varnish, so that I'll have something to do in between making you cups of coffee . . .

Seriously: all of our 'pending' cases are non-urgent, but there are a couple of new jobs that you need to make a decision about. The Stapleton file is halfway complete – you remember, it's a credit fraud that Alphamax Insurance asked us to handle? I've run preliminary checks; motor, taxes, property sales. But 'Mr Stapleton' seems to be one of a multiplicity of aliases, and I need now to go further – into marriage certificates, personal property deeds – you know the routine . . . It's a challenge, Parco. This guy is the man of a thousand faces, to be sure. And the Alphamax fee is fat. Tell me I can go ahead, and you'll make my day!

It would be nice if you came round to tell me in person. I've bought a Freebird Microwave Tagliatelle that I can nuke if you turn up suddenly, and there's a chilled bottle of Valpolicella to accompany . . . Oh, and if that's no incentive, last weekend I bought myself this little leather micro-skirt and black thigh-boots which I haven't worn yet, so . . .

Let me tell you, I don't go to this trouble for every man I know. The last time was when the Calverton Panthers Basketball Team dropped in unexpectedly. But that's another story.

Just come, OK?

Oh, by the way – a *big* by the way (sorry, should've mentioned it sooner, but this is all stream-of-consciousness stuff, you know): Eleanor Van Allen called round to 'terminate our services' – that's how she put it. She's paid up to date and was very firm about us not pursuing our enquiries any further. I asked if the matter was resolved, and she said that yes, it was. She had decided not to leave her husband and not to go away, so there was no point in us keeping the alternative number she gave. And that was that. Can't say I'm sorry, Parco: the lady was starting to get me just a smidgen jealous . . . Oh yeah, I thought you said she'd been beaten up or something? There wasn't a mark on her this afternoon.

That's about it. I'm into my own time now. See you tonight?

> Hopefully,
> Theo.

PS: if not, then in the a.m. (you bastard!). T.

No one objected to John Pearcy strolling into Police Headquarters looking as though he'd just spent a week on the streets. No one asked him about his red-eyed, pale-complexioned state; no one offered sympathy or told him to fuck off home and get to bed. He knew, and his colleagues knew, that if he needed advice or a shoulder to lean on, he would ask for them, and they'd be there. State-employed street cops were a tight-knit bunch, but were never intrusive. Every man on the force who had not been promoted up into a world of paper understood that the hardest battles you fought were in your own head; rationalizing what people did to one another, and what you saw of it, took some doing. Plenty never managed it for the full span of a career, but folk didn't interfere while you tried – unless you opened your mouth and asked for some help.

The desk sergeant registered Pearcy on to the premises.

He made an informal call to Hanlon's office at the morgue and was told that the man was busy right now. Pearcy identified himself to Hanlon's lab assistant, who gave him the information that the DNA breakdown of cell samples taken at the scene of crime was proving a tough nut to crack: Hanlon would issue a full report when it was completed, but meanwhile would Pearcy be kind enough to keep him appraised of any new developments at his end?

It was an unsatisfactory phone call. Pearcy felt frustrated and no less frightened for having made it. He brought his mind back round to his purpose for being here, and took the elevator to the fourth floor, where the computer records' office was located.

Carole Sweetman was a friend who had in the past, and not so obliquely, made it clear to Pearcy that she would like to be more than that. At the same time, she respected his relationship with Karen, knowing that he was not using it as an excuse. Whatever other faults John Pearcy possessed, he was no coward, and had told her plainly that he found her as attractive as hell, but that he was in love with his wife and did not have the nervous energy to see his life complicated any further. So they got on fine, both appreciating that the warmth between them was genuine. On this occasion, Pearcy was particularly glad of it, though would have bluffed and lied his way to getting what he wanted if necessary.

Carole, pretty in her uniform and looking as fresh as when she'd come on shift seven hours earlier, knew better than to ask after Pearcy's health, or to query the validity of his present request.

'Peters, Patrick Joseph' presented no problems. The monitor flashed up a 'Scanning, Please Wait' message and spilled all there was to know about the man inside thirty seconds, Risico's life history in green pixels.

' "Risico"?' The girl frowned.

'Says here, look, it's an alias he sometimes used . . . I only know the name from a James Bond story. Maybe Peters fancied himself as a supervillain.'

'Yeah, maybe . . .' Pearcy smiled down at Carole's cascade of auburn hair. She was busy with the keyboard and was taking no notice.

'Here we go, John. All that you want – though some of it's in subfiles. Any specifics?'

'Not really . . . I'm looking for connections. Associates he used regularly. Names, however tenuous. I need something solid to chase.'

'Don't we all . . . OK . . . Let's see.' Carole pushed buttons and beamed up at him. 'You know the PNC stores a database of fifty million vehicle records, almost ten million sets of fingerprints, and details of eight hundred thousand reported crimes, solved and under investigation? Forty thousand computer operators in police stations right across Europe have twenty-four-hour access to the mainframe, which can deal with fifteen thousand requests simultaneously . . .'

'Bloody wonderful,' Pearcy said. 'So why are crime rates rising?'

'Good point. Ah, *voilà*!'

Pearcy suddenly cut the banter and stared hard at the screen. Lists of names, dates and locations had appeared, connective speculations on the expertise Peters employed in his long and successful career.

'Someone's worked pretty hard to assemble this lot. I'm impressed . . . Has to be a cop, because these linkages are the way a cop's mind works – everything included from definite relationships backed by hard facts, right down to hunches with not an iota of proof to support them . . . Or should I say, right *up* to hunches . . .?'

'You'd be surprised,' Carole added. She worked more magic with the machine. 'Here you are – the text credit and flow-system patents are under the name of Joshua Randles. I went to one of his lectures: he's a professor of criminology at Oxford; also writes thrillers under the pen-name of Jack Wainer.'

'I'll be damned,' Pearcy whispered.   –

'This is a new science, combining computer software capabilities, with psychology, sociology, statistics – you name it, connectronics incorporates it: the holistic way to catching perps, blaggers, pervs, psychos and crazies . . .'

Pearcy grimaced, indicating ironic mirth. 'I ask once more, why the rising lines on the graphs, Carole?'

Before she answered, Pearcy again turned his attention to the VDU display, talking to himself rather than the operative as he abstracted what he wanted.

'This guy Conway is a regular . . . His name is linked with Peters' from way back. A heavy, all muscle, no brain . . . Follows orders . . . An early record of armed robbery, assault with a deadly weapon, disturbing the peace – ha! I like it . . . Then he drops from the frame for a few years . . . Quite a few, until he comes under Risico's control . . . Photographed brandishing a pump-action shotgun during a bank job in ninety-four . . . Case dropped due to alleged police corruption of evidence – Jesus wept!'

'It was what the politicians needed to privatize the force, John: the rotten apple they were looking for to scatter the entire barrel . . .'

'OK . . . OK . . . That's the brawn . . . Risico's the mind . . . There's got to be a workman on the team: no theorist, but someone with hands-on of security systems, explosives, electronics . . .'

'Here's your guy,' Carole said, pretty definitely. ' "The Electrician", aka Wes Weldon . . . Another mystery man in the early days, until he went down for wiring up his two-timing girlfriend to an incendiary device . . .'

'Holy shit . . .' Pearcy couldn't believe what he was reading. 'There was no timer . . . Weldon left her naked in her flat, her face within reach of a water feeder . . . The fire-bomb – '

'Went off when she urinated. She died pissing herself.'

'Carole – '

'Don't worry, I read this kind of stuff every day. I'm thinking of competing with Mr Wainer in the crime-writing stakes – except that I don't think anybody would believe the plots! OK, so Wes Weldon gets sent down to Gartree for two years: there was only a suspicion of murder, so they sent him down for a handful of other, more minor offences. But look, Peters was doing time in the same institution during that period.'

'All right, we're doing fine. How can I check whether all of these men were gathered at one time and place? That'll give me spin-off data to work on.'

'Simple. I just type in all the names and the software scans the subfiles for – ah, no sooner said . . .'

'The railyards robbery in June – what's this? – Conway killed outright, shot in the face. Weldon gut-shot, died in hospital . . . A kid called Neil Cernan killed also.' Pearcy smiled fiercely. 'And a security guard, Denny Crane, wounded in the incident and sustained second-degree burns to his body . . . Subsequently employed by Richard Van Allen, since it was a consignment of artefacts destined for the Calverton Museum that Crane was protecting at the time. Fucking bull's eye! Oh, I beg your pardon, Carole.'

She grinned up at him pertly. 'Don't apologize, I like to see a man happy. So, have you got what you need here?'

'Just about, though I'll require more detailed biogs of these names. Oh, and, er, a hard copy of it all, if poss?'

Carole shrugged. 'It's a job's-worth situation, I'm afraid, John. I need authorization to release data. Um, however, I do need to go to the ladies' room for a few minutes . . . And you know you can push my buttons any time you want to . . .'

Pearcy blushed and Carole Sweetman felt duly flattered. When she returned, Pearcy was idly looking around the room. The monitor display had been cleared.

'Thanks again, Carole, I appreciate it.'

'No problem. Maybe you'll escort me to the Policeman's Ball one of these days, eh?'

'Maybe I will.'

Pearcy walked to the door, then turned.

'Hey, Carole – '

'Huh?'

'When I asked you why the crime rates were skyrocketing – I interrupted you. You say you wade through this data daily. Any theories?'

Carole Sweetman was thirty-one years old, had a kid brother still at school and two parents who had never abused or neglected her, and who still lived together in a bungalow just south of Croydon. She was a normal, bal- anced, stable young woman, who looked at Pearcy now with perky green eyes and a face you could find on the cover of any middle-class female coffee-table magazine.

'Yes, as a matter of fact. The human race is sick, John, and getting sicker. And unless something comes along to wipe us off the crawling face of this dirty little planet, we're on the road to hell – and we're going down all the way . . .'

Bill Howard woke with a cry.

Something was suffocating him. His cock, aroused and erect, was being worked with an expert rhythm. For a span of maybe five awful seconds he was in confusion and fear, desire and terror driving through him like magnetic opposites.

The Medusa was a mask clamped over his mouth, pouring her breath into him, her serpent-hair writhing around his face. She was perfume-sweet, a horrifying shadow half in his mind and half sprawled over his bare body, on which the sweat of dreams was cooling.

He struggled wildly, pushing her away, and in his drowning helplessness, and to his utter humiliation, as he realized the nature of his illusion, Howard ejaculated under Helen's jerking fist. He groaned, she echoing the sound, stimulated herself in witnessing the height of his pleasure.

'You were quick.' She whispered it, insisting herself closer, eager now to be lying on the leeward side of her own ecstasy. Howard wiped a hand over his face, clearing his thoughts and misty eyes. Helen kissed him and his fear ebbed, though soured the passion he would otherwise have fully enjoyed.

'You scared me. I was dreaming . . .'

'Sorry, love. I woke. I needed you . . .'

Howard slid two fingers into her and she sighed. Yes, she was ready and had wanted him. Sometimes Howard himself woke in the deep night, randy as hell, charged with a dream-borne passion that swathed himself, his partner and the whole situation in a cloak of intense eroticism: love made on the brink of slumber, half in fantasy and half in the real world, being the best way he knew. He guessed that girls were no different.

Helen's climax arrived with a shudder: she arched herself upward against his hand, her lean, strong thigh muscles standing out beneath the satiny skin, her clawed fingers twisting up the sheets. Tears squeezed from between her closed eyelids, then she slumped, relaxed and spent, back against the mattress, smiling luxuriantly.

'Even when your mind's on something else, Bill, you're good for me . . .'

Howard kissed her, as though to apologize, reached for a Kleenex, and pulled the blankets back up over them.

'I dreamed of Gorgons,' he said simply, feeling as absurd and embarrassed as he had when confessing night-terrors to his mother, years ago. 'So horrible . . . So unimaginably ugly – because they parodied our form. Humanity with the heart ripped out . . .' Howard chuckled. 'Listen to this: I sound like the intro-blurb to a late-night horror flick!'

'I don't mind if you want to talk, Bill,' Helen said. 'But it's your turn tonight to make the tea.'

He did so without arguing. Although it was only four in the morning, and his schedule had been busy with the translation as well as his regular studies, Howard knew that he could not recover sleep again that night. Even if he was able to, he was not convinced it would be peaceful.

He made toast too, a piled plateful which he brought on a tray, together with a reasonable selection of marmalades and jams, plus some individually wrapped pats of butter, which made Helen look at him awry.

'You've pinched these!'

'Guilty. Student habits die hard. You'll also notice your sugar comes in separate sachets – for hygiene and convenience, madam. One of the greatest luxuries in my under-grad days was to go to bed armed with a pot of coffee, a whole loaf of toast and a selection of stolen sundries. I had the TV propped on the cupboard at the bottom of the bed, and a "Do Not Disturb" sign hanging on the door.'

Helen laughed as she pictured it. 'And what's your great-est luxury now?' she wondered. Howard shrugged.

'Same. Except I like a blonde beside me to share the toast these days . . .'

They ate and drank in silence for a little while, each lost in thoughts of their own. Howard's took him back to the work he was doing for Van Allen; to the strange world of Greek mythology and the tales of the Gorgoneion that ran through it like black thread through a golden tapestry. Why was the image such a powerful one? And why did it seem to reach a peak of development in Crete four thousand years ago, then melt away into thinly diluted and much-corrupted superstitions?

'Maybe it didn't,' Howard said, an idea straight from the subconscious.

'What's that, love?'

'I was just thinking . . .' Howard explained the run of his thoughts while Helen munched on toast, keeping the bedsheets drawn up above her breasts, because she knew he was in one of his serious moods.

'And so it occurred to me that perhaps the symbol of the Gorgoneion need not have peaked in pre-literate Crete: the Cretans themselves certainly go back long before that time – probably coming from somewhere in the Levant, quite likely as refugees from the troubles in Egypt, at least four thousand years earlier . . . And also I thought; why did I assume that the mythos of Medusa and her sisters was stron-gest in its Ancient Greek manifestation?'

'I don't know – why did you assume that?' Helen was fed up of being serious. She let the blanket slip down an inch or two.

'The fact is, the fear of the Evil Eye – the petrifying force embodied in Medusa – is *incredibly* ancient. Eye shapes have been found in cave art dating from the palaeolithic period. And it may well be that the history of the image is continuous, coming up through the centuries right to the present day. In its modern form, it may be the unwholesome face of Big Brother, or the way western culture almost reveres physical and facial perfection, or – '

'Or the mystical Third Eye of the Aquarian Age! Old wisdom in new clothes . . .'

'OK,' Howard said, 'I give up for now.'

'Oh, come on, Bill, I was trying to help you there!' Her pouting face made him smile.

'I know you were, baby. But the problem is that I just don't have enough information myself. I'm working with fragments, trying to pin huge theories to a few scraps of incompletely translated codified text.'

'So just keep translating . . .'

'For as long as I can, sure. But Van Allen is different just lately . . . He hasn't mentioned looking for the Hagia Stone: he seems so preoccupied. And that guy Patrick really gives me the creeps. I mean, Castillo makes my flesh crawl, but Joe Patrick is on a different scale of weirdness entirely.'

Howard sighed, put his empty plate at the side of the bed and brushed crumbs from his chest and lap.

'I simply think my time is limited, that's all. And so – ' He shot a glance at Helen. 'I guess I'm going to break in after hours and take a few photographs.'

He expected her to object, argue, protest: instead, a sparkle came into her eye that he hadn't seen before. Helen clapped her hands and the sheets dropped away entirely.

'Now you're talking some excitement, Bill!'

He reached out and stroked her, and her nipples rose at once with a life of their own.

'Isn't *this* exciting?'

She moved towards him.

'Oh yes. But excitement comes in different guises . . . And I'm going to help you: I'm going to be there, and no arguments.'

'All right. No arguments . . . And thanks, Helen . . .'

She was licking her way down his body, but paused, wet-mouthed, to gaze back up at him.

'We feed off each other, honey. That's all.'

Some hours earlier, at a little before 10 p.m., Eleanor Van Allen slowly drove away from the house that once, a lifetime ago, she thought she'd left for the last time. Now, as before, her mind was unclouded in its purpose, and her thoughts of the future glowed rich with promise.

With Richard's help, she had scrolled through the long list of addresses in the Accommodation Office at the university. Here were kept on disk details of houses that students could rent, or buy co-operatively; together with information on the hundreds of people in the area who let rooms during term-time; also a list of applicants turned down by the Accommodation Officer for any number of reasons. An hour's work had produced an address that was ideal. Eleanor phoned through to the house's only occupant and explained that a party of foreign students was arriving soon in Calverton on a three-month exchange package, and would need lodgings together for the duration. Would it be at all possible for her to discuss the matter, although she would not be able to call round until quite late in the evening . . .

The journey through the countryside was a pleasant one, out into the just-autumn darkness with the smeared glow of Calverton dropping behind. This part of the county was relatively hilly, and Ketley village, her destination, followed the line of the ridge above the wide Wyland Valley.

Eleanor located the house easily; 'Ketley Lodge' was signposted, and stood at the bottom of a winding gravel drive deep among trees, hidden apart from its tall chimneys and TV aerials. The database had revealed that the Lodge belonged to Major Colin Goldsmythe, RN, DSO (retired), and his wife Vivien, who had lived on alone in the big house after the Major died. She had spent years previously involving herself with voluntary work of various kinds, which disposed the university to put her on their files. The house, however, was rather remote and Ketley suffered, like virtually all outlying villages, from a total lack of public-transport facilities. This tipped the balance the other way: no students had ever stayed there . . . But there would be no reason, Eleanor thought, why they couldn't start now . . .

She parked the car on a stand of cleared ground at the side of the house and walked round to the front door. The huge bulk of the place was lost in the dark, beyond the pale spray of light given out by a single lamp in the porch. No glow was showing from any of the windows; Eleanor guessed that Vivien Goldsmythe lived in a few rooms at the back, most likely keeping herself to herself. But then, it wouldn't matter in the slightest if she was known: her face would still be seen in Ketley village; her voice would still be heard. The fact of her death would be kept from all but the Children of the Bidden.

Eleanor pushed the bell-stud and heard the ringing far down in the depths of the house. She was on time. Vivien would be expecting her. A light came on along a distant corridor: a pale distorted form showed in the coloured glass panel of the front door, sliding closer as though swimming up through water. The hallway light came on. The door opened to the limit of its security chain.

'Hello?'

'Mrs Goldsmythe – this is Eleanor Van Allen, from the university. I telephoned earlier to make this appointment . . .'

'Yes, yes, I remember. Can you identify yourself?'

Eleanor controlled a burst of temper. Stupid bitch had been watching too many Crimebuster commercials.

'Of course, just a moment . . . She passed through a small laminated card with her picture, name, address—

'This says Calverton Museum.'

'We're closely associated with the university, Mrs Goldsmythe. I, uh, I think I have more ID here if you like. . . Driver's licence . . . Cash cards . . .'

The door opened fully and Eleanor was bathed in the light.

'It's all right, dear. I believe you. But you can't be too careful, you know.'

Vivien Goldsmythe stepped aside and beckoned Eleanor in. The woman was in her late sixties, Eleanor guessed, bulkily built with a rosy complexion and long greying hair tied back in a bun. She was wearing a tan tweed skirt, hose the colour of strong tea, and a pea-green turtle-neck woollen sweater with heavy cotton shoulder patches.

'One of the Major's,' Vivien explained, to satisfy Eleanor's look of curiosity rather than through any self-consciousness. 'Saves on the heating, you know . . . Anyway, come through to the lounge and we'll have some tea. It's at the back – lovely view of the valley, all the way down to Kenniston . . . I must say, I'm very glad you approached me when you did. I could really do with some cash – not simply for myself, you understand; but I'm helping support a house for deprived youngsters in the city, and we're hoping to buy a snooker table before the year's out. Not a full-size one, of course, but even three-quarter size is appallingly expensive . . .'

Eleanor let the woman chatter on while she opened the large briefcase she was carrying and delved her hand inside.

'I must say, my dear – Eleanor, isn't it? I hope you don't mind first names? I'm Vivien – no, I must say, Eleanor, you look much more striking than your passcard photograph. Not older or anything. Just different—'

Vivien Goldsmythe turned as they reached the roomy lounge. A TV set in the corner was running an old musical, the sound turned low.

Eleanor pushed the creature stiff-armed into Vivien's face, before she had time to scream or understand. Grasping tendrils held at once. The flesh of the animal rippled and heaved as ventral glands secreted thick mucus over Vivien's mouth and nose, over her entire face. The aim was not to meld with this human, but to destroy it; and so the poison came next, driven swiftly and in copious amounts through a hollow barb from the creature's underside.

The woman's body stiffened and crashed backwards, one worn carpet slipper falling off as the legs and torso spasmed, quivering; lay still. The acid was injected, spurting power-fully beneath the hardened mucus crust. The air close to the body took on a red and liverish smell. The guest animal changed colour, from the waxy pallor of dead flesh to a healthy pinkish hue, and beyond to a gorgeous crimson tinged with violet. Protofeatures quickly melted towards a recognizable configuration, the creature's dorsal surface splitting horizontally, opening up to a monstrous barracuda smile. Seconds later, Vivien's face, startlingly transformed, stared up at Eleanor, who had watched the process with fascination.

'She—' Thin fluid rilled from the corners of the mouth. The woman's brain was gone, liquefied now and ingested, but the Child of the Gorgoneion had absorbed much in the brief moments of its attack and kill.

'She – had hope – for the – future . . .'

'So do we all,' Eleanor said without passion. 'I will summon the others. The house is ideal for the spawning.'

'Blessed be the Children of Phorcys and Ceto,' the wonderful face intoned. Its eyes were ever-deepening, blue darkening to shades almost beyond blueness. Freed of the strictures of concealment, its form was fluid, running through profound race memories of a thousand faces; the fringe of tentacles waved in an ecstasy of feeding.

'She – tastes good—' the animal said, its mouth upturned with pleasure. Eleanor laughed at the inadvertent ambiguity of that remark.

'Don't be greedy. Others need to gain strength also.'

She looked down at the remains. The creature was sliding away from the collapsed shell of the head, down over the still-substantial bosom. Eleanor felt no shock or outrage at Vivien Goldsmythe's demise. It was as it had always been, the survival of the fittest. Besides, this had been Vivien's last and greatest charitable act.

Chapter Eleven

For now we see through a glass, darkly; but
then face to face: now I know in part, but then
shall I know, even as also I am known.

I Corinthians 13:12

Theo was beautiful in a different way when she was angry. Her cold-steel unapproachability turned Parco on as much as or more than any flaunted sexuality: precisely because she kept her distance, he wanted her. Badly.

His attempts at explanation of the night before were met at first by a breezy indifference that was pure sham and as enduring as a box-kite in a blizzard: when Parco continued with his apologies, Theo's temper flared and she told him, using some of the most smoothly articulate obscenities he had ever heard, to please remove sections of his person from her sight and leave her alone.

Parco retired, bruised, beaten and more solidly infatuated than he had ever been, to the inner office, where he dialled Eleanor Van Allen's number every fifteen minutes until his call was answered.

'Yes?'

'Eleanor? It's Jim Parco . . .'

'We have nothing to say to each other, Mr Parco. Our business is concluded.'

There was something in her tone that troubled him. Fleetingly he was reminded of Theo's coldness. He would win with her, eventually: her ice was to warn him, to teach him a lesson. But he knew he'd need to play it carefully with her, and with Eleanor also.

'I realize that, Eleanor, and I fully intend to respect your wishes. I will not attempt to extend my enquiries further into your husband's affairs – '

'I appreciate that.'

' – But I feel I should tell you that the police have been appraised of my findings to date. I suggest you advise Mr Van Allen to hire a good lawyer, for himself and for you. Having kept the knowledge of his activities to yourself, you are also implicated.'

'All of this is clear to me.'

Parco sighed. 'I'm sorry, truly.'

'There is no need for sorrow, Mr Parco. It is an empty emotion, like regret, celebrating a past that is over and done with. We must all look to the future.'

'I admire your optimism.' Parco let the smile show in his voice. In his mind's eye, Eleanor's elegant face remained impassive, outwardly shunning the compliment. There was a long silence. 'Eleanor?'

'Mr Parco, you would do well to put the telephone down and forget about me. Your case is closed. You have impressed me with the effectiveness of your detection; Richard was quite convinced that his operation was sealed and secure. So, you may congratulate yourself – Take your pretty secretary out to dinner to celebrate. If you go to Forrester's Restaurant, please be my guest. I have an account there . . .'

'The problem is,' Parco said, approaching the nub of it now and the reason for his call, 'I have achieved very little. You employed me for a specific purpose, to answer a question that still goes unanswered.'

'I was mistaken. My husband was obviously under more strain than I realized. The Greek connection was not as reliable as he'd hoped, you understand, and so Richard was worried for the integrity of the entire enterprise.'

The lie was plausible, likely, and obvious.

'You just told me Mr Van Allen thought his operation was secure . . .'

A moment's hesitation.

'At this end, yes. Michaelides is proving a risk, however. And now, Mr Parco,' Eleanor said, her voice sharpening, 'I have much to do. Really, I'm too busy to continue this conversation. I thank you again for your loyalty to my interests. If it comes to a prosecution, then believe me when I say that I'll never lay the blame at your door. We went into this with our eyes open, Mr Parco . . .'

'I understand that, but—'

Parco found himself talking into the purr of a dead line.

He wondered, a half-hour later, whether Theo would stick the flowers up his nose and smother him with the pizza he'd brought back.

'Extra anchovies,' he pointed out, his final card. 'Your favourite. Mmm, smells good.'

She took off her work glasses and looked up at him.

'You think you can bribe me with a pizza and a bunch of freesias?'

'Two bunches. And there's extra black olives, too. I read they were supposed to improve the temper . . .'

'You're impossible, Parco, do you know that?'

'Yes, Theodora. And you're amazing. Now, do we eat, or fight?'

'Let's eat,' she decided, taking the pizza box out of his hands. 'We'll fight later on my home ground. Now, you put those flowers in water while I divide this food unfairly . . .'

Parco obeyed without a word of complaint.

*

Joe Patrick watched the man work in silence, and tried to understand the complex amalgam of emotions that swept through himself upon seeing the sacred words of the Gorgoneion brought into the light of human understanding. Here were names that his host could comprehend, as well as the one undertaking the translation. That one – Howard – kept his thoughts well hidden behind a façade of academic intensity, but Patrick could tell that he was consumed with excitement, curiosity, perhaps even a little with dread. For here were the secrets of the ages revealed to plain sight; the truth of the fact that mankind had never lived alone in the world as the only intelligent predatory species. For millennia past, he had ridden with a companion; one so closely bound to the ways of humanity that man had long since consigned the union to the obscurity of legend and vague superstition. As for the Children, where they had once thrived in their thousands during the Old Time, dark ages of weakness and ill-fortune had dwindled them to a few individuals eking out an existence in the face of all the ills to which mortal flesh is heir. Plague, pestilence, the depradations and depravities of the human race had all taken their toll on the spawn of Phorcys and Ceto. Entire nests of Children had been wiped out as civilizations crumbled and crashed, and the tides of human change and expansion swept across the world. Man proliferated into every far-flung outpost of the globe, while the might of the Gorgoneion was shrunk tight as a mouse's wintering heart in desert sands and dry caves, curled inside the skulls of dead hosts or the amphorae of the reverent burning with the terror of the gods. But the breed was nothing if not tenacious: individuals could survive in silent hibernation for centuries, their bodies dessicated as rock or bone, dreaming their dreams of resurrection and glory.

From time to time, here and there, those dreams were kindled, only to be dashed in a horror of outraged slaughter – human and Gorgoneion dying together at the hands of the incomprehending and afraid. Never since the sun-bright grandeur of Greece and Mycenae had the Children had the chance to revel in their true place at the height of creation.

Until now.

The flesh of Patrick's face squirmed and writhed askew in the anticipation of a future that was bright with triumph. The host body beneath trembled, its smothered voice struggling at the insistence of a suddenly terrified mind.

Howard's concentration was broken momentarily by the noise the man made behind him. He held a deep revulsion of Patrick, a profound distrust. And now the man's scufflings caused Howard to glance round, in time to see Patrick hurrying away, out of the little workroom and, as the door eased closed, across the labs to the dark storerooms at the back.

Howard moved quickly, stepping to the window set high up in the wall, which admitted a slit of light at ground level. Through the dust-grimed glass, Howard could look out over the side lawn of the museum into a shadowy tangle of laurel bushes: beyond were public seats, and the quiet walkway down towards the city centre.

He slipped the window catch, taking care not to disturb the dust on the ledge, then returned to his bench, where he had time to employ the shirt-sleeve trick before Joe Patrick returned.

John Pearcy called round to Parco's office in person later that morning. Theo saw that he was pale and tired, his eyes bright with an inner burning that she had recognized before in the eyes of paranoiacs and those that are afraid. He explained that he'd been trying to call, but the line had been engaged. He needed to speak to Jim urgently . . .

'Let me buzz him first, John, if you wouldn't mind.' Theo kept her voice calm, her smile light and bright. Pearcy's jacket was unzipped, and had bulged open so that Theo could see the butt of a hand-gun protruding from his inside pocket. Judging his mental condition, the trauma he'd suffered, Theo reckoned that right now he was a danger to himself and to the public at large.

Pearcy was agitated, his breathing shallow and fast, his face alive with the nervous energy that animates people on the final downhill run to emotional burn-out.

'OK, buzz him then. Tell him I've got to see him – he'll understand, Theo. He'll see me.'

'I'm sure he will. Can I fix you a drink – tea, coffee?'

'No,' Pearcy snapped, then reined in. 'I'm sorry. No, thanks. Just tell him—'

Theo dabbed the intercom button and heard the tone sound through the door separating the two offices. Parco responded a moment later.

'Jim, I have John Pearcy out here. He's very keen to speak to you—' Pearcy mouthed something. 'Yes, he says it's urgent. OK, Jim, right away. You can go in, John, Parco's just as keen to see you.'

Pearcy thanked her again and smiled brittly. The skin was grey around his mouth, and Theo hoped that Parco had picked up the hint of warning in her rare use of his first name . . .

Even before Parco could run through the formalities of greeting, Pearcy had dragged the Police National Computer printout from his pocket and was launching into the findings. Parco allowed him five seconds before raising his hands.

'John – John! There's no point blitzing me with this stuff. We need to work through it carefully—'

'Fuck "carefully".' Pearcy gave a hard laugh. 'We've got an angle here on the origin of these things, don't you realize that? They're coming in via the railyards: it's the weakest point. Customs and Excise is spread so thinly at the ports these days that by the time freight reaches Calverton, not even the most cursory checks are made. Besides, what do security forces look for? Drugs, bombs, illegal immigrants . . . These killers won't show up on any scanner, and they're small enough to be passed over by teams searching for refugees . . .'

'All right,' Parco said. He indicated the chair beside him and Pearcy sat down shakily. 'Look, John, I'm with you on this one, OK? You've done some good work making these connections—'

Pearcy tapped his head. 'Thank the old microchip, and a sweet gal named Carole . . .' The laughter came again, crackling up out of Pearcy's throat; aberrant, pointless laughter.

Parco regarded his friend with concern. He sensed the fear that was crashing through the cop, threatening to sweep him away in its undertow. It was, sickeningly, a common occurrence among police officers that after years of iron-willed defiance of such fear, they broke suddenly under the strain, often from a minor incident. Not that Parco thought Hanlon's theories were insignificant . . . But they were speculative, and until Parco witnessed one of these animals himself . . .

'All right, John. Let's accept for now that these creatures

have entered the country via the railyards. Would they have been deliberately sent? By whom? And how?'

Pearcy shrugged. 'Who knows, Jim? Probably deliberately, unless they're intelligent enough to hide themselves away in packing crates . . . But the other point I was coming to was that Denny Crane and 'Risico' Peters, both tied in with this business, were involved in the railyard robbery a few months back . . .'

'And Risico has disappeared,' Parco added, slowly, working towards the brink. 'And Denny Crane went to work for Richard Van Allen . . . Oh my God – Van Allen's Greek pipeline . . . Eleanor thought it was secure . . . How many of these things has he brought into the country? And does she know about them? Jesus Christ – *does she know!*'

Now it was Pearcy's turn to frown. 'What are you saying, Jim?'

'If you've got an hour to spare,' Parco said steadily, 'I'll fill you in on how far this thing might have gone . . .'

At the end of that time, Parco was convinced of a number of things.

As *outré* and bizarre as Hanlon's and Pearcy's ideas might be, they became plausible given the weight of evidence that Parco had now accumulated in his head. The cross-correspondences between what he'd uncovered about Van Allen's activities and the recent city slayings was a coherent structure that did not so much require a suspension of disbelief, as demand acceptance that it was real.

Parco also knew that the time to move in was not yet. Given that Richard Van Allen was bringing these unholy creatures into the country, a new kind of clean-up operation would need to be considered; something between a drug squad swoop and a rabies control disinfestation procedure. To imagine that he, Parco, and Pearcy could turn up like the Lone Ranger and Tonto to save the day was ludicrous. There was the question of gathering more intelligence – what were Van Allen's plans now? How many people were affected, or infected, by these leeches (and to hell with Hanlon's 'symbiont' notions: these were parasites!); was the problem confined to Calverton at this end of the pipeline? How extensive was it at the far end? Where the hell else on the planet was this thing happening? And crucially, could it be stopped at all?

There was, finally, the problem of convincing the powers that be that Parco and Pearcy should not be taken away quickly in a white van and locked up somewhere with a top-security decal on the door. Hanlon would back up their assertions with hard fact, but, as yet, not enough of it to warrant any kind of large-scale action.

Parco was therefore forced to conclude that his best course of action would be to do what he had been doing all along – and what it was his job to do; watch, listen, gather facts, stay in the shadows . . .

He explained this to Pearcy and the man nearly went through the roof.

'What if there's a hundred of them today, Jim? Animals breed. Next week there could be a thousand. In six months, a million . . .'

'Don't you think I've reflected on that?' Parco kept his voice calm. 'But if we move in now with guns blazing and a single creature slips the net, we're back to square one.'

'But at least we'd be alerted. Everyone will know about them!'

'Yeah.' Parco nodded wryly. 'That's if we're not muzzled at the outset. Government clean-up squads are pretty efficient at covering tracks, John. It might be in the country's best interests to keep the lid on – which means erasing all traces of this phenomenon. Which means early retirement for you, me, Hanlon, and anyone else who's involved: and I'm using the word "retirement" in its most sinister sense . . .'

'You believe that?' Pearcy was incredulous and unnerved at the same time. It made Parco smile grimly.

'If I can believe in unknown killer parasites that eat people's faces off, then I think I can stretch my imagination to that, yes.'

Pearcy sat quiet a moment, the rage taken out of him.

'I think I want to get Karen and the kids away,' he said then, very quietly, and looked up at Parco moist-eyed. 'Really, Jim, I want them out of it.'

'That's understandable. Also reasonable,' Parco said. 'You got somewhere in mind?'

'Karen's parents retired to Dumfries a few years ago. They're always urging us to take a holiday. No reason why the children can't take a week off school – and Karen could do with a break after what I've put her through. They'll be safe up there . . . Me, I reckon I'll stay on and "monitor the situation" . . .'

Parco grinned at him.

'I was hoping you'd say that. I'm going to need a reliable partner once Theo's out of the way . . .'

'You're sending her to safety too?'

'If I can. But she's an independent woman, John. A holiday will have no pushing power behind it at all . . . Though she was keen to take the Cline case . . . Maybe if another one came along just like it . . .' Parco had almost been talking to himself. Now he shook himself out of the reverie.

'Anyway, that's my problem. Can I suggest that you go

back home and make your plans for Karen and the kids: pack a bag and join me back here whenever – I'll give you a key and the number for the alarm . . .'

'OK. What about you?'

'I'll work on Theo, as far as I can: but I also need to keep tabs on Richard Van Allen and his wife . . . I'm beginning to realize just why Eleanor wanted me to drop my investigations on her husband . . .'

'You take care then, Jim. We know how dangerous they can be.'

'The parasites, or the Van Allens?'

'Maybe both,' Pearcy said. Both men laughed without any humour. Parco nodded towards Pearcy's jacket pocket.

'Talking of dangers – are you going to be careful with that piece?'

Pearcy took the gun out and hefted it.

'Smith and Wesson Military and Police Special. Medium frame six-shot revolver, .38 calibre, with a two-inch barrel. Also, hollowpoint bullets – they mushroom on impact . . .'

Pearcy handed the gun to Parco, who in all his years of work had never used one of these things, information being his only weapon to date.

'I'm not sure I'd advise you using this, John . . .'

Pearcy pulled a small box of extra cartridges from another pocket and passed them over also.

'I won't be, my friend. These are for you. When the time comes, I'll be packing something a lot more powerful . . .'

Vaughn Castillo had now reached the point where pique had bubbled over into jealousy; where outrage had turned into simple rage.

He had worked for Richard for over ten years; obediently, efficiently and with the utmost discretion. And yes, he had long expected something other than the remarkably generous salary that Van Allen allowed him, and the elegant compliments his superior paid him with flattering regularity. Richard's charm and charisma had been evident from the outset; and from the outset, Castillo's heart as well as his loyalty had belonged to him. A phase of pure awe had mellowed into lustful longing, and during these years Castillo had been at his most provocative, despite Richard's seemingly unswerving devotion to his bitch of a wife. Indeed, perhaps surprisingly, Van Allen had responded subtly but with definite interest to Castillo's approaches, although the understanding between the two men had always been implicit and had never matured into anything physical.

Now, Castillo began to see that Van Allen had been leading him on, exploiting his weaknesses to gain Castillo's trust and secrecy. These of course had become increasingly important as Richard's businesses had branched out into new and more dangerous areas: Castillo knew well enough that Richard had crossed the line of legality and was now generating fortunes far outside the ambit of the law. But Castillo had kept these truths tight shut in his mind, as much as his overweening love of Van Allen had withdrawn to a simmering hurt that had come now to fester into the wish to hurt back.

The puzzling events of the past few months had hardened Castillo's attitude against the other. First, Van Allen had employed that ruffian Crane, ostensibly in the capacity of security guard; but right from the start the two had shared an intimacy of trust that it pained Castillo to see. And now, this stranger, 'Joe Patrick', suddenly appeared on the scene to occupy a similar position close to the centre of Richard's operations.

Castillo felt quite justified in his anger, which he knew was tainted with a venomous streak, created by Richard's apparent disregard of the pain he was causing. Well, the time had come when he must be made to face the truth, and in so doing acknowledge the feelings of the man he had ignored for so long.

It was mid-afternoon. The museum had been quiet throughout the day, and now, as Castillo walked the familiar galleries and displays towards the rear offices, he estimated that not more than a dozen members of the public were here. It saddened him rather to see the place looking so run-down, both in terms of its lack of patronage as well as in the relatively inferior nature of the exhibits, that once, in hey-days long gone, had been so grand, so fine. It felt like an ending, in which he, Castillo, was caught up and helpless to prevent.

He entered Richard's office without knocking; something he'd done previously as a matter of course. Now, in the midst of his surprise, he found Joe Patrick stripped to the waist and Van Allen standing up close to him, his hands pressed to the man's body.

'Oh – what – what are you doing, Richard?' Shock and bruised pride made a rich mixture that brought quick tears to Vaughn Castillo's eyes. Van Allen let his hands remain on Patrick's hairless chest, but he turned his head slowly to gaze at the intruder. There was no towering rage – but his calm was equally frightening.

'Did you realize, Vaughn, that the earliest known figurine is thirty-two thousand years old? It depicts a pregnant female, and is carved from a reindeer antler that was found at La Ferrassie in the Dordogne . . .' His smile was dark and seductive. Castillo, unnerved though he was, wondered what he had stumbled upon here – and he was not altogether dismissive of the possibilities.

'I – I didn't know that, no,' he replied lamely. Van Allen's hands began moving in slow spirals over Patrick's body, up to the shoulders, down to the hips.

'The miracle of birth has long since been revered and held in the highest esteem. All creatures know at some deep level that it is the root of their own existence, and the survival of their species. For many, many generations – beyond the creation of the La Ferrassie figurine – the principle of fecundity has been granted its rightful importance in the great cycle of life and death. Ignorantly, of course, it has been vested within the human female: primal symbology of all cultures exaggerates the breasts and child-swollen belly – although certain philosophies long since thought to be perverse have reflected the view that such female centrality must be destructive . . .'

Castillo smiled weakly. Now he had no idea what Van Allen was talking about. Deep waters. Dangerous undercurrents. But the sight of the man's big hands massaging Joe Patrick's tiny dry nipples was acutely arousing. Castillo moved closer, closing the office door behind him.

'Richard, please, forgive my intrusion. I had no way of knowing that you were, er, otherwise engaged . . .'

'This is no intrusion, Vaughn. It could be, though, a revelation.'

Castillo's skin prickled and the old, old feelings began to clench in his guts; anticipation of what was forbidden yet irresistible. He allowed his erection its rein and noticed Van Allen's glance down there, and his smile.

'Richard – you know how much I've always admired you. Always . . . wanted you . . .'

'Want. Need. What are these things really when set against what is essential?'

Again, Castillo was lost, floundering. But the aura of sex surrounding the three men was now almost overwhelming to him. His breathing shallowed and quickened; his entire body felt trigger sensitive. He could feel Van Allen's strangely scented breath on his face; could smell the sweat from Joe Patrick and his own thickening aroma of longing.

'What – do you want me – to do?'

'Desire is insidious, Vaughn. It controls you, makes you powerless. Even when it's recognized, it's ignored.'

'Richard—'

'Don't you think,' Van Allen said, 'that it is much better to accept that what must be done, should be done quickly, and without regret?'

Now Castillo felt he understood. Van Allen turned his back on Patrick and moved Castillo round, facing the way he had come. Patrick's hands rested on Castillo's shoulders. Van Allen stepped forward, stooped slightly and gazed into Castillo's eyes.

'Vaughn. You have served me so well. Will you serve me now, with all of your heart, in a way that you never thought possible?'

The blue eyes absorbed Castillo entirely. His will seemed to fade and evaporate under the power of that gaze. His lips parted. Richard's face was so very close.

'Oh yes,' Castillo whispered. 'Oh yes, oh, my love, oh yes . . .' His hard on was like hot iron, its heat filling him so completely that sweat appeared at his temples and trickled down to his jawline.

He felt Joe Patrick's hands start to shudder. And there were noises that he did not completely understand. He began to fumble with his own belt buckle, but then Van

Allen kissed him lightly, eased away, and kissed him again as his tongue pushed the yielding lips apart and penetrated to his throat.

Castillo gasped. It seemed that, behind him, Patrick was going into spasms so violent that Castillo himself was shaking with their force. He kept his eyes tight closed and surrendered himself to the dreams that had now been made flesh for him.

Van Allen's hands were in his hair, holding his head up, back. And – Castillo groaned – now it was happening. He felt Richard tearing at his trousers, pulling away the confining cloth so that he could see, and take, and use . . .

But – his hands were also tangled in his hair; Joe Patrick's still gripped his shoulders. What could be –

What could be?

Those hands were huge, the fingers impossible, too many and too thick to believe; the palm so wide and heavy. Castillo, soaked and agonizingly erect, cried out in confusion as a wet rubbery mask was clamped over his head, suffocating him into black panic.

Then something replaced Richard's tongue in his mouth, sliding to touch his palate, pushing his own tongue down, swelling out to bloat his cheeks and gullet and windpipe . . . Castillo became filled with spiderwebs and pain.

The soft sighing of his own breath, or the tides of desire that Richard had named, faded into a voice that was many-faceted; a jewelled voice composed of a million. And his vision, returned to him now even though his eyes had been open for several minutes, made the room ripple as though a viscous jelly had been poured into his sockets. Blood and stars drifted across: everything looked dreamlike – though Castillo was beyond caring, for reality now lay inside him.

'It is done,' Richard said, dismissing Castillo's sexual

yearnings, since Castillo no longer existed. The man once possessing that identity adjusted his clothing and the two Children of the Bidden turned to look at Joe Patrick's remains.

The skull was a blood-filled crater, scooped out messily so that streamers of flesh festooned the cavity walls and rim. The man's upper body seethed beneath the tight, blued skin; while lower down, Patrick's grey work trousers moved constantly with the activity beneath.

'The time approaches,' Van Allen told the other, calmly but with an underlying excitement. 'I must move him to the safe house. Help me to get him to the car, then remain here and alert me if there is danger.' Van Allen smiled. 'Do not worry. The Children care for their own. You are not alone here – the Bidden has seen to that. And soon, tomorrow, there will be another host to serve our purposes . . . Now, take his head.'

They lifted Joe Patrick's body and carried it towards the rear exit where Van Allen's Daimler was parked.

Halfway across the room, the skin of the abdomen split and the spawn of Phorcys and Ceto clamoured to see this new world of theirs, in their hundreds.

Eleanor Van Allen listened to what her husband had to say, then agreed with him briefly and terminated the conversation. She broke the connection, keyed up another number and waited patiently for a response.

'Hello – Accommodation Office? Oh, hi. This is Eleanor Van Allen here. Yes, that's right . . . I'm phoning because I think I may be able to help you over your shortage of lodgings. Yes – yes, I'm sure you do. I believe you have on file a Mrs Vivien Goldsmythe who lives alone at Ketley Lodge in the village of Ketley, south of – You remember it? Good. Well, really, I'm asking you to reconsider your previous decision not to use the Lodge for student accommodation. I understand that transport is a problem, but . . .'

Eleanor allowed the Accommodation Officer her interruption, then carried on smoothly.

'When I say I can help, I mean that in a very practical sense, Mrs . . . Mrs Fisher, thank you. The situation is that my husband is planning to host an archaeological convention at the museum shortly: he has a number of, um, guests arriving from Greece. All specialists in their field. What he's hoping for is to arrange for students from the university to accompany his guests during the course of the convention. Now it would be much more useful all round if students and guests could share accommodation also . . . Pardon me? Oh, well, I thought of Ketley Lodge after Mrs Goldsmythe approached me directly. We're both involved in charity work in the city. Mr Van Allen is quite happy to arrange transport for the duration – apparently the museum has a minibus that can be used . . . Yes, yes, quite. And he's hinted to me of something more permanent if this arrangement succeeds . . . Oh, you will? Well, I'd be most grateful, Mrs Fisher . . . There are eight bedrooms, all large. What? Oh, no more than half a dozen guests. You will? Thank you so much. Please call me when you've decided.'

Parco ran through the nasty little ritual of unloading the gun, cleaning out the cylinder, checking the sight alignment and replacing the bullets, for the tenth time that day. He'd had visions, when Pearcy began talking about the use of the weapon, of disassembling the whole machine like he'd seen on the movies: Pearcy explained that modern hand-guns required no detailed maintenance, but basic care of the weapon, making the feel and balance of it familiar to the hand, was vital, so that the user neither over- nor under-estimated its capabilities.

Parco replaced the final shell with a sigh. He had no doubts whatever that he would end up using the revolver, probably soon, most likely in a state of blind terror for his life, rather than with the controlled cool efficiency he had also seen on the movies. But then, all of Parco's childhood heroes were dead – or just not the men they were. He spoke his reservations aloud to John Pearcy, who'd looked back at him in a way that caused Parco's heart to freeze in his chest.

'When you open up with that, Jim, whatever's moving in front of you will deserve to die. And it's hardly a question of heroism. Life or death rarely is . . .'

'I reckon I feel worse about this than about anything else I've ever done. It's unreal, John. I believe it, but I don't think I expect to see it.'

Pearcy stood up heavily, wearily, his smile ghastly and pale.

'When you see it, you'll believe it then.'

After he'd gone, Parco spent time trawling his list of addresses for a referred case that would get Theo clear of this mess until the crisis was over. One way or another, he told himself.

There were a few possibilities in the offing, one of which, involving suspected industrial espionage with a computer-fraud angle, looked complex and challenging enough to appeal to Theo's sense of adventure. Parco put out a few more feelers and compiled a brief which he rough- then final-drafted, and hard-copied for Theo to take home over the weekend. It would mean several weeks away, working in

London and Brussels: a job she would relish and he would hate, for their various reasons.

His plan then was to catnap for an hour, then to risk a final meeting with Eleanor Van Allen to confirm his worst suspicions and validate Pearcy's scenario. What he'd said to the cop had been true: he believed this incredible invasion, but somehow it lacked the substance of the furniture in the room, the city bustling outside the window, the warmth of his own hands . . . It was too alien to imagine as something other than a vague horror with which he was involved through a tumble of circumstance . . . Yet what Pearcy said was equally true: when he saw it, he'd believe it. And that was a thing he wanted least in all the world to happen.

Parco buzzed through to Theo and told her not to pass on calls; he was going into conference for an hour. Theo chuckled as usual at the coded phrase and said she'd wake him after that time . . .

There was never any need. Parco's internal clocks were pretty precise and very reliable. He adjusted the venetian blind to limit the incoming light, sat in the lobby chair in one corner of the room with his feet up on the coffee-table, slowed his breathing until his eyelids closed; and oblivion followed of its own accord.

Sixty minutes later, Parco woke. He was always mildly groggy, but after a coffee and a wash he'd recharged enough for another six to eight hours' work. Though God knew this time how long it would be until he next saw his bed.

Theo was right on time with the coffee.

'And Barry Hanlon will be calling back in the next few minutes,' she added. 'He rang earlier, but I said you were busy.'

'OK, Theo, thanks.' As she put Parco's cup down on the little table, he leaned forward and captured her hand in his.

It was impulse, but it had been building inside him for days, weeks. Maybe for ever.

She looked surprised, pleasantly so, and did not draw her hand away.

'Parco? Does overwork bump up your tenderness quotient?' It was a gentle sarcasm, his seriousness equally so.

'I don't tell you often enough how valuable you are to this agency, Theo – or how precious you are to me.'

Now she detected the complex flood of feelings on his face, and worry tainted her own. Theo frowned and knelt beside him.

'What's eating at you, Parco? These killings? The Van Allen case?'

'All. All of it.' He wondered how much she had picked up and put together herself; whether she had deduced from scraps of overheard conversation and this file and that the full implications of what was happening. It would be easy enough to ask her – but that would mean telling her everything; he would never leave her half-blind.

'What are your plans for the weekend, Theo?'

'What are yours?' She leaned against him, smiling up. Her perfume was tinged with the sweat of the day; a muskier, earthier, more potent concoction. Parco wished with his soul that it could be a normal weekend of ambling walks, meals in quiet restaurants, petting in darkened rooms with the TV running on unnoticed . . .

'I was hoping you'd cast your eyes over a case that's come our way,' he said, hating himself. 'Cruse Diamond pitched us this ball. I thought it was right up your street, Theo. And, as you confirmed, since our caseload is so light at the moment . . .'

Her mood shifted to the far end of the spectrum, as Parco had expected it to. He knew she suspected ulterior motives from the sudden green chill of her eyes. He prepared himself to bullshit, to argue, and not to give in.

The phone rang next door. It would be Hanlon.

Theo stood up and stalked out silently.

Parco went to his desk.

'They're intelligent, self-aware, highly adapted beings that have no other analogue on this planet.'

Parco wanted to slam down the handset. Hanlon's note of intense excitement sickened him. The facts themselves left him numb.

'Are they mammals, or what?'

'The DNA is of a mammalian complexity, Jim, but the lifestyle and behavioural characteristics of the creatures don't fit that . . . And yet, can you conceive of any *non-mammalian* animal developing such a degree of self-consciousness? . . . They're something else,' Hanlon went on after a silence. 'I'm talking from the gut now, but I say they can't be mammals. Perhaps a new kind of cephalopod – or an incredibly ancient kind . . . I'd need years to study them properly, Jim – '

'And I want to wipe the fucking things out as soon as I can track them down!' Parco responded, his voice rising. 'For God's sake, man, you saw what they did!'

'You're right, of course. But the benefits of such a study . . . It would be criminal to destroy every trace . . .'

Parco's voice became ominously quiet: Hanlon was behaving like a kid with a new toy or, more dangerously, a scientist with a new discovery. Fame, wealth, reputation – and damn the consequences of that!

'Hanlon, if even one of these parasites survives . . .'

252

The reply came back at once, and Parco understood that the bastard had thought it all through . . .

'If we could actually *ensure* the destruction of all of them, then I'd be tempted to agree with you, Parco. But how can we guarantee that? They could be anywhere – everywhere. Think about it. Their invisibility up till now might be due to their scarcity, or to their cunning. One of us in a hundred might be carrying a symbiont, or one in ten, or—'

'Then I'm tempted to agree with John Pearcy. Whatever effort we make to destroy them will alert people to their existence. OK, so some escape – but if we can hold one corpse up in front of the TV cameras, we'll have won a kind of victory.'

'A Pyrrhic victory, Jim,' Hanlon replied smoothly. 'If these creatures are sentient, as I believe they are, and have evidence for it, then they'll be forced to adapt in the light of changing circumstances. They could once more vanish from our sight, occupying some new and subtle niche in an ecosphere that in truth we barely comprehend.'

Parco felt bludgeoned by this double-talk, sceptical of it. It sounded like a man with ambition trying to stick fingers in a crumbling dyke of secrecy. The lid had been kept on until now to gather evidence, to avoid panic . . . Well, Parco felt that he wanted to panic; wanted to scream out the danger so that every fucking man-jack with any influence would take notice. Hanlon had sold his bill of goods too well: the last doubts were vanishing in Parco's mind.

'Evidence . . .' Parco sneered the word. 'If you've got evidence, then convince the people who count, Hanlon. You're preaching to the converted now . . . I presume there was some foreign tissue on Bakker's body?'

'Discarded cells. That's how I was able to run some simple tests on the DNA . . .'

'I'm ending the conversation now, Hanlon,' Parco said. 'I have work to do.'

'Parco – one last thing.' Parco heard the note of desperation, and hesitated.

'I know that you regard these as obscene and offensive predators. But you don't know, you don't understand. Our bodies swarm with life, most of it benign, some of it beneficial. Millions of amoebae are sliding over your teeth right now; their job is to ingest bacteria. In your gut you have other bacteria that help to break down the food you eat. Your very blood cells act like independent organisms, destroying invading germs, breaking down cancerous tissues . . . Parco, there are as many creatures living in and on your body as there are people living on this planet. Think about it – five billion organisms, without which Jim Parco could not exist for more than an hour or two. You reap the benefits of this world of life without realizing it. Perhaps, just perhaps, these creatures you want to destroy have been paying for their keep in many marvellous ways. It might be that without them, we'd never have developed intelligence at all! Parco – will you think about it at least? Parco!'

Parco put the phone down without making any promises. He drank the last of his now-cool coffee and buzzed for Theo. No answer. He went through into the other office and found that she'd left, having taken the Cruse Diamond file with her.

He went down to the garage to confirm that her car was gone. His own, the Saab he'd once been so proud to possess but which he now so rarely used, smelt coldly metallic and neglected. Parco opened the driver's door, slid into the leather seat and felt its familiar contours, and tried the ignition. The starter motor hacksawed briefly, then the engine caught and idled with the same rich clarity as it had always done.

Parco backed the car on to the tarmac, stepped out to close up the garage, then drove across town towards the Van Allen house.

The afternoon was smouldering down towards dusk, but even looking from across the less-than-daylit street, Parco could tell that Eleanor's facial injuries had vanished. She looked flawless once more. Beautiful.

He climbed from the Saab and crossed the road to intercept her as she locked her front door and walked to the end of the path. She noticed him and smiled without surprise. Parco's guts were closed tight as a fist, and his heart was pounding. He knew the reason why – he knew exactly why – and this was suicide if all that he believed had any meaning –

'Mr Parco. Jim. I did ask you not to bother me.'

'I know you did. But you *do* bother me, Eleanor. You bother me by suddenly pretending everything's OK, when I know it isn't.'

'I understand all that you've said about the evidence you've amassed against Richard. I understand that you are duty-bound to pass on this information to the police. Naturally Richard and I will make a fight of it: Richard's resources are greater than you might imagine, so I think we can mount a good case to counter your own. Now, if that's all you wanted . . .'

Eleanor's polite perfect smile never wavered. But now her eyes lost interest in him and looked beyond him to the street, to the city beyond.

'I really do have a lot to see to . . .'

'Eleanor, I haven't come here to talk business. I'm quite

sure you have the wealth and intelligence to shoot the police lawyers out of the sky. Besides, any public scandal would cause the university severe embarrassment. You may well succeed in keeping the whole thing under wraps.'

'Quite.'

'But I wanted to see you again to say that – to say that you bother me in other ways, also.'

'Oh . . . Oh, I see.' Her brief laughter was lightly coy, darkly seductive. God, Parco thought, if only this was a normal encounter. 'There's really nothing you can—'

Parco moved closer, occupying intimate space, and looked into her eyes that seemed to gather up the twilight and throw it back in a violet glow. Such night-time eyes: you could almost watch the stars come out in them.

'Eleanor, you have disturbed me from the start. You disturb me more now. I felt earlier that you were keeping something from me, but perhaps the time for secrecy is over.'

'The time for secrecy is never over, Jim.'

'I don't agree.'

Parco put his body up to hers and slid his left arm around her waist to the hollow of her back. His right hand moved under his jacket to the gun settled in its leather holster at his belt. How long would it take him to withdraw the weapon, step away and either detain her or stop her permanently? And how fast could she react, should she realize his plan?

He kissed her gently and was trembling like a schoolkid out on his first date. Eleanor's soft breasts pushed against him as electrically as her hard hip bones. Her lips felt cool and were slightly apart. Parco prolonged the kiss to the limit of his endurance, and still the woman failed to respond in any meaningful way. The demon on her shoulder stayed silent.

Parco broke the contact and stood back. His shirt was damp with sweat. He felt exhausted and incredibly relieved. His embarrassment and disappointment were feigned.

'I'm sorry, Eleanor. I seem to have misunderstood the situation. I thought – '

'I know what you thought, Jim. And once perhaps we might have made something of the opportunity. But times have changed and there are other things in my life now. New horizons.'

'I see.'

She walked the few steps to where her car was parked at the roadside. Parco watched her as she started the engine and drove away.

The wind of the new night blew chill across his face. The tail-lights of Eleanor's car flickered red momentarily before moving out of sight. Her elegance – her elegance and beauty had been the same as he'd always admired. But the woman herself was changed.

Parco knew that he had not just been speaking to Eleanor Van Allen.

Howard watched Helen Remmick's wriggling backside just as she had watched his. This time she succeeded in pulling herself through the narrow gap of the open window, where he had failed.

Howard had warned her about the drop down from the ledge, and the wooden table with its clutter of objects beneath. Considering she was working in darkness and in unfamiliar territory, she made remarkably little noise. A few scuffles emerged from the blackness, the rattle of a potsherd, a delicate feminine sneeze. Howard scroamed out on the ground in a sniper's position and thrust his head through the basement window.

'Helen – are you OK in there?'

'Sssshh, Bill. I can hear you. I'm all right. It's pretty dark in here, so I'll wait for my eyes to adjust. And then – '

'Then go out the door and walk right on. You'll see two more doors: the first's a storeroom, nothing in there but brooms and mummified pharaohs—'

'Bill, I'll bloody brain you!'

'Sorry, sorry. The second leads to a kind of little corridor and a back lobby. At the far end is an outer door that's usually locked, but it'll have the key in it. That's all – just find that door and turn the key, and I'll be waiting there for you.'

'What about the security guards?'

'Guard,' Howard corrected. 'And I guess the only person who fits that description now is Joe Patrick. God knows what Van Allen's playing at; he's running the place right down . . . Anyway, that's neither here nor there. If you feel nervous, there's a knife in the right-hand drawer of my work-table.'

'What do you use that for?'

'Carving my initials in the wall – what do you think? Now for heaven's sake get a move on. I'm not lying here to work on my tan.'

Howard smiled at the neatly delivered package of curses that came his way. Then there was a brief miscellany of sounds, followed by the faintest click as Helen pulled the workroom door gently closed. Good girl, he thought, she's taking it seriously enough; although someone like Joe Patrick would perhaps only try to grab a feel under the pretext of apprehending the intruder, should he catch her;

and Howard had some money in his pocket if further persuasion was needed for him not to ring the cops.

Howard stayed full stretch on the ground for another minute or so, straining his ears to catch the smallest detail in that bland landscape of silence. It was mesmeric, also pointless. He whispered good luck and I love you to her, then scrambled up and hurried through the shrubbery to their place of rendezvous.

After Helen closed the door to Howard's workroom, she stood with her back pressed against it, pushing her senses out into the depths of the darkness, listening for details; the knife was held out firmly in front of her, its handle against her hip, her right arm programmed to use the damned blade if anything – if *anything* – should suddenly loom out at her.

The air hung dry and dusty; this a kind of background smell on which were carried stronger but more fleeting aromas; wood polish, a chemical stink that tickled Helen's nose and reminded her of science lessons years ago in school; faint, very faint threads of cigarette smoke . . . But then imagination began to intrude and Helen saw in her mind's eye this mysterious security guard whom Howard had mentioned, walking slowly through the museum's empty galleries, his eyes bored with dead and inanimate things, his mind wrapped around visions of catching some poor tramp come in from the cold, or a couple of kids doing it for a dare, or a lone and foolish undergrad whose only protection against his whim was a woefully inadequate penknife and a mouthful of terrified pleas.

Dammit. Dammit! Helen cursed her own nervousness and the uncontrolled run of her thoughts. At this rate she'd panic herself back to the basement window and out on to the lawns and down the street to the nearest pub. And then of course she'd never forgive herself, and neither would Howard, whose ribbing would be merciless.

She stepped away from the door, feeling better, more independent, with empty space around her. She had hoped for greater light, but what underglow there was allowed her to measure the height and width of the corridor, though its far end was hopelessly lost in gloom.

She took each step carefully, working with the silence as though it was still waters, on which she was determined not to cause a ripple. Now the chemical smell was fading, and a cool draught blew into her face and through her hair from the unknown country beyond the boundary of her vision.

A door appeared on her right, the broom cupboard Howard had mentioned. Helen forced herself not to think of mouldering mummies with eyes that still saw and rotted hearts that still lusted, and moved on quickly towards the second door, the one that she wanted.

The breeze was growing stronger. It was just a draught, she told herself, that's all. Someone's left a window open probably, or it's just the chilly evening air sliding in under doorways and pouring down to these lower levels. That's it. That's all it is. She decided that being firm with herself was the best way, as her mother had been firm with her – and still was, even though the good counsel came across country these days as regular letters and phone calls . . . Now work hard, Helen, won't you? Don't get behind in your studies, but at the same time make the most of the social side of university . . . Although do be careful, darling. Don't go smoking any of that hash, or whatever it's called – and for goodness sake, if you're going to have a boyfriend, take precautions. Use those – well, you know what they're called. I'm sure you can get hold of some, but if not, then tell me and I'll go to Boots . . . And eat properly, and don't drink too much, and –

And don't go breaking and entering, Helen thought, her own mind-voice replacing her mother's; even for someone you love. She conjured up a picture of him, waiting in the cold for her with the simmering impatience that often seemed to exist just below the surface. He would surely be there by now, ear pressed to the wood for the smallest sound of her approach . . . While here she was dawdling along, not keeping her attention on the mission she'd been given . . .

Helen hurried another dozen paces, and the corridor came to an end. She reached a T-junction and stood bemused and annoyed with herself for her lack of care.

But thinking about it, had *she* made a mistake, or had Bill? She was convinced there had only been one door on her right: so had Bill given her poor instructions – meaning that she should take the second turning right, which would be the passageway she'd just come across?

Helen clenched her teeth and let anger replace the vague unease that had settled in her guts. This was ridiculous. This was bloody stupid! Maybe she should retrace her steps and check for the error. But it would be quicker to take this right-hand turn and explore there; it was certainly heading in the right direction anyway, and if there was a back window she could at least signal to him . . .

Somewhere in the distance, a person sighed. A simple sound that swept away all thought of decision or a calculated plan.

The fear leaped inside her and the muscles in her groin tightened in a spasm. Oh God. Oh Jesus, it was that fucking guard . . . And as soon as Helen had thought it, a swarm of other possibilities chased blackly through her mind. The handle of the knife felt slick with her sweat. Helen smelt her own fear and was ashamed of it, but was unable to control it. She was standing now in the open space of the junction. The sound came again – from the right. Without thinking, she ran left, her breathing shallowing until her throat was constricted and a terrible sensation of choking brought her to her knees.

This was the greater danger. Helen had been through a panic attack once before, years ago on a roller-coaster ride at the fun-fair. That terrible hurtling had made her want to die, just to lock it out. And she almost had. Father had slapped her to shut off her screaming: Mom hugged her tight, tight and close and warm, until the whirling subsided and there was room for her to breathe as the terror eased off and her perspectives settled back to normality.

Helen recognized the symptoms now and stayed on all fours, head hung, panting; but slowing the pace after some seconds so that she wouldn't hyperventilate. Her heart ceased its manic hammering, her arms supported her weight with more confidence as their trembling eased . . .

But whatever was out there had heard, and was moving in her direction.

Helen scrambled up and hurried on, ignoring the doors she passed for fear of the noise she'd make in trying them, and the seconds' delay at each. She turned left or right at random, and succeeded in confusing herself much more than the unknown pursuer she'd dressed in the darkest clothes her imagination could create, thus completely losing her way.

There came a point at which the nauseous suspicion in her stomach became a far more sinister certainty, that the thing in the darkness was on her trail and gaining ground. A whimper broke from Helen's lips, while sudden heat bloomed across the tight crotch of her jeans, as intimate as a lover's hand. She saw herself raped here; dying here. Perhaps both. The urge to scream built up a pressure that was almost irresistible. A rain of fat wet stars burst in her eyes and her head was spinning and the knife began to ease from her cold fingers growing numb . . .

She hit the swing-door at full pelt so that its slamming open boomed around the roof like a gunshot in a cathedral. And now the acoustics of her footfalls were different also. The draught had vanished, and Helen sensed a huge emptiness about her . . . The central vestibule of the building, she surmised: relief soaked into her as a balm to her fear as she suddenly found her bearings and swerved towards the ground-floor gallery that would return her to the rear of the complex.

Helen took ten steps before the side door crashed again, and instinct froze her to the spot.

She dropped to a crouch, calming herself with a sheer effort of will. A lone white streetlamp shone its watery light through the arched windows over the main doorway of the lobby. Helen had never noticed that lamp before, but now she offered up thanks for its existence to whatever undefined deity watched this fleeting drama from on high. The faint illumination gave her eyes something to focus on and measure by. She watched as a mouse in a moonlit field watches for the night-owl, terrified but determined – determined because she was not dead yet.

Out of the silence came sound. Out of the stillness came movement.

A human silhouette walked slowly across the floor, pausing halfway to scan its surroundings. Helen hoped it would be searching at head-height and might not spot her tucked amongst shadow. She kept her knife very still, for fear of a single stray gleam betraying her position.

The man – so she decided by its masculine profile – turned a full slow circle. She could hear him breathing. An odd, bellowing rhythm; maybe because he had been running too. He continued moving to Helen's right, into obscurity once more . . . Then reappeared yards closer, his head and shoulders now outlined crisply in lamplight.

He was so close . . . Helen felt she could easily leap up and out and drive the knife-blade deep into his face. That would stop him. And it would end the bleak dread that was rising again to consume her . . . Better a brave try and heroic failure than to suffer this torture a moment longer . . .

Two more steps, and the man stopped again. Now he was all but looming above her, and still gave no indication of knowing she was near. Helen steeled herself to act, desperation forcing her hand. Her muscles, clenched hard, were ready; her mind in the act of commitment.

Then it all changed, so that the growing madness inside her was belittled by the insanity in front of her eyes.

The shape of the man's head had altered: and, even as she stared in complete amazement, this transformation continued so that the skull bulged around its entire circumference, and a portion broke free at one end – some kind of fingerlike projection that was quickly joined by a dozen others in a midnight parody of the sun's radiating rays.

Something like laughter and the bubbling of swamp gas crossed the space between Helen and this being. It spoke in a liquid language she failed to understand as the mass of the head started shuddering and thrashing atop the stooping shoulders.

Then torchlight exploded into Helen's face, triggering the manoeuvre the metamorphosis had delayed.

The knife jabbed upwards piercing an eye, and monster and torchbeam went spinning away.

Vaughn Castillo's howl of dying agony was mirrored by that of another. He whiplashed out of range, the blade still embedded, stumbled over his own feet and fell heavily to the ground, ridding himself of life and torment together.

The torch had not smashed: it splashed a wedge shape of light far across the floor, by the weak yellow wash of which Castillo's splayed body trembled, while that of its guest moved on for a few seconds longer. Then both were reduced to the cold lifeless clay from which all arises, and to which all returns in time . . .

Helen let the tidal wave of sobbing overwhelm her. This was more than she could bear. It was a million miles and a million years from the sight of Bill Howard's peeved face urging her on to find the key to a door that now she would never find. Yet even so, that distant, meaningless instruction moved her, sent her stumbling back in any direction – any direction at all away from what she had killed. And would she in truth ever know, some detached part of her mind now wondered?

The knife was gone, and nothing could persuade her to retrieve it. She had left the torch behind, but that light was not so much a haven as a return to the moment of slaughter. She wanted the darkness now: she wanted the solitude and safety of her brain's deepest corners . . .

Helen stumbled against a fluted column and clung to it with outstretched arms as she sagged into a foetal crouch at its base. Trauma wiped clean the slate of memory. Shock swept away all sense of time and space and drew her down towards the only thing that held meaning for her; towards oblivion.

Perhaps she slept, perhaps not. Hours and seconds were no longer part of her world. But at some time later, Helen woke to the soft stroking of fingers through her hair, and to someone whispering, whispering softly as her mother had used to do when childhood fears grew larger than youthful courage.

Helen smiled, snuggling into herself, sliding her hands around her breasts and under her arms. She was a baby again, giggling at nothing, drooling a silver string of saliva down on to her red woollen jersey. If only she could stay here for ever!

But it was not to be. The whispering was becoming insistent now and urgent. Helen moaned softly with displeasure, and lifted her head to see what Mummy wanted so late into the night . . .

And she was soon rewarded by complete knowledge of the intruder's purpose, and by a caress beneath which any mother's kind words and all of man's promises paled.

Bill Howard's foot-tapping impatience had risen to a bright-eyed anger, and then to a quickly growing worry as he stood by the locked rear door waiting for Helen to arrive.

As much as anything, he was getting cold and had been hungry at the outset. It was too much! No doubt the silly bitch had lost her way, or had scared herself into some cupboard or stockroom, convincing herself that bloody Joe Patrick with his creepy eyes was on her tail . . .

Howard considered banging on the door, although that would defeat the whole purpose of having sent her . . . Maybe he should just pack up and go home: that would teach her a lesson! But then, possibly something *was* amiss . . . Beneath the muffled rumble of traffic from the city, Howard had thought he'd heard a noise; a gull screech far away, a car emergency-braking, a female scream . . .

His increasing burden of concern tipped the balance of

action. Howard decided not to bugger about doing nothing here, but to find the first unbarred window and break his way in. Damn Joe Patrick and damn the cops – if Helen was hurt and he did nothing, he'd never forgive himself.

After a moment's hesitation, Howard set off, planning to check the front of the building first. It may well be that she'd reached the main vestibule, and was either still there waiting, or had left an indication. Besides which, he could only reach the far side of the museum by crossing the forecourt; the back being blocked by railings and thick shrubbery.

Howard, like Helen, had no torch – so he was surprised to see a splay of flashlight coming from inside the vestibule, and at floor level. More than that, there was enough illumination for him to make out the feet and lower legs of a body being slowly dragged away.

Howard looked again, to be sure, cupping his hands to the glass. And he *was* sure, and a kind of dread settled inside him.

Suddenly he realized that everything had gone wrong. It was all a mess. Ringing the police would be the best plan now.

Howard turned and a stone-hard fist crashed into his face. There was blinding light, a bolt of unbearable pain, and then a darkness that swept away both.

Chapter Twelve

And I saw a great throne, and him that sat on
it, from whose face the earth and the heaven
fled away, and there was found no place for
them.

Revelation 20:11

He woke fighting dreams, wrenching away from the
snakepit of nightmare. As the visions lost their vividness, they became grasping hands with which
Howard struggled.

There was an oath, and the cold barrel of a gun was
placed gently against his forehead.

'Easy does it,' came a voice. 'Just slow down, son. Or I'll
take your head off with this . . .'

He believed it too; could sense the man's panic over and
above his own. Howard quietened and began to come to
terms with his pain. His left cheek throbbed wickedly and
the eye above dribbled tears, while his nose felt like a lumpy
mash of flesh. His own sticky blood smeared his mouth,
chin and jacket. And the back of his skull confined a raging
headache where he'd struck the metalled forecourt on
falling.

'OK – OK, man . . .' The machinery of his voice cranked
up slowly and shakily. It didn't sound like him at all. His
good eye focused; the other was half-closed through
swelling.

He was slumped in a car, rear passenger seat, with his
attacker beside him. The man, as he'd surmised, was scared,
the gun unwavering but held on a hair trigger.

'OK,' Howard said again, letting himself subside, letting quiescence be his one and only protection.

'You're going to talk to me,' said the stranger. 'I'll ask and you'll talk. And believe me, if you try anything – if – if anything happens . . .' The very presence of the weapon completed and confirmed the statement. Howard wondered what the guy expected to happen: but his own time to question was not yet. Later maybe, if he got out of this fix alive.

'First, name. And why you were sneaking around out there.'

Howard eased a glance out the window.

'Where are we – I've left someone behind – please!'

'Not far from the museum. Less than a minute's drive. This "someone"; tell me about him.'

'Her. A friend of mine. A girl called Helen Remmick. My name's Bill Howard, I'm studying at the uni. Did you see her?'

Parco shook his head. His first act after flooring Bill Howard had been to look inside the museum lobby for signs of life. But the place appeared deserted.

Howard seemed genuine, with nothing suspicious about him. But the creatures Parco was tracking were cunning – the ultimate tricksters. He dared not take a risk.

'There was no one,' he allowed, reacting to Howard's reflex towards the door. 'Uh-uh. I mean it, pal. Be wise and follow this through. Now keep talking. Why were you there?'

Howard's indrawn breath almost crumbled to sobbing. Unless he was willing to accept that Helen had fallen and knocked herself out, or something equally absurd had happened, then reason forced him to conclude that she was in a greater danger than he right now . . . But at least he understood the *nature* of his peril. He doubted whether Helen did, or even could, at this point.

He talked after a long pause, quietly retracing the track of his ideas from the time at which Van Allen had first asked him to translate the Hagia Stone. His companion interrupted him hardly at all, except on one or two occasions to clarify a technical point that Howard had failed to explain fully.

Parco listened with rapt attention, and was at once pushed towards despair, yet uplifted to have met a man whose knowledge – couched in mythology but still practical – might yet tip the scales in their favour.

So, it seemed that Hanlon's filthy parasites went back a long way. A long way. They were known in antiquity and had been slain then ... Creatures as mortal as man, as voracious and perhaps as intelligent; their path to survival had driven them to dark corners and the most stunning camouflage imaginable. While humankind went forth and multiplied, the Children of the Gorgoneion found a subtler niche. Folklore and legend patchily traced their descent from the Golden Age of Ancient Greece, the time of their last great flowering, but then the threads unravelled and were lost. Vague notions of the Evil Eye, splintered super-stitions amidst a Dark Age desert of understanding, hearsay bleached of any meaning; these were all that remained of the horror until Nikos Michaelides of Theodorus Antiquities stumbled upon, not merely stories of the Medusae, but the real thing. Once infected, Michaelides would be compelled to scatter the seeds far and wide – but carefully, so carefully. Van Allen's antiquities' pipeline formed the ideal oppor-tunity. Two cells of parasites; two nests, rather than one in the old homeland, so as to increase the chances of success . . . And how close Van Allen was to success right now; he and his band of chained souls . . .

Howard came to the end of his tale, and Parco lowered the gun. He saw the strain on the younger man's face, the skin stretched by more than Parco's unthinking blow; the one seeing eye bright with grief and hope, alternating second by second . . .

'Now, please,' Howard asked again, listlessly, 'can I look for Helen . . .?'

Parco walked with him out of the deserted office-block car-park and down the lonely walkway to the museum. They checked a dozen doors for ingress: Parco shone his light through darkened windows wherever he could, but the place was tomb silent, and as empty of the living, he concluded.

'What now?' Howard wondered, aloud but to himself.

'We return to my office and pick up some kit that will get us in here quickly. Then I have a couple of other house calls to make . . . I'd appreciate you coming along, Bill, really. Apart from anything else, I've my side of the story to tell yet.'

Howard hesitated, shrugged, then nodded.

'All right, Mr Parco. If you've got wheels, you could maybe help me to check where Helen's gone.'

'Son,' said Parco, 'I think you'd better realize that she's not around any more . . .'

'She's got to be somewhere.' Howard pointed into the night, at a space beneath a tree. 'My car's gone, and Helen had the only other key.'

Theo sat reading the Cruse Diamond file without absorbing a word of it. Her face was tight and pale, and inside she was seething. Cynicism and bitterness more than any female intuition were telling her that Parco was playing games; selfish and cruel games, if not dangerous ones. She was in no doubt that she was being elbowed out of the way while her boss, good old reliable Jim Parco, bless him, was chasing the tail of Eleanor Van Allen . . . Not that Theo could entirely blame him . . . And with that thought she smiled, and a touch of colour bloomed across her cheeks. There was, undoubtedly, something about the woman that was deeply compelling. Deeply – disturbing . . .

Theo reached for her glass of wine on the side-table by her armchair. The blues album she'd selected played on, but now the self-pity and sharp anger she'd felt initially had mellowed to a kind of wistfulness, a subtle sense of nostalgic loss. It was vague, because she'd held few expectations of any life with Parco – but powerful visions of a strong and successful future. And she would achieve that, whoever she partnered to get laid.

Now Theo yawned languidly, startling as her doorbell rang. Talk of the devil, she thought; but then considered that Parco was hardly likely to visit when he'd dismissed her so peremptorily earlier. If not him, then who . . .?

She uncurled her legs and walked barefoot across to the door, her mind flicking through possibilities pace by pace.

Theo stopped as the bell buzzed once more, and her heart beat up faster at the evocative whiff of perfume as she reached down unhesitatingly for the handle.

Barry Hanlon tutted with annoyance at the telephone's persistence. He was working alone in the lab and no one had bothered to switch over to the answerphone. He checked his watch, which gave him twenty-five minutes to ten, decided that this could well be important, so left his bench and took the call.

'Mr Hanlon?' Unexpectedly, a woman's voice; vaguely familiar. Hanlon recalled liking its sexy undertones.

'Hanlon here.'

'Theo Vines – Jim Parco's partner.'

'I remember you, hello.'

'Hi. Um, I'm not exactly clear on the context of this message – Jim left me some notes, one of which was to telephone you if I'd not heard from him by nine-thirty.'

'Oh, right. Fire away, Theo.' Hanlon felt fear thrill through him at Theo's news: fear and a wild kind of hope. If Parco in his madness wiped out every trace of the symbionts, then all that remained would be the few poorly preserved cells taken from Bakker's remains, and the poisons together with the crusty secretion removed from the landlady's face – evidence that few zoologists would find credible. On the other hand, if Parco and John Pearcy tried, and failed . . .

'I'm sorry, Theo,' Hanlon interrupted, 'could you repeat that?'

'I said that Jim left an address; it's, ah, Ketley Lodge in the village of that name, about ten miles south—'

'I know it. Did he say he was going there?'

'Not to me, Mr Hanlon. But he's written here that it's vital you should know about this location. I can't even tell you why . . .'

'No need, Theo.' Hanlon's excitement was barely contained. 'Thanks for calling. The message makes complete sense.'

'I'm glad of that. To tell the truth, Jim's been so distracted lately, I've started to worry about him . . .'

'I'm sure he's fine. Thanks again. Goodnight now.'

'Goodnight, Mr Hanlon,' Theo said, and gently put down the receiver.

Ten minutes later, Barry Hanlon drove away from the pathology lab that was situated to the rear on the ground floor of the city mortuary. The car-park was reached via a short ungated alleyway, and at this time of night was an empty quadrangle.

Helen Remmick watched Hanlon's car make a hurried right turn into the mid-evening stream of city traffic towards the centre of Calverton. She climbed out of Bill Howard's Beetle, stepped round to the boot at the front, removed a full can of petrol and a crowbar, and crossed over the road.

Howard wondered frankly what the hell he had gotten himself into. During the short hop in Jim Parco's car from the museum to his office, Parco had let slip a little of what was going on, but only a little; enough to signal to the other that there was danger here, that it centred around Richard Van Allen, and that Parco and his closest associates were working alone; which was to say, isolated from the normal processes of criminal investigation. Just why that should be so, Parco wasn't yet telling.

The two men entered the office building and went upstairs to Parco's suite of rooms. John Pearcy was already there, as nervously exhausted as the tall PI, and carrying a gun that was substantially bigger and looking, if possible, even more deadly.

Parco himself expressed surprise, but not condemnation: he didn't question his friend's motive, just how he'd come by such a weapon.

'Just call it unclaimed property,' Pearcy said, with

humour too dry to merit the tag. Nevertheless he smiled, such that Howard was prompted to ponder just who in this room, apart from himself, was on the side of the angels.

'Remington Fireball,' Pearcy continued quietly, not with any pride, but as though to reassure himself. 'Highest muzzle velocity of any commercially available hand-gun. Two thousand six hundred and fifty feet per second.' He looked up. 'Loaded with hollowpoints, it'll stop anything that lives at half a mile. An improvement on a standard night-stick, eh? Or counselling . . .?'

'He's a cop,' Parco said, half-turning to Howard; as though that explained it all. Howard smirked like a gawky schoolkid who'd stumbled into the hard boys' den.

'A cop and a private investigator . . . I guess you're after Van Allen, right? I thought he had some fingers in some illegal pies.'

'It's a bit more involved than that, Bill.' Parco glanced at Pearcy. 'Why don't you tell him about it? I've got a couple of things to do before we set out.'

'Where to?'

'The museum, then the Van Allens' house – then I don't know where, to be honest. And I'll make some coffee. Whisky or brandy with yours, Bill?'

'Scotch, please.'

'John?'

'Whisky with my brandy. But don't worry, that won't impair my judgement . . .'

Parco grinned and went through to the other room. He called Hanlon first on the off-chance, waited thirty seconds then keyed in another number. Theo answered at once.

'Parco?'

'Yes, it's me, Theo – '

'God, I've been so worried! I was angry with you, Parco, you hurt me . . .'

'I know, I'm sorry, but—'

'Hanlon called me.'

'Hanlon? How come? I mean, what did he want?' His thoughts were racing now. Just when he felt he had some kind of game plan, another obstacle appeared to trip him.

'Slow down,' Theo said. 'Just let me explain. I got into town, thought about the way I'd acted, and came back. To apologize, Parco. But you'd gone, so I decided to wait a while. I started tidying my desk, because if I *was* going to take the Cruse Diamond job as you wanted me to, I'd need to leave things pretty shipshape for you . . .'

Parco smiled. It was just like her.

'That's when I took the first phone call – '

'Hanlon.'

'No, it was someone from the World Association of PIs. Guy called Sweetman. Jim, he told me that your contact Mylonas is dead.'

'Jesus Christ.' Parco whispered it; curse, prayer and expression of hopelessness in one. Aloud he asked: 'Any details?'

'No, except it looks like murder. He was stabbed. Also his office was torched at about the same time – burned out. Nothing left there.'

'OK,' Parco said. He was having difficulty controlling his urge to scream down the phone at Theo to get out; just drive away from there and keep going and don't look back . . .

'Hanlon telephoned minutes later. He said that he'd tracked Joe Patrick to a place called Ketley Lodge – it's in Ketley village. South of here, Parco. You'll see it on the map.'

'But how did Hanlon know about—?'

'Hanlon also told me to leave town. I laughed at him and he got angry – no, desperate, I suppose. He kept telling me to leave town and reach safety . . . Parco, I don't understand. I knew something was eating at you, but this sounds too serious for you to handle alone. I want to help,' Theo said, a heart-wrenching plea. 'Let me help you, Parco. The Cruse Diamond case is a ploy, isn't it, because *you* want me to leave also . . .'

'I'm not going to lie to you, Theo,' Parco said, knowing he would be unable to anyway. 'Something is happening that's like – it's like an epidemic: like a disease.'

'Parco—'

'No, now you let me finish. Richard Van Allen was smuggling in more than valuable antiquities. He was also knowingly bringing in living creatures, parasites that somehow infect and survive on people . . . Now, this is nothing like we've ever seen before, Theo, although it seems that these things go back to ancient times. Goodness knows, but they probably changed the course of human history then, and may well do again if we don't stop them – and him.'

There was a brief silence. When Theo next spoke, Parco could tell that she was having difficulty keeping her voice calm and level.

'If I'm going to run, then I want you to run with me. Please, Parco. If any of this is real, then you know you don't stand any chance. Van Allen is a powerful man. He'll have protected his machine very effectively.'

'Maybe not,' Parco said. 'If we can make a strike when he's not expecting it, then there's a possibility we can defeat him. At least, love, I've got to try.'

Now there was no reply, just the sense of Theo, silenced,

at the far end of a complex of optical fibres, not knowing how to answer Parco's determination.

'I'm going to send all my documentation down the line to your PC at home, Theo. That way, you'll have a copy as well as the one here. I'm not sure of the security of this office right now... As soon as it's downloaded, I want you to go to Police Headquarters and give the disk to CS Maynon. Don't bother to explain it to him; simply ask him to read what it contains. By that time, I'll know one way or the other whether I can bring him proof that's a little more substantial.

'Theo, will you do that?'

'I'll do it,' she told him at last.

'Good girl. So, all being well, I'll see you in the a.m.'

'Take care, Parco,' the woman whispered. 'I'll be waiting for you.'

Parco dropped the handset into the modem cradle attached to his office PC, accessed the files and set the modem to transmit. He hovered at his desk until the first page of text pulled down over the screen, then went across to his corner table. During the four-step journey, he decided against coffee, picking up two bottles and three glasses instead before rejoining the others.

Thus, he failed to see sudden movement in the VDU's pageful of text. Without warning – though warnings would anyway have been pointless – a solitary 's' slipped out of position and dropped to the bottom of the page. Before it reached the end of its fall, another letter shook loose and tumbled down; and another, and twenty, and a hundred ... Words and phrases rotting swiftly on the screen as the viral sabotage-program took hold. Connections and details, cor-relations and arguments were quickly reduced to jumbled nonsense ... Then the virus swept on at lightspeed down the phone line and through the network, corrupting data right across the city and beyond.

In the Old Time, the slowness of communication had been an effective weapon of the Gorgoneion. Today, the speed of the transmitted word served much the same purpose.

There were no lights showing at the front of the house, the Lodge being one with the shadows and the trees. Hanlon had killed his Range Rover's main beams and engine, and now coasted quietly down the slowly curving drive to a suitable parking place at the bottom. The silence and emptiness meant nothing, he reflected: for all he knew, Parco might have been and gone, or had yet to arrive . . . And, in any event, he was here based on wild speculation over Theo Vines's phone call. In Parco's world, this address could be just another dead end.

He had brought with him a chloroform pad and a scalpel, and felt weaponless. But that was his anthropic view of things. How could one *begin* to think like these beings, given that they were sentient – as Hanlon was now sure they were? The twin-helical structure of their DNA was every bit as involved as that of *Homo sapiens*: while the sheer scarcity of evidence for their existence spoke of complex behaviours modified by sophisticated minds. And so, were weapons necessary at all? Was it just possible that these creatures were open to human reason; to the persuasions that Hanlon was offering in return for the opportunity simply to learn?

His one hope during the drive down had been to capture a symbiont for study. The scalpel was there to remove it from its host, so passionately did Hanlon desire that aim. But his triumphs might far exceed that early objective . . .

To converse with these creatures; to build the first fragile bridge of understanding – this would be glory indeed.

He refrained from using a flashlight. The hull of the house bulked large against the backdrop of a sky polluted with citylight, and was quite easily discerned as his eyes adjusted. He walked quietly, the scalpel held before him, across the width of the gravel sweep, past some single-storey redbrick outbuildings, then around the side of the Lodge to the rear.

A path of crooked flagstones guided Hanlon's feet, and around him the garden was a jungle. Cultivated plants untended had taken on some of their ancestral wildness. He walked through an arched trellis of roses: their too-sweet scent rich and cloying in the air. Lean runners caught at the cloth of his jacket and trousers, snagged at his hair and scored one side of his face. His impulse was to struggle and rip free, but his nerves were taut as it was, and something that was excitement and fear both broke liquidly in his guts and threatened to drive him back to the car and away from this place altogether.

So he stopped, took time to untangle himself, then stood still until he was composed, before moving on.

To his left as he walked, the ground sloped away, down and beyond the boundaries of the estate to farmland and the Wyland Valley river. A village or small town came into view, like a nest of lights glittering between hills. Hanlon surmised that during the daytime the view would be truly magnificent.

He rounded another corner. Light slabbed the grass ahead. French windows stood open with long lace curtains billowing out in the night like veils of milky ectoplasm.

Now his heart raced as his resolve to continue was tested

to its limit. But he had to. Had to. If he retreated now, he would never know, and would never forgive himself . . .

He walked on, coming level with the edge of the windows. Looked in.

And saw the woman dancing.

She was dancing in silence to internal rhythms, the only sound the swish of her silken legs against the material of her blue cocktail dress. Mid-forties, Hanlon guessed, tall and possessed of an elegance that matched her height; honey-gold hair and deep-red lipstick; fine-featured . . . She spun and swayed around the rather drab homeliness of the room; this blandness enhancing its occupant's glamour; the woman's isolation and self-absorption lending the scene a lazy eroticism to Hanlon's fascinated eyes.

He watched her, equally absorbed, until her unknown melodies ended. Then she moved out of sight, prompting him to peer round to follow her.

She was standing before a mirror, studying her face as all women do – and all men, though less frankly. A highly polished fingernail traced the line of an eyebrow, then her hand planed the curves of her cheek and the shape of the lips as they pursed. She pushed a finger into her mouth, deep in, following it with two more. Hanlon frowned, puzzled, as normal feminine vanity became something different.

The woman swept back her hair, running her fingers through its strands. Her eyes in the mirror seemed very bright, and piercingly intense. The hands drew back to cup the whole face, while the hair continued to move and undulate—

And then Hanlon realized, and reeled from the shock of his understanding.

She was not alone at all, not by any means. Her hidden

companion was with her more truly, more intimately, than any admiring man could be. How close can husband and wife ever grow, even through long years of marriage? No bond made in heaven would equal the one that Hanlon now witnessed. The stirring of the woman's hair increased, until a dark-red protuberance broke the surface and waved feebly in the air like a hatchling's questing limb. Other appendages joined the first, as though the woman's face was clamped by a huge hand, and these, the fingers, wrapped around the back of her skull. And she revelled in it, found fulfilment there; enjoying a partnership that Hanlon, with perverse and passionate envy, longed to share.

He eased forward another inch, the better to see. And was seen.

The woman turned around to him and smiled. Apart from the sheer grotesqueness of the coronet of flesh that surrounded her face, the smile was radiant and warm. Hanlon tried to smile also but couldn't quite make it. The wonder of the thing left him stunned. He felt like a fool before her, with the puny scalpel still gripped in his sweat-slick fingers, the chloroform pad in his pocket . . . Like meeting Hitler's war machine with a butterfly net. Sudden shaky laughter broke out of him, and the woman cocked her head curiously.

'We are Eleanor Van Allen.'

'My – name is – Hanlon . . .'

'Yes. The pathologist who works at the mortuary.'

Hanlon's mouth dropped open.

'How do you know that?'

'Because everything *you* know about us is true. And everything you believe.'

She took a step towards him, this beautiful woman in the

figure-hugging dress; and the thing that was on her and in her. And Hanlon retreated, unable to prevent himself.

'I need to learn. I want – to know about you.'

'Then come in and learn. But you must understand that there is only one way you can know about us. Really know about us.'

He knew at once what that meant. Now the scalpel came up as though in someone else's hand and Hanlon's eyes became slitted.

'No! You won't take me like that – I need to see you from my own perspective. I'll have credibility with the rest of them – with society – only if I am myself. Can you understand that?'

'Your credibility means nothing to us,' the woman said: or rather, the host and its parasite guest. Which of them, he wondered, was controlling the voice, this chilling and mesmeric flow of words? Did she move of her own accord, or after silent consultation with that which rode upon her?

Whatever, they were moving forward now with intent; the woman's hair churning, her face changing colour with a vividness and speed that disgusted Hanlon as much as shocked him. Salmon-pink tainted with brown; all brown; the livid purple of blood-engorged flesh.

'Back off,' he told her, a hoarse whisper approaching a scream as she came on. 'Back off, I'm warning you!'

The scalpel flashed. She laughed at it.

Hanlon flung the blade and bolted into the dark.

He sought distance rather than direction, his momentum hurling him on, and quickly found himself lost and on a downslope tangled with thick rhododendrons that gave way to trees. He ignored lashing twigs and whipping leaves and looming trunks, leaped fallen branches and sudden clumps of tufted grass. He ran till his lungs were scalded and his legs felt like bars of twisted iron. But the vision of her could not be outsped; it hung in his head like a tumour through which his perception of all else was distorted.

Without warning he broke into a clearing, above which the night breeze moved among the trees with the sound of the ocean. There was thin grass and loamy earth under Hanlon's feet. He had burned himself out with terror, and now let himself fall, crumpling like a pile of empty clothes into exhaustion.

He blacked out briefly, and might have slept, but for the crack of a broken stick that woke him like a gunshot, moments later.

He scrambled up on to all fours, then leant back on his knees, probing the blackness for further sounds.

Through the webwork of branches, Hanlon could see the big house at the top of the slope, defined by a symmetrical grouping of lit windows. He had come about a hundred yards, and across difficult ground that the woman in her unsuitable clothing might not be able to negotiate . . . That said, she or someone else was making the attempt. Careful footsteps were crushing leaf litter just beyond the edge of the clearing. Another twig cracked as easily, as softly, as a bird's bone breaking. Then there was nothing: she had stopped to listen, playing the same game of tolerance. And the advantage was hers.

Hanlon guessed her position by this fragmentary collage of noises. She was hidden by trees as well as the night, whereas he was kneeling unprotected in the middle of the clearing. More than that, the symbiont's eyes might be better than hers, or his: perhaps at this moment it was staring right at him in plain sight, enjoying his confusion and fear.

But maybes never won wars. Hanlon reminded himself of

his old history teacher's maxim. He could debate the question and die, or act now with the possibility of survival.

He eased himself forward, on to his hands, and waited for the wind to gust once more, so he could push upright and move away under cover of its distraction . . .

It rose again, soughing the canopy, then fell away to silence. He waited for the next lifting in the trees – but realized his mistake before it came.

The scream shattered upward from his chest like a spray of broken glass.

Hanlon had time to twist round and see the many complicated movements thrashing in the undergrowth and in the thick forked branches above.

Then the huge breathing solidified to a pig's eager grunting and something big, something monstrous, swung down at him and took off the top of his head.

Hanlon's screaming stopped, but he lived long enough to witness the ancient face of Medusa, before a red wash of blood flowed down over his eyes, followed by a darkness as deep as any man can ever know.

John Pearcy did not at this point bother with the niceties of the law. He jemmied out the old window-frame with a single wrench, using the crowbar and his elbows to smash away the last of the glass and sharply projecting wood. Squirming through, he jumped down into darkness, dropped the bar and swapped it for a flashlight and his Remington, which gleamed like blue oil in his right hand.

Howard followed, muttering a mixture of curses and fearful speculations on the possible consequences of their action.

'Stow it,' Pearcy snapped at him briefly, and Howard

shut up as Parco lowered himself down on to the gallery landing.

They'd gone in through a first-floor window, which had been accessible via the flat roof of a boiler room at the back of the building. The smooth drumming of the heating system helped to mask the noise of their entry, while a casual inspection of the rear of the museum might not immediately reveal the act: any glass falling outwards would land on the roof.

Now the three men stood close to a wide and elegantly curving flight of stone stairs that led to the ground-floor vestibule and display areas. Despite the heating, turned low for the night, the air felt chilly. Parco shivered under the thin material of his windcheater. He accepted the sense of Pearcy's caution, and pulled out the Police Special he'd been given, the mild contempt he'd first felt at the nature of the bullets transformed now to a distant kind of relief.

'Come on,' he enjoined the others, and edged forward with them a pace behind; the echoes of their cautious footfalls creating the illusion of many men at their side.

'Van Allen's study's through there,' Howard offered, pointing. 'It's where he'll be.'

Parco nodded, not bothering to reply that he already knew it, and had already picked it as his first destination.

They walked on, hurrying now along the last yards of corridor, turning the corner.

'Jesus!' Pearcy said. He snapped off the flashlight and they all stared at the bright slit of light beneath the study door – and the shadow that crossed, once, twice in the space of a second.

'I'm going in.' Parco said it without hesitation. 'John, cover me as I open that door. Howard, stay to one side, out of his firing line if he's armed also.'

Parco didn't wait for their confirmation. He walked to the door, reached it and pushed it open.

Richard Van Allen was sorting through a sheaf of papers at his desk, discarding some and putting others into a slim black briefcase. His calm swift efficiency had been interrupted, and now he let the papers fall from his fingers as he stood upright to face the intruders.

'If you don't leave now, I will call the police and have you arrested.' The bluff was flawless, Parco thought, beautifully controlled.

'I am the police,' Pearcy said. Van Allen looked at him disdainfully, then smiled.

'But not, on this occasion, the law.' He let his eyes shift a fraction to Parco. 'I suggest that the eager pursuit of your case against me has overstepped the bounds of common sense, Mr Parco. You must, like every other man, allow your evidence to be tested in a courtroom. Did you perhaps expect to find proof here tonight?'

'Cut the bullshit, Van Allen.' Parco felt the urge to disturb that façade of sophistication: to put his hands to the man's sneering face and rip the mask away. 'That's all finished. This has nothing to do with smuggling antiquities – not directly anyway . . .'

He lowered the gun, let it hang at his hip as he went on.

'Tell me, did Michaelides warn you about what was in that one particular shipment – or was it a complete surprise?'

Van Allen feigned a quizzical frown, and pretended to consider.

'Really, Mr Parco, I can't imagine what you are referring to—'

The painful detonation of Pearcy's gun made Parco and Howard flinch as though a bomb had exploded. The room seemed to rock with the boom of it. In the afterflash that was drilled into Parco's eyeballs, and through the expanding shell of blue smoke, he saw part of Van Allen's left shoulder erupt, as though it was liquid and a stone had dropped into it. A splatter of bloodspots speckled the wall behind, and the man spun across his desk with the force of the impact.

'God Almighty, man!' Howard yelled: whatever they'd said Van Allen was, he had not come here to witness an execution.

Parco silenced his protest with a shake of the head. He knew that at this point, when they had committed themselves so far to believing what was unbelievable, making reality show itself, or else breaking the illusion, was an all-or-nothing gamble. He knew what Pearcy was doing and why he was doing it. And would not stop him.

'It's over,' Parco said quietly, speaking to Van Allen's slumped back. He could see that back heaving with dragging breaths, and the hand of his injured arm trembling, blood-soaked.

'We understand what you are. We know that you've sealed the Greek end of the pipeline and killed Mylonas. We know where you're building the nest to breed your next generation . . . Like I say, Van Allen, it's over.'

A silence fell between them, and slowly Van Allen turned himself around, using his good arm to ease himself away from the heavy desk.

Parco moaned softly. The man's face was contorted and purple, as though with apoplexy. But the eyes, those damned eyes that had brought him so far, and would have taken him so much further, to where no man could touch him – they still regarded the three with a calm hatred that was not affected by the agony.

'Nothing – is – over.' Van Allen smiled at them, infuriatingly. 'Where – there is one nest, there might be – many. And I – am – no more than a servant of – the Bidden.'

'The thing that spawns?'

'The Mother of the – Children . . .'

'What the fuck's he talking about?' Pearcy wanted to know, his voice harsh with loathing now that his fear had found aggressive expression. He was thinking of Bakker, Spears, Harris, Shelton . . . And needed no further excuse or reason to blow this bastard away: him, and the foulness curled up in his guts dreaming of Olympus.

'It's in the stone,' Howard said then. 'I've read it on the Hagia Stone – the Coming of the Bidden and the Dawn of a New Age . . .'

Pearcy spat on the carpet. 'Mystical shit! These are like any other vermin; rats, roaches – you bring in the pestmen and you wipe them away . . .'

'Pitiful – little – man.' Van Allen spilled a laugh, weakly. 'We had a history before – you – had thoughts in your head. We revered the gods even as you fouled your – caves!'

With an oath, Pearcy shot again; same arm, taking it off at the elbow. They all, Van Allen also, watched it spin and thud against the wall. And now the blood spouted, hosing with the rhythm of the heart through the ragged stump.

Parco felt sick, but he could see the changes intensify. A certain agitation in Van Allen's face, which was darkening further, and swelling, the entire facial skin tightening like a swollen bruise.

'It's on his face,' Pearcy breathed, teeth clamped tight. 'I'll leave the face till last.'

He discharged the Rem once more, blowing away Van Allen's left foot. The man howled, collapsing to his knees. His mouth – that mouth was altogether too large, the cry of pain torn from it not normal.

Howard made a retching sound and backed off to the door.

Pearcy aimed, fired, and took a pound of flesh from Van Allen's right leg. The man spurted blood from all his wounds; looked to be melting in blood.

And now his face was black and something was ripping free of his clothing – a snake-thick cable shuddering loose from Van Allen's shattered shoulder, then the other; cables lashing out from around his waist and chest; a severed tentacle coiling-uncoiling up from his leg.

Then Parco knew, and was horrified as he lifted his gun.

But Pearcy fired before him, inflicting his butchery on Van Allen's twisted midnight face, erupting it in a bright coronet of brain tissue and bone fragments, slamming the body back against the front of the desk.

It should have been over. Instead, it began.

Another mouth opened in the dead man, a huge, red, tooth-filled wound exploding sound into the room; the full-blown bull roar of the Bhavani Gorgoneion.

Pearcy began to scream at the size of the thing. It had lived on Van Allen, occupying most of his body space. It tore apart from the host and launched itself forward, moving in a way that he could not understand; many-armed, its body swathed in waves of sweeping colour change, some of them startlingly beautiful: and always that noise, the bellow of vengeance from one who had dreamed before the first human thought appeared on Earth.

Parco lifted his weapon and kept on firing, emptying the cylinder into the bulk of the creature, thankful at last for the awful barbarity of the hollowpoint shells. Each shot caused massive damage, driving red-hot sprays of metal through the alien flesh with energies he knew only as numbers.

Still it came on, but slowing finally, its efforts taken up in dragging what was crippled of itself and bleeding towards the place where its enemies stood huddled: enemies that it needed, and always would, for life itself to proceed.

When it paused, Parco held back his last shell. One eye regarded him from hip-height at two yards' distance; the other eye was missing, its socket weeping gore. The creature's remaining workable appendages kept it lifted up, so that it might gaze upon its destroyer; and what Parco saw reflected there could never be described.

'We – say that while one lives – all – live . . .' The bubbling liquidity of the voice was no longer Van Allen's, and indeed owed nothing to humanity. The full strangeness of the beast was overpowering.

'Be sure, Par-co – that – you find us out com-pletely. Or else we – will destroy you . . .'

The creature sighed; the great dorsal slit that was its mouth contorted shockingly and blood-streaked mucus welled up in a sticky grey surge. It dropped to the floor, limbs stirring weakly, the octopoid colours fading now to a dull greenish brown like copper left out in the rain.

And yet the eye that was the colour of skies when the Earth was much younger would not close. Parco wondered what thoughts were running there behind it; what plans yet this being was constructing even as its final seconds trickled out with its blood on the floor. The mouth began to open again, but nothing intelligible emerged.

Parco straightened his right arm and with no further hesitation put a bullet through the Gorgoneion's eye: out of pity or out of utter revulsion, he would never be able to say.

Each of the men looked pale, with shadows around eyes that had become exhausted by the ordeal. Pearcy walked over towards Van Allen's desk, his face averted from the carnage, and lifted the telephone. Parco was behind him. He pulled open drawers, came across a small silver handgun and a box of cartridges, and these he tossed across to Howard. Then he began where Van Allen had left off, sifting papers that would – if all this were not enough! – constitute the proof the world required.

Pearcy's call went through. He gave his name and said, 'Is CS Maynon in the building? It's urgent.'

Parco stared at him, listening to the tiny voice of the desk sergeant telling Pearcy that the Chief Super was conducting an interview at that moment, and had asked not to be disturbed.

Pearcy started to get belligerent. Parco cautioned him with a shake of the head. 'We haven't got time for this, John. It's probably Theo he's interviewing.'

'We need to know—'

'We need,' Parco said firmly, 'to get out to Ketley Lodge and put an end to this business. Tell the man to get a message to Maynon: he's to send a unit out here – and however many more he can spare to Ketley. If Theo's still in there with him, she's probably got him half-convinced. That computer data hung together pretty well.'

Pearcy nodded briefly and complied. He dropped the handset and watched as Parco gathered up the last of the papers and snapped the briefcase closed.

Howard was standing between the slain Gorgoneion and what was left of Van Allen's body. Parco considered sending the man home: he had bright tears in his eyes and was shaking gently.

'You OK, Howard?' Pearcy asked, noticing too.

'They were human gods, you know,' he said, not taking his eyes from Van Allen's ruined carcass. 'Zeus, Hera, Poseidon, Hephaestus – man's aspirations personified. Olympus was where we wanted to be – climbing back into grace to be there with them . . . But look,' Howard said, sobbing it, 'look what it's come to. Such . . . desecration! And – Helen – she may – be . . .'

'Easy, son.' Pearcy walked over and turned him away; led him out through the office door and into the corridor.

Parco, by this time, had reached a state of total calm that lay beyond the horror of what had been done here. He seemed to be able to see and think with crystal clarity, and he knew that Howard was right. Van Allen's corpse was skeletal, burst apart and ravaged like prey taken by lions and left in the sun for the jackals and vultures to pick. This wasn't symbiosis: this was extreme predation, where people's bodies were used and destroyed with no more thought or consideration than was shown by the bubonic plague bacillus.

And like the black death, it would sweep around the world if the Gorgoneion was not stopped now, and completely.

Chapter Thirteen

Chilling wind, and across the fields, faces.

after Onitsura, Zen poet

They crouched beneath trees and looked down at the Lodge. A single exterior lamp bolted to the wall cast a spray of light over the porch area. No lights were showing inside. Off to the left, Parco could make out the squatter shapes of old outbuildings; stabling, maybe, or storerooms. He guessed that the ground would slope away behind the house, and thinking about it, recalled seeing the place from the ridge road across the valley one time; a lone redbrick three-storey manor ringed by trees, with a pelt of deciduous woodland below that grew right down to the river. Then it had been high summer, a lifetime away: and indeed, if he had not been through the events of this night, Parco would think that the Lodge looked innocent enough now. Maybe the occupants had gone into town; or perhaps they lived at the back, which was why the windows round the front were in darkness; or maybe . . .

'So what do we do?' Pearcy asked softly, breaking into Parco's thoughts. 'I don't see Hanlon's car.'

'Means nothing. He might have been and gone, or it could be, if they got him—'

'Yeah. I don't suppose they'd give the guy much time to explain himself.'

'We must assume they are not open to negotiation,' Parco said. 'And neither are we.'

He stood up.

'OK. We're all armed now, and between us we have two cans of petrol. Our main aim is to verify this as the nest, and

294

burn the place down. Don't worry, Howard,' Parco added, feeling the man moving beside him, 'we go in to look for Helen first. But I've got to tell you, if we see just one of those things, then I'd put her chances at zero . . .'

'I know that . . . Do you think I don't know that!'

They all knew it, of course, as surely as they knew what their own chances were of getting out alive. But somehow, Parco was barely concerned with that. He was prepared to go in and do the job: anything else would be a bonus. And should that not happen, then his only regret would be not seeing Theo. Not saying goodbye to her.

He made to move forward. Pearcy stopped him.

'One more thing, Jim . . . Look through the trees – over there . . . See it? That white shape, just showing in the light from the porch.'

'Barely. What about it?'

'It's a butane gas cylinder. The village has no mains gas supply. Most of the houses will be using these cylinders – much cheaper than electricity for heating. The point is, if that thing blew, it would take out this house and anything alive inside it . . .'

'Christ, John! But how—'

'Either a well-placed bullet, or a bloody big fire lit underneath it.' Pearcy cocked his head at Howard. 'His gun won't do it. Yours might, at rather dangerously close range. But this mutha . . .' Pearcy hefted the Remington and Parco sensed him smiling. 'Trouble is, there's no way I'm going to wait around out here while you two heroes go indoors. On the other hand, I somehow don't feel comfortable trading weapons with our friend Bill . . .'

'All right. It's worth knowing. We all go in. Let's stick to the plan. If we see a single creature, we leave, we blow that cylinder – create as much damage as we can before calling the emergency services. Maynon might have the cops out here by then anyway. Bill, carry one of these petrol cans. I'll take the other. You watch our backs, John. Agreed?'

'All for one,' Pearcy quipped, though his legs were weak and his guts felt full of hot liquid shit, just waiting for a reason to reach the outside world. He chuckled awkwardly, the only one who did.

Parco led them forward, closer to the house.

A front door left ajar would have looked too much like a trap. As it was, they three-quarters circled the house before finding a conservatory window hanging open; and beyond that, another door into the back of the house, with lamplight showing through the keyhole. It still might mean nothing, Parco told himself, over and over, like a mantra: this could still be plain old b-and-e, and if we're really lucky some wizened guy with a fire-iron will come hobbling out to see what all the damn fuss is about . . .

He leaned in through the window and was able to twist the key in the conservatory door. They entered in silence; Parco found that the inner door was unlocked.

He looked at his companions and saw the sheen of sweat on both their faces. Now it was happening, something had changed inside him. Before, he had fought his fear all the way to get himself this far: it would've taken no effort at all just to turn around, collect Theo, spend a frantic twenty-four hours winding up the business, and then away – anywhere – and let the world get on with things. Perhaps in five years, or ten or twenty, his door would open and someone that was neither man nor beast would come in and smile and smile and be a villain. Well, by then he would have had a good life and enough of one . . . What would they want with an old man, these Children of the Bidden . . .?

And anyway, he'd make sure he kept the Smith and Wesson with him always, well-oiled and loaded . . .

That was how he had felt about it. But suddenly some kind of balance had tipped in his heart, so that instead of running from dread he was drawn towards it. Face your nightmare: that way you exorcize it, or at least understand the worst that it can do. Not that the fear was lessened – no, it intensified by the minute. Yet in this new state, Parco was able to smile with some confidence at Pearcy and Howard, and find the will to turn the handle of that inner door and walk through into the weakly lit corridor beyond.

It smelled damp, and dusty strands of spiderweb hung around the bare low-wattage bulb dangling on its grey length of cable, showing up the cracks in the ceiling. The walls were decorated in a fifties floral design, ornate but dowdy with age; and behind the paper the old plaster had lost its key and was crumbling to powder, sagging the drops outward in bulging moisture-stained pouches. The red quarry tiles of the floor looked in no better state; they were beaded with sweat as profusely as the men who walked over them: many had cracked along their spines and clinked faintly as the broken pieces moved together. Beneath them would be the cellar, Parco thought, his mind spinning dark yarns: a foul, black place of slime-coated brick and wet mud floors. You'd find plenty of niches and corners down there – plenty of places where They could hide, where They would survive any fire that you could set.

His skin crawled at the thought of spaces below him, above him, crammed with these disgusting animals, their many limbs and tendrils constantly moving.

He stopped, simply to take a breath and sweep this garbage from his head.

Pearcy came up level. 'OK?' No more than a whisper.

Parco nodded. 'Come on . . .'

Another choice of doors. The one on the right opened into a walk-in pantry with the same musty smell as the corridor. A few groceries, cans and packets of dry goods stood on otherwise empty shelves. An air-brick high up near the ceiling looked blocked by ancient grime.

The other door led in to the kitchen, and here the stench made them pause. Someone had been badly sick in this room, or else . . .

'Switch the light on,' Pearcy said, making his voice deliberately loud because the tension had made all of them china-fragile: one good scare would shatter the last of their resolve, and that would be that.

Howard complied while Parco covered his back, squinting into the gloom until the fluorescent strip flick-flickered whitely, blinked out, then came on and stayed on, buzzing loudly.

Pearcy groaned at the mess on the table, the remains of a meal and a chicken on a wooden board, covered over with tin foil. A loaf of bread beside it was spotted blue with mould and was powder-dry. The meal itself, left unfinished, had rotted down into a jellylike pool of congealed gravy which by now was sprouting a vigorous growth.

'Jesus wept,' he muttered. 'Something stopped whoever it was from finishing this.' He walked over to the stove, lifted the lid on a saucepan balanced on one of the rings, and wished he hadn't. This was where the main stench was coming from, chicken giblets boiled up for stock, then left and left until they were greyish-green, hung motionless in blackening water.

'You're right,' Parco said. 'The occupant was interrupted and never returned.'

'So where – ?' Howard began, but knew that the others were thinking the same thoughts. He shut up.

'It's looking worse, isn't it? Move on?'

'Let's get it done,' Pearcy said. He shouldered open the door across the room and took the lead, along a further stretch of passage, then turned right into a larger, colder room where the air smelled stale rather than rank: but it was darker here, and when Pearcy tried the light switch, he found it didn't work. 'Damn this . . . Curtains, Bill, please.'

Parco thought it best to stand where he was. His eyes were still adjusting, and he didn't have the layout of furniture fixed in his mind. Slow details were emerging, due to the fact that the front porch-light was shining somewhere above and off to the left, glowing like faint fire through the room's heavy drapery.

Howard reached the curtains, put down his can, and hauled them open. But they swung heavy and, as they moved, twisted their folds inward to show the material hung with the faces of dead men. A score of them. Two score.

And the dead eyes opened blue, and circlets of limbs were suddenly busy.

The face closest to Howard hissed at him, and dropped.

'Fucking hell!' Howard shouted, screaming, jumping back. 'Fucking hell, fucking hell!'

Pearcy loosed off a round, just one, that shook the room and sent a length of drape, rail and rings attached, surging through the window, which exploded outward in wood and glass, pieces of it flung far over the trees.

It was a bad move. The gun was too powerful here: it shredded heavy velvet and pulverized wooden frames, but the detonation shook loose many of the night-cold animals: Pearcy could hear them hitting the suspended wooden floor with a series of wet thuds. Then came the scufflings. Then more sharp and dangerous hissings, like being trapped in here with snakes.

Howard was still swearing, his blasphemous litany almost comical. He hadn't the presence of mind to use his weapon or do something with the canister of petrol. Parco realized in fact he had no presence of mind left at all, just the dull passivity that comes with the proximity of death.

By the shafts of light from outside, Parco detected movement close to Howard's feet. He dropped his own can, took up a stable stance, held his gun double-fisted, fired once, twice, and felt a bright brief triumph streak through him as two of the animals burst asunder in a splash of flesh and flame. The bullets, ploughing onward, smashed out holes in the floor after taking a sizeable corner off the bulky parlour chair against which Howard was pressed.

'Out!' Parco yelled. He aimed and fired again, missed his target. 'Get out now!' There were more of them falling by the second; wriggling into life, releasing their grip on the drapes – always landing right, like cats, before darting towards cover. Each of them had a face of yellow clay; a death-mask not yet animated by any human host. Then Parco saw one of the creatures use its colour-changing mechanism. A flow of crimson spread over its body as it swung a clutch of limbs around the leg of the sofa that partnered the ruined chair. It scuttled under a cushion and stopped.

Parco pointed and shot. The creature squealed as its innards blew apart.

Now he was at the door. He watched Howard flailing around in the dimness, uncoordinated and helpless with panic. Pearcy, hesitating briefly, discharged the Remington twice more, blasting the second curtain through the hole where the window had been; two rounds blazing like artillery. And by the strobe of the double-flash, Parco's darting eyes glanced upward, and he froze.

The ceiling was alive with Gorgoneion, massing like crabs at feeding time.

He screamed a warning and fired at the same time – a similar burst of two shells before the hammer started clicking on empty chambers.

Then a thread broke delicately deep inside him. He guessed, in this intimate pocket of silence, that Howard was as good as dead, and that Pearcy would just have to take his chances. Parco told himself he'd seen enough; that every facet of the nightmare his imagination had tilted to show him was real, and that now he had one job left to do, which was to reach the cylinder of butane gas and breach the integrity of the vessel. He needed a few moments to gather these last strands of courage, reload the gun and carry out this final act of defiance.

And so Parco, not in a daze, but thinking as calmly as he had ever done, turned his back on the other two men, closed the door behind him and walked along the same corridor, through the kitchen and out through the back of the house.

Howard felt the weight of a creature crawling over his foot, and his revulsion was complete. Everything was out of control. Parco screeching like a madman, the cop, Pearcy, shooting that cannon so that his ears were pierced with excruciating pain; the air thick with smoke and the dangerous glitters of flying glass . . . And these animals all around him – still coming off the walls and out of the furniture, spitting at him . . . And their faces . . . Oh God, those awful faces . . .

Howard released the last thin reins of reason and fired wildly, hardly able to see in the dark and with one eye damaged. But he needed to do something; couldn't simply stand there and be suffocated by them in their tens and hundreds . . .

The animal on his foot began to clamber quickly up Howard's leg. He shrieked, hacking at it with his hand. Its eyes were open and regarded him passionlessly; its mouth twisted outwards and fastened on to his fingers. Simultaneously, it unwrapped its fringe of tentacles from around his thigh and locked on to his wrist and lower arm.

Howard seemed intoxicated, reeling stupidly, bumping into hulking shapes in the gloom. Pearcy took in the situation and guessed that Howard was lost – and quite likely so was he. He'd heard the door slam behind him and sensed that Parco was no longer there, the bastard! – But then, deeper waters ran here than he'd ever before encountered: had any of them entertained a hope of doing the job *and* escaping with their lives?

Pearcy knew that Parco was trying to reach the cylinder. He knew too that the Police Special, even with hollow-points, might not be able to punch through the steel. He'd need the Remington for that . . .

Pearcy stared back briefly into the room, grimacing as more of the animals wrapped around Howard's legs – and there was one on his hand now, and Howard was lifting it to head-height and – Jesus! The creature was mimicking Howard's own face, a terrible tragicomic mask . . .

Time had run out. Pearcy had seen Howard put the petrol can down by the window. He quickly estimated its position, working solely on instinct, and fired, and missed. But the flash had pinpointed it for sure.

He turned, yanked open the door, turned back and fired again.

The wave of flame barely touched him, he was out so quickly.

A giant hand pushed Howard stumbling to the window-ledge, then lifted him up and dropped him over the lip.

One second later, fire spewed out above him, followed by roiling black smoke laced with dying alien screams.

Without thinking about it, Howard dragged himself, close to the wall, along the front of the house. His legs felt wrong – not in pain, but tingling strangely . . . And his left hand was heavy, numb –

He remembered. The creature was still there, crimson-faced, the crimson streaked with white score-marks. Its expressions were melting like butter, fluidly merging one into another, moving through its repertoire of human agonies, and beyond, so that Howard couldn't stand it any more. Amazingly, he'd held on to the little .22 Browning all along. And now, knowing perfectly well what he was about to do, he put the snub-nose barrel to the animal's face and pulled the trigger.

The report was wetly muffled by flesh, but the vibrations sped swiftly up his arm, closely followed by a scalding sensation that was more than the pain of a bullet wound. The thing was releasing its digestive acid, that much more than the slug causing him to arch in the extremity of his torture until his back muscles cramped, then relaxed him back to the dirt, shuddering.

Howard dipped below the pain, flotsam in a storm-tide, and lay for many seconds before surfacing. As it gripped him once more he cried out, knowing it was too much to bear; knowing he was dying . . .

But someone was there to respond to his cry, and cold hands came down to cradle his face, and a voice whispered soothingly for him to be still, to be calm.

Howard looked up at images haloed in porch-light and webbed by his quivering eyelids. It took him a moment to recognize her, but once he had, the sight of Helen here, now, ripped grief up out of him. She had never looked so beautiful or so concerned, her face etched with an echo of his suffering. She knelt beside him and lifted his head towards her lap. From this angle, Howard was able to survey the distant landscape of his body. His feet were reduced to bloodied bone, the shoes and socks burned off. From mid-shin upwards the blackened cloth of his jeans was still smoking, matted to his skin and weeping thin fluids. And more than that. Cold was creeping through him, up the length of his injured arm, pooling like dry ice at his shoulder; deep cold flooding down into his back and chest, tracing its killing frosts along every rib; etching traceries of ice on the muscle of his heart.

It was the Gorgoneion, of course, injecting more than acid into him in its own death spasms. Parco had mentioned the virulent neurotoxin the creatures used to disable their prey. It paralysed in moments, brought oblivion winging over inside a minute or two. And no antitoxin was known. And no hope was left.

At least it cools the heat that's burning me up, Howard thought; like a cold shower on a hot August night . . . Perhaps that fond image made him smile, for Helen was smiling too as she cradled him, bending over him tenderly. Her hair hung long and heavy, tickling his face: it was whorled into rings and spirals by the effect of the light. Angelic.

'Love,' she said quietly, sharing these last moments. 'Oh, my love . . .'

And Howard would have been fooled, if the dark coil of flesh had not appeared out of the midst of her hair and come snaking down above his eyes.

No Helen.

We'll go through the door together.

Darkness was rushing over him. Howard concentrated on moving his left hand, jamming the gun barrel clumsily between her hideous, beautiful jaws.

Smoke, fire, noise, had stirred the creatures out of their deepest and most secret corners. Pearcy felt the quick heat of the spraying, flaming petrol through the one-inch thickness of pine behind him. Others had sensed it too.

The corridor back towards the kitchen was now seething with Gorgoneion; and even as Pearcy watched, the weakened rotted ceiling sagged and split, revealing more writhing masses of curling tentacles dangling like torn cables in the air before him. No way out there – nor ahead, since the front door was secured with bolts and locks that would take too many seconds to work.

Upstairs then, and out through a first-floor window.

Pearcy took the stairs two at a time, his boots thudding on the worn carpet. He still had no mental map of the house in his mind, but this dropped into place at the head of the stairs as the landing gave on to several rooms with an unlit corridor leading off to the right. Too dangerous: no time to fumble for a light switch. Stick to the glow – to the porch-light illuminating the front of the house to his left.

He turned that way, relying on the wisdom of his trained body to move him safely forward; pausing to check back, eyes flicking constantly this way and that for movement, hidden corners, bland slabs of shadow; left and right and upward and ahead. He held the Remington easily; his wrist bones felt oiled and limber, in control of the weapon. He'd paused to reload on the stairs, and now enjoyed an increased sense of confidence as the confusion of noises below grew muffled and died away.

But what could he hear . . .? The sound of the wind streaming off the shoulder of the ridge, down through the trees, coming square-on to the frontage of the old house. Yes, Pearcy could detect the draught on his skin; strangely scented, the breeze made unwholesome by blowing past mildewed curtains and over dusty, worm-eaten boards. He wrinkled his nose in distaste, mildly disgusted without really thinking about it.

Ten paces on Pearcy reached the end of the landing. A door to the right was locked, the one straight ahead swinging ajar, stirring minutely in the airflow.

He pushed it open but held back as the door hinged aside into darkness broken by a vague rectangle of light – the window, with drapes across, and the way to freedom.

He remembered the moment Howard had pulled on the drapes downstairs, and fear locked him into indecision. Two seconds away – the window was that close. A half-dozen good quick strides and he'd be out . . . Then rejoin with Parco and blow that fucking cylinder. So close, so easy . . .

But now Pearcy heard sounds on the stairs; many tiny chitterings, a dry sliding of limbs – and then a spill of language in what reminded him of a child's unbroken voice. The words meant nothing, but the complexity of the sounds revealed a syntax and a tone – obvious intelligence.

Another option blocked. Pearcy wiped his sweating

right-hand palm down his thigh, then gripped the Remington and made his decision. As one door closes . . .

He stepped into the room, one, two paces in.

Then something closed the door behind him.

He thought that featureless black would be the most
testing he could experience, possessed of the knowledge
that he was not its only occupant. But the fear was nothing,
insignificant, compared with what he witnessed when the
overhead light came on.

They were everywhere, studded into the walls and the
floor where they gazed curiously up at him, as though he
was a giant striding in some strange kindergarten play-
ground. A wardrobe, tall and boxy, swarmed with them,
their fleshy tentacles flung around its angles and outspread
like a rock awrithe with octopuses. Some of the creatures
smiled at him, and Pearcy found that the most chilling
image of all.

The flash picture of the lair did not all register at once.
More details surged into Pearcy's head. He began to notice
features, expressions. A few of the animals reminded him of
people he'd . . . Sweet Jesus! There was Hanlon's face, high
forehead, black goatee; even the pathologist's rather sadly
lugubrious eyes . . . And amidst the host was Bakker, disem-
bodied and jammed between two motionless Gorgoneion
whose faces were utterly inhuman and demonic . . .

Deep chords of memory struck inside Pearcy's mind . . .
More than people he'd known, he now recognized images
from legend, from the mythic bedrock on which the occult
lore of mankind had been built. The fallen angels of Para-
dise; Dante's demons from hell's crowded galleries; Asmo-
dai to Zinimar: all, all of them. Watching him.

Pearcy knew there was no point in backtracking. No
point in doing anything except either to wait for one or

other or all of these creatures to move upon him: or to put the Remington to his temple before that happened. There was his one decision, plain and simple. But for the moment he stood, his state driven so far beyond the normal that he was able to see a certain beauty in the terribleness surrounding him, and not just the reflex horror of lifting an old garden stone. It was a beauty quite outside his experience, having no points of contact with his culture or his world. But yes, it was there, and it was the beauty of life's tenacity and its triumph in one form over another. He realized that now. Perseus was and had always been a fantasy to keep away the monsters beyond the fire's glow.

He made no sound, and, moving slowly, lifted the gun.

'There is another way, you know.'

The voice behind him spun Pearcy round. The one who'd shut him in.

'No – please—'

'Really, there is . . .'

And she was the living embodiment of her words, this woman in a normal blue dress, with a normal woman's curvaceous figure and an attractive downspill of blonde hair. Her eyes were compelling, her smile one he might wish to be offered by any woman at any time. But her head was marred by a crown of undulating fronds whose movements stirred that blonde hair and cast shadows down over her fine cheekbones and neck. The face of the Medusa, made awful by human fear when, in truth, it was the *contrast* of what was human and what was not that terrified him.

'I don't – I – can't – '

Pearcy tried to squeeze out the words as the woman took a step closer. His arm unlocked and he completed the raising of the weapon, pointing it at her now, instead of towards his own head.

The creatures around him stirred, murmuring. He felt tiny pressures on his boots and about his ankles. They were asking him, in their way; persuading him to cross that barrier to become what she was and what – God help them – what everyone might yet become.

Pearcy's last act was to offer his denial by putting a bullet through Eleanor Van Allen's head. He watched it disintegrate before him, even as the thunder churned the walls and floor and every surface into pandemonium.

The Gorgoneion surged at him.

Pearcy stamped at them with his boots and felt them break and squash under his heels. He fired the Remington again, again. Then glanced up as the lampshade swung crazily, flinging shadows around in a wild gyration.

The thing suspended above was vast, a reddish mass bulging towards him. It possessed a gargoyle's hideousness, with bulbous eyes swirling colours insanely like oil slicks, and yellow tusks curving down and back on themselves from jaws out of which bright saliva hung in strings. Its tongue lashed in that cave of a mouth as it poured its abattoir breath down over the man.

Pearcy's gun dropped from his fingers. The whole area of the ceiling was gathering, from corner to corner, folds and folds of its membranes.

He opened his mouth –

And did not scream. His throat was no longer in existence.

Parco had seen Howard thrown from the downstairs window and witnessed his destruction of the girl. The flames continued to dance and flare in that room, but they would consume the house too slowly, giving the animals ample time to scatter.

Now came the multiple report of Pearcy's Remington upstairs, followed by silence that stretched across a minute – then two.

Parco faced the fact that his friend also was dead, and that neither man would be coming out to help him. Maybe they'd thought he'd chosen the coward's way, but that was not true. He turned away from the house to look at the white hull of the butane cylinder thirty feet away through the trees. Taking that out was all he had left, the one purpose for being here.

He remembered what Pearcy had said about the uncertainty of the Smith and Wesson's power against the steel. Without any doubt, if Parco went right up to it and hit it square, it would blow. But he'd die too, instantly: and if the cylinder exploded and did not destroy the house, then he would no longer be around to substantiate his data on file or Theo's pleas to Maynon . . .

So, how far could he compromise? He counted his bullets again and again reached six; six shells, six chances. Zero feet was out. Ten . . . fifteen, that would probably kill him too. But who was he kidding? Twenty feet was about the distance of the house from the cylinder. Pearcy expected the force of its eruption to saturate the building with incandescent, flaming gas. Twenty feet was suicide.

Thirty? Maybe suicide also. Or worse – a scalding wave of fire that would strip the skin from his body and leave him writhing raw and in agony, but not dead. That went beyond Parco's contemplation; it made his testicles crawl in his pants and lit an exquisitely horrifying ecstasy in his chest.

He was not sure if it was the way of the coward or the

hero that made him take aim at thirty feet, steady himself and fire.

He closed his eyes, flinching. But there was no sound of impact, either on metal or in wood.

Fuck it! Parco thought. Five chances now. He steadied his hand again, and saw that however hard he tried, the gun was still quivering minutely – but that movement would be magnified over thirty feet, enough to send the bullet rocketing into the dark, way off its target.

Hurriedly, with the thought of a thousand animals skittering away through the grass and the woods in his mind, Parco scanned round for an armrest.

There – another ten feet back, a fallen tree that would do the job and provide the cover he craved.

He ran for it, leaped over and hunched behind. Parco's pulse was going crazy inside him, and although he felt unbearably hot in his jumper and windcheater, his face was chilled and his knuckles, as he clenched his fists, throbbed with cold.

'Well, let's warm the suckers up,' he said, speaking to the night and its unseen inhabitants and to the gods that watched over all. 'Now, come on, do it right . . .'

This time he waited, getting the gun to align and making sure it was unwavering before he eased back on the trigger, squeezing not snatching, keeping it firm—

The boom echoed off over the valley, Parco's arms jerked upward with kickback, and almost instantly afterwards came the loud hard 'spang' of the shell striking home. But no explosion. Parco's spirit began to sink.

He aimed up again. Fired.

This time the metal rang on a different note as the hollowpoint ricocheted off the cylinder's curves. Parco swore softly and tried to keep his concentration fixed on the three shots he had left. He was tempted at this stage to imagine rustlings among the leaves close by. And was that a door to the house, opening, closing again with a thump?

He decided that if the next two shots failed, he'd make sure with his final shell. Ten yards, five: it didn't matter. This was the coward's way after all, wanting everything when the danger loomed large that the people of Calverton and the whole country might end up with nothing.

He squeezed off another shot. A miss.

A fifth one a second later – and the sun rose ahead of him and rushed towards him blindingly bright, and so swiftly that he barely had time to drop down before the woods were picked up and swept aside in a howling gale of brilliance. Flags of flame hung in snapping banners about the trees; the noise went on and on forever, roaring, thundering: and Parco felt that he was no more than a tiny speck of flesh sent spinning away out of the meagre little dream that had been his whole reality. It seemed to him that he was a dust mote lifted by pure chance into a beam of celestial light, and there in its brightness turned into light himself, a transient spark that blinked and guttered and faded into nothingness.

Then thought itself closed down and Parco's body relaxed.

He woke to the great surprise that was life; moved, and groaned at the mass of pain his body had become. He held back a moment, studying it, and then felt a profound gratitude that it was not the agony of burned flesh, but the simple and straightforward buffeting he had received from being flung through the undergrowth by the shockwave of the explosion.

Parco eased his head up. The woods were full of glim-
merings; small fires, drifts of sparks, billows of sweet wood-
smoke. Looking beyond these, he could see that the house
was gone, smashed aside and utterly destroyed . . . He
thought about the cellar, and how that most certainly would
still be there, harbouring its hidden evils. He and Howard
and Pearcy had been naïve to think that every creature could
be wiped out thus . . . But then again, the blast would have
rocked Ketley village – its foundations and its complacency.
And it would surely have been seen as far away as Calverton.
The emergency services were no doubt speeding to the
scene right now . . . So, Parco couldn't have been out of it
long, for the trees and the night were still quiet, apart from
the cracklings of the flames.

He hunched himself up so that his back rested against
an oak trunk. Some branches from the tree, snapped and
scattered, as well as a nest of smaller sticks, lay in chaos all
around him; the entire grounds of the Lodge had been
rearranged in that brief outburst of light.

Parco smiled despite everything at the work he had done.
And now that smile was stamped frozen on his face as more
light seared suddenly through the darkness and picked him
out from among a million crisply drawn shadows.

Headlights, blazing full-beam into the trees . . . And
someone walking down the path they cut . . . Someone
coming closer, tramping the grass, hurrying towards him.

In a surge of hopeless panic, Parco cast round for the
gun. But it was long gone, lost who knew where and useless.

With a chuckle that was pure fear, Parco started scrabbling away, clawing out of the light as his vertebrae crackled
and the bones of his broken left leg ground their splintered
ends together.

He heard a final rush of running footsteps, and cool

hands were on him, gripping his shoulders, easing him round.

For an instant he tensed himself to lash out.

Then he laughed aloud and relaxed into the familiar sight of Theo's face. 'Oh God,' he whispered, 'oh God,' the syllable ending in a sob. Now he could bear any hurt. Now it was all worth struggling against again.

'You've failed you know, Parco,' she was saying to him, kneeling close so that he could smell her perfume through the drifts of burning wood. 'You haven't won . . .'

'Yes.' He could afford to agree it. 'There's still danger, Theo. We ought to get out of here – '

'Maynon is dead,' she was telling him. 'All the computer data corrupted . . .'

He paused, hearing in the distance the mad and welcome whooping of fire-trucks and ambulances. Theo heard them too.

'No time left.' She bent as though to hug him and Parco, wincing, lifted his arms to her.

'You never really understood me, Parco, not even in London when we – ' She smiled, and Parco thought of London, and Theo thought of Eleanor Van Allen's visit to her flat the night before.

'I love you, Theo.' It was all he had left to give her, this woman of faces.

'Goodbye, Jim,' the Child of Destiny replied.

And her face was black as her lips came down for him, reaching, reaching, to make him hers.